DARKSLAYER
Part One:
The Demon Chasers

Volume One of the
Chronicles of Mídhris

G. M. Deveril

DARKSLAYER
(Parts 1 and 2)

is fondly and most gratefully
dedicated to
The Reverend Doctor Bonnie Ring
and the Congregation of
Saint Cuthbert's Episcopal Church,
Oakland, California

You journeyed with me into the darkness
and back into the light

—GMD

.

ACKNOWLEDGEMENTS

The genesis of this series, and this tale, goes back four decades to late nights when I was a graduate student. It would be impossible to name all those to whom I am indebted. Liz gave me the hero journey theme that shaped the original tale that comes much later in this series and is echoed on a grander scale here. The fantasy works of C. S. Lewis, J. R. R. Tolkien, and Katherine Kurtz all influenced my imagination, both consciously and subconsciously. My mother took me weekly to the Fresno County Free Library where, among other works, I checked out many a volume of mythology before I ever got to junior high school. Early readers of this story include Kathy Booky, Janet Braziel, and Bill Lynn—all of whom offered insights and helpful suggestions. The work is better for their efforts and its remaining flaws are mine alone. Jack Hutchinson told me I simply HAD to publish on line and without that push this might still be languishing on multiple thumb drives. That I can write with any sense of style is owed principally to Alan Amend who taught humanities at Fresno High School. I am indebted to them all.

The dedication speaks for itself. When I conceived this tale in the early 70s I was too young to understand depression and the struggle to return to the Light. Over the last six years I was finally able to tell this story. A loving parish and a skilled therapist made this tale possible.

Mídhris

The Mithermere

Nialt

Tolvith

Aonghe

Crumbly

Fjorn

Thioth

Nimmoth

Siot

Vothnell

Ulnor

Mimmoth

Vorthall

Hlv

Vios

Fishtal

Cuggl

Norden

Worbl

Ewdon

Nithl

Iarmir

Kjellith

Cimir

Timnel

Tesser

Hespros

Thilnos

Issenport

Fioille

Kelanos

Khast

Liarroth
[Thyelos]

Shevéli

Rupow

Druvádi

Humen

Viziv

Rilech

Syndon

Orith

A Guide to Mithron Pronunciation

The proper names and language of another world can be challenging. Those who are fascinated by language may want to peruse this pronunciation guide. **The one rule any reader should keep in mind is that the letter "J" always has the sound of the English "Y" in "you," even if it follows a vowel.** The name "Njothir" sounds like "nyote+here."

Our "J" sound is represented by "GG" and our "CH" sound (as in church) is represented by "Ç." Only fantasy or linguistic purists should worry about anything else. Accents carry grammatical information but do not change pronunciation.

A = a in father

B = b in boy

C = c in cat

Ç, ç = ch in church

CH = ch in Bach, never the ch in church

D = d in dog

DH = th in these

E = e in met (short) or a in gate (long)

F = f in fog

G = g in go, never g in gin

GG = g in gin, never g in goggle

GH = voiced version of ch (not found in English)

H = h in hat, unless following a consonant as in ch, dh, th, sh.

I = i in pin (short) or i in machine (long)

J = y in you, never j in judge.

K = k in kite

L = l in lane

M = m in map

N = n in note

O = o in rote

P = p in pin

Q = k in kite (in Druvic script)

R = r in Spanish or Italian, with a slight trill of the tongue

S = s in sing, never s in reason

SH = sh in shine

T = t in tip

TH = t+h in "not here" or "hot house" (sometimes reduced to th in "thin" in Anglicized words such as Mimmoth)

U = oo in noon

V = v in van

W = w in wax

Y = French u

Z = z in zoo

ZH = z in azure, s in measure

PROLOGUE

Stars shatter me, shred me, leave me defenseless and overwhelmed. I walk into the night, look up at that fragmented fire, splashed against the darkness, and something clutches my heart, desperately trying to hang on to some piece gone missing. The constricted throat, the familiar pressure only released when tears run freely, an aching longing for the unnamable—there is no avoiding it.

Family lore says my ancestors worshiped the stars. Perhaps they still call to me. I sometimes feel as though I wrestle with a demon. Or a god. Jacob at Bethel? My great-great-great-whatever walking into the darkness on Mount Rggan? Who knows? How do you slay a demon or gain a blessing? Where is peace, the tranquil resting place? I have yet to find it.

Without the stars I am nothing. Walking beneath them I ache with a tenderness beyond words. Words are all I have. Here are the words: my family story, a tale of two worlds.

CHAPTER 1

Lofty peaks circle the lands about the vast inland sea, sheltering inhabitants of that region from most of the larger world and standing in silent witness to their tales. Even these, in their vast and ancient knowledge, cannot tell the ages of the worlds. For that one turns to the stars.

Stars are the precursors, energy manifested as matter whose death forms the stuff of other worlds. These brilliant cousins are not timeless, though they come as close to it as anything we know.

The ancient inhabitants of Mídhris turned, by some primal knowing, to the stars as their source and witness. Some worshiped the great daystar and most adored the spangled lamps of the night. Constellations were named and stories told about them. Seasons were marked by them and societies organized around their rhythms. Life was ordered, crops harvested and fish caught, buildings rose and fabrics were woven, arts and cultures developed.

Then, in the latter years of the High King Avroth II and during the reign of his son Horgil, while Liktor ruled in Kelanos, there came a darkness into the northern lands about the Mere.

The sun continued to rise each day and stars continued to shine each night. The moon maintained her monthly dance of concealment and unveiling. The world seemed the same and yet it was not. This was a darkening of the spirit among mortals, something that sapped energy and imagination. None could name its cause.

Perhaps it began with the plague years when the certainties of life were shaken by sudden death of young and old alike. Fevers and ulcers came equally to chief and churl, to the frail and the firm, to milkmaid and warrior. No prayer seemed to avail, no amulet or recited charm provided defense, no medicine offered respite. The living scarce sufficed to bury the dead and as they hurled the stricken bodies into mass plague pits one would easily believe they buried their hopes with them.

The toll was high though the pestilence did not stay long. Passing from village to village, region to region, it rarely lingered beyond one year, perhaps two, and those who survived were never touched by it again. The ordinary routines of life gradually resumed but rebuilding of lives proved harder now.

As if arising from the dark thoughts of many, there appeared in the eastern depths of the Forrest of Norrast a spirit of despair that became palpable. Rarely visible to the eye but always sensible to the heart, this spirit sent out tendrils like a black mist drifting through the midafternoon. This bitter smoke did not sting the lungs or cause the eyes to water. It attacked the human will, eating away at all force and drive, eroding hope, inflaming indifference and torpor. Lovers were less ardent, dreamers lost in the drift of a lazy stream. On rare occasions this spirit became sufficiently tangible to pass across the sun and turn the sky dark or to obscure entire swaths of the star path by night.

Whatever it was, it was given a name: the Chegjan. The basic human need to identify, to name, to cope, perhaps to control, required a classification and the Chegjan was deemed to be a demon and the source, rather than a manifestation of, the despair that gripped the peoples.

Into this world came a young man by the name of Ian and this is his story. It was preserved in The Deed of Ian, an epic poem that is here adapted into prose.

The original begins with a young ruler by the name of Njothir, whose father was among the last in his region touched by the plague. Over the centuries the bardic lament's first stanza was adapted as a drinking song, the original terror and sense of dread thoroughly suppressed and long forgotten in its ironic use as a prelude for revelry. This strange permutation of word and music may have expressed our desire to prevail over darkness and remember that it is possible to do so, for little else could explain the dancing lilt in a tale beginning thus:

Dorch' iroh 'n laitha choj nudh ti nij
Ovni n oichevi cojdivi di'n aithna
Thjo vù jethig Njothir du'n talla ti'n a'ir
At li tjò tjern faic tri bas merdh lag cai'l

Dark the days in the misty north
Fearful the nights in forests deep
When Njothir came to his father's hall
To see his lord lie still in death

CHAPTER 2

Circling buzzards confirmed Njothir's fears before his band reached the rise from which he could look down on what remained of the village of Vathna. The raiders had not paused to burn; they had only slaughtered and pillaged. Sensing they might still be near, Njothir spurred his war horse toward the eastern hamlet, seeking clues of the bandits' flight. The dead could be honored later.

Not that there would be that many dead, given the plague's toll from the winter. Vathna held but half the population of two years before. One third had succumbed to the mortal fever and many survivors had moved west, seeking hope in larger communities. Here at the edge of Rathdar's realm life seemed too precarious to remain. This day's horror proved their fears well founded.

Those who had survived the rigors of winter and the deadly fever that scourged the land now lay slaughtered upon the muddy earth, their gaping wounds still fresh. Njothir silently commended them to the star path they were now traveling and to Hjelgi, Shepherd of the Dead, that they might safely join the ancestors. He then called on Vrotni, the Fierce Mother served by all warriors, as he followed the raider's fleeing tracks.

The cowardly opportunists had not made it far into the eastern forest when Njothir approached. The lawless band, one of several pressing on Rathdar's people from the Northern Waste, took advantage of isolated hamlets weakened this year by plague as well as the rigors of winter to steal food and furs, horses, cattle, clothing, household goods, and usually a few villagers as slaves. Those chosen for slavery were usually the prettiest young women and an occasional strong child. The rest they slaughtered with complete indifference. Njothir detested everything about such men.

So it was that Rathdar's son rode at the savages in a war fury worthy of the Fierce Mother avenging her children. His own band was not large but it rose to match Njothir in his courage and skill and they quickly dealt with the raiders as the raiders had done to the people of Vathna. Only one of Njothir's companions fell that day, Herkeld son of Herdal. Him they placed upon his horse as they returned to Vathna accompanied by the three women seized there. Their laments were endless and one, when she saw what was left of her village and kinsman, grabbed a dagger and slew herself to be free of the memories and the horror of what had been done to her.

Njothir and his men gathered the dead of Vathna onto a makeshift pyre and lit the sacred fire. Waiting no further, they remounted with the last two survivors and headed west.

The swift approach of a lone rider not long thereafter caused Njothir to stiffen in alarm. It was Rutnir son of Ivor and the pained tension etched above his fine black brows proclaimed ill news. Rathdar had been stricken with the plague and was now facing the long journey.

Rathdar's heir lashed his steed into action with no word to his troops, setting out ahead of them all. Racing toward his father the young warrior allowed the steady rhythm of hooves and the irregular creaking of the leather in his saddle and armor to lull his fevered mind into a state of semi-shock. He and his people had absorbed many losses but nothing prepared him for losing his father and chief. Njothir submerged himself in the powerful energy of his horse and the pattern of his own breath, hoping to escape the spreading tendrils of darkness.

CHAPTER 3

Vorthall of the Norrungs was the home of foresters and artisans. It was an open sprawling place in the midst of the great Forest of Norrast, a pleasant break from the dense trees that spread many miles in all directions. Trade roads spread from Vorthall, piercing the woods and holding peoples together in a spider web of commerce

Vurdni Ironfist founded Vorthall many generations ago, deeming the gentle curve of the Nurgen and its easy fords a favorable habitation for a people that feared no enemy. The Norrungs were a fierce people, fond of peace yet skilled in battle. Vorthall became the center of the scattered tribe and the home of its chieftain.

Rathdar had ruled from this prosperous village, seated in the chieftain's hall on a low rise with a good view but no serious fortifications for war. Those had not been needed for almost two centuries. Warriors were few but well-trained, necessary protection for the people but not the chief occupation of a now domestic people. Most warriors possessed peacetime skills, whether they were mighty with axe and adze or workers in iron or leather. The Norrungs also wove much cloth, trading with peoples to the northwest or the south for wool.

Amid such peaceful trade it was always wise to have warriors traveling with merchants. Njothir was known for his abilities with both sword and axe. In spite of many follies in his youth he now rarely acted in haste and his judgment was trusted. For this he was known as Njothir the Righteous. If the need arose he could fell several men or a goodly tree faster than his peers, making him a valued friend and a dangerous foe.

The plague had descended from the distant southeastern hills, following footpaths and waterways until it reached Vorthall. Its second victim among the Norrungs was Drenneth, daughter of Nothun, First Wife of Rathdar and mother of Njothir and his younger sister Njothila. Her loss had shaken the leader of the Norrungs and elders noted that he had become a shell of a man, hollowed with grief. They respected him in this but knew the people were weakened by it.

Many other victims followed, as had been the case wherever the burning came upon mortals, the characteristic lesions forming by the second day. Perhaps one among a hundred who felt the fever survived. Most suffered its tormenting fire, accompanied by weakness and delirium, until the convulsions came on the fourth day. At that point it was reasonably certain the victim would not see noon of the fifth day. Those untouched by the foul pestilence were marked forever by the horror and helplessness of watching others suffer through its fatal course. Not a few skilled in healing turned to herbs that shortened suffering by shortening life, as they realized that no leaf, root, flower, oil, or potion had yet curbed the deadly fire.

Vorthall shrank from roughly eight thousand souls to five thousand over the course of two years. Hundreds who had fled their villages and come to Vorthall for comfort or new beginnings formed a partial offset to the lost populace but the Norrung capital had become a very different place than it was when Njothir was a boy.

Njothila was just coming to womanhood when they lost their mother. In addition to the grief she shared with her father she also felt a gnawing anxiety that she might lose him also, if not to the plague then to despair and madness. She watched him closely and only began to hope when a year had passed since her mother journeyed to the stars.

Rathdar walked among his people, leading the struggle to hold the clan together, fighting for life and surviving as a proud folk. For this he had been named Rathdar the Faithful, but one man's faith could not hold out forever against the growing darkness in the collective soul. Here too the Chegjan had come on the heels of disaster, seizing its advantage in time of loss and confusion, infesting as surely as the plague and eating away at the health of the people.

When his day came and the evil fire touched Rathdar's flesh, the Norrungs felt it as a deathblow to them all. Rathdar's heir and a party of the men were away, defending the Norrungs from raiders that had come from the east. Elders were lost in their own dark thoughts and offered little counsel. Ivor's son Rutnir sprang to horse and rode out to notify his foster-brother Njothir even before his sister Ringskild urged him, as she in turn went to the side of the chief's daughter.

Njothila was beside herself and the keening of her clanswomen echoed into the surrounding forests. The fever ran swiftly in their lord, attacking him to the marrow. The final battle did not even last four days.

The princely body of Rathdar, son of Ronir, son of Pjernval the Mighty, was scarce washed and laid upon a bier when thundering hooves announced the arrival of Njothir to Vorthall. As he leapt from his horse it was quickly escorted away and tended by no squire but by the warmaiden Ringskild herself. Njothir tore the doors open and stormed into his father's hall, bearing with him the scents of the forest and the steam of his own driven body.

Was it the Chegjan pouncing upon this grief-torn encounter that instantly reproached the faithful son for not saying farewell to his father and lord? No man, woman, or child among the Norrungs saw guilt in their defender, yet Njothir conjured it within himself, invoking with it every moment of regret between father and son. He, the noblest among his people, had failed his lord in the hour of need, betrayed his blood, and violated the code of his people. All this poisoned his first moments of beholding Rathdar, pale and motionless before him.

A mighty cry leapt from the warrior's chest and he flung himself upon his father's shrouded body. His sister, having never left her father's side, now joined him, embracing the men dearest to her and piercing the rafters with her lament. The flower of their people, they had become orphans, strong but confused bear cubs in a vast forest, with no clue of where to turn their powers.

.

CHAPTER 4

Having seen to Njothir's horse, Ringskild joined the mourners in the great hall, her own long raven tresses disheveled in grief. Her face was covered with ashes, a ritual usually observed only by close family, and the Norrungs could see how Rathdar's death touched her. The more insightful at reading hearts could also tell her sense of closeness had more to do with Njothir than with their dead lord.

Ringskild held back, allowing brother and sister the consolation of sibling grief. She was not touched by the Chegjan, having sworn by her own ferocity as a woman warrior to oppose it with all her might. Those who had seen her in battle vouched for her skill, courage, and deadliness, noting as well that she had all the potential of a berserker, though that had yet to be manifest.

She allowed grief and anguish into her heart but closed the door to anything that might weaken her will. Ringskild met loss with building anew, injustice with vengeance, and insult with steely disregard. The plague was her personal enemy as much as raiders, brigands, and traitors were. As the daughter of Ivor saw things, the new darkness that seemed to accompany the plague was to be studied and opposed, not feared. Though of the same generation as the orphaned cubs of Rathdar, Ringskild could easily serve as a mother bear.

When Njothir finally stood, his young face already haunted, he remembered to reach into a cold brazier and mark his face with the ashes of grief. Though late to his father's death, he would honor his lord. His char-colored forehead and cheeks, motley with sweat and fresh tears, now matched those of his sister and of Vunill, the chieftain's Second Wife. Then Njothir noticed another ash-streaked visage in Ringskild and he took new strength from her presence. As children Ringi and Njori had terrorized Vorthall with their pranks. She had been his slightly older playfellow and battle companion, a soul mate whose brother Rutnir had fostered with Rathdar and Drenneth. More than that, she was his secret oath-sister, a bond no less sacred than blood. The warmaiden deserved the mark of near kin. As his manners returned to him, Njothir remembered the service she had just given.

"I thank you, cousin, for seeing to my horse. Eager to behold my father, I should have served it ill."

"It is my honor as a warmaiden to care for such a fine charger, and an honor to serve the family of our lord. Your horse is well groomed and fed and stabled." She held Njori's eyes as though her heart had things to say without words, releasing him when she noticed the tension come into his face as his eyes moistened afresh.

Njothir broke his oath-sister's gaze and turned next to Vunill, inquiring, "How fares my second mother?"

"I fare ill, my husband's son, as do all our people. This loss is hard beyond bearing, yet I thank you for your concern. All things are prepared."

"Little sister, how shall we fare now?"

"That is beyond mortal knowing, my brother," Njothila responded. "Not well, I fear, but we shall fare as we shall fare. It is good to have you home, though I would this were not your welcome."

And so, though the Chegjan hovered in the shadows, the newly bereaved began to reweave their world and face their lord's final journey.

When Rutnir and the rest of Njothir's party arrived with the only two survivors of Vathna, they were granted a brief space of time before Rathdar's body was carried by eight warriors from the hall onto the pyre outside. Among the Norrungs, women ululated and warriors beat their swords upon shields. Vunill followed her lord in the white garb of a widow, her grizzled hair streaming in disarray. No tears streaked the ashes on her cheeks for she had cried herself dry in the past few days, though silent sobs seemed to rack her body as she walked. Njothila and Njothir kept pace behind her, clinging to each other's hand as if to draw mutual strength in that physical tie. Ringskild and Rutnir were at the head of those carrying their lord's remains.

Moments before reaching the pyre, the cortege was interrupted by Hranild the seer walking between the readied heap of logs and the dead chief with his companions. She had obviously not strayed. Though Hranild was blind, she had a better sense of place than those whose eyes were open to the light. The procession halted before her and was silent. She seemed to scan the heavens and the assembled Norrungs, then spoke.

"Children of Rathdar, hear me."

Though all eyes fell upon Njothir and Njothila, the greeting used an ambiguous title given to all members of a chief's clan. Hranild's words could have been addressed either to Rathdar's heirs or to all the Norrungs. She continued:

The darkness has come to Vorthall and the vast Forest of Norrast.
No power of this world shall undo it.
You shall not overcome it, though it shall be overcome.
Who seeks glory shall lose it.
Who forsakes victory shall have it.
Faith shall be your shield if you will bear it.
Hope shall be your weapon if you will wield it.
Love shall be your chieftain if you will follow it.
The stars await us all whether we will or no.

With that the ageless woman looked toward the eastern sky. All eyes followed and the Norrungs beheld a great eagle approaching and circling over Rathdar and his people. By the time they looked down Hranild had hobbled away and the procession resumed, quietly now. The people of Vorthall pondered the seer's words and the eagle's appearance.

As Rathdar's body was laid on the pyre, the crowd rejoined in the ritual keening and shield beating, letting the heavens know by their tumult that a great man was ready for the star journey. As the time came for the first glimpse of the evening star, Thomdar the star singer stood at the head of the pyre. When the star was sighted he began a Hymn to Hjelgi, Shepherd of the Stars, leader of souls from this world to the next.

When the hymn ended Rathdar's pyre was lit. Other star singers chanted Ushni's Lullaby, welcoming Rathdar into the halls of the Queen of the Dead. Vunill spoke quietly with Rathdar's children.

"You must allow me this. I was never blessed with children like your good mother and though you have both been dear to me I no longer have anything to live for. If I have any mother's blessing to give it is freely yours, my children. I will journey with my husband." She then kissed Njothila and Njothir and climbed upon the pyre, embracing the rising flames as she embraced Rathdar's beloved body.

Custom accorded this right to any chief's wife, though it laid no obligation. Most women survived their lord and only a few chose to join this way in death. Vunill's final act of love was never forgotten. Shields thundered and the women's lament doubled until voices were spent and the flames died down. The stars welcomed the new pilgrims.

.

CHAPTER 5

The Norrungs mourned their lord a full moon cycle, as was their custom, before calling the clan together to elect a new chief. During this interim the children and foster children of Rathdar continued to wear ashes and leave their hair in disarray, while those in the council who had survived the plague sought to guide the people.

Ringskild lost herself in her weaving for she was gifted in this and knew how to turn her deep passions into fine cloth. Njothila pondered her role in society, now that she was a woman and an orphan, and fretted that she may be forced to choose a husband before she was ready. Rutnir took on additional responsibilities as a young warrior, leading patrols against raiders. Njothir brooded, pondering his place in a world that seemed cruel and indifferent to the fate of mortals. He spent many hours riding alone in the forest, observing the animals and trees that were the livelihood of the Norrungs. Four days after his father's funeral he found one fine straight fir and felled it, calling upon friends to help with the horses in dragging the great log back to the village.

There Njothir applied himself in a frenzy, shaping the tree as he willed. It was a simple but noble design with the head of a fine horse at the top and a long chain of interlaced knot work down the huge pole. In places he carved runes telling of Rathdar's ancestry and his two wives. When it was finished to his liking, he colored the carved knots with the juice of crushed leaves and ashes, then polished and oiled the entire pole. A deep hole was dug in the earth and the honor tree raised. Njothir hung his father's shield upon it,

Njothila adorned it with garlands of green, and it was anointed with mead by a star singer. This was a new thing, not the custom of the people, yet all the Norrungs approved of Njothir's act, noting that the wood-skilled warrior seemed to stand tall like the carved tree that now memorialized their former lord.

While the young foursome and Rathdar's extended family busied themselves and pondered their own thoughts, the rest of the Norrungs seemed to drift day by day. The decimation of the plague had meant fewer sources for pelts and wool from the north, fewer hands to harvest wood or dig for iron, fewer traders to purchase their goods, fewer to tend and harvest fields. Life seemed more uncertain than it had been just a couple of years ago and hope seemed to dim. The Chegjan's presence seemed always to be lurking, like a fleeting shadow at the edge of one's vision. You could never look straight on at the illusive being yet you were certain you had seen something.

Parents were careful when speaking of the dark demon lest they frighten their children, but the little ones noted the tension in adult voices and the increasingly frequent gestures to ward off evil. The easy atmosphere of feasting and comfort with one's neighbors became diluted and old friends seemed just a bit more distant. All this had certainly been among the effects of the pestilence as its indifferent death blows severed the living from the dead, shattering families and filling each soul with haunting questions, "Will I be next? Or my neighbor? My child? My beloved? Who is marked for death? Who will live? Could I carry on if I survive?"

The usual energy was thus not present when the ritual month of mourning ended and the Norrungs gathered to choose their new chief. Tribe members from the vast forest region came to Vorthall and it was easy to see their numbers were not what they had been. Still, the traditions must be kept and ancient ways honored.

A light rain marked the morning of assembly. Njothila had barely slept the night before and rose early, washing the ashes from her face and donning her best clothing. As stubbornly independent as she was, she allowed one of the older women to deal with her hair, for it had become matted in the month since her father's death. This took some time, so it was as well that the young woman had risen early. The elder used the medicine of several plants in the cleansing and restoration of Njothila's chestnut tresses until the maiden was revealed in fierce and radiant beauty, no longer the wild child she had been before the plague days. A few sharp words from Auntie Gethalen, Lord Rathdar's elder sister, convinced Njothila to allow the patient groomer to anoint her with fragrance as well before decking her with her mother's jewelry. When they were through with her, she looked a chief's daughter, worthy of the Norrungs.

Njothir had silently striven with his own long thoughts for a month, nor did he ever share them, even with Ringskild. This morning he rose to face whatever the stars decreed. He stood in the early rain at the hour of sunrise and the heavens washed the ashes from his countenance. Returning within his hut he changed his leggings and tunic. He then hesitated before, for the first time, draping his shoulders with his father's great cloak, woven years before by Drenneth, his mother. It was not his father's clasp, however, with which he fastened it but that of his mother, a golden ring and pin that Rathdar had given her when Njothir was born.

He did not pass muster when Ringskild spotted him. Having been something of an elder sister to him all their lives—though only by two years—she let the bravest of the Norrungs know that he had done nothing with his hair and she promptly went to work, untangling, combing, and gathering the warrior's ruddy hair into a thick braid, similar to her own dark one. Satisfied, she informed him the Norrungs now need not bear shame for him and gave him a soldierly slap on the shoulder. Njothir did not fail to notice that Ivor's daughter herself appeared a fine Norrung warmaiden—tall, strong, proud, dangerous, and rather beautiful. The ashes no longer covered her burnished cheeks and fire was in her eyes.

"Thank you, my sister," was all he said.

Ringskild nodded and said nothing, then turned to join her brother.

Rutnir had little preparation to make. He was not courting that day, nor planning to stand for chief. His ashes were gone, his hair adequately tamed, and he wore his best tunic and a cloak of midnight blue wool. Whatever the day's assembly may bring, he felt ready to get on with life. Rutnir greeted his sister as she approached, wisely choosing not to question the collection of emotions that seemed to be playing across her face. Together they went to the meeting place, grateful that the morning's drizzle had ended.

Everyone was familiar with the assembly stone, a great flat rock on which speakers could stand amid a broad level space on a rise at the north edge of the town, close to the Nurgen's bank. The stone rose no more than the length of a forearm above the ground but that was platform enough. Today a stranger could find it as a steady drumbeat announced the gathering and called the Norrungs together. When all had met, a small boy led Rathdar's horse into their midst, decked in a fine blanket edged with silver bells and covered in greens of the forest.

A crone came forward and sprinkled the horse with scented water as the star singer began to chant the praises of the chief's steed. He sang of the thunder of its hooves and the bright music of its neighing. Its legs were the pillars of the world and its body the very earth itself. Fire was the life of the horse and its blood the rivers and seas. The wind was the dancing of its tail as it coursed through the heavens and its mane formed all grasses and plants. The World Horse was the soul of the Norrungs, the singer concluded, gift of the stars.

Other songs praised mountains, trees, and rivers as the soul of the Norrungs, but this was the song for the choosing of a new chief and it sounded good and right this day. Three young maidens had replaced the crone in the course of the singing and these crowned the steed with flowers. When all this concluded a young warrior approached the horse, bearing a sharp obsidian knife. He raised the knife but did not plunge it into the great beast. Back before memory this ritual had certainly begun in sacrifice but the people had long since ceased to waste good horses. In this enactment they acknowledged the gift of the world and all that was in it, and they honored their former chief indirectly, for he had been the soul of his people also. Instead of a mortal blow, the nervous horse encountered a ritual tap on the nose and a great cry released from many throats at the star singer's signal. "Live, Norrungs!"

Though the people knew this ritual did not end with literal sacrifice, there was always a great release of tension when it was completed. Hordal the lawkeeper then mounted the assembly stone and addressed the people, praising Rathdar and Drenneth and Vunill, speaking of the many losses among the people, and of the challenges faced by the Norrungs. This, he said, was a time in the life of the clan that called for a good leader. He paused for a long time before posing the traditional question: "Who among us should stand for chief, to lead the Norrungs in life and death?"

An awkward pause followed. Though the tribe was smaller than before, there were good men available, but leading in such dark days was no small consideration. None seemed prepared to set himself forward or ask friends to name him. Some looked to see if Hranild had any comments but the blind seer said nothing. Many of those present at Rathdar's funeral recalled her words that "Love shall be your chieftain if you will follow it," but electing love made no sense, nor could any think of a name that meant or echoed "love."

At last Vartal the miller spoke up. "We do not follow the ways of southern folk or peoples in the far western lands who pass leadership from father to son. In this we are wise, for generations of power do not build up to oppress us. Each chief among us is elected freely by this assembly of the people and we will talk and meet until we can agree. In this too we are wise. Yet I think that we shall find no braver warrior, nor fairer judge, than Rathdar's son, Njothir. He is young, very young for such a post. Nevertheless, he has proven his worth and I would have him lead us."

While a few outlanders asked the people of Vorthall about Njothir, most of the people knew him or knew of him. It seemed good to the assembly and there was little discussion. Before long the chant rose among the Norrungs: "Njothir! Njothir! Njothir!"

Njothir felt all eyes upon him. As at his father's funeral he squeezed his sister's hand for strength. He had known this might happen and he was of many minds in the matter. When the cheering waned, Hordal addressed the crowd again.

"Will the Norrungs have Njothir, son of Rathdar, son of Ronir, as chief?"

A great roar went up. Hordal then turned to Rathdar's son and questioned, "Njothir?"

Njothir drew a deep breath but no word came at first. The entire assembly waited anxiously. When his eyes met Ringskild's she fixed him with her gaze and nodded. Njothila nudged him with her elbow. Finally Njothir turned to Hordal and replied.

"I did not seek this, Norrungs, nor do I know that I am worthy of so great a charge as you would lay upon me. The mind of the stars is not mine and I know not what lies ahead of us all. Yet I will serve you faithfully so far as I am able."

He would have said more, but the people had heard all they needed for the moment. Njothir was led up to the assembly stone where all could see him. Amid the cheering he was anointed and a golden torc was placed about his neck to mark his new status. Njothila was led beside him, relieved that her brother would now be chief, for he was not likely to make her marry against her will.

Rutnir was beside himself with glee for his foster brother and best friend. But it was Ringskild's moment, for she now stepped forward bearing the cloak she had been weaving day and night for this occasion. It was made of many yarns and depicted the animals of the forest on its borders and symbols of the trees, all things sacred to her people. Njothir reluctantly parted with his father's cloak, handing it to his sister, then allowed Ringskild to place the new chief's cloak upon him. She did retain his mother's clasp, but now Njothir stood on his own, not mantled in his father's garb but chief of the Norrungs in his own right.

At that moment the sun broke through the clouds as if in benediction of what had passed. The hearts of the Norrungs were higher than they had been for some time. Njothir, however, was certain he had seen a dark shadow from the corner of his eye and he feared for his family, his people, his world.

CHAPTER 6

The coarse texture of the heavy wool blanket touching his chin entered Ian's consciousness first, but it was not what had stirred him from sleep. He tried to ignore both sensations and settle back into sleep, drawing warmth from his brother next to him in the deep shadows of the autumn night.

He felt himself sliding into unconsciousness when it returned—a sense that their bed, no, the whole cottage had just jolted.

"What is it?" Steven whispered sleepily when Ian bolted up in bed.

"I don't know," his younger brother replied softly. "Do you feel anything?"

"No."

Both boys tried not to wake their cousin Henry with whom they shared the bed, though he usually slept like a log and heard nothing. Aunt Susan similarly shared their sister Annabelle's bed in the next room and those were both light sleepers. There was no noise from that side or from the bedroom of the boys' parents.

"And you don't hear anything?" Ian persisted.

"Not unless it's that cursed dog next door. Go back to sleep, Ian."

"I can't. I'll be back shortly."

And with that Ian Dyrnedon, a lad who just turned fifteen last Lammas Day, rose in his nightshirt, shivered briefly as he changed into his shirt and trousers, slipped on his shoes and a heavy coat, pulled a cap over his head, and stepped out into the November darkness. The night itself was still and the moon shone in silence but Ian had been awakened by some deep vibration as though the earth had been rung like a bell. Nothing else seemed to move and his brother had obviously noticed nothing, yet Ian still felt the rumbling within himself. Yes, that was it: a rumbling and a great bass roar below the threshold of hearing, though all of nature appeared calm to the eyes.

Ian scanned the heavens, glanced at the denuded trees, and surveyed the nearby cottages of Dibble Lane. By now more than one dog was barking but otherwise all seemed normal. Still, he could not shake the strange feeling.

What he did not know on that Monday morning between midnight and dawn was that on the other side of the world the sacred Fuji-San had erupted through a vent on its side and would continue to spew ash for the next two months. All Ian knew was that something very big was happening here in Dribley Parva.

He closed his eyes to focus his mind and hearing. The roar grew louder and the barking increased in fury. For a second he felt dizzy as though the earth had shifted beneath him yet his feet still pressed on damp but solid earth. Then it seemed as though the neighborhood dogs had doubled or trebled in number and were all running wild, howling in a frenzy. Ian opened his eyes and saw a dark streak cross the waxing moon. There had been plenty of rain in the last week but Ian noticed the ground was dry. The boy looked around him as several dogs ran by and only then did he notice he was not in Dibble Lane and his family was not sleeping behind him. The only thing behind him was a stand of fir trees and the crumbled remnants of a low stone wall.

This made less sense than what had preceded though it was clearly more congruous with what he felt inside. Beneath Ian's feet the earth seemed to move in a slight slow wave and he could now see a dancing in tree branches. The great low roar also seemed at last to be coming from somewhere. Ian turned and saw a distant glow on the far horizon that reflected a deep orange color from the dark churning clouds above. A sudden flash was followed by a cracking sound, but these passed, and the deep rumble began to fade. An unseasonably warm breeze rushed his way and Ian's face grew taut with puzzlement.

Was this what Mt Etna was like? Ian concluded that he must be witnessing a volcano in the distance, except that there was no active volcano in his part of England and the whole thing had to be a dream.

The confused boy looked about for some shelter and finally curled up under a tree, wrapping his coat about him, and shut his eyes, trusting he would awaken in bed having only heard the rumble of Harry's snoring. None of the rest was real.

CHAPTER 7

Sarah Dyrnedon played the role of Chanticleer heralding the dawn as her cheerful voice came through the door, "Time to rise, lads, busy day ahead."

Harry, as usual, was impervious to minor noise. Steven kicked him awake and tried to roust his brother in the same manner. His foot encountered no Ian.

"Get up, Harry," he urged, then asked himself aloud, "I wonder where Ian's got to?" Being the eldest of the three boys, Steven took the center of the bed for warmth and was accustomed to shoving Ian out ahead of him but this morning he faced no obstacle. When he encountered their sister Annabelle, Steven asked if she had seen Ian about this morning.

"No. Why do you ask?"

"For starters I didn't get to kick his lazy arse out of bed this morning, but I remember that he woke up last night, dressed, and slipped out. Haven't seen him since."

"How very odd. That's not like him, being so fond of a warm bed and all. Perhaps Mum or Dad has seen him."

"Perhaps."

As if on cue, Mum called out to all the household, "Breakfast!"

With her sister's assistance, Sarah had the table set and porridge and tea ready. Mr. William Dyrnedon settled at the head and prepared to say grace, then halted.

"Where's your brother, Steven?"

The sixteen-year old, who had hoped not to be asked since he had no answer, faced the head of the family and replied, "I have no idea, Father. He wasn't in bed when we got up."

"Well, he can't have vanished, go find him." Steven was thus sent off before he could take a bite while his father, a devout Catholic from the days of the Old King and still one under Anne, crossed himself and began, "For these and all our many blessings…."

By the time Steven returned without Ian the household was in turmoil. In spite of her husband's fatherly blustering, Sarah saw to it that Steven was fed as all parties prepared to look for the missing boy. The anxiety was mitigated by their knowing that the village was rather quiet and secure and Ian was resourceful. Each felt confident that Ian would show up within the hour. As the sun reached its zenith that day, Mr. Dyrnedon finally notified the constable that Ian had not been seen and a general search was raised.

All was in vain and ultimately the tragic episode was summarized in a brief notice:

> **Local Lad Disappears**
> Friday, 28 November 1707
> On Monday last Ian William Dyrnedon, aged fifteen, second child of William George and Sarah Elizabeth Dyrnedon of Hellebore Cottage, disappeared without a trace. His brother Steven and sister Annabelle remain safe with their parents. There is, as yet, no suspicion of foul play. Authorities trust that parties with information about the boy will step forward with their assistance.

The family never heard more.

CHAPTER 8

Ian felt the hot breath on his neck and braced himself for Steven's kick. Some things in life could be relied on.

The kick did not come and Ian kept his eyes closed. Given the strange nightmare he had just been through, the boy was reluctant to face the day and convinced himself that he needed more rest. The warm breath became a licking tongue.

"Stop it," Ian warned, certain that Steven would not stop teasing once he began. And the tongue was especially disgusting. "*I hope I taste terrible,*" he thought silently. The tongue did not return but Ian heard a shuffling of leaves by his head and all his senses became alert at once. He opened his eyes to see the legs of a large gray dog standing next to where he lay on the ground. The familiar smell of the bedroom was now the musty smell of soil in autumn and fallen leaves adorned his bed, not sheets. God help him, he was still dreaming or the dream may have been real. The beast had drawn back when Ian grumbled at what he supposed to be his brother.

The dog stared, its tongue hanging to one side. Ian stared back into the pale blue eyes. It was a handsome dog and rather looked like a wolf, though he could not imagine a wolf waking him for breakfast. Then again, wherever he might be right now, he did not want to be a wolf's breakfast.

Slowly Ian raised himself from the earth and looked about. He was in a wooded area facing this rather questionable dog. The stone wall from his dream was still there, running along the ground, undressed stones fitted without mortar and speckled with lichen, a visual barrier only.

The sun had not yet risen, though it would very soon. The heavy cloud of the night before had thinned somewhat. Ian dusted himself off the best he could and addressed the attentive canine.

"Well, old chap, where do we go from here?"

As if in answer, the dog turned and began walking, though without a sense of the sun's position Ian had no idea in what direction. With no better idea to offer, Ian followed. When the dog availed himself of a tree, Ian did the same only to watch the dog revisit the tree and claim territory back from the boy. This provided the only humor of the morning, a morning that proved especially tiring after a short night's sleep and no breakfast.

Breakfast. What Ian wouldn't give for his mother's porridge at this moment. And what must his family be thinking? His father would be furious and his mother frantic. If only he could hear them calling to him right now. Ian strained to listen but only heard woodland noises: an occasional chirping bird, the rustle of leaves when a breeze stirred, the sound of a small animal he could not see passing through the brush.

Every now and again Ian paused to reassure himself that the earth lay still beneath his feet. The ground had made no movement but the night before had left him questioning reality at every turn.

Ian began to wonder if he were totally daft to be following a beast through strange woods but it seemed so companionable a creature that he assumed it must belong to someone. In that case, it would surely lead him to someone. In this hope, he stayed with the four-legged guide. An outspoken jay seemed at one point to disapprove of Ian's companion and trailed them a while, scolding every second.

The dog favored animal trails winding through thick brush and Ian wearied of pushing through branches. At one point he set out on a broader trail and the dog shot round to block his way and snarled.

"Since when did you become a border collie and I your sheep?" Ian asked.

The dog stood its ground. When Ian took a step toward it he noticed the retracted lips and sharp teeth. Dogs did not especially frighten Ian but the thought of testing those fangs with his own flesh did not appeal.

"Have it your way, then," he said and turned to go in the direction the dog had taken before Ian's detour.

Assured of Ian's compliance the animal retook the lead.

Upon reaching a small stream both of them drank. It felt good to have some fresh water though Ian would have loved some breakfast to go with it. This led to renewed thoughts of his mother's cooking. How was he to get home by following a dog? But which way was home? Any home at this point.

They continued, working their way up a long rise that eventually became a rocky slope. The dog managed to find a winding path around boulders, occasionally leaping to the next ledge. Ian clambered after it. Pulling himself up onto one large stone slab, Ian spotted a snake partly camouflaged by a bed of leaves windblown into a long crack in the rocks.

It lacked the zigzag pattern of an adder and appeared larger than a common grass snake. Its scales were in shades of eggshell, slate, and an earthy tan and a pale ochre stripe ran the length of its sides. It was coiling as though in readiness to strike and Ian's mind fought vainly to overcome an instinct to freeze.

Before Ian could analyze the situation or act the dog pounced on the reptile, grabbing it just behind the head with its strong jaws, clamped down, shook it, and then tossed it into a nearby clump of shrubs where it twitched a few times and relaxed into death.

"Thanks, old boy," Ian heard himself say. The dog looked at him with what might pass for a canine smile, its tongue hanging to one side.

They continued to mount the rocky ridge where the dog paused as Ian caught up. Trees were still thick, for they had journeyed through nothing but forest, yet through a couple of openings in the trees Ian could see what looked like a valley before them. The overcast sky of early morning had given way to scattered clouds and in the sunlight some distant aspens looked like dancing gold coins.

Having caught their breath the two descended. Ian's hunger had grown but he was disinclined to catch and eat a raw rodent, as the dog had done at one point.

Finally, at midmorning, they came to a clearing with a couple of small stone cottages. These appeared quite primitive, but Ian was grateful for any sign of human habitation. He hallooed and was answered.

"Young man, look at you."

Ian glanced down, dusted himself off, again, and looked hopefully toward the stranger's voice. The words of friendly reproach had come from a plump and cheery woman looking out a cottage door. She was simply dressed in a dun-colored dress with a brown apron and dark kerchief from which gray wisps strayed. "Come, come," she said, waving him forward.

"How do you do, ma'am."

"Better than it seems you do, lad. Stars be merciful, I'd swear you've spent the whole night out in the woods."

"I'm afraid that's true."

"Well, bless me. Where are my manners? Why don't you hang your coat on this hook and sit for a minute?"

As Ian sat she bustled about and soon had a thick slab of bread and an apple in front of him, along with a cup of mead.

"You just eat and get yourself back together. I can tell you're exhausted, though I've no idea how you came to be walking about with a wolf. I'm not fond of them but they usually avoid us humans."

The lad did not comment immediately, absorbed as he was in addressing his hunger. The bread was hearty and coarse but satisfying, the apple crisp and tart. Ian paused from chewing to taste a swig of mead and reply to the friendly woman.

"I can't really say how I came to be walking with it, but it woke me up this morning as I lay sleeping under a tree. But I thought it was just a large dog."

"Oh no, lad, that's a wolf all right, though he acts tame enough. If it gets near my chickens you'll hear about it. But what were you doing sleeping in the woods?"

"That is stranger still, ma'am. I woke up in my bed at home, thought I heard a deep booming noise, and went outside. Dogs were barking but nothing was happening. I closed my eyes for a minute and when I opened them the noise was louder and the ground moved. It was then I saw the glow under the clouds."

"Ah yes, Mount Firestorm off in the eastern hills. It did act up in the night. I could see it too. But wherever is your home?"

"Yorkshire, ma'am, Hellebore Cottage, Dibble Lane, Dribley Parva. But this doesn't look anywhere like home."

"I daresay, boy. I've lived here all my fifty-three years and never heard any of that. Not even sure I can pronounce the names." This seemed to amuse her and Ian allowed himself to smile.

"Well, I am Gwenda daughter of Fintall, wife of Geredh son of Sendhor, and mother of Njella, Nedreth, and little Sendhor, named for his grandfather. Who might you be?"

"My name is Ian Dyrnedon," he began, then adapted to the woman's style, "son of William and Sarah, brother of Steven and Annabelle."

"Good then, we know you have some family."

Gwenda eyed the lad, just on the edge of manhood by her guess. He was on the tall side, lean but healthy enough in spite of his current state. He had a narrow face and blue eyes. No sign of a beard yet but a few light brown curls stuck out of the edges of his cap. His hair was oddly chopped short as though he had no dignity whatsoever, not even a hint of a good Norrung braid. His were definitely the clothes of an outlander but he was unlike any traveler she had known and did not seem hardened enough to be one of the eastern raiders.

She sounded reassured and relieved at word of his family but Ian became agitated. Where was his family and where was he? What must they be thinking? Were they looking for him? How might he get home again? Such questions tumbled in his head, re-energized by the recent food and drink.

"Where are we?" Ian ventured.

"Dear me, that lost are you? You can see we are hardly a village here, just a couple of hunting huts with no more name than Fintall's Clearing, for my father. We are in the Forrest of Norrast in the land of the Norrungs."

"I've never heard of the Forrest of Norrast or the Norrungs."

"Never heard of the greatest forest in the Lands about the Mere? That is about as curious as seeing you walking with a wolf. You don't practice dark arts, do you, Ian?"

"Heavens no, ma'am. But I am very confused today and concerned about my family since I don't know how to get back to them."

"Probably suffered a good bump on the head, is my guess. It should all come back. And if not, there's plenty to do here. You can join my boys hunting."

"That's very generous of you, but I would rather go home."

"Of course you would, lad. I just don't know how to help you get there."

31

And so they puzzled together until a howling arose outside. Gwenda and Ian leapt from their places and came outside to see the wolf giving alarm. "It's not my chickens," Gwenda shouted, "but stars deliver us, I don't know what it is."

What it was soon became apparent as a band of eight armor-clad men rode into the clearing, trailed by four other horses. Three of these had unarmored riders: Gwenda's husband Geredh and their sons, Nedreth and Sendhor, both just a few years older than Ian. Geredh was bleeding and his sons appeared pale.

"Come, Mother," Nedreth urged. "These are men of Chief Njothir and they have only just rescued us from a band of raiders to the east. It is no longer safe here. They are taking us to Vorthall for safety."

"Your father?" Gwenda questioned.

"He is injured but should heal," Nedreth answered, dismounting. He and Sendhor helped her gather the most precious belongings as Ian was introduced and joined in the packing. Sendhor's glances indicated suspicion regarding the stranger but there was no time to deal with that. Several chickens were grasped and added to the stores. Gwenda mounted a horse and Captain Rutnir, a man not much older than Ian yet clearly in command, ordered Ian to ride behind him.

The armed band then headed west, with Gwenda trying to explain to her sons what little she knew of the stranger and Ian trying to make sense of the world he was caught up in. Rutnir, so affable in Vorthall, was all business now, a disciplined young warrior in no mood to answer questions, and he let Ian know as much. Now and again the young Englishman caught a glimpse of a gray shadow trailing them.

CHAPTER 9

Ian had been on a horse before but all he had known were farm horses or carriage horses. This was a great black warhorse with a white blaze down its nose. They were clearly not plowing a field or bearing everyday burdens. The man to whom he clung had become, for the moment, his sole anchor in a strange and swirling world.

The vague disorientation that woke Ian the night before had grown to overwhelming proportion, dislodging the youth from every familiar point of reference. The somewhat comforting hospitality of Gwenda had suddenly evaporated before the tangible evidence of danger and violence. Ian cast a glance at Geredh's face, drained of all color, and the combination of anxiety and determination on the other faces about him. Was this still a dream? If so, it was not a happy one. But it did not feel like a dream. There were no soft edges, no familiar elements woven into it.

This Rutnir seemed but a few years older than Ian. Ian was tall for his age, and wiry; this warrior was taller still and seemed bursting with power. His arms would befit a blacksmith though his refined facial features and thin brows did not fit that image. Ian could sense tension in the man's body, like a tightly coiled spring. In the moment that Rutnir had ordered Ian to mount the younger man saw flashing dark eyes that expected instant obedience. Now Ian saw only the back of Rutnir's head. A braid of dark brown hair that could almost pass for black trailed from beneath a metal helmet.

This was not exactly the knight in shining armor figure of old tales. Rutnir's body armor was mostly hardened leather with metal pieces at the joints, such as the shoulders. The shield slung beside them was also covered with heavy leather and iron bosses. Ian held on and inhaled the sweat of horse and man, of moist earth from the previous day's rain. This was too real. He wondered whether the soldier was his savior or captor. And what had happened to Ian's home?

Was his family scouring Dribley Parva at this moment? What had Steven told their father? His mother must be frantic by now, fretting over her second child. Cousin Harry was probably plotting how he could now have half the bed instead of a third. Oh, there would be hell to pay when he got home again. If he got home again.

Ian had no idea where home was from here. Where or what was this Vorthall toward which they rode and who was Chief Njothir? Why had people attacked Gwenda's family?

The road seemed little more than a muddy trail threading its way among the trees. This was an untamed world, something out of an old history book or fairy tale, except the injury to Gwenda's husband and the fear of all around him proclaimed it all very solid and present. Unaccustomed to riding a horse for any length of time, Ian was becoming saddle sore but knew better than to complain to those who appeared to be saving his life. From what, he could not say. He had no understanding of "eastern raiders" though it clearly referred to some sort of brigands.

Each mile took them farther from this vague threat. Farther also from Hellebore Cottage and Ian's family. At one point Ian felt a tremor arise within his body, an uncontrollable shudder of lostness. "It's all right, lad," Rutnir said. "You're safe now."

What could be safe in this foreign place surrounded by strangers? Could any place ever be safe again if going outside one's own home could lead to this? This was like one of Aunt Susan's stories of children carried away into some fairy land but these warriors were no fairy folk. Had he been snatched by demons or dark forces?

Ian made a cramped and surreptitious sign of the Cross with the fingers of his right hand and silently began to pray: *Pater noster qui es in caelis…*. He completed the prayer with special emphasis on the words "*libera nos a malo,*" but nothing seemed to change. The sign of the Cross did not make the demons, or warriors, or strangers flinch, much less vanish. He did not want to show weakness or fear but he could feel his eyes moisten. Ian chose in that moment to resist, internally at least, whatever darkness lay behind this cruel trick. He silently recited as much as he could remember of the litany of saints, beseeching every friend of God with a piety and fervor he had never known in his young life.

Saint Michael the Archangel did not descend with legions of angels to rescue him, however. The only warriors to be seen were these he rode with. They had no wings, only swords and shields and leather armor. They, it seemed, were to be his only rescuers. He prayed to Jesus and Mary that these strangers were not on the side of evil and turned his attention once more to the strange countryside through which they traveled.

They had ridden about an hour before Ian spotted other habitations. A crude shelter carved into a low bluff was the first—its facing made of stones carefully stacked with clay filling the cracks—followed shortly by a hut like those at Fintall's Clearing. It was a squat, round wattle-and-daub affair with a large gap in its thatch, zealously guarded by a three-legged dog that sounded its warning before Ian could even see the dwelling. Its yapping rose in frenzy as the riders went by then suddenly ceased. The angry bouncing of the dog also stopped. Ian glanced at the now slowly hobbling dog then followed its gaze toward the wolf in the distance that still trotted parallel to the warriors and their wards. He wondered why a dog so ferocious in defense of its territory would becalm itself on seeing a wolf rather than redouble its efforts. Not another sound came from its throat.

They rode on and the mountain that had dominated the landscape to the north when they were back at the Clearing had diminished behind them. Eventually more huts appeared, dotting either side of a stream that cut across their path. Some of these had walls of rough-hewn planks and others were mud-walled like those Ian had seen before. The few windows were shut from the cold with oiled skins scraped thin and stretched taut. The cries of an unhappy baby drifted through the air and a handful of curious children waved at the warriors. Ian spotted a couple about his sister's age, a girl and a boy, pulling a cart weighted down with firewood they had evidently gathered in the neighboring woods. Their faces were disquietingly expressionless, even as they turned their heads to glance at the passersby. The pair continued hauling their burden behind one of the huts. Crows floated among half-denuded branches.

This, Rutnir informed Ian, was the Tuga Stream and here they paused to water the horses. The riders walked upstream with dippers to slake their own thirst. The warriors reached into their saddle pouches and took out strips of dried meat, sharing them with Gwenda's family and Ian.

Strengthened by this refreshment, they all remounted and took advantage of the easy ford to continue westward. They had scarcely emerged from the stream when all the riders suddenly veered to the right and proceeded in a wide curve off the wagon track they had been following. Ian had noticed no signal to trigger such strange behavior and inquired.

"Why did we just leave the path?"

Rutnir nodded toward a cottage on the left side of the path. It appeared quite ordinary, another simple dwelling of tightly fitted stones. A cluster of birch trees sheltered it on one side while a vegetable garden extended along the other. In front of the door stood a pole with tattered red and white strips of cloth attached, hanging limp in the absence of any breeze. A lone chicken scratched the dirt among some cabbages.

"Plague house," said Rutnir.

Ian had heard tales of the Black Death and shuddered.

"How can you tell?"

"The red and white bands tell us a house has been visited by the fiery death. The pestilence came to our lands a few years ago and is now rarely seen but we do not take chances. This house may be abandoned now and there may be no evil left; still we avoid it."

"I see," Ian responded, wondering how many may have perished.

He also began to wonder "when" he was as much as where he was. That he was nowhere near Dribley Parva seemed obvious, but it was also apparent that he did not see any signs of the eighteenth century. It was unlikely this crowd had heard of Queen Anne or the ongoing War of the Spanish Succession. The colonies across the Atlantic seemed nearer now to home than the forest he found himself in, but even the colonies had buildings such as those Ian was accustomed to seeing. All he had seen here were scattered cottages, with no churches or pubs or anything very civilized.

A very few cultivated fields appeared along the way and one orchard with the last lonely leaves still clinging to the trees. Ian noticed several well-tended vegetable gardens beside whitewashed huts, but the landscape mostly consisted of trees and more trees, broken only by small meadows. Those rare folks he spotted tending the land cast glances at the small band of warriors passing with their new charges then turned back to their tasks. There were only two small groups of travelers heading east and these hailed the group, calling them cousins. Ian wondered how everyone could be related. Rutnir warned these travelers of the presence of raiders.

Ian had never seen a forest go on so long. Heavy in firs around Fintall's Clearing the woods gradually shifted to pines and occasional stands of oak as they journeyed. There were a few pauses. Ian spotted what he thought a broad river ahead but it was the sky glinting off a lake instead. They approached the shore where the lake was still narrow, fresh from the mouth of the Agbo Stream that drained the plain west of Mount Hnorg. The lake ran south for a couple of miles, broadening until it met the Woodstream River. This was a lush area and Ian noticed plentiful waterfowl among the reeds and skimming the smooth surface of the lake. Here they only had to deviate by half a mile to find a ford in the stream just above Lake Agbo.

On they rode through varied terrain: field, thicket, stony passages, and yet more forest. Traveling so long with little conversation increased Ian's anxiety. Nothing and no one was familiar. He might as well have been a captive. Perhaps he was. There was no sign of the Yorkshire he knew, of home, or of hope. Rare glimpses of the wolf padding along through the woods had become the most familiar thing in this very strange day if only because the wolf was his one constant. That only raised more questions and was little comfort.

Finally Ian could take the silence no longer.

"My family is back there somewhere," he began.

"Stars save them," said Rutnir. That seemed an odd prayer but Ian almost said "Amen."

"Will I be able to go back to them?"

"Perhaps. Not today. Probably not soon."

"I've never been away from them," Ian confessed. He thought he felt the warrior's body stiffen for a moment.

"I'm sorry," said Rutnir. "It's not easy to lose family."

Rutnir's tone was gentle yet Ian sensed a rebuke. He thought about this for a while before speaking.

"Is your family all right?" Ian asked.

"My sister is well. Our parents and our brother are dead."

"I am sorry," said Ian.

"I am sorry we must take you away from your family. We could not leave you at Fintall's Clearing."

"I think I understand that, sir. I am very confused. Gwenda tells me we are in the Forest of Norrast but I have never heard of it before and so I don't really know where I am."

"We'll have to sort that out with Lord Njothir, then," said Rutnir.

Ian took that for the end of the conversation and sank back into puzzled silence, observing the world about him and trying to understand what had happened to him. The cries of birds seemed familiar enough and, though he knew nothing of this forest, the trees seemed like those of home. When they forded the third stream, the one Rutnir called the Felni, with its water rushing over smooth stones, he wondered if they would ever reach this place they called Vorthall.

A hint of something resembling civilization materialized when the riders came at last to the Nurgen valley and Vorthall of the Norrungs. Ian noticed scattered homes had appeared with more frequency. They had passed several wagons laden with goods and begun to encounter more travelers. The road suddenly emerged from a dense stretch of woodland and curved, offering a view of far more than a handful of huts. Ian felt tension drain from Rutnir's body at the sight. The habitations of Vorthall were on the far side of the Nurgen, following its course and tightly clustered. The town stretched along the far bank to Ian's right where he lost sight of it around the river's curve.

Sundry moorings dotted the riverbank while shops and houses stood between the river and the palisade that enclosed the city proper. Shallow bottomed boats could be seen in either direction. To Ian's eyes there was nothing that seemed like a proper wall about the town. He had once visited York with his father and brother and seen the stone defenses left by the Romans, weighty and impressive tributes to an ancient civilization. There was no real defense here, just a nominal wall of vertical logs tightly planted, perhaps twice the height of a horse. Ian spotted a few guards watching from the top of the wall so there had to be a walkway around it. A battering ram or a fire would make short work of it, thought Ian. These people could not have serious enemies. The raiders that inspired fear earlier in the morning might threaten isolated communities but not Vorthall.

The sight—and scent—of smoke rising from hearth fires seemed comforting amid the strangeness of everything else. This also held promise of warmth for they had ridden long and shadows were overtaking the day.

Ian was surrounded by strangers and could not tell if they were his saviors or he their prisoner. They had preserved him from brigands and murderers while carrying him farther and farther from Hellebore Cottage. A shift in their demeanor told him the sight of Vorthall was a good thing, to them at least. He hoped it bade him well also.

Rutnir and his men pursued the gentle decline of the last stretch of road to the broad ford where they crossed to the south edge of Vorthall. The water here was deeper than in any of the streams they had crossed so far and they emerged onto the road on the far bank with the horses' bellies and their own legs dripping with cold water.

They rode perhaps five hundred paces from the river's edge, winding their way amid the buildings outside the palisade. People intent on their own errands bustled about them, stepping aside for the armed party with no particular notice, as though warriors on horseback were an everyday affair. Ian watched their faces of those who hawked wares at the roadside and those who made their way along the road. He noticed the etchings of anxiety on some, a weary look of resignation on others, and wistfulness on yet others. What he did not catch sight of was the energetic movement one might expect at a hub of commerce.

They came to a crossing of many roads and turned right toward the western entrance to the town. This was half a mile from the downstream end of town. Rutnir greeted the guards at the gate. They returned his salutation with a respectful tone. Ian wondered how important the man he rode with was.

Once inside gates they threaded their way among close-set dwellings and shops and headed directly toward the great hall standing on a rise near the center of town. Huge timbers framed it and Ian noticed carvings at the top of the porch columns and on the ends of crossbeams. Off to the side stood a lone pole of carved knotwork with a horse head at its top. Two grooms seemed to materialize and help some of the warriors with the horses as the party dismounted. With a jerk of his chin Rutnir motioned for them to enter the hall.

Ian could barely move. He had ridden horses but never for so long. With pained steps he stayed close to the young captain, an anchor amid all the confusing newness, while Sendhor and Nedreth helped their semi-conscious father from the horse and Gwenda hovered anxiously. Rutnir ordered a page to send for a healer as two of his men hastened off to return with a pallet.

Here Geredh's sons gently laid him, nor would they allow the soldiers to carry him. With one son on each end of the pallet, the group passed the guards and entered the hall.

"Rutnir, thank the stars you have returned. Are all the men safe?" This inquiry came from a tall man, scarcely older than Rutnir, with broad shoulders and ruddy hair forming a long braid. His trousers were of coarse cloth like that of the other men Ian had been riding with and his tunic was simply made, though of a fine fabric the color of mahogany. A great sword was belted at his side and a golden torc circled his neck. Animal and forest patterns decorated the great cloak he wore on his shoulders. His posture and energy bespoke authority unusual in one so young.

Was this the lord of the Norrungs? He seemed unlikely. There was no wig of magistracy, no distinguishing uniform, no retinue such as Ian would expect of an English lord. Should Ian bow?

Ian chose to wait and see, taking his cues from those around him.

Rutnir answered the man.

"They are, my brother. We encountered some raiders east of Fintall's homestead beyond Gretnir's Stream. They had just surrounded the honest huntsmen you see here and who have traded with us before. We routed the raiders but not before Geredh son of Sendhor had suffered a great blow. We gathered his wife, Fintall's daughter, and this stranger and have brought them to the safety of Vorthall."

"You have done well. Vorthall needs honest souls in times like these. Let Geredh be cared for. I take it the young man in foreign garb is our stranger. Bring him closer."

Gwenda went with her husband and the healers and her sons remained in the chief's presence, not knowing if they needed to defend themselves or swear allegiance. Ian stepped forward and thus it was that the Yorkshire lad found himself before Njothir of the Norrungs, a ruler but eight years older than himself. The chieftain surveyed the boy from his cropped hair to his unusual shoes, noting oddities such as buttons and pockets. Ian seemed healthy and alert enough, though nothing like warrior material. Anxiety was written all over the boy's face but there were no particular marks of guile, nor did he act like someone with a need to conceal.

"And where would you be from, stranger?" Njothir finally asked.

"From Dribley Parva, Yorkshire," Ian replied, "but I don't think it is part of this world."

"Not part of this world? Are you a shape shifter or person of power?"

"Not that I know of, sir. But the land where I come from does not seem like this land. It has mountains and trees and rivers and all that, but, well…. I don't know how to explain it. I heard something, a deep roar like, and left the house to see what it was. I listened and shut my eyes to focus on what I heard, then when I opened them my family's house was not there, nor our neighbors' homes, and I was here in your land. I thought I was dreaming, so I went to sleep under a tree and woke up when a wolf licked me in the morning." At this the sons of Geredh gave a low, mocking laugh.

"A wolf, eh? This is a very strange tale you tell. I can think of many reasons a man might lie about where he comes from."

This was not promising but Ian stuck to what he knew.

"Indeed, sir, I can think of some myself, but I am not lying to you. I just don't understand what happened to me. All I know is that I followed the wolf until I came to the cottage where Gwenda fed me."

"There was wolf outside the cottage," Rutnir interjected, "howling and snapping when we rode in as if giving alarm. It seemed to follow us back toward Vorthall as well, staying just within sight."

"Well, if my captain and foster brother vouches for that part of your story I will take it for true. But it seems even more likely you and your wolf might both be shape shifters. Or worse." Njothir let this thought sink into Ian's consideration before continuing. "Who are you, lad?"

"My name is Ian William Dyrnedon, sir, son of William Dyrnedon."

"Those are a lot of names, and strange sounding ones. I trust we may call you Ijn son of Wiljm. I am Njothir son of Rathdar, chief of the Norrungs. I should like to keep you near and observe you. Rutnir, is the boy armed?"

"We did not have time to see, my lord, though if he has a weapon it was not used against me on our ride hither. I will check." Rutnir then proceeded to search Ian quite thoroughly, turning up only one weapon: a small pocket knife. "The blade is sharp, brother, but it is certainly neither an instrument of war nor very serviceable for either defense or acts of betrayal."

Njothir raised his brows and looked straight at Ian, who gulped and spoke.

"It belonged to my father, sir. He gave it to me some years ago as it is very handy. I have always carried it with me in case something needs cutting. But I have never used it as a weapon." Ian was both horrified and amused at the thought. This was a very poor weapon.

Njothir gave an amused snort, "Indeed, I imagine not. You may keep your knife with you, for all men have something for slicing a bit of food. You are warned, however, that it must not be used against any of my people, even in jest, or you will forfeit your life."

Such an idea had never crossed Ian's mind, but he took the solemn warning seriously. With wide eyes he replied, "Of course not, sir."

"So," Njothir continued, "you do not know where you are or how you got here, and presumably have no clue how to get back where you came from. This makes no sense, but I will worry about it no further at the moment." He turned his attention to the other young men.

"Sons of Geredh, tell me of your hunting this morning."

Nedreth and Sendhor then recounted how they and their father set out, as usual, seeking small game. They had gathered a rabbit from one of their traps and downed a couple of ducks with arrows when a flock of geese caught their attention, honking across the morning sky. The noise of the geese covered other sounds as four raiders burst from cover and attacked them, presumably for their food and weapons, but possibly in a search for healthy slaves. It was impossible to tell the motives of men these days.

The young men put up a goodly fight but their father, feeling his age, was not quite swift enough to fend off a couple of hard blows from a great ox of a man. Into the midst of this free-for-all rode Rutnir's men, slaying two of the raiders and dispersing the other two. Rutnir informed them that they could no longer be safe in their hunting cottage and urged them to join with the Norrungs of Vorthall while lawlessness was abroad. The boys might have argued but fearing for their mother and considering their father's injuries they agreed. The entire party then returned to the cottage to collect Gwenda and found themselves saddled with the stranger as well.

"We have a sister, sir," Nedreth added, "but she married two years ago and lives now with her husband's family to the west. There was news we are uncles now but we have heard nothing lately. And that accounts for all our family."

"May the stars keep her safe as they have led you hither. You are welcome among the Norrungs, grandsons of Sendhor and Fintall. We need strong men and good hunters, not to mention loyal sons. Times are dark and many seem to be giving up on life. You may find good wives among us and help us in the restoration of life. There are houses emptied by plague yet safe enough for new dwellers. Let one of our men help you find one before nightfall. My sister Njothila can lead you now to the house of the healers to rejoin your father and mother."

At that point all three young strangers to Vorthall noticed the young woman with downcast eyes who had been busy nearby. She stepped forward when Njothir mentioned her name. He explained and she nodded her head, then turned to visit the house of healers, Geredh's sons walking behind her. Sendhor and Nedreth seemed quite eager to be in her company and Ian wondered why he felt so disappointed to be remaining near the chief of the Norrungs.

CHAPTER 10

Even with the flexibility of youth, Ian found it a challenge to adapt to life among the Norrungs. While many of their social customs seemed arbitrary or incomprehensible, he managed to pattern himself on those around him. His own anxiety and Norrung suspicion of outlanders gradually diminished. The worst obstacle was the ache in his chest that would not go away and arose each time he thought of his family.

His sense of loss would surprise and sweep over him with no warning. It might come at the scent of bread baking—hearty bread that he learned to enjoy but nothing like the loaves his mother baked. He longed to wail with a voice that would reach the stars though he feared to do so. He had neither met nor heard of a single family in Vorthall that had not lost members to the fiery death. How could he fuss over his grief in light of this widespread loss? Rutnir, his rescuer, and his sister Ringskild had lost their father to the plague just months before Ian arrived in Vorthall and their mother to the wasting sickness three years earlier. Lord Njothir and his sister were orphaned young as well. Ian took his cues from these, who were becoming a new family, and tried to carry on with each new day as best he could.

His quick mind and skillful hands allowed him to learn much of woodworking from Kjevar, one of the master craftsmen of Vorthall. Ian was especially adept at inlay and advanced halfway to journeyman status within a year. He was less clever at hunting but enjoyed the sacred quest for food nonetheless, learning from Njothir and others the respect with which all things, including one's future dinner, must be approached.

With the exception of the chieftain's friendship and his mysterious origins there was nothing marking Ian as unusual. Gwenda continued to welcome him though her sons remained suspicious of the outlander. Geredh mended and rejoined his sons in hunting, though all hunting parties heading more than half a day east of Vorthall now included at least a couple of warriors, a constant reminder that the world was not as safe as it had once been.

Ian could not say at what point he felt that Njothir had ceased observing and evaluating him but he noticed the chief had ceased calling him stranger and begun to address him as brother. Perhaps Ian's obvious bewilderment about this new world and its customs convinced the chief that the stranger was neither dissembling nor present with evil intent. Maybe Njothir enjoyed having the ear of someone not tied into the history and politics of the People. In any case, those near the chief treated him as their lord's foster brother.

Njothila, daughter of Rathdar, was almost always present in Ian's life. They lived, after all, in the same house, the chieftain's home adjacent to the great hall. She was close to him in age and, as sister to an unmarried chief, had many duties at Njothir's side. Ian found himself chatting comfortably with her, sharing more of his feelings than he did with most Norrungs. She, in turn, seemed to find this stranger fascinating and less likely to threaten her with a political marriage than the other young men of Vorthall. They could tease each other without offense, something neither experienced with most others. Njothila also gave Ian one of his greatest surprises.

It was an early spring morning before the world had truly warmed again. Njothi, as her family and closest friends called her, was sitting at a portable desk just outside the chief's dwelling, taking advantage of the light. She wrote rapidly and Ian, who had rather enjoyed his non-academic education with the tribe, paused in passing to look at the lines flowing from her quill. It was an incomprehensible scrawl unlike anything he had ever seen.

"What are you writing?" he asked.

"I am making a note of the decisions of last night's council meeting; can't you tell?"

"No, I can't make sense of any of it," Ian stammered, feeling challenged by her question.

Njothi looked up. "Oh. I'm sorry. I didn't realize you cannot read." She said this gently.

"But I can," Ian protested. "I just can't read this."

"What do you mean?" she queried.

"Back home I could read. I didn't do much reading but I can read and write. Your letters are different from ours."

"Really? Would you write something for me?" She proffered the quill.

It had been many months since Ian had read or written and he now felt unsure of himself.

Njothi spoke again: "If you'd rather not…."

"What should I write?" Ian responded, certain he could write at least something simple.

"I was just about to write that 'Word reached Vorthall of the death of Avroth II, King of Thyelos.'"

"Very well," said Ian as he put the quill to vellum and sounded out the words as he wrote them. Njothila's eyes widened as she saw the foreign shapes slowly emerge on the parchment, so very unlike her flowing script. Then she gasped.

"What did you say?"

"I said 'word reached Vorthall….'"

"But you didn't," Njothi countered. "You were making strange sounds."

Ian looked at his script. It was proper English. Then he rehearsed in his mind what Njothi had just recited to him. It was not English at all. She had expressed what he was writing down but in another tongue.

They stared at each other and then looked down at the parchment again.

"It's the same thing," Ian began.

"But it is in your language," Njothila concluded.

"How do I understand you, then?" Ian asked.

"I have no idea," she said, frowning. "Unless…."

The pause seemed much longer to the frustrated English lad than it really was and the Norrung woman seemed to enjoy making him wait. Finally she continued.

"Unless you were bitten by a rachthor."

"A what?"

"A rachthor. They are terrible beasts that lurk in caves and other dark places and feed on humans. They say that if you survive their bite you can understand all speech, including the tongues of animals."

"Wouldn't I remember something like that?" Ian asked.

"I should imagine so. Maybe one of your ancestors was bitten by one and the rachthor's magic flows in your veins."

Ian resorted to logic, though it had not always served him as well in this strange world as it did in his own. "We don't have rachthors in England."

"Well, that is the only explanation I can think of," Njothi said.

"I guess it will have to do. But I can't recall understanding animals, unless a cat is begging for food or a dog is barking to tell me to stay away."

"Well, everyone understands those," Njothi conceded. "Still, if it wasn't a rachthor it must be something like it."

"I shall take your word for it," said Ian. It was the only explanation they had.

CHAPTER 11

The mysterious fever had continued its expansion beyond the lands of the Norrungs and the presence of the Chegjan grew with it. In addition to lassitude and despair there were new manifestations of its waxing power. Fits of collective hysteria or group delusions were now appearing randomly in villages as people took on strange beliefs or unexplained behavior. Violence and mob actions erupted spontaneously, leading to horrendous deeds that left the perpetrators aghast at their actions afterwards. Rumors multiplied and fear gripped the land.

A new phrase arose in the common vocabulary as the Chegjan was characterized as a "mind eater." This was an attempt to make sense of the fits striking the people. Labeling it changed nothing but doing so gave the comfort of calling such behavior by a name, barely reducing the fear of the unnamed.

Then, just as the snows were beginning to melt, the Chegjan demonstrated a new power. A sheep was found slain near the Ercoille River, its entrails missing. The shepherd attributed this to wolves. Other shepherds soon noticed similar evidence of attacks on their sheep and nearby villages became alarmed. No one had seen wolves and the occurrences grew in frequency and scope beyond anything seen before. As this was happening a perpetual mist seemed to gather in the atmosphere and the sun shone less brightly. Fear gripped the people along the tributaries of the Wicket River, including the

Ercoille and Njim, and traders and travelers spread news of these alarming developments in all directions.

The day word of such horrors came to Vorthall, Ian was scouting for trees suitable as future roof beams. He had exited the upstream gate of town and headed into the woods, following Kjevar's instructions to locate an old stand of mature growth.

As outlying dwellings became fewer, he passed an ordinary hut housing one of Vorthall's more extraordinary inhabitants, Hranild the Seer. She was sitting on a large, lichen-mottled stone with a bearskin about her shoulders and head uncovered, soaking in the morning light. At her side lay a finely carved staff to which deer hoof rattles had been attached with a leather cord. The sightless eyes in her deeply lined face followed the sounds of the morning, giving the illusion at a distance that she beheld the world around her. Only a closer look would reveal the unfocused and filmy reality.

The harsh call of a raven in a nearby tree caught Ian's attention and he spotted the old woman looking in his direction.

"Hello," he said. Hranild laughed before answering.

"I was wondering when you would come to me, Stranger."

"I beg your pardon?"

"I knew you were coming, but it has seemed a long time waiting for you."

"I'm afraid I do not know you, missus."

"My mother named me Hranild the day her mother buried my afterbirth below the tree in which yon raven now sits," she replied with a low chuckle. "Others have called me many things over the years, but Hranild is good. I do know you, however, young man, for your coming has been prophesied."

Ian was momentarily at a loss for words, then regained his manners. "Then you would know that I am called Ian son of William beyond the Forest. I know nothing of prophecies and your words puzzle me."

"I fear that is part of my gift and curse, for what I say is often puzzling. Sometimes I confuse myself, yet I must speak, whether I understand what I am saying or not. This does not get easier, you know. I have seen many years, far beyond any decent allotment of days. Many a night I have argued with the stars yet still they have not disclosed why I must keep living. If you ever find the answer, young man, please share it with me.

"Well, be that as it may," she continued, "I thank you for your name, Ian. Calling you the Stranger lacks the satisfaction of a proper name. It sounds very dignified and mystical, but I have laid dignity aside long ago and weary of mysteries. Frankly, I hope you may be the last of them. Mysteries, that is.

"You were not born among the Norrungs, you are no child of Vorthall nor of any place in the great Forest of Norrast. Yet you are the hope of our people, of all the peoples around the Mere. When Rathdar died I had no idea what the words that came to me meant but when you came among us I knew it was you.

"That nasty thing, the Chegjan they call it, will grow and grow until something stops it. Plague runs before it like a herald and despair trails behind wherever it goes. It has weakened mortal hearts and begun to consume minds. Worse will come. Though no power of this world shall undo it, you, my boy, are not of this world. You have the power to undo this evil thing."

Ian began to protest Hranild's ranting but she remained unperturbed. Using her staff to aid her, she eased herself up from her rocky seat, struck the ground with her staff, causing the rattles to sound loudly, then transfixed Ian with the command of her voice. "Come, Ian son of William beyond the Forest, you must take me to Njothir."

"I came by here on another task, Hranild. You must excuse me."

"Of course you did, lad. Life is always interrupting our tasks. But you shall not be excused. Your trees will still be here another day; the more important question is whether the people will be here if nothing is done. Don't dawdle," she added as she set out, needing no guide in her darkness.

"Grandmother," Ian rejoined as he fell in step beside her and used the polite Norrung address for an older woman, "what can I possibly do against a demon?"

"I have no idea, grandson, but I know you are the one who will undo the foul thing. For one thing, you have not asked for this task or sought it. You are not without ambition but I doubt you would know glory if it bit your ankle and that's a good thing. The demon grows very proud and a proud warrior would only be nourishment for it."

"I don't want to nourish a demon."

"I doubt you shall. Now hush and let me think."

With that the pair followed the path back toward the great hall, the raven flitting from tree to tree alongside them, croaking most of the way. When the bird's cry was especially strident, Hranild paused, listened, and announced, "Ah, your friend is very faithful."

"What friend, grandmother?"

"Why, the wolf that has watched over you. Look to the right on the edge of the woods."

Indeed, as Ian glanced where Hranild indicated he saw a gray shadow pause among the trees.

"I have not seen him since he led me to Gwenda."

"No? You must learn to look more carefully, boy. I'll wager you have never stepped outside the walls of Vorthall and been out of his sight, though how he eludes the hunters is beyond me. My cranky bird does not seem too fond of him, but I can assure you this wolf is your brother. His presence is a good sign in a time of many evil signs."

As they neared Njothir's hall Hranild paused suddenly, then announced, "Ill news draws nigh." At that moment Ian caught the noise of a party of traders approaching, their pack horses laden with goods from the northwest and their carts heaped with bags of wool for the spinners, dyers, and weavers of Vorthall. Hranild and Ian continued on their way, arriving just before the merchants did.

Njothir emerged to meet the merchants and a grizzled man with a black beard dismounted to greet the leader of the Norrungs.

"Hail, Rathdar's Son. I am Tjurn of Mimmoth, an honest merchant come to do business among your people My kinsmen and company bear wool and silver, amber and obsidian for the weavers and craftsmen of Vorthall."

"Greetings, Tjurn, I am told that you are known here. You may do honest business freely, though I see concern written in your face. I am my father's son and you may trust my word. Or do you bring troubling news with you?"

"Troubling indeed, Lord. The wasting fever continues to spread and that is ill enough. The demon has begun to do more than drain mortals of the spark in their hearts, it is gnawing at their minds and causing a different pestilence. There is a plague of strange behavior, leading to betrayals and terrible deeds. Neighbors suddenly turn on neighbors, maidens are violated, folk are found slain in their beds, some take their own lives, and in a few small villages folk have tortured and slain someone on whom they blame all their woes.

"There is a darkness in the very air, though it seems barely noticeable here in Vorthall. In the north the days are dim. Since the last full moon sheep have been found dead and gutted on the mountainsides over a wide region. I might say that a plague of wolves has descended but none have been sighted nor have we heard their howling. It is feared that this too is the work of the Chegjan, now devouring beasts as it has been devouring hearts and minds. I do not know what to say, but I hope your people are safe now that the wasting fever has passed through here."

Ian had listened to Tjurn's evil news and heard Hranild's murmured acknowledgment that his report matched whatever visions she had been granted.

"If this be the case," Njothir replied, "it is no wonder care has darkened your countenance. I would such news had not accompanied your goods among us but there is no fault in the one who brings bad news. You are welcome and I thank you for the warning."

The formalities completed, Tjurn and his companions departed toward the market square. Njothir turned toward Ian and the seer. "Grandmother, it is surely not by accident that you stand here with Ian when news such as this arrives."

"Nothing happens by accident, Lord of the Norrungs. This young man purposed to scout for trees this morning and probably supposes he happened by chance to pass my way. I think it is time."

"Time for what?" both Ian and Njothir asked simultaneously.

"To act against the Chegjan."

Njothir responded. "Your words are often confusing and sometimes misleading, though that is the nature of visions. I have never suspected you of guile, Grandmother, though I know you have a subtle sense of humor some might call perverse. I am certain you come now in good faith but I cannot see how we might act against such a demon."

"You are wise beyond your years, Njothir, and a good chieftain. You know I do not flatter nor seek to deceive. Either would violate my calling and debase us all, chiefly myself. You judge aright that my messages are difficult to decipher. Many a night I have sat beneath the stars seeking to understand what comes to me and mostly I am no wiser at dawn. If I knew exactly how to battle the foul darkness that weakens all who lie in its path, I would tell you forthrightly. Alas, that has not been given me. But I do know who will defeat it and he stands before us."

"No," Ian countered. "Surely I cannot overcome this foul thing, though if I knew how I should do all I can to help the people. This is now my world too, though I came here as a stranger."

"And that is why you are the one, my boy," Hranild answered. "At your father's death, Lord Njothir, I was given to understand that no power of this world would undo the demon. Ian is not of this world. I knew that you, my

Lord, the bravest among us, would not defeat it but that it would be defeated. Ever since this lad came among us I have awaited his visit to see whether he might be the one. Today he came by with other purposes in mind, not seeking such a quest nor desiring the glory that awaits the victor. I knew in my bones that he is the one chosen by the stars."

A silence ensued as the three pondered the old woman's words. Njothir was an ambitious warrior though he shared glory easily with his companions. If a foe was defeated, he cared not who struck the blow. That a boy, scarce become a man, should champion the Norrungs and all the peoples of the lands about the Mere posed no threat to his rule, so long as Ian did not thereafter challenge him. He doubted the lad would do so, if he judged character aright. If wrong, he could deal with that later.

Njothir eyed the lad from another world critically, assessing potential strength, endurance, alertness, and mostly the inner fire that made each soul unique. Ian had proved himself loyal, respectful of others and of the ways of the Norrungs, willing to contribute his share to the life of the people, quick to learn, flexible, and trustworthy. The boy was a passably adequate hunter and a skilled woodworker, but there seemed to be no warrior skills in him.

"With what weapons does one fight a demon, Grandmother?" Njothir asked.

"As I recall, the message was this," she began:

> Faith shall be your shield if you will bear it.
> Hope shall be your weapon if you will wield it.
> Love shall be your chieftain if you will follow it.

"Do such weapons as these stand any chance, Seer of my people?"

"I doubt any but these will affect it, Lord."

"Ian, does any of this make sense to you?"

"Yes, my brother. They are the virtues of our faith in the world I come from. We believe they are the only three things that last when all other things fade and perish."

"It seems a strange but wise faith. Do you think you can bear faith and hope into battle with the darkness?"

"All I can do is try."

"Indeed, that is all any man or woman can do. If love is to be your chieftain and not Njothir son of Rathdar, then I am content to be only your elder brother, Ian from Beyond the Forest, though I would not casually yield lordship to any mortal."

"Njothir of the Norrungs, I have borne you faith and service since you took me in and will continue to do so. You have been my family in a world where mine could not be found. I could not betray this kindness."

"Then, my friends, we need to take counsel. The Seer has spoken, a spark of hope abides. Let us fan it into a flame."

CHAPTER 12

As Ian walked from his home, Njothir's home, to the Great House next door he felt more apprehension than the first time he entered it. He glanced thoughtfully at the carved oak doors and wondered how much of their symbolism he truly understood. By now the immense tree trunks that supported the hall were familiar. They formed long columns and rose incredibly high. The timbered roof was tiered, rising from what would have been side aisles in an English church to a mid-level and finally the central, well, nave. Clerestory openings provided some indirect light and allowed smoke to escape but they were shadowed by huge eaves that kept the elements out. Windows high on the side walls were covered with oiled skins, offering a bit more light by day. In this forest context it was as impressive as a minor cathedral and Ian occasionally felt his arm begin to cross himself as he entered. Tonight he did not hesitate to invoke the Trinity as he passed under the porch.

Most Norrung homes had floors of packed dirt, softened with scattered rushes. Here great flagstones rested solidly below the feet of all who had business here. Alcoves lined either side and trestle tables and benches made business possible when they were not laden for feasts. Fire pits ran up the center, offering warmth and light. Torches in cressets, braziers, and hanging tapestries and furs added to those sparse comforts. Shields and weapons hung on the walls, for the Great House was also a storehouse. Other goods were in the back rooms, generally shielded from the public eye. At the end of the long hall was a dais, but it was low lest any chief bethink himself too lofty and the chief's chair was like any other and hardly a throne.

That night leaders among the Norrungs were gathered, forming a circle around one of the fire pits, faces etched with concern as Hranild spoke. She repeated her assurance that Ian from Beyond the Forest, whom many still referred to as the Stranger even after having accepted him in their midst, was the one to overcome the Chegjan. The task before them all was to decide how to help that happen and ascertain if Ian would, indeed, accept such a dangerous responsibility. The dancing lights and shadows of firelight played across the brooding faces of the Norrungs' leading warriors and sages, star singers and heads of clans.

Ringskild was the first to speak up when the challenge was presented and counsel was taken.

"My Lord, you have often heeded the words of one who is like an older sister to you, I beg you to hear me now. The Norrungs need their leader in these difficult days. You must remain here to sustain the hearts of the people. Send me to protect Ian as he journeys to the northern lands to meet this foe. Choose whatever other warriors and companions you see fit, but you, our chief, must remain at Vorthall. I pledge my life to this quest for the sake of all our people."

Others murmured and nodded in assent to her urging for none wished to see the Norrungs without their leader should he accompany the Stranger against the Chegjan. Njothir was troubled by this and felt himself caught in knots, a tangle of conflicted feelings. He knew the Norrungs needed him present if they were to hold together in the face of general fear and the raids along the eastern edge of their lands, not to mention the ongoing effort of rebuilding after the plague. Still, as a warrior he wanted at the very least to be part of the forces against the foe, and he bridled at Ringskild's treating him as a younger brother.

She was his elder and she was both brave and often wise, so listening to her counsel was not a problem. It was the sister issue that troubled him. He suspected she viewed him as a man as well as a brother and he had come to see her as a woman, a desirable one at that. Her fierce beauty and strong spirit excited him, though amid his many duties and the people's challenges he had not spoken to her of this. For him to yield the quest to other warriors was one thing; the thought of possibly losing Ringskild was yet another. This was one time he would rather she not pursue glory in battle. The sightless seer smiled at him as though reading his heart and this did nothing to comfort Njothir.

Vorgun, the eldest clan head among them spoke next. Tradition called for him to be heard first but he was accustomed to the brashness of Ringskild and forgave her in light of her skills as a warmaiden. He was from the Badger Clan and had seen more than fourscore years under the stars. His hair was white as snow and formed a cloud behind his face. Vorgun's beard was little more than a wisp like a sparse tuft of wool attached to the end of his chin.

"The warmaiden is brave and bears weapons well in battle. If she rides with Him Who Comes From Beyond the World it would be as though you rode with him yourself, Lord of the Norrungs. I have seen many things befall the Norrungs, both good and evil, but never a threat to the world equal to the foul demon that follows the fevered death. My clan has ever been a hearty one, stout of both heart and body, yet we and all the clans of the Norrungs have been weakened. No one among us doubts your courage, Lord, or your willingness to face any foe. Even so, I do not know if we should survive without our chief among us and thus I join the maiden in urging you to let others ride forth."

Njothir listened somberly and waited out a pause for the next to speak. It was Thomdar the Star Singer, who had appeared asleep. None were fooled by this for, like Hranild, he listened to an inner voice and saw what many could not, though unlike the blind seer his vision was excellent.

"As the stars circle high above us, so their ways are beyond our reach and understanding. My entire life has been devoted to observing and adoring them, though I remain a novice. Their dance has been in ominous combinations for six years now. At first I did not understand for it was a while before the plague came among the Norrungs. It seems part of the dark pattern I have perceived. My heart began to hope again when a new element emerged and I returned again to my nightly records. As the smoke from Mount Firestorm cleared and we entered the Dark Month, the Bard Star was exceptionally clear. It was at this time that Ian came among us. I have watched it carefully and then last autumn the Bard Star wandered near Senjir the Dancer, just touching the top of her head as the moon was full.

"Though I have said nothing of this publicly until now, I have quietly watched this Stranger over the months. Senjir's Dance is the dance of creation in which all things pass from one phase to the next. If the Bard has crowned her while singing for her then something mighty is going to change. Perhaps the Chegjan will be undone and light will shine again where darkness has been growing. Ian from Beyond the Forest did not appear by chance. I believe Senjir has taken him from his world and placed him here in a time of great peril and that Hranild has explained why.

"My only caution is that if he goes to face the foul demon there should be a singer with him as well as such warriors as may be chosen. This is a sacred quest and more is called for than the swords and shields we normally use. I would suggest my nephew, Pjortan, a devout and courageous youth whose holiness matches that of venerable men and women in spite of his tender years. He would be a support for Ian when it comes to the 'shield of faith' Hranild has mentioned."

With that, Thomdar sat down and those seated about the fire pondered the possibilities and dangers of a battle unlike any other contemplated by the Norrungs. Njothila refilled the drinking horns of those gathered but this was no feast and thirsts were temperate. She seemed especially interested in the ground when pouring mead into Ian's horn, never letting her eyes meet his. Ian was disappointed at this, having taken a liking to the playfulness and independent spirit he had seen flash in them on occasion. He could not dwell on this, however, with weightier matters at hand. He was the main topic of discussion that night, like it or not. He did not like it, but he was resigned to whatever path the Dancer had set him on.

Talk continued and options were pondered. Njothir was forthright as he admitted he longed to go with Ian on this uncertain journey yet he bowed to the wisdom of his people urging him to remain to lead the many rather than risk his life with the few. What he did not admit that evening was his reluctance to see Ringskild go.

Perhaps the moment of greatest anxiety in all the discussion was when Njothir asked Ian if he were truly willing to face the Chegjan. A thick silence followed as none spoke and most took only shallow breaths. Many emotions had flickered across Ian's face during the preceding hours of debate yet there was no indication in this moment one way or another. The youth's struggles in many directions seemed poised in a delicate balance and then he opened his mouth and his voice shattered the tension that hung in the air.

"I will, my lord."

Many a breath was released at these words. Ian continued, "No revelations have been given me to tell whether this is my path or not, but others have seen what I cannot. Perhaps this will give meaning to whatever forces have torn me from my former home and placed me here among you. It may be that I shall fail but anything that brings hope back to the people is worth the effort. May this show my thanks to all the Norrungs."

CHAPTER 13

Thomdar smudged the base of the looking platform with cedar, as he did every morning before dawn. That day, however, he did not ascend the platform to sing the hymn to the daystar. He ceded that role to his nephew Pjortan, a youth of twenty-six winters who had trained as a star singer all his life. Pjortan had sung the dawn hymn many times but never before on behalf of his chief and all the Norrungs of Vorthall. Now he stood solemnly as his uncle censed him with cedar and looked on him with a mixture of love and pride.

The young priest bowed to his uncle and to Njothir, then turned to ascend the stone steps of the looking place, moving as though in a trance. He was of average height, lanky and built for endurance. Pjortan loved to run and often served as a messenger among the star singers. His hair was a dark brown, thick upon his head but sparse on his face, and his cheeks ruddy. Pjortan's smile, when it flashed, had great charm but his usual expression was a calm half-smile. This particular morning his face seemed caught somewhere between earth and the skies, profoundly undisturbed and seemingly exalted.

Reaching the top of the platform he bowed toward the four directions then stood attentively, facing the eastern hills. At the first sign of the sun's touch on the hilltops he began to breathe deeply and when the light touched the crown of his head his tenor voice rang out, clear and rich in the morning air.

> My heart's desire mounts the heavens
> The fire of love floods the world with light

Birds announce your coming while the veil of night
Still covers the land and earth slumbers
You shatter the darkness, scattering shadows
All things bathe in your glory
Nothing can hide from your sight
You embrace the distant isle
And the snow-capped mountain
Giving warmth and light to great and small
Disperser of the morning mist, giver of joy
Upholder of truth and source of justice
No deceit can stand before you

Kindle anew the life of every creature
Melt the ice of our hearts and water our souls
Daystar, lifegiver, accept this morning song
Raised with gratitude from earth to sky
Journey bravely forth, we welcome you
Brightest of stars, beloved of heaven and earth

I lift my face to you in adoration
Radiance! Gladness! My heart's desire!
Glory to you, great fire that brings the day
Dazzling wonder of the world, hail and welcome!
Look upon us with your blessing
We are your children, help us walk aright
Bless my morning song
Bless your people
Shine over all the earth
Shine in our hearts

Pjortan raised his face slightly and spread his arms during the last stanza as if embracing every possible ray of the sun's first light. As the song concluded he held the pose a moment longer then turned to descend, his face as radiant as if he now shone with an inner light.

Thomdar's description of the youth's devotion seemed no exaggeration and Ian felt a mantle of faith cast about him at the thought of the star singer journeying with him toward the dark being he must face. The earthling wondered if he would ever believe so profoundly in anything. He had accepted fully the faith he was raised in—the English Catholicism that was a vestige from the days of James II—but had not given it much thought. The faith of the Norrungs was strange to him but not at all offensive. At its worst it could degenerate into superstition or fatalism but Ian had seen that in English churchgoers as well. At its best, star worship seemed to ennoble those who practiced it and form worthy virtues in their personal character and social values. Ian joined in Norrung public devotions and continued to recite the rosary when he was alone. He had come to believe that Jesus and Mary and Hjelgi the Star Shepherd all watched over him. Amid such strange circumstances he welcomed all the help he could get.

Help came in many forms, beginning with the wolf that led him to Fintall's clearing and Gwenda who fed him. Rutnir and his band had rescued him and Gwenda's family from raiders and Njothir had received him, first as an oddity and then as a younger brother. It was now clear that many in Vorthall had been keeping an eye on him and only a few of those were motivated by suspicion. Rutnir's sister the warmaiden was willing to risk her life to guard him and the chief's sister seemed to smile when she saw him. Now a small band was setting forth to help him find and defeat a force that threatened their world. Ian wondered how he, a youth with no skills in battle and a stranger to this land, could repay their help and be of any use in a quest that seemed foolish at best. And yet, it was needful. Ian sighed.

"A thoughtful sigh, young brother," Njothir said with an encouraging smile. All were trying to be hopeful though none knew how hope could be realized. Njothir gave Ian his blessing, as did Thomdar who beseeched the stars to guide his heart as well as his steps. As Ian turned to go, Njothila approached.

"Ian," she said in a voice uncharacteristically shy. "I have not been chosen to go with you but I pray you take these."

She handed him two eagle feathers wrapped in a heavy wool scarf of her own weaving, patterned geometrically in light and dark grays and tan. She may not have had Ringskild's artistry as a weaver but it was warm and would be welcome as they journeyed north. Ian caught sight of a pattern on one end that he had never seen in Norrung weaving. Njothila had copied his rosary, black beads woven with black wool and a gray cross for his silver one. Ian had not realized she had ever seen it but she must have caught him praying and noticed closely. The pattern was not quite exact, so he did not suspect the chief's sister of "borrowing" his beads, but it was close enough to confirm that she paid more attention to him than he thought. Feathers worn in one's hair was not part of war dress but a sign that one came in peace. Ian was somewhat confounded by her gifts, but all in all he was pleased.

"I thank you," he replied, hesitating to call her sister. That was not exactly how he was beginning to consider the beautiful young woman who stood before him, especially as he wondered if he saw a slight misting of her eyes. Was that sisterly concern, or perhaps something more? Ian blushed, prompting Njothila to do the same. He added, "You are very kind, daughter of Rathdar. I shall think of you when I wear it."

Njothila turned a deeper red and returned to the chief's hall without another word. Ian sighed again, bowed to Njothir—who seemed to be resisting a smirk—and mounted the horse that had been provided for him.

As the sun's rays descended upon Vorthall and its inhabitants, the strange band set forth, Hranild's raven croaking overhead at their departure. Ringskild led the group as their organizational head. Among those skilled in both battle and hunting were two other warmaidens, Vunskridh and Meldreth. The women were matched by male warriors: Hildir, Volthir, and Mechdar. Guiding them all toward the lands of the north was a well-known Norrung trader, Jannir son of Stejni, a man so affable he was universally liked. Wilda would see to meals, mending, and general mothering of the youths in the group and her husband Nordil served as groom. Nordil was also a falconer and Fjurthil, his prize falcon, accompanied them. Extra horses carried supplies or drew the cart in which Wilda rode with the demeanor of a queen touring her realm. Wulfdar the healer had been selected to look after mishaps since he was also clever at leatherwork and repairing armor. Pjortan upheld the group's piety and was likely to help with a positive spirit.

In the center of the motley gathering rode Ian the Stranger, feeling very strange indeed to be at the heart of this bizarre journey. His heart raced and his imagination ran wild, something seasoned warriors and travelers had learned to moderate. He took comfort in touching the scarf Njothila had given him and in occasional glimpses of a familiar wolf traveling alongside them at a distance.

The Demon Chasers

Warmaidens
Captain Ringskild
Vunskridh
Meldreth

Warriors
Hildir
Volthir
Mechdar

Ian the Stranger

Jannir the Merchant
Pjortan the Star Singer
Wulfdar the Healer
Wilda the Cook
Nordil the Groom
Fjurthil the Falcon
Vladje the Wolf

CHAPTER 14

Ian was grateful that morning that during his time at Vorthall he had ample opportunity to ride and hoped that saddle sores would not be part of this journey into the unknown. The horse assigned to him was a sturdy and steady bay mare, which suited him as the chargers ridden by Ringskild and the other warriors were more horse than he was prepared to handle. Their high spirits and battle lust could get out of hand with an average rider at the reins. Pjortan rode beside Ian on a coal black gelding with small silver stars on its bridle, symbolic trappings that signified the singer's sacred role in society. The singer was pleasant company as was the seasoned warrior Volthir on Ian's right. Ian noted wryly to himself that he not only rode between them but was also emotionally somewhere between Volthir's alert caution and Pjortan's confident faith.

Volthir of the Vedniradhs was one of those people both men and women noticed. Slightly taller than Ian, Volthir stood out among Norrungs for his black hair in large ringlets, black eyes, the fine black hair that extended to the back of his hands and fingers, all contrasting with fair skin. He and other "black Norrungs" were admired by a people characterized by lighter hair in shades of brown, gold, and red. Volthir came from a family of miners, traders, and workers in gemstones—trades that had garnered wealth over generations. He was considered exceptionally handsome and he knew it. Though touched with some vanity about his looks he remained generally humble, caring little for his social status or personal worth beyond enjoying the favors of women. He neither expected nor demanded favors or deference and gladly leapt to the fore in service to the common good.

Volthir had noted the wolf paralleling them as they rode and mentioned it to his companions. Ian said it was the wolf that had led him to Gwenda's cottage and thus, as chance had it, to Vorthall. "Hranild says this wolf is my brother and a good sign," he added.

"Then I will tell the others lest they slay him," Volthir responded and made a quick circuit of the party to explain their four-footed companion. Ian thanked him and Volthir explained. "We can all see that the wolf stays beyond bowshot but I myself would have gladly taken his pelt if you had not spoken. Hranild is honored among our people, no matter how much she troubles our peace. Some of her visions are dire but her heart is good and I cannot imagine her speaking falsely. Your wolf will come to no harm from us now."

"I wish her visions did not include me," Ian rejoined. "Life would be simpler, and safer."

Pjortan joined in. "We cannot wish the same, Ian. Life can never be safer than it is and is rarely simple. You, however, represent hope in a time when it is rarely found. Without hope we should have declined and wasted as a people and the plague has left few enough of us as it is."

With such somber thoughts the trio fell into silence as the adventurers traveled west on a road that roughly followed the flow of rivers, first the Nurgen that looped around Vorthall, and then the Woodstream that meandered through the western territory of the Norrungs before heading southwest to join the great Norrast. As they approached the first of the Three Sisters, a landmark grouping of hills on their right, the road continued west as Woodstream turned south.

After their midday meal, positions on the road shifted. Meldreth the war maiden now rode beside Ian, her hearty laugh lifting the youth's spirits. Meldreth had her share of battle skills but what made her popular was her seemingly endless store of tales and jokes, most of them ribald. Ian wondered what the jolly strawberry blonde with twinkling green eyes looked like when not armed, imagining a tavern mistress gaily entertaining travelers who would never suspect how dangerous she was with a sword, spear, or bow.

"I'll wager the lads didn't tell you the tale of the Three Sisters, did they?" Meldreth asked.

"No, cousin, they did not," Ian replied, glancing toward the three hills to the north.

Meldreth shrieked with delight at his polite form of address. "A handsome lad like you has no use for lady cousins, boy. Just think of me as a woman. You can do that, can't you?" At this she winked and Ian was not sure if she were teasing him or suggesting a carnal proposition. She laughed again at his hesitant expression.

"Relax, Ian. War maidens cannot afford to let down their guard to lead youths astray, I'm having fun with you. Though," she added in a huskier tone, "if we were at home I'd love to teach you some movements in a friendly struggle." At this he simultaneously felt a slight arousal and a furious blush creeping up his fair angular face.

Meldreth simply smirked. "Boy, I swear by all the gods of war that you are safe enough with me. I am charged with getting you wherever we are going and back again safely. Still, there's no harm in sharing stories to pass the time, so long as we stay alert to any danger."

"The three sisters," Ian urged, hoping a return to the story at hand would ease the moment.

"Ah yes. Well, we are going to be passing three hills and this is the tale.

"I once heard it told," Meldreth began, in the manner of Norrung storytelling, "that there was a poor but honest couple who lived in the north of the forest...."

The warmaiden spun out a complex tale of the couple and their three daughters, the adventures and misadventures of each girl, their loves and betrayals, the intense loyalty they felt toward each other, and the fate that claimed them all. The gods, taking pity, transformed each into a mountain, the very ones Ian was now looking at, as a warning to young women who trust too easily. Meldreth concluded the story in an ominous tone to match its cautionary moral.

From behind them came Nordil's voice, "You should tell the lad this applies equally to young men who trust too easily. I swear women are equally dangerous, especially beautiful warmaidens."

Meldreth joined those around them laughing at the rejoinder, especially when Ian blushed again. She shouted back, "Your Wilda might not take it kindly that you know of beautiful warmaidens, Nordil."

Amid the general merriment Wilda's voice joined in. "He's a man; he notices. But I notice him noticing and if he values his life, noticing is all he does. I know how to make a capon out of a cock." Chortles and hoots followed and even Fjurthil ruffled his feathers. The release of tension was welcome but as the jollity subsided minds returned to the dangers ahead. A few silently prayed to the stars that they might still laugh closer to the journey's end.

As Shach the daystar descended beyond the horizon the party did not stop moving as there was a village further along the road. While still on his horse Pjortan sang an evening hymn, explaining some of its less obvious significance to Ian, who always seemed eager to learn more about the new world he now inhabited. It was not quite dark when they saw homes and flickers of firelight before them. They had reached Nigdell, a minor hamlet beside the road where a stream named the Little Nigl flowing toward the southwest. The denizens of Nigdell could tell the strange party, half composed of seasoned warriors, came in peace. Ringskild had raised a peace pole before approaching them. It was a shaft of sacred ash decked with evergreen branches, eagle feathers, and yellow streamers—a sign recognized throughout the lands that circled the sea. The peace pole betokened messengers, travelers, merchants, or pilgrims who came in peace. To use this sacred emblem falsely was punishable by instant death. The warriors of Vorthall also bore eagle feathers in their hair, an additional sign that they were on a peaceful mission, though all knew they could and would defend themselves if needed.

An elder of Nigdell came out to meet them, flanked by torchbearers.

"Greetings, strangers. Or should I call you cousins, for I see you ride with Jannir?"

Jannir, who rode beside Ringskild, replied, "Greetings, Grandfather Harknel. May the stars bless you and your family. These, indeed, are friends who travel with me. We journey toward the northern lands where the dark demon attacks both beast and human."

"A brave desire for a fool's journey, my children, but you are welcome here."

The formalities observed, barter and purchase obtained lodging and food for the night. As the party was parceled out among several homes Ian noticed that he was never left without the presence of two warriors. He wondered if this were a coincidence or resulted from an order by Ringskild or Njothir. He did not mind. As he settled in the dark to sleep, their presence and their weapons were comforting.

Vorthall to Siot

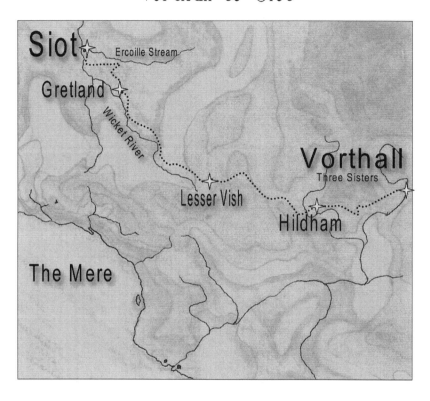

CHAPTER 15

When Ian rose in the middle of the night and went outdoors to relieve himself, he was not aware of two sets of eyes observing him. His companions knew he got up and would look for him if he did not return shortly but were ordered to allow him reasonable times alone such as this. It was Ringskild's turn to keep watch on the cottage where he was lodged and she kept him discreetly in sight. The other eyes were not human, but they were not the perceptions of a demon either. It was his brother, the wolf. Ian walked out to a cluster of tall brush to answer nature's call. The wolf, seeing no one with him, approached and marked a scraggly pine. Ian remembered how he and the wolf had done this the day they met. He did not take this as a territorial challenge but as a sharing of creatureliness across species.

"Hey, brother," Ian whispered and the wolf came up to him, its tongue hanging to one side of its mouth. Ian crouched down and the two eyed each other. Ian reached out and the wolf let him touch its fur. Suddenly the wolf, hearing something Ian did not, dashed back into the woods. Alarmed, Ian turned to see what it may have been, only to see the silhouette of Ringskild in the distance. She had wondered what might be delaying him until she saw the flash of the wolf running away in the dappled shadows and moonlight.

Ian knew then that he would be protected, and probably overprotected from this point on. He snorted a stifled chuckle and returned to the cottage. Ringskild withdrew without a word. The sleeping companions were just about to take their weapons and look for him when Ian returned to bed. The earthling let out a loud sigh and allowed himself to sleep.

The next morning Hildir and Vunskridh went out before dawn, managing to snare a couple of rabbits and shoot a wild turkey. Game was abundant in the area and their outing provided extra provender for the day's journey.

Ian watched the two hunters return, their silhouettes contrasting. Vunni was tall and slender, straight hair the color of spun gold, her eyes dark and alert. Hildir was as thick as Vunskridh was slim, not solid in the manner of Mechdar but overlaid with muscle, a man of near legendary strength whose armor and clothing scarce seemed to contain him, much as Vunni's skin scarce contained her energy. His face and arms were sun-darkened, his beard a light brown and carefully cropped. Hildir's stride was relaxed, as though he were taking in the early morning sights; Vunskridh's tense, as though she might pounce on fresh prey at any moment.

These handed their spoils to Wilda, who praised their efforts effusively, her blue eyes twinkling and full lips drawn into a wide smile. Medium brown curls framed a round face that reminded Ian slightly of his mother but what struck him most was Wilda's cheerfulness, very like his mother's habitual mood. Wilda was both comfort and painful reminder, a mother substitute who could not truly replace the love he knew at Hellebore Cottage over sixteen months ago.

Wilda was skilled at adding herbs and root vegetables to game and the hunters looked forward to enjoying the fruits of their combined efforts. The travelers left Nigdell just before sunrise. Pjortan had sung for the morning star and, as with the evening hymn the night before, welcomed the daystar as he rode. His singing was not as elegant as the morning before when he stood on the looking platform in Vorthall but his devotion still touched all who rode with him.

During the afternoon Wilda put Ian to work cleaning and cutting roots for the evening meal as he rode in her cart, his horse tied to follow it. Ian used the pocket knife he always carried and found it comforting to do something so basic and so far removed from demon-slaying.

Because villages were not always spaced one day's journey apart, the second night was spent in a clearing beside the road. A nearby brook provided water for horse and rider alike and liquid for Wilda's cooking. She produced a flatbread, cooked quickly on an iron plate set on stones to rest over the fire. This with a hastily cooked turkey and rabbit stew nourished them all. Pjortan sang to the evening stars, Meldreth got everyone started on some drinking songs, though mead was consumed sparingly that night, and finally all retired, sleeping on the ground. Ian had never lived like this, even in his year among the Norrungs. The companions were as good as one could ask for but the comforts promised to be few. He wondered, before falling asleep, how long this journey would last. He chose not to ponder how it would end.

There was little enough sleep and Ian was rousted early, as were all the others. Jannir wanted them to reach Hildham by nightfall and it would take an effort to do so. Once again Ian found himself riding next to Pjortan, so he asked him about the heavenly deities. The star singer was happy to oblige and, beginning with the season of the winter solstice, recounted the names and stories of the constellations that formed the circle of the year. By midday Ian's head was swimming with names he had not heard before, though the stories were vivid, especially as Pjortan told them. The young singer's deep piety did not seem to hinder his sense of humor or willingness to narrate the more salacious and scandalous mythologies of his people. The pause for a noon repast was quickly upon them, though their rest was brief and they were on the road again.

And so it was that by the third evening the comrades of Vorthall entered the village of Hildham. All were grateful for Jannir's reputation among the folk with whom he traded as his presence allayed most suspicions of strangers. Additionally, in the disorder that still lingered after the plague had passed, the sight of warriors accompanying almost all who journeyed had become more commonplace.

Hildham was a much larger village than Nigdell though far from a town like Vorthall. It was located on a rise about which Dirtach Stream looped as it flowed southeast to join Woodstream. The inhabitants were more cautious than Harknel of Nigdell in their greeting but an inn was found to lodge the entire party. After his night in the forest Ian was pleased with more comfortable lodgings, at least until the snores of companions in close quarters forced him to reconsider his definition of comfort.

Wulfdar the Healer lay next to Ian in the men's quarters and noticed Ian had trouble resting amid the erratic rumbles. He spoke in a very low voice.

"Ian, would you allow my healer's art to assist you in sleeping?"

"I would, uncle, if you think it will help," the youth replied.

"It may or may not but I should like to try. Let your body relax and close your eyes. Think of nothing but your breath coming in and going out." As he spoke the older man laid one hand on Ian's forehead, very lightly. "That's it: in and out, all of creation gathered in your breathing, its gentle rhythm, in and out, in and out."

The soothing voice of Wulfdar and whatever skill or magic lay in his touch combined with Ian's rhythmic breathing to lead the youth into a deep relaxation. As Wulfdar's voice trailed into silence and his hand was lifted, Ian had become one with the earth and stars, at peace and asleep.

To his surprise and delight, Ian awoke the next morning refreshed and ready to travel. The group left Hildham by a slight decline toward a stone bridge spanning the Dirtach. Once across the swift brook they followed its willow- and alder-clad bank upstream for a while before the road turned west to pass between the Watchers, two mountains guarding the inner forest from the plains descending toward the Mere. The path they were following would not lead southwest to the Mere at this point, however, but west and slightly north toward the headwaters of the Wicket.

A hostel on the slopes of Fiarvachje, the Southern Watcher, provided shelter that night. The travelers took their evening meal facing across the valley toward its counterpart, Nivachje, and indulged in a bit more mead than they had been taking. The evening hymn was a bit later that night as there were no near hills to the west and the setting sun delayed its departure. All watched the evening from this pleasant vantage point, sharing stories of travel and adventure, maintaining the pretense that this journey was not much different from others. Ian begged scraps from the meal and tossed them outside the hostel for his lupine brother. Finally all slept except those taking turns keeping watch.

Perhaps it was the extra draught of mead before bedtime; perhaps the stars had messages for the unusual pilgrims. In any case, dreams came to several that night.

Mechdar was considered ancient among warriors, having seen forty-seven turning-of-the-year celebrations. Most servants of Vrotni, blessed to live so long, had yielded their weapons by that age. Mechdar fought on, using his seasoned battle skills to make many a foe regret underestimating him. The muscles on his barrel-chested frame were toned and his reflexes as swift as most younger men. Ian often spotted a twinkle in the dark, observant eyes framed by pitted and sun-wrinkled skin. Mechdar kept his beard trimmed to a thumb's breadth while the hair on his crown had thinned over time from a dense forest to a straggly stand of scattered pines.

A widower, Mechdar's heart now belonged to the many grandchildren whom he was loathe to leave behind in Vorthall. Three of them were shared with Auntie Vunskridh since her elder brother had married Mechdar's daughter Dagnil. Each night he fell asleep commending the cherished bairns to the keeping of the stars.

This night he struggled as a great weight pressed down upon him, feeling the breath slowly squeezed from his lungs and sight departing from his eyes. He jerked awake, gasping, desperate to fill his lungs with air once more. Though fearful to return to sleep, he finally did and was at peace until dawn.

Happier images came to Meldreth, the saucy warmaiden, for she beheld the form of a young warrior, brave and handsome, fearing only her wiles. This was a battle she could enjoy, toying with an opponent who longed to be overcome. Ringskild jabbed her awake to put an end to the sensual moans she emitted in the night.

"Again?" Meldreth inquired, more proud than abashed.

"Yes, you battlefield hussy," Ringskild reprimanded, smirking.

"You are only jealous," the former whispered.

"I have dreams of my own."

Pjortan, not surprisingly, dreamed of the stars. One of the lesser constellations seemed to glow especially bright and dance in a midnight sky. It was Morvladh, the Great Wolf, who figured in one of the more intricate myths. This night it seemed that Morvladh radiated like Uncle Thomdar's descriptions of the Dancing Torches, a wonder Pjortan had not yet seen.

Ian also was visited by a wolf in his dreams only this was his companion. As on that first morning in this new world, Ian felt the hot breath of the wolf on his neck, then the lick that awoke him. As on that day, the youth opened his eyes, but he was in the darkness of the hostel. The wolf was not there, nor were those crowded about him either his brother Steven or his cousin Harry. This had not been an unpleasant dream and Ian easily drifted back to sleep, focusing on his breathing as Wulfdar had taught him.

In their travels the next morning the companions chatted of dreams. Ringskild began it all, chiding Meldreth. "I swear, at first I thought some guest at the hostel was rutting and found you in the night. If I hadn't jostled you, you'd have awakened everyone with your cries of pleasure."

Meldreth gave her usual response, a hearty laugh. "If everyone had such pleasant dreams none of us would want to waken."

Nordil noticed Mechdar's troubled expression and gently asked, "Brother, what distresses you?"

Mechdar looked at the groom. Nordil was a slender man only a couple of years younger than Mechdar. Nordi's blond hair had thinned and half of it had turned white. His eyes were a blue so pale as to seem startling, his nose long and his face thin. He reminded Mechdar of Nordil's father, Kendan son of Vregna, a fowler and breeder of horses. Kendan had the same narrow face and pale eyes.

The groom had lost both brother and sister to the fiery death. Vregdir, Nordil's brother, had married Wilda's sister Ustrel and she had perished also, followed the next year by two of their children. The remaining niece and nephew had been taken in by Wilda's other sister, Cenda, a widow with no children of her own. Nordi and Wilda's own two offspring had died in childhood and all their love had been redirected into their role as aunt and uncle.

Mechdar knew all this and understood the flashes of grief so often seen in Nordil's eyes. The question posed to the warrior was not pointlessly inquisitive.

"My dream was not so pleasant, cousin. I thought I should die. Some immense weight, I know not what, pressed upon me, forcing the very life out of me. My lungs were crushed and I could find no air, my sight was failing, my ribs were about to crack from the burden that flattened me. Waking was a great relief. I tell you, Nordil, the air of this world never felt so sweet as it did when I drank it into my lungs last night."

"A heavy dream, indeed," Nordil agreed, failing to repress his wordplay. Mechdar frowned as if to convey offense that his friend would inject humor while discussing something so haunting. Nordil, sensing affront in Mechdar's expression, quickly apologized. "I did not mean to amuse myself at your expense, good brother. It was a fearful dream and I am sorry that it came to you." Mechdar then laughed.

"Thank you, friend. I know you do not mock me. It is just that my heart, and I say it myself, is heavy today with the memory." At that they both emitted a rueful chuckle.

"Then let us enjoy the morning air and the beauty of the day, my bother," Nordil concluded.

"Have any of you seen the Dancing Torches of the Sky?" Pjortan asked, using a phrase common for the Northern Lights.

"Ay, I have," shouted Jannir, across the company. "Some years ago I was far north enough in my travels as a merchant to see the shifting colors of the Dancing Torches as they frolicked about to some silent music, or at least music that I could not hear.

"You have all seen banners in the wind, rippling like the waves of the Mere, snapping and popping if the breeze is stiff. But when the air blows gently the bright fabric stirs softly and slow enough for the eye to follow its rise and fall. This slower wave with its secret rhythm, certain but not quite predictable, is like the Dance of the Great Torches, rippling across the sky. Their colors are ever changing and yet you can see through them, like cloth that was thin to begin with and is now worn. The Torches weave their way about in the silent darkness of the night, like sorcerers drawing you into their spell, so that only by strong will can you tear your eyes from their magic."

All had fallen silent as Jannir told of this wonder that only he among them had ever witnessed. When he had finished, Pjortan heaved a great sigh and exclaimed, "You are blessed, Uncle Jannir, to have seen such a thing. My Uncle has also seen them and your description matches his, though I think there must be a singer in you as well as a merchant for you spoke of them as one who worships. I hope the stars might grace my eyes with such a sight before my time to journey to the sky."

"You may, lad, you may. If any should see the Torches it should be a singer such as you." Jannir then added, "But why, worshipper of the stars, do you ask about the Dancing Torches?"

"We were talking of dreams and I saw something like I imagine the Torches to be in my dream last night. Beautiful dancing lights seemed to surround the Great Wolf in a midnight sky. There was no moon but the stars of Morvladh shone intensely, far brighter than usual, and my heart seemed purer and happier for seeing this. The shimmering lights seemed to shower me with blessing, embracing everything I knew."

Wulfdar joined in, "The stars speak to you, Pjortan, as you sing to them. Was Morvladh not the boon companion of Athna, the Hunter? You hunt with your heart and not with weapons, in accordance with your vows. Perhaps Morvladh will help you find the heart's prey, that which you desire."

"You are a good interpreter of dreams, Wulfdar, what you say is pleasing to hear. I would you might give our cousin Mechdar a brighter meaning to his troublesome dream."

Vunskridh spoke up, "Pjortan, you are too compassionate for your own good. Thank the stars you have warmaidens watching over you."

At this Pjortan blushed and Hildir protested. "You forgot to mention warriors, Vunskridh."

"I did not forget, cousin. Yes, you are useful too."

"Peace, cousins, I pray you!" Wilda interjected. "As the only married woman here I claim the right to say men are more blessing than curse, and let us not dwell on the curse. But, my brothers, you know we women are most needful. And I will testify that we have here some of the best fighters among all the Norrungs and I am grateful for each of them. Furthermore, if you do not stop this now, a quarrel will grow and my Nordil and I might be caught up in it. I would like to rest in peace and affection this night, thank you very much."

Her outburst was so vehement that all wondered why she spoke so strongly, but the sexes declared a truce without a word more being spoken. It was then that Ian spoke of his dream.

"My brother Pjortan dreamed of Morvladh, the Great Wolf. I too dreamed of a wolf only it was my brother the wolf. It seemed I was reliving that first morning in this world and he awoke me, then led me to company, shelter, and food."

Volthir noted that the wolf had followed them faithfully in their journey and wondered what caused the beast to behave so strangely.

"It seems the stars have granted him to befriend our brother Ian," Pjortan declared, "as Morvladh befriended Athna. We have all vowed to protect this wolf and perhaps our two dreams were linked. Perhaps this wolf is an appearance on earth of Morvladh, for all we know."

"If so," Volthir added, "Morvladh may be listening to our words."

Indeed, the wolf seemed to be nearer the company of travelers than usual. Ian decided to test Pjortan's theory.

"Morvladh, my brother, come here," he called, but the wolf did not respond.

"Vladje"—Ian shifted to the affectionate form of "wolf"—"your brother calls to you. Come."

At this the wolf drew nearer. Ian swiftly dismounted and crouched down as he had done the time they met at night with Ringskild watching. "That's it, Vladje. It's your brother Ian calling. None among us will hurt you, they have all promised."

As if he understood Ian's words, the wolf approached the earthling.

"Here, I saved something for you," the youth added, pulling a bone from his journey bag. As Ian held it out, its few shreds of meat beckoned and the wolf came closer, eyeing all who watched him so intently.

"It's all right," Ian reassured. "Come on, Vladje, you are among friends. Let us journey as brothers, you and I."

The wolf walked up, sniffing, then snatched the bone from Ian's hand. "Careful, brother, I have other uses for my paw," Ian said. All watched in wonder at this incredible scene. When the wolf was satisfied that no more meat was to be found on the bone it came up to Ian, placed a paw on his knee, and licked his cheek. The wolf jumped back when chuckling rippled through the onlookers but as none moved it then placed its head on Ian's knee and allowed him to pet its silver and gray fur.

"My brother," Ian said.

CHAPTER 16

Vladje, as the wolf was now known, gradually became more comfortable with the travelers, though only Ian and Wilda were ever allowed to pet him. Those who tried guarded their fingers thereafter. After a few days he even rode in the cart with Wilda, saving his energy to hunt by night. Since none could be certain he was not a physical manifestation of a lesser deity, all treated Vladje with respect. Some even swore that he expected and demanded it, getting testy when it was not duly offered. Ian thought this was all imagination or superstitious nonsense but he honored the wolf in his own way, with the mutuality of equals and a growing affection.

None dared mock openly when, on rare occasions, Vladje would howl along with Pjortan's hymns, though Ian would offer a mild rebuke, saying, "Vladje, behave." If a wolf could smile, Vladje did. Taking no chances, Pjortan began composing a new hymn to Morvladh and Athna, ostensibly to honor his dream though possibly to honor their new companion. The distinction was hazy.

Between Vorthall and Hildham there had been sundry merchants going the opposite direction. This continued to hold true but others were scattered among them, people leaving plague-stricken areas behind. On the sixth day of the journey Jannir saluted Shundar, a fellow merchant based in Gretland-on-the-Wicket. Shundar was a rail-thin man with an ascetic look that obscured his innate friendliness. Though older than Jannir, his long hair remained a dark brown bordering on black, providing him with an impressive braid hanging down his back. His eyebrows resembled a thicket grown out of control but the eyes beneath them were expressive, shrewd, and playful.

"Jannir, you crazy fellow," Shundar shouted back, "what brings you from the banks of the Nurgen toward the west these days? Not much trading in plague county."

Affection colored Jannir's voice as he responded, "Shundar, you old horse thief, are you bringing any honest goods among my people this time?"

This exchange caused the two old friends to laugh heartily. They rode ahead of their parties to meet and traded a few more insults before the Gretlander asked Jannir why he traveled with such an odd party rather than his usual assistants.

"Ah, cousin, this is not one of my usual trading journeys. I guide my friends on a mission from Njothir, our chief."

"That explains the extra warriors, and I am glad enough to see the peace pole, though warriors of Vorthall are ever a welcome sight to a merchant on the road. Unlike some," he added in a lowered tone, "who lack good Norrung honesty."

Jannir commiserated over the plight of merchants in regions where warriors were hard to distinguish from brigands then, without elaborating on their mission, introduced his companions. Shundar, being an experienced merchant who understood the virtue of discretion, did not inquire further. He did allow that in addition to his fellow merchants and employees there were unusual members of his party as well, most notably several stragglers from Lesser Vish. These had abandoned what was left after the plague had ravaged their hamlet and were now traveling with the merchants in hope of finding a new home.

"So they be honest folk, I warrant they will find welcome in Vorthall," Jannir asserted. Ringskild affirmed this.

"We too have lost many good folk and could use fresh blood as we reweave our life together. You should be there within a week. Tell Njothir son of Rathdar that Ringskild daughter of Ivor commends you to him."

"I thank my lady," a pale woman of some thirty-odd years said. "We were the last to leave Lesser Vish and saw in Shundar a chance to find some haven. He was kind enough to allow us to travel with him in return for abandoned goods from our village that he might trade."

She was one of five who had joined the party of merchants and appeared to speak on their behalf. A younger woman stood beside her and three children clung to them. Shundar explained that both women had lost their husbands and most relatives in the plague and saw no reason to stay in the place of their birth now that all others had fled. The women seemed care-worn but hopeful, the children frightened and uncertain.

One of the children, a small boy, gave a shriek of alarm when he noticed Vladje's head next to Wilda in her wagon. "Woof! Woof!" he cried and began to shake. Ian was quick to respond.

"It's all right, my little cousin. He won't hurt you. You see how peacefully he sits next to our sister Wilda. This wolf saved my life and he goes wherever I go. He was looking at you because he does not know you but he did not growl, so that is how I know you are a good boy. He growls at bad people but right now I think he is smiling." With that, Ian rode over to Vladje and leaned over. The wolf licked Ian's face and Ian chuckled. The little boy's eyes were wide with wonder, though he kept a firm grip on his mother's skirt.

Shundar shot a glance at Jannir that was both skeptical and amused. "You keep stranger company than I thought, my cousin. Had I not known you for some decades now, my tongue would wag from here to Vorthall and beyond. I shall keep my speculations to myself but I hope the day will come when we drink together and you can tell me more. May the stars shine on you all and give you good fortune in your mission. We must move on. Be well, and see you leave Thjothar's wife alone this trip."

Both merchants roared at this old joke and the two parties passed, each pursuing its own goals. Hildir urged Jannir to explain about Thjothar's wife but was not expecting the answer he received. "Ha, Thjothar and his wife keep an inn. Thjothar is insanely jealous and that is what is so amusing. His wife is twice as ugly as midsummer day is long and no one can imagine going near her for anything but another glass of comfort. What Thjothar sees in her, I cannot imagine. All the merchants joke about making Thjothar a cuckold but the stars help the man who ever does such a thing. I would rather dally with the Fierce Mother or the Dark Queen than with that woman. The Raven would have to peck my eyes out before leading me that far astray."

Ian remembered from Pjortan's tales that the Fierce Mother was the goddess of war and the Dark Queen ruled the dead. He was trying to remember what role the Raven played when Pjortan, noting his expression, said cryptically, "Her flight is fanciful but she mates for life." Ian then recalled that the Raven was the goddess of love and the thought of her pecking out one's eyes was a perverse comment on Jannir's part. Ian joined in the general laughter.

After a day and a half more of traveling they reached Lesser Vish. No dogs barked at their coming, no fires burned, no children played, none came to meet them. The village was abandoned indeed, victim of the plague's ravages. Someone had raised a prayer pole in the central square but attached to it were strips of white, the color of death and mourning, not the traditional banners of prayer. An air of desolation hung about the place and an evening mist seemed to drift among its homes as evening drew nigh.

Debate arose over whether the group should take shelter in the empty homes or stay outside the perimeter of this hamlet of death. No agreement was reached and Ringskild finally announced that, in deference to those who feared to lodge there, they should all camp just outside the hamlet and remain one group. Division was as deadly to their purpose as plague had been. Several faces betrayed disagreement with the decision but one would have to be either foolish or very brave to take her on and she had been set in charge of the expedition by Njothir and the council. Before they camped, however, Pjortan stood near the hamlet's prayer pole of death and sang to the stars that his prayer might cleanse and bless the place, setting it free from the trauma it had witnessed.

Vladje surveyed the site chosen for the night, marked a few trees, circled and lay down. Taking their cue from the wolf, the two-leggeds decided to follow his example and sleep in peace to the extent possible in such a star-forsaken place. All were eager to set out early the next morning.

CHAPTER 17

It came like tendrils of smoke filtering through the trees, a hint of mist in the chilly air. Gradually it thickened throughout Lesser Vish to fill the spaces in the night, veiling the sacred lights above and shrouding all that was near. Volthir, who kept watch with Nordil, swore he could actually taste the fog that silently claimed all around them. Sounds were muffled and no birds were heard that morning. By dawn the companions from Vorthall had abandoned their camp to follow the road west toward Greater Vish on the edge of the upper Wicket River.

A small thing acquires significance when the context is favorable. Morning mists dissipate on many an ordinary day, yet a cheer broke out that day when the sun finally pierced the overcast heavens at midmorning. Jannir spontaneously led the group in a few drinking songs, in spite of the fact that they were not drinking at the time, and a few felt as giddy as if they had tippled. Haunted by the atmosphere of Lesser Vish, the travelers besought the stars that no such mood lurked about its larger sister village.

In spite of fate of its neighbor, Greater Vish seemed ordinary enough, given the times. It had been ravaged with plague and its people seemed to lack energy or will, but this was common enough wherever the Chegjan had visited. The village had been reinforced by many of those who had fled its eastern neighbor. For all the uncertainties of life, the added souls bolstered the community. Jannir stopped first to greet several comrades, including the family of Shundar's sister, then settled the travelers in pleasant enough lodgings among the merchants of the village. All slept easier that night.

Another four days journey following the Wicket's flow north and west brought them to Gretland, a much larger settlement than they had seen since leaving Vorthall. The trader suggested they spend two nights there and rest before facing the crowds of Siot. Plans were changed when news arrived from the north.

As the travelers were finishing breakfast, conversation at another table grew animated. A robust man with a straggling white beard and florid cheeks loudly asserted, "I tell you, I saw it with my own eyes. Would I repeat a tale handed down to me with such certainty?"

"You've been known to," retorted one of his companions, somewhat younger but a physical match. The first man's face flushed as he uttered a string of curses, questioning the lineage of anyone who would question his word. The laughter at the table reassured the party from Vorthall that this was not a deadly quarrel, only jesting among friends. Nonetheless, it bore watching and the warriors among them instinctively calculated possible tactics should a brawl break out.

"Degh speaks true," a third man interjected. "I was on the Ercoille but ten days ago and it was spreading then." This chap, of much softer speech and casual manner, lent verisimilitude to the blustering Degh's claims.

"And what did you see of it, Tjorn? Are the tales really true?"

The lanky man with a leathery face and soft brown eyes took a deep breath before answering. "I was visiting a cousin near Pjall, north of here on the Ercoille. He and his family have herded sheep in the area for stars know how many years. I could tell times were truly hard when I first laid eyes on him. The poor man's face had a haggard look and he seemed spooked—the slightest thing startled him. A sudden bird cry would set him shaking. I asked him to show me what had happened. We rode out to one of the lower pastures and there at the edge of the meadow, near a clump of miserable shrubs, I saw the remains of four sheep."

"And you're sure it wasn't the doing of a pack of wolves?" one of the listeners inquired. Ian almost leapt up to demand satisfaction upon hearing the blame automatically go to Vladje's brethren but Meldreth kept him in place with a strong hand on the youth's leg. Under other circumstances, and especially with Meldreth, one might suspect a sensual motive but this was clearly the soundless command of a warrior. Ian kept silent.

"I've seen the work of a wolf and the work of savage men, but tell me this— have you ever seen a sheep not only ripped open but with its bones melted?"

"Ah, Tjorn, how many drinks have you had this morning? Bones don't melt, you fool." This from a woman at their table with the air of someone who brooks no nonsense. "Now I know you are in league with Degh, trying to scare us all with silly stories."

"Magda, have you known me to mislead? Or, for that matter, to cast my lot in with Degh here? How many wagers can anyone recall when I have not bet against him? But though I cannot truly vouch for what he has seen or not seen, I can speak of what my own eyes beheld. I know bones char but do not melt, yet these appeared to have gone soft like wax too near a fire. And what's more, there is no shame in saying my stomach rejected what felt like the previous week's meals after I saw it. And yes, this last was exaggerating. But the rest is true, though I wish to the stars I had never seen such a monstrosity."

Degh confirmed Tjorn's story, saying, "The world knows me for speaking more than I should and sometimes saying more than I have seen or heard, in that you know me far too well, my brother's wife." This was aimed at Magda, who frowned. "And I confess, unlike Tjorn I did not notice any melted bones or whatever horrible thing happened to the hapless beasts, but I did see a carcass unlike any I have heard of, grotesquely misshapen in whatever foul death had overtaken it. And others have told me this is happening more widely every day. Not even scores of wolves could do this sort of thing and I shudder to think any human capable of such savagery."

"Perhaps it is some evil magic. Has anyone heard of spell casters about?" None had and even the mention of dark arts made the crowd uncomfortable.

"Some say it is a demon, and we all know its name—the Chegjan," added Degh darkly.

The mood at the table shifted from convivial jests to somber consideration of the fearful underside of life and the shadows of the human heart. Ringskild broke into the mood, asking Tjorn, "Good cousin Tjorn, we have heard tales of the roaming darkness and the things you speak of. Would you guide us north to see this? We will pay for your assistance."

At first Tjorn shook his head, unwilling to face the sickening spectacle again. Then Meldreth put her wiles to work, "Surely a man such as yourself could travel a short way in the company of good companions, with the protection of warriors. I will personally vouch for your safety." This last was said with heavy undertones and not a little positioning to display her ample chest. Tjorn seemed to consider her sword belt and leather armor, and certainly the proffered bosom, and then made the mistake of turning to Meldreth's eyes. She gave him a look of lust and smiled and Tjorn consented, asking a rather high price to lead them to the Ercoille and his cousin's flocks.

The obvious seduction brought more taunts from Tjorn's companions and some of the jollity of the party was restored as all prepared for what the day would bring.

Tjorn led the party north from Gretland toward the Ercoille and Meldreth kept at least part of her implied bargain, riding beside him and indulging in coquetry, if such can be said of a warmaiden. She carefully maintained enough reserve that Tjorn could never say she promised more than pleasant conversation. Indeed, that was all he was going to get, beyond the silver coins he had been paid to guide the party. He would allow thereafter that the wages were good and the company a delight, though in the retelling he never prevented his companions from imaging there were unspoken rewards as well. Those who had seen them in Gretland that morning easily assumed there were.

As the day wore on the group's energy flagged. After nearly two weeks of travel they had a sense of how hard they could push each day but on this particular day a deep fatigue seemed to be developing in each of them. Before the afternoon was over, the horses had been spooked several times.

Anxiety rose, as did the fur on the back of Vladje's neck, but the most skilled scouts among them could discern no cause for the collective uneasiness.

The clouds were not dramatic, just a wash of gray overhead, yet they seemed to press the heavens down upon the riders' heads, oppressing their spirits. When Fjurthil was loosed for exercise and a chance to hunt, he did not soar up as he usually did, but hovered low and returned quickly. No amount of urging from Nordil could encourage him to fly higher or further.

The two warriors who battled without the usual weapons, the singer and the healer, did what they could. Wulfdar passed a restorative salve among them, a pungent and pleasant unguent the company used to anoint their faces. The natural oils were a blessing to weathered skin but it was the scent that helped restore the spirit, a blend of mints, evergreens, and other herbs.

Pjortan chanted hymns to ease the mind and invigorate the heart. Hildir and Vunskridh raised a few battle songs. Each effort helped somewhat but it was still with a great collective heaviness that the party arrived at Pjall. A meal and some mead made all feel better, though it was decided to visit Tjorn's cousin immediately thereafter rather than settle in for the night.

The night was approaching when they reached Hnakil's home. He embraced his cousin and asked why a return visit had come so soon. Tjorn explained what he knew of the strangers from the Norrast.

Ringskild picked up after introductions. "We are sorry to learn of the fate of some of your sheep. Our chieftain has sent us to inquire of all things related to the dark demon and we hoped to see for ourselves what we can."

No mention of their more ambitious mission or Hranild's prophecies was made, nor had any stranger been taken into the group's intimacy on the matter.

Hnakil could not tell if this were a manifestation of bravery or foolishness, but he nodded and welcomed them all to his home. Ringskild assured him they would not take advantage of his hospitality and asked merely that they might camp near his house. The obligations of hospitality led him to object repeatedly but in the end, conquered by the fact that his home could accommodate but a few of them, he relented. A quick glimpse of what appeared to be a wolf near their supply wagon may have influenced the agreement to allow his guests to lodge out of doors. Reassured that they had all eaten, Hnakil offered a round of mead and with thanks the travelers made camp.

CHAPTER 18

The uneasiness of the day before continued as the travelers arose and prepared to ride out with Hnakil and Tjorn. The once wealthy herder explained that he had no idea what they would find on that day. The previously desecrated sheep had been burned and their ashes buried, yet a few more were found almost every day.

Tjorn had not exaggerated his cousin's forlorn look. Whatever horrors the Chegjan or other sinister forces had wrought, the impact drove a savage plow across the countenance of a handsome man. The result was startling. Hnakil's harrowed visage inspired involuntary sighs in all who met him, as though the man invited all into his despair.

It took some convincing to explain Vladje's presence to a herder. All agreed it was better for him not to join Ian on this outing and Ian solemnly bade the wolf to stay at Hnakil's home with Wilda that day. Since Vladje had never been known to let Ian out from his surveillance, no one was certain the beast would stay, but with a short prayer to the stars they set out.

The beauty of the hills and meadows around Pjall was notable, even if the mood of those who surveyed them was glum. A few shafts of sunlight pierced the clouds to illumine random portions of the landscape yet overall the day matched the mood, muted and sullen. As the horses paused to drink from a small stream, Hnakil informed the group that the flocks should be found beyond the next hill.

Indeed, they were, and one of the sheepdogs paused in its herding to greet the master then hastened back to keeping the woolly beasts in line. The men and women of Vorthall looked over a fluffy sea, the source of the wool they dyed and wove back home. It was not a sight found in their forest, though very small flocks could be found in the meadows of Norrast.

Hnakil rode over to one of his shepherds to see if anything had happened of late. The small, tanned man jerked his head to one side, indicating the direction in which they might find something and the party followed Hnakil over a small scrub-covered rise. In the shade of a large boulder lay the body of what once was a sheep. Flies hovered over the mangled carcass. Mechdar and Hnakil dismounted and approached, causing the flies momentarily to disperse in a small black cloud before returning to their task. Mechdar searched the scrub until he found a stick with which to prod the remains. At first glance it had appeared that what was left was not much more than a sheepskin, stripped of meat, organs, and bones, a shriveled thing without much shape. When Mechdar lifted part of it there was obviously more substance but not much. As the warrior shifted the carcass he could see that it had been eviscerated. What troubled him, even as it confirmed what Tjorn had told the day before at Gretland, was that the ribs had seemingly melted together.

"This is what we have been seeing," Hnakil said almost in a whisper.

"Holy Hjelgi," Nordil cursed, invoking the Star Shepherd.

Ian noticed that Ringskild seemed like water on the verge of boiling, her eyes blazing and her face flushed with emotion. "Damned be whatever did this. May the Fierce Mother strengthen us against it," she uttered between clinched teeth. Vunskridh's hand was on the grip of her sword but her eyes were wet with nascent tears and those near him could hear Volthir's jaw popping with tension.

Pjortan had only glanced at the benighted sheep's remains then ridden toward a clump of nearby trees. At first the group thought he wanted privacy to be sick but he only cut off a branch and returned. Dismounting, he circled what was once a sheep three times, waving the branch and singing a hymn to Hjelgi. Nothing could undo the horror that had taken place here but he could at least honor the victim and enact his grief. Hnakil stood bemused, overwhelmed by all that had been taking place yet caught in the praises of his patron deity. Tjorn touched his shoulder gently to wake his cousin from the spell.

After Pjortan's feeble but sincere tribute, buzzards resumed their circling and the riders returned wordlessly to Hnakil's home.

There, at least, they found some respite from all that was somber. Wilda has discovered that Vladje seemed to approve of children and Hnakil's youngest two had been playing with the wolf. The rest of the household, raised in a tradition that knew wolves to be the enemy of their livelihood, had looked on in wonderment. Hnakil's sister-in-law had even dared once to pet Vladje but learned that Wilda and Ian remained the only adults granted that privilege. The children squealed with delight that they were allowed a treat forbidden to adults, a complete reversal of the usual order of things.

Hnakil, when apprised of all this, remained suspicious of the furry beast—in his own courtyard, no less—but was seen to smile occasionally at the joy of his children. His wife, who had witnessed most of this, took his arm, leaned upon his shoulder, and beamed that some happiness should come into their lives in such a dark time, wolf or no wolf. Wilda, afraid Hnakil would come down on her with wrath when he found out about the afternoon's entertainment, was relieved that the herder was puzzled and concerned but too drained of life to be angry. To Hnakil's relief, Vladje meekly left the party and followed Ian outside the house to camp a second night. The wolf slept with Ian, reassuring Hnakil that at least this predator was not wreaking havoc with the herds.

The following morning the party thanked Hnakil for his hospitality and Tjorn for his guidance. Gifts were left for their host and the promised silver handed over to Tjorn. Wulfdar made a special present of herbs to Hnakil's wife, explaining that infused into a tea they would help her husband heal of the horror on the hillsides. The children said goodbye to their furry new playmate and the Norrungs headed west toward Siot. Tjorn later rode south to Gretland with new stories to tell of the strangers and the wolf.

That day's journeying only brought them to Nishtell, the last town on the Ercoille before Siot. Encounters along the road confirmed that strange occurrences seemed to multiply. One merchant, a short, lively fellow who seemed to talk with his hands as much as his mouth, informed the Norrungs that he had barely escaped a riot in Siot when a pottery merchant suddenly went berserk. Instead of overcoming him or calling the authorities, the crowd adopted him as their leader and rampaged through the bazaar, tossing tables, trashing merchandise, and injuring or killing those who got in their way. The excited merchant had fled for his life and decided to avoid Siot in the future.

"I tell you," he concluded, "This is the Chegjan's work. It was bad enough when the plague coursed through the land but now we have madness and violence."

Ian's heart quailed at the thought of going up against anything that could cause such destruction, especially a faceless, bodiless power. How could it be found, much less overcome?

Nishtell buzzed with news of the turmoil in Siot. Later reports said the riot died down and the crowd dispersed. Even the man who first ran amok came back to his senses. Unfortunately, many were injured and perhaps two dozen killed in the melee. Evidently this sort of thing was happening in other towns, unpredictable fits of madness and violence erupting and subsiding. In addition to the initial damage done, such outbursts left the populace in a constant state of anxiety. All this was aftermath of the demon. Its vanguard followed the plague and was now further west.

Ian spoke in spite of his doubts and fears, most significantly his own sense of inadequacy for whatever lay ahead, "We must hasten, Norrungs. We cannot let this continue unabated. Whatever I must do, let it be done. I only hope the stars reveal what I am to do, for I still have no idea."

His valor was appreciated, though none present had any idea how to defeat a demon. Not even the rich mythology Pjortan carried in song and story, not to mention in his heart, provided an answer. By dawn they were on the road again.

CHAPTER 19

With Nishtell behind them and the sun intermittently breaking through clouds to warm their backs, the companions continued west. They decided to skirt the center of Siot, where the Ercoille joined the Wicket, keeping to its outlying encampments. Mob fury seemed less likely to thrive where people were less concentrated and it seemed unlikely they would miss much news, given the tendency of merchants to ply as many tales as they sold wares, plus whatever tidbits travelers might share.

Given its location and role as a nexus of trade and travel, Siot-on-the-Wicket bore the earmarks of any trading center. Even from its southern outskirts the Norrungs could see the vestiges of its energy before the plague, with people coming and going in larger numbers than one would see at Vorthall. Fortifications surrounded the center of the city, situated on the rise within the fork of the confluence. Iron-colored clouds wreathed Siot like a mournful crown, giving no rain but pressing down on the once-thriving city.

Nearly all they encountered on the way had something to say about the recent riot. There seemed to be as many versions of how it arose as there were tongues to recount the tale. Fewer variations arose in telling the course of the violence, though the details deemed important and worthy of emphasis exposed the speakers' interests. One could hear agreement on the toll of the melee, if not in numbers at least in its emotional impact. Fresh wails of lament had risen throughout the market area and beyond. Those who had taken part in the frenzy soon hid themselves, overcome with shame and horror. Everyone viewed neighbors with suspicion and soon charges and countercharges began to multiply. The horrible question all those capable of self-reflection now faced in solitude was whether they might be susceptible to the sudden madness and find themselves next to go on a killing spree.

Realizing that this was but one instance of the Chegjan's evil influence, the companions tarried only one night outside Siot, replenishing supplies then taking a ferry across the Wicket toward the lands of the setting sun.

The ferryman was long and lanky with shaggy brown hair streaked with gray through the middle, his face nut-brown from days in the sun, and a friendly manner. The ford the companions took was one of two near Siot and the ferryman easily recognized Jannir.

"As I breathe air and the water flows below me, if it isn't Stejni's son! What news do you have from the eastern forest?"

"Little enough worth the telling, you old son of the river. How are you, Snith? Is there enough traffic these days to keep your family clothed?"

"You know how it is among us river dogs, Jannir. Water flows, whether we will or no, and so do life and the traffic I live by. The river crests in the wet season and trickles in drought and my trade has its own rhythms. Still, my wife and children have yet to go naked, nor have we had to beg."

"I am glad to hear you all walk the earth, for losses are heavy in the land. Will you bear my friends and me to the other side? I wager a flask of decent wine may be added to your fee today, for we are eager to be on our way."

"Many of late have been eager to leave the city sitting in gloom up there. I tell you, the sudden madness has spooked the whole region and I hear Siot is not the only place where this has happened. A flask of wine, you say? And decent? Well then, your friends have always been mine, cousin. We'll have to divide up, though. I can't take that many horses across at one time. Step carefully, now."

And so Snith befriended yet another group of strangers, herding them across a ford too treacherous and, in all but a few weeks of late summer, too deep for crossing on horseback. Like many who serve others, Snith's exterior friendship was gained by payment for services rendered, but Jannir knew that a deeper tie was formed over time with those he learned to trust—and sometimes those who had the best stories to tell. Jannir enjoyed this latter bond with the ferryman, so family stories were exchanged along with talk of the Chegjan and the journey of the party from Norrung. Vladje, who decided at some point that Wilda was an alpha female, lay docile and out of sight in her wagon. When all had crossed, the promised flask joined the usual sum of coins, leaving Snith richer and happier.

They did not journey far beyond the ford since the two crossings required by the size of their party consumed a fair piece of the day and the hamlet of Mjerth was not far from the Wicket. There the travelers retired early in order to cover more ground the following day.

Over the course of recent days it became evident that the Norrungs were moving into a different world as the thickly wooded hills of their home gave way to lighter woodland easing into the plains clustered about the Mither River. The vast Forest of Norrast they knew as home became more distant with every day of journeying beneath the daystar's path. For Jannir this was part of his life as a merchant, pursuing many roads in the quest for goods and customers. Youngsters like Ian and Pjortan found the continual shift of scenery and variety of humanity to be endlessly fascinating, while the warmaidens and warriors who watched over the group's safety felt the strain of constant wariness among the unknown.

In succeeding days they crossed the eastern and western forks of the Piç, pausing for food and rest in Chrun and Megh. The latter was a less restful pause, for there time was spent repairing a wagon wheel on the verge of breaking.

Fjurthil enjoyed this part of the world, flying high and wide and taking many a tasty bird that could not match his arrow-swift descent, talons outstretched. Opportunities for hunting were many and Vladje proved a good ally, spooking prey that fled from the wolf only to find the arrows of the Norrungs. He was generously rewarded for his assistance and seemed to enjoy the sport, though for all his cooperation he still would allow no adults but Ian and Wilda to touch him. By now the entire company had grown comfortable with the four-legged predator among them, even the horses, and there was a fondness for him. Vladje, for his part, accepted their praise and cuts of fresh meat but remained sufficiently aloof to remind one and all that he was not domesticated.

From Megh the party moved toward the region of the Njor River, pausing at Njorc on the river's upper loop and Shultal further downstream. Stories of the Chegjan preying on sheep, goats, and cattle continued to filter through the conversation of passing travelers and the inhabitants of villages along the way. The mistress of a drinking spot in Shultal seemed to the Norrungs to be fond of her own wares when they heard her recount a startling new event. Others confirmed her tale, however, and all were alarmed to hear that what had once been named "sheep's death," that is, the horrific demonic evisceration of animals that left their bones fused like melted wax, had now happened to a local baron north of Nimmoth. His servants found his grisly remains in the courtyard early one morning and the tale spread like wildfire.

Shaken by this latest development, the travelers sought to cleanse their minds as well as their bodies when a pleasant stream between Shultal and Nith provided the opportunity to bathe. Horses, clothing, and goods were guarded in turns as the party frolicked in the water, grateful for an especially warm day in late spring and the cool depths of the pool where they refreshed themselves.

Ian marveled that a society so modest in public dress was so casual on an occasion such as this, finding it difficult to envision men and women, respectable ones at least, bathing in sight of each other back home. With that thought he felt one of his recurring pangs of homesickness, wishing that now and again his brother would kick him out of bed instead of having a furry paw nudge him at dawn. At the thought of even missing his lump of a cousin, Ian decided it was time for his meandering thoughts to turn back to the world of which he was now a part.

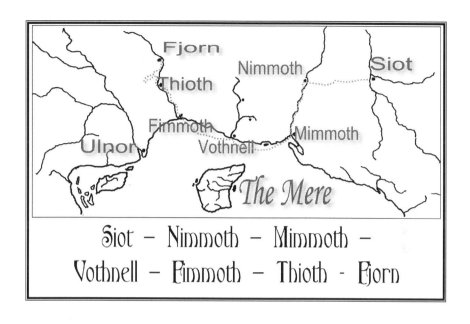

Siot – Nimmoth – Mimmoth –
Vothnell – Fimmoth – Thioth - Fjorn

CHAPTER 20

Renewed by the cool cleansing waters of the pools, the party forged ahead toward Denev, their last stop before reaching the Mither, the River that gave its name to the Mere. As Jannir alerted the group that they should see Denev after the next curve in the road, Pjortan began a hymn to Vuchtall the Bear, god of healing. Wulfdar recognized the chant immediately but did not interrupt. Pjortan's timing was excellent as Vunskridh spotted the village just as the last note faded in the twilight air. Containing his curiosity no longer, the healer asked Pjortan why he sang this particular hymn at that moment.

"Because there are great ills ahead of us, my cousin. I have been watching the skies, night after night, and they have hinted at something out of joint. Perhaps it is a recurrence of plague, perhaps something else, but my instinct says we approach a sick place and I felt it wise to call upon the Healer before we enter."

Wulfdar had no comment to add to these forebodings and wordlessly furrowed his brow.

"We thank you for your prayer, Pjortan," Hildir said, breaking the pensive silence.

There was no visual hint of anything awry in Denev and the evening was a lovely one. The country air was pleasant and tinged with a scent of blooming trees. Nonetheless, as the travelers entered Wilda could hear a low growl from Vladje and all were especially alert for trouble of any kind.

Jannir chose an inn he had used before, noting that its quality and character had been gradually declining. Scattered among the tables a rough lot sat or stood, a few caught up in a quiet quarrel that might or might not have been friendly. A game of knucklebones kept others focused, though drink may have blurred their focus a bit. A fastidious person would have thought better of dining in such unsavory company but the Norrungs knew that one had to live in a world comprised of all types. This particular evening Meldreth refrained from flirting with the men. Nordil felt a swift nudge in his ribs when Wilda caught him looking at a feather woman in a pale rose-colored gown that rippled at even the slightest movement. His wife's jab caused him to blush, then laugh. Nordil's appreciation of women was expressed so openly that he lacked the stealth to betray Wilda. She chuckled too, but there was warning in her eyes.

The food was hearty, heavy with onions and pepper, and the drink strong. Laughter broke out from time to time, hearty and usually mocking. Oaths were part of the rhythm of the knucklebone table. Ian was unaware that a hand reached for his purse but the thief did not escape notice. Before the cutpurse could withdraw his arm Vunskridh had a dagger poised so that pulling back would impale his wrist and Mechdar swiftly had another dagger at the thief's throat.

"I would think twice before upsetting the lady, friend," warned Mechdar. "She has a very quick temper, especially around dishonest men."

Eyeing the warmaiden, the cutpurse broke out in a sweat that quickly drenched his small frame. "Might I move?" he queried.

"So long as your hand is empty," Vunskridh replied.

It was a very unsteady hand that released Ian's purse and drew back. Indeed, the man's entire body seemed to tremble under the blazing eyes of the warriors.

"Much better," added Vunskridh. "Perhaps you would prefer to dine elsewhere this lovely evening."

At that, the unnerved man, whose leggings indicated even more terror than his face as a wet spot grew down his thigh, left the room, followed by a larger companion with a light scar on the side of his head. When they were gone all in the room drew a collective breath. Ian thanked Vunskridh and Mechdar and a voice from the edge of the room proclaimed, "Well done, milady."

This was the voice of a tall, scruffily handsome man with copper-colored hair and a small scar on his chin. He was clad in dark brown homespun set off by a finely tooled sword belt, gold rings in each ear, and a tattooed snake coiled about his left forearm. As unrefined as he appeared, his voice was elegant and he bowed courteously toward Vunskridh as he spoke. The smile as his head rose was clearly flirtatious and the warmaiden bridled. In an icy voice she replied, "Kind of you to notice," then added, "sir," with a mocking nod.

Meldreth lost no time whispering to her fellow, "Keep an eye on him, but my, he's nice looking." To this Vunskridh gave a hint of a blush and Meldreth said no more.

Rattling knucklebones became a background rhythm to the night as meals were finished and lodgers prepared to retire. Wilda stepped out to the privy and found a large figure blocking her path when she made to return. It was the man who had left earlier with the cutpurse. Wilda recoiled from the disfiguring scar bordering on the man's left eye and wrinkled her nose at his foul breath.

"Forget the silly girls," he said, "you are a real woman, the kind to take a man to the stars and back again."

Before Wilda could cry for help the man's huge hand covered her mouth as his body backed her against a wall. His other hand began to take liberties and Wilda regretted the folly of stepping outside alone. She prepared for the worst when hope came from the darkness. She heard a familiar growl.

When the attacker turned, Vladje leapt for his throat, connecting on the first try. The man let out a furious roar as Wilda looked on in relief and horror. As others rushed out with drawn weapons and a torch, they saw the scar-headed man twitch one last time then lie still, the last spurts of blood shooting from his neck where a large chunk had been torn out. The wolf had already become a shadow in the night.

Nordil and Ringskild rushed to the weeping Wilda, a woman never known to tremble but now resembling aspen leaves in an uninterrupted shudder. Nordil was all remorse at having let her out of his sight, now feeling double guilt for having looked at another woman earlier in the evening. Ringskild gently asked Wilda if the man had attacked her. She nodded in the affirmative and Ringskild knew what must have happened. So did the other Norrungs, familiar with the bond between Vladje and their collective mother.

Other inn guests were confused. Those who knew something of the man and his ways could surmise the first part of the story, especially with Wilda so distraught. The gaping wound from which a pool of blood had poured was a puzzle, bearing no resemblance to a sword wound or most forms of human combat. What it resembled was the attack of a predator: a lion or a bear or a wolf. Questions began to flow but they were briefly stilled when the copper-headed man spoke.

"So, Djort finally received his due reward."

No one gainsaid this observation for the man, evidently named Djort, was detested by women and looked down on by all but the worst men.

With the commanding tone of a captain, Ringskild turned to the redhead. "You knew this man?"

"We all knew of him," the man replied, "but few would qualify as his companions. The cutpurse who seems to have vanished was one. The world will not be sadder for Djort's passing."

"And you would be…?"

"Vishgar, at your service, my lady." Again the man bowed.

"And I am Ringskild, daughter of Ivor, foster-daughter of Rathdar, late chief of the Norrungs," she replied, establishing her position and seeking to raise the level of conversation.

"My manners have failed me. I beg forgiveness. I am Vishgar, son of Ioreth the woodcarver, from Ushtet near Aonghe. I am honored to behold the skill and quality of the Norrungs this evening. Though I am not from this area, please convey the regrets of all present that the gentle lady suffered the attentions of Djort. He was a vile creature, and vile seems to be the manner of his death. It is fitting."

"So it seems," Ringskild replied, not rising to the implied invitation to speculate on Djort's wounds. "Would that the stars always came to our aid so swiftly when the unrighteous act."

It is unlikely that Vishgar missed the warning in her voice, as no one else seemed to. She judged Vishgar to be a slippery fellow with a silver tongue, charming but potentially treacherous, and she was not about to take him on his superficial terms. Nor was she wrong, for he was indeed a criminal, though not the ordinary sort. When not trading on his father's artistry in wood, he organized men of few scruples to commit theft and fraud. It was a living, but Vishgar did it as much for the joy of planning and carrying it out as he did for plunder.

The look of sympathy he gave Wilda, however, was not false and the contempt in which he held Djort was obvious. With a muted smile he bowed to the ladies and bade them a safe night and good sleep.

With Ringskild and her band clearly in charge of the moment, the onlookers took their questions elsewhere. Djort's body was tossed unceremoniously in an adjacent field, spat upon, and left to its fate. Wulfdar provided a strong draught for Wilda's nerves and Nordil obtained extra cuts of meat from the kitchen for Vladje that night. Knucklebones and whispers kept the night from silence, but the Norrungs kept watch and slept as best they could.

CHAPTER 21

Morning was more subdued than the night before, to no one's regret. There were no feather ladies taking breakfast and the knucklebones were finally stilled. Vishgar was nowhere to be seen. As the company rode out of Denev, Jannir apologized for their lodgings and the entire incident.

Ringskild assured him no blame accrued to him for there were, undoubtedly, many worse places to stay and rascals can be found anywhere. Wilda, though still shaken, freely offered forgiveness for anything the merchant may have done and affirmed that although her peril was great, no harm had come to her beyond the fright. Nordil hovered near her all day.

Glad to be quit of the entire episode, Pjortan sang the dawn hymn with great fervor, adding a song in honor of Morvladh, the Great Wolf. Vladje appeared to recognize the latter for he added a few howls of his own. He then bounded up to Wilda's cart and snuggled next to her with great affection. She melted in tears again, though this time they signaled relief and gratitude.

"You saved me, sure, my furry fellow," she said, "and I will ever be in your debt." Vladje replied to this with a very wet lick and Wilda laughed, forgetting for a brief moment the terror she had experienced.

"We need a song for Vladje, Pjortan," Meldreth suggested, but it was not the star singer who composed the song. The warmaidens and warriors, with an occasional phrase from Jannir, took turns adding bits and snatches together until by noon they had a serviceable song in honor of the wolf. They borrowed the tune from a well-known drinking song and tossed in some traditional riddle elements, the latter chiefly from Volthir who loved nothing better than a good riddle. A few fanciful additions to what was actually known of the wolf worked their way in as the battle-skilled poets could not resist working in nearly every idea that occurred to them. Volthir was fond of the misleading opening line, based on Ian's version of how he met the wolf— "His kiss awoke the stranger." No one, hearing that beginning, would suspect this would not be a love song that would later include a verse about ripping a man's throat open. Elements of the legends of Morvladh worked their way into the growing ballad and laughter vied with artistic arguments, keeping minds off the unease that clung with them from their time in Denev. Pjortan had been right to warn them of illness, a sickness of human behavior.

Vladje seemed unaware of the exaggerated praise being heaped upon him in verse, taking advantage of Wilda's lap, his favorite pillow, and napping after the fierce watch he had kept all night. After the singing of the song during the midday meal break, Vladje was sometimes addressed as Lord Wolf, but so long as good scraps came his way and no one got too close, he seemed unaffected by it all.

"Ah," Wulfdar philosophized with a smile, "the gods and their companions are above our praises or cursing, but they enjoy our offerings."

By mid-afternoon they had descended the plain to the banks of the Mither River where they came to Nimmoth, a trade center linking the east-west roads with the waters that ran roughly north to south. Pjortan reassured his companions that he saw no omens in the sky in this place and Wilda saw no hackles rise on Vladje.

Nimmoth had been settled at a spot where the river, in its meandering course, was especially broad and shallow, providing easier fording. It was a clear and exposed location but also one no enemy could approach undetected and Nimmoth had been at peace for many years. Whatever political shifts occurred among neighboring peoples and tribes, all seemed to value a relatively neutral place for the exchange and transport of goods. Nimmoth sat on the west side of the Mither and the Norrungs crossed to the city, arriving by late afternoon. This was easily done with simple fording of the shallows to a small island, crossing the old bridge leading to a second island,

and then a ferry across the deeper channel where ships plied the waters to the area of the docks and warehouses. Here, for all the attrition of the plague in the past year, an endless stream of goods and people seemed to move purposefully in every direction. Only Jannir's experience told him things were slower than in the past.

Jannir guided them through the bustle of the dockside to the Merchant's Gate and into the city proper, past the trade quarters and bazaar toward the main square. Here the civic buildings in dressed stone provided a marvel to the forest dwellers' eyes. They had never seen such extensive stonework, nor so intricate, for all the artistry of the Norrungs. Pjortan was fascinated with the star tower rising from the highest point in the city, enabling singers to watch the heavens from a splendid vantage point, as well as to call out to the city in prayer. Finally they came to the Street of Inns, where Jannir trusted things not to have declined as they had in Denev.

As they managed to find lodging in a somewhat quieter inn than most, Nordil kept close to Wilda, not even letting her out of sight to visit a privy unless a warmaiden went with her. His wife protested that this was overdoing it, but she loved him the more for it and was grateful half their party was comprised of chosen warriors to keep them all safe. The group also conspired to sneak Vladje into their quarters to sleep near Wilda, which spared the scene he might have caused since he would not let her out of sight after the night before.

Ian considered the twinge of jealousy he felt to be unmanly and convinced himself it was normal for his special guardian to watch over Wilda under the circumstances. He did not share the moment of selfish emotion with anyone, ashamed that he even felt it.

Mercifully, Nimmoth provided a night of secure and profound sleep, though two kept watch at all times, as had been the case throughout the journey. The following day was spent taking advantage of Nimmoth for restocking journey provisions and making minor repairs. Amid the jostle and random noises of a crowded street Vunskridh of the sharp eyes, as she was occasionally called, touched Volthir's shoulder, then indicated a direction ahead of them with a jerk of her chin. "Do you see that great blond brute yonder?"

"Indeed, cousin. The one with the curly hair and huge shoulders?"

"Yes. Is that a familiar copper head beside him?"

"Stars bless me, I believe it's your admirer, Vunskridh."

"Hah," she replied in a dismissive tone, but Vishgar and his tall companion disappeared in the flow of humanity.

Meanwhile Nordil located a smithy and saw to any needed repairs or replacement of horse shoes. Wilda, well protected, spent the morning acquiring provisions and the afternoon mending garments. Wulfdar took advantage of the crossroads city to acquire additional herbs and potions, exchanging information and techniques with local healers.

Ian found the Woodcarvers' Lane and spent a couple of hours admiring the varieties of technique and the beauty of woods, asking questions of the masters if they were willing to share. A few were jealous of their secrets but most, from their love of the material with its varieties of hardness and softness, grain patterns, and all that made each piece a unique expression of a once-living tree, relished sharing the joys of the craft with someone who was not going to set up a competing shop in their own area. Ian also purchased a carving tool for cuts he had not seen back at Vorthall and hoped to incorporate into his future work. There was a reaffirmation of life in taking a step on behalf of a future beyond the Chegjan and his spirits were lifted a notch as he and Hildir left the Lane to see more of the city.

With the scent of fresh wood still in their nostrils they paused to quench their thirst at a small alehouse.

"Look yonder," Hildir said softly. Ian looked about but sensed no danger and gave Hildir a quizzical look.

"She's looking our way," the warrior added and Ian scanned the room once more with better focus. He saw a young woman with flowing brown tresses and a gown the color of ripe wheat. The dress was tightly cinched at the waist by a strip of sea green and her generous chest, ample for a frame so slender, seemed on the verge of escaping the fabric that held it in place. The expression on her face was playful and she was, indeed, glancing their way from time to time.

"Ah," said Ian, recognizing that Hildir was raising hopes, not alarms. "She must find warriors irresistible, cousin."

"A man may hope as much," the older man replied, "though she may be fancying the tender and inexperienced morsel standing next to me, more would be the pity."

Kirlat, for such was her name, rather fancied them both, personally and professionally. She was one of the city's many feather women, ever on the alert for sources of income and preferring the young and handsome customer whenever possible, though that was, sadly, not often enough the case. The craftsmen's section of Nimmoth was at least more prosperous than some parts of town and she was well known in this alehouse.

What she saw across the room was a pair of strangers. One stood out for his build, a model of strength and barely contained energy, his large arms rippling with knotted muscles, a finely trimmed beard on a rugged brown face, and the alert look of a man accustomed to danger. His hand was never far from the weathered scabbard from which his sword hung. She would have known him for a warrior anywhere, even without the eagle feathers in his light brown braid proclaiming that he traveled in peace. The man radiated vitality and she knew he would give great pleasure to any woman he favored with his attention. The thought began to excite her.

Standing next to the virile warrior was a beardless youth, not yet grown into all his manly power, but stunningly handsome. His face was angular and clean shaven, with a long straight nose and a wide mouth that easily broke into a slight smile. His eyes were as blue as the Mere, accented by eyebrows that formed small peaks, his skin fine, his hair a curly brown where it was medium length and forming a thick braid in the back. The greenness of youth bespoke little experience of life, and that was a challenge to Kirlat. She wondered what it would be like to teach this youth some of the refinements of lovemaking and her nostrils flared at the thought of this. The smile she gave the two strangers was full of promise.

Ian smiled back, with a touch of hesitation, while Hildir's mouth revealed an even row of good teeth and knowledgeable desire. "Ah, yes," thought Kirlat, "now if only they have good money." Gradually she worked her way across the room, sharing jibes and laughter with all as she threaded among the thirsty and the hopeful.

"She approaches, Hildir," Ian said.

"This is good," replied Hildir, his voice taking on a husky tone as he began to imagine possibilities. "Relax, cousin, she likes us."

"I can tell that, and she is a fine lass. What do we do now?"

"Follow my lead, lad. The only problem is we cannot linger to enjoy her company, nor can we probably afford it."

"Do you mean she is a feather woman?"

"No other kind would smile so easily in a place such as this, boy. But, oh, I would be comforted by her if I could."

"Based on her smiles, I'm sure you could, Hildir."

"And fail my charge to keep you safe, Ian? As much as I would have her, I cannot risk that."

"Could we both have her, cousin?"

"She would be happy to oblige, I am sure, but tell me, have you no promises to another?"

"None, Hildir."

"Are you sure, boy?"

Ian frowned. He had made no promises to any woman of Vorthall. But then he thought of the day they left, and the present Njothila gave him. There was a quality in her friendship that seemed unlike the friendship of others, though she had been as a foster sister to him. There was no promise there, but as he recalled the way she looked at him there seemed to be some hint, something that had always made him feel she waited for him to return. Nothing had been said, yet he had taken strength from thinking of her during the days and nights of the journey.

"Well, not really, cousin," he finally responded.

"In that case, Ian, I suggest we enjoy the little game we are about to play without becoming customers of the afternoon. We must soon return in any case."

By then the lovely Kirlat of the easy smile and enticing form had drawn closer. Her eyes danced over the men before her and her expression combined humor, welcome, and the possibility of more.

"Good afternoon, strangers. What brings you to this alehouse?"

"Thirst, good lady," replied the warrior, nodding with a smile.

"This is a good place to find refreshment and pleasant company. Are you visiting Nimmoth?" This was a rhetorical question, as their dress proclaimed they were from another region.

"Indeed we are," said Hildir. "Is this your home?"

"My home is wherever I find welcome in the world," Kirlat replied, her eyes darting between the two men.

Hildir recognized the invitation in the remark and responded playfully, "A woman so lovely must surely find welcome wherever she goes," and concluded this with a smile and a slight tilting of his head. Kirlat nodded, acknowledging the compliment and the game they were playing.

"Your young friend smiles but seems wordless," she parried.

"I was struck dumb by your loveliness," Ian finally managed to utter.

"Why, thank you, cousin. I see you do have a tongue, and I am sure it has given pleasure to the ladies." This produced the blush she was sure would come and confirmed her suspicions of his inexperience. She and Hildir both chuckled at Ian's embarrassment.

Hildir took pity on Ian and responded, "He is discreet and shames no woman by easy talk."

Ian knew this was a misleading evasion but was grateful for the attempted rescue.

"That is a good thing in a man," said Kirlat. "And you, man of arms? Do you keep the confidences of your women?"

Hildir almost blushed himself but only answered, "A gentleman always does, sweet lady."

This jousting of words, interlarded with emotions, desires of the flesh and desires of profit, was interrupted by a voice from the doorway.

"Hildir, Ian, it is time to return!" Ringskild's message was delivered casually but Hildir recognized the command in it. His captain cut fantasies short and ended their time with the beautiful woman standing so close and promising so much.

"But of course," he shouted back, equally casually, stifling his inner curses. "My lady, it is time to rejoin our companions. You have made our visit to this alehouse a true delight."

"I would it were possible to entertain you gentlemen further," Kirlat replied, "but your lady clearly awaits. The stars keep you."

"And you, lady," Ian answered but Hildir, recognizing Kirlat's veiled inquiry, answered her question.

"Neither my lady nor his, sweet woman, but our companion and my captain." Kirlat could see by Ringskild's dress and eagle feathers that she was, indeed, a warmaiden. The feather woman's smile broadened and radiated the warmth of many promises.

"I see. Journey well, strangers. I hope we meet again."

"Thank you," Ian stammered.

"As do I," grinned Hildir, taking her hand and kissing it gently. It smelled of the lingering hint of perfume and quickened his pulse. Reluctantly, he released Kirlat's hand, bowed his head, and turned toward the door. Ian followed him out.

Kirlat heaved a sigh at the double loss, neither the pleasures of these men nor their silver would be hers that afternoon. She turned back to the crowd and sought some ale herself.

As the two men stepped outside, Ringskild raised an eyebrow and chastised her companions. "Lord Njothir did not send us to seek comfort in Nimmoth, cousins."

"No," replied Hildir, "but eyes were made to behold beauty and a man must have dreams to survive."

Her rebuke delivered, Ringskild now laughed. "Fair enough, good cousin Hildir, but if I have no time for a feather man then my comrades cannot have time for a feather woman. Let us save our dreams for the time of sleeping and finish our errands."

Mechdar, who was with Ringskild, clapped the other men on their shoulders, "Dreams are wonderful while they last, cousins. Is it not often a shame to wake up?"

"Indeed," the outland youth replied and his elders all chuckled, aware no stories of dalliance had yet accrued to Ian's reputation.

"Did you get her name, cousin?" Ringskild inquired.

"If you did, please share it," added Mechdar with a leer. Hildir gave an exaggerated sigh before answering.

"Alas, cousins, no."

"More's the pity," Mechdar commented.

Ringskild dryly said, "Perhaps as well," but Hildir softly said, "Alas."

The four finished their rounds in Nimmoth and returned to the Street of Inns.

CHAPTER 22

As the Norrungs slept in the inn, Kirlat completed her day's business and retired to the small room she called her own. Although the customer base had been severely reduced by the plague, her choice to cater to wealthier clients enabled her to stay decently clothed and adequately fed, unlike many of her less fortunate sisters. To even have a room of her own was a luxury and one she guarded carefully.

Settling into her bed, she did not fall asleep easily that night. Her mind kept returning to the two strangers in the alehouse. Were they toying with her as she was playing with them? For her it was a living, for them mere amusement. The youth was charming and delicious but the older warrior had kindled something in her. Kirlat had learned not to form emotional ties with customers, though she was fond of some regulars. The dream of settling down with one man was a fantasy she considered too indulgent to pursue. That the warrior was interested in her physically was obvious, and his manners were refreshing. The kissing of her hand had caused a faint tingling to spread throughout her body and the memory of that instant still seemed an icy fire on the back of her hand. What might it be like to have a man like him, not for one night but every night? With a deep sigh, Kirlat shifted position and finally drifted asleep with thoughts of Hildir's muscled body next to hers.

Hildir, for his part, was thinking of her as well while his day came to a close, though not going quite so far as to imagine being married to Kirlat. He did not even have her name and the possibility of a feather woman as a wife had never occurred to him. He did, however, fantasize more than an evening with the woman in the wheat-colored dress and her long, unbound brown hair. Another commonality in their imaginings was shared laughter. Hildir fell asleep with a smile on his face and her perfume still in his nostrils.

Ian thought of another woman that night. As he removed the eagle feathers from his hair before retiring, he considered Njothila, who had given them to him. Hildir's questioning whether Ian had promises to a woman, and the warrior's gently asking whether he were sure, haunted the youth's thoughts. He had made no promises, either to Njothila or any other. Yet he had spent a fair portion of his first year at Vorthall in her company. That was only natural since he was the young chieftain's personal ward, and she the chief's sister. This would not, however, explain the easy conversations that had taken place between the boy entering manhood and the girl who had become a woman, nor the frequency of their encounters. They clearly enjoyed each other's company. Had this youthful companionship implied an unspoken promise? Ian realized this had not occurred to him. Still, he had counted on her friendship as she seemed to count on his. With all of this unresolved, the adopted Norrung drifted to sleep, his mind lost in the chestnut tangles of Njothila's hair.

Refreshed by a day spent in preparation instead of journeying, the companions embarked on a different mode of travel, boarding a riverboat to head downstream toward Mimmoth and the Mere. The hope was that it would be faster to travel by boat along the Mither coast to Ulnor and then journey on horseback along the road paralleling the Ulava River than going directly west overland. This decision resulted partly from tales of lawlessness and distress among civil factions in the vast triangular region between Nimmoth, Thioth, and Nialt. Dealing with outlaws, anarchic mobs, or some warlord's thugs would not make for haste in the journey toward the dark being they sought.

Boarding the boat went smoothly and the captain, Gleth from Crumbly-on-the-Mither, had a reputation in Nimmoth for honesty. Jannir had met Gleth at least once before. He and Ringskild spoke to the captain privately before embarking, explaining that they had a wolf with them whom the twelve considered sent by the stars. Vladje's rescue of Wilda was briefly recounted and Hranild's claim that the wolf was Ian's brother. These stories puzzled Gleth and he asked Pjortan to take a singer's oath that the tales were true and Vladje posed no known harm to the crew and passengers. Pjortan willingly complied and Gleth was permitted to catch a glimpse of Vladje as Wilda's wagon came on board. Vladje sniffed the air and let his tongue hang when he saw Gleth and the Norrungs viewed this as the wolf's approval of the captain.

"You have a reputation for being an honest fellow, captain," said Ringskild. "With Vladje's confirmation we are certain it is true. We trust the judgment of the servant of Morvladh."

"May the stars watch over us all," Gleth replied, wondering how many other strange things he would witness on this river before journeying to the stars.

Assisted by the others, the warriors took advantage of this time to check all gear and make minor repairs in armor. Some weapons had been freshly sharpened in Nimmoth and everything was now polished and made ready. Although no others could hunt while on board, Fjurthil stretched his wings and brought a few birds back to Nordil, receiving his reward in the process.

As the day wore on beneath a slightly overcast sky, Gleth and his crew expertly navigated their way down the Mither, avoiding shoals and watching for the rare patch of rougher water. Downstream from Nimmoth the river was fairly broad and smooth, with only a few narrows. Unlike some spots to the far north, these were not particularly problematic. The passengers watched the varied landscape of the river's banks glide by: willow- and shrub-clad slopes, grassy expanses, bluffs, pebbly beaches, muddied fords, thickets, and plains.

A new pairing occurred among the companions as Pjortan seated himself on a grain sack near Vladje that afternoon. The singer was careful not to touch or threaten the independent wolf. For an extended stretch the two sat in silence, observing the scenery as they drifted past it. Eventually Pjortan began to speak in a low voice, conversing as he might with an old friend, sharing thoughts and questions, revealing inner struggles, pausing for a response. Vladje did not speak, yet seemed attentive and sympathetic. Once or twice a questioning look passed over his lupine features when it would have been appropriate to prompt Pjortan for more information, evoking a mild chuckle from the human.

The discussion was never shared with others, nor did any interrupt or attempt to overhear. The singer clearly wanted private time with the wolf, whom he, perhaps more than the others, viewed as at least a representative of a minor deity. At length, apparently satisfied, Pjortan bowed toward Vladje and rose. All of this led to speculation, especially among a couple of sailors who found it not only puzzling but somewhat humorous. None, however, dared inquire into what appeared a holy matter.

As the day wore on they drifted past grain fields and gardens that bordered the river, docking for night by Niftor, then resuming their journey toward the Mere the next day. Warmaidens and warriors practiced battle moves in the stern, to the distraction of the Gleth's crew. Norrungs took advantage of the day to take naps, gathering strength for the days ahead. That night they came to the Bay of Nioril and city of Nimmoth.

Mimmoth was the greatest trading center along the northern seacoast. Located on the delta of the Mither River and enjoying the shelter of the Bay of Nioril, it was ideally situated as a link between the central northern regions and all the lands about the Mere. Mimmoth was also one of the oldest settlements in the region and held, by the cachet of its age, a respected prominence among northern cities. Its titular ruler was styled "the Tjernmor," or Great Lord, but the evolution of civic structure and rise of the merchant class had led to formation of a Council that held most power in the city and its dependent regions.

At dawn the next day Gleth collected from the Norrungs the rather significant toll required to allow the ship to depart from Mimmoth. Ringskild handed it over reluctantly, and only after confirming with Jannir that this was the established custom and correct amount. Convinced that Gleth's honesty had been confirmed, the proud warmaiden smiled winningly and said, "Onward, Captain Gleth! We sail to uncertain fortune but we cannot turn back."

Gleth handed the required fee to the customs agent, who counted and recorded it meticulously, and ordered the moorings loosed.

Still pondering Ringskild's words, Wulfdar was heard to mutter, "Uncertain fortune, indeed. Such is true of us all. The stars process in their cycle and do not turn back."

"Ay, cousin," responded the star singer. "However twisted our path we travel in but one direction. I am only glad I do not know whether our journey to the stars comes sooner or later."

Ian, who stood next to Pjortan, joined the conversation. "The choice will not be mine, but I should choose much later, thank you, cousins. I would like to see more of life beneath the stars' path; this world is still new to me."

"And where we journey next is new to all but Jannir. Though I have seen many days, I receive each one with a grateful heart," the healer said.

Jannir broke into these weighty considerations to state the obvious. "The Mere! My cousins, we have come to it at last."

The Norrungs' eyes widened. A vast expanse of water opened out before them as they glided between the lighthouse of Mimtor on their right and the hills of the Nioril Peninsula off to the left. There was nothing beyond them but water and sky. Distance and morning mists obscured the nearest landmark, the Isle of Vios, lying WSW of Mimmoth. Its highest point, Mount Hiovith, reached to almost four thousand feet but its peak was one hundred miles from the voyaging Norrungs.

Once out in the Mere they could travel by sail and so they swiftly skirted the coast toward the west. Gleth led the ship close to Nimos, between that coastal town and the Isle of Vjoç, thus avoiding the hidden rocks on the seaward side of that island. They then proceeded to the mouth of the River Tugh and the port of Tugdal, where they moored for the night. The captain presented his warrant from the payment of toll in Mimmoth and the authorities of Tugdal recognized it without further tax, though not without a couple of small silver coins.

As the daystar neared the end of its daily journey, the Norrungs could look due south of Tugdal and see the faded outline of Vios, the island now being much closer and mists having long since dispersed. It was a magical view for the forest dwellers, especially the dancing shades of sunset upon the waters of the Mere. Gleth and his crew were as grateful as the Norrungs for an auspicious first day on the Mere and all slept well that night.

Early the next morning they left Tugdal and set sail for Fimmoth, a good day's sailing toward the west. From there they could resume overland travel, should they so choose, following the path of the River Fiona. Or they might continue to Ulnor.

Ian, who had never been on a ship before, was fascinated by every detail—the creaking of the rigging, the dancing of the waves, the spreading wake behind the boat, the trick of catching the wind. He and the other Norrungs took turns helping at the oars when there was no breeze, learning quickly to appreciate the toil of sailors. Nordil marveled at the flight pattern of the terns, soaring until they spotted a fish, hovering and bobbling for a brief moment, then plummeting toward the water in hopes of returning with a fish. The mewling of gulls formed part of the music of the Mere. Ringskild, the resolute leader of the entire adventure, experienced the radically unsettling sensation of seasickness, her commanding visage turning pale and all her warmaiden's dignity fading as she clung to the railing.

As midday drew nigh a sudden shout added to all the newness the Norrungs were experiencing. A lookout spotted two ships approaching, white pennons flying from both masts. Gleth observed that this would make them the ships of Furk, lord of Vothnell, but he had no idea why they were making for his merchant ship. All aboard came to full attention, peace poles prominently displayed but with weapons handy in case defensive action was needed.

As Furk's ships came alongside to flank Gleth's merchant vessel, one could make out the black battleaxe on the white banner of Furk. An armed man shouted across, "Ahoy, do you realize you are crossing the waters of Furk of Vothnell?"

"Indeed, sir, I know we sail past Vothnell and the holdings of Lord Furk, but I have never heard of the waters belonging to any but the goddess Vuoru," Gleth replied. "I am Gleth, son of Glendar, merchant of Mimmoth and captain of this vessel. Our course this day is for Fimmoth, not Vothnell."

"That," replied the other, "may have been your plan, Gleth son of Glendar, but I am afraid I must insist you return with us to Vothnell. My Lord Furk would share his hospitality with you and I am under orders to escort all vessels thither."

Ringskild, who had recomposed herself as this confrontation neared, struck the deck lightly with her peace pole. Gleth added, "You can see that we journey in peace, good sir."

I would expect as much," answered the Vothneli, "and I know you will join us peacefully."

CHAPTER 23

When the moon was but five days old, Thomdar scanned the heavens in hopes of finding some clue concerning the adventurers. Wigdor, the Sky Chief, had gradually become more central to the nightly pattern of the stars, succeeding Raven in the dance. The singer pondered a passage about Wigdor in an ancient hymn: "…watching over oaths, checking the hasty blood of young men." He offered a prayer for his nephew Pjortan and Ian especially, youths on their first venture into a greater world. The venerable holy man also prayed that the stars would grant the keeping of faith among all whom the travelers would encounter, that the Norrungs might be spared from betrayal.

"Ah," he grunted with amusement. "As if my feeble hopes could change the course of heaven or keep those I love safe. Were that the case, no plague should have touched Vorthall nor any guests come to the halls of the Dark Queen. Does not Wigdor also test the wisdom of the aged? Perhaps I should beseech him for myself, fool of an old man."

While thus conversing with himself Thomdar noticed the shadowy finger of a cloud reaching across the moon. Ruanel, the Silver Queen was not yet half full. The shining portion of her disc was soon touched by a second finger and then the cloud veiled her altogether. Stars, of course, were also obscured and Thomdar considered this at most a minor sign. He held his vision skyward as the shadow progressed, thinning at one point to allow a diminished vision of the moon.

At that point the singer thought he saw the Silver Queen, now but a gray majesty, grow as though she would fill the sky. The cloud obscuring her was like smoke swirling to suggest patterns. Thomdar was held by the sight as one watching a fire can be lost in the flames, thoughts dancing in the shifting light. Eventually the shadows congealed into the form of a man, well proportioned and noble in bearing. The center of the man then seemed to blossom, with tendrils reaching in every direction, then collapse as though his bones had vanished and the skin slumped into a shapeless pile.

Thomdar blinked and the moon was but her usual size, emerging from the darkness to illumine once more the treetops of Norrast. "Wigdor, keep me from folly," he prayed, "my old mind is straying."

He had not yet heard that "sheep's death" had finally touched a human and was unaware that the heavens had told him of it before word could pass to Vorthall.

The vision he had dismissed, however, troubled his sleep in the hours before dawn and the following day found him strolling thoughtfully along the banks of the Nurgen. Other singers noticed the distracted air of their leader but knew better than to ask him yet what troubled him. It was not until Thomdar missed the midday meal that Fjorvel decided to approach. She was of the next generation of singers in Vorthall, a woman greatly respected and trusted.

"Uncle," she began respectfully, "the daystar has completed more than half his journey and you did not eat with us at noon. I pray you share with me whatever concern pulls your heart from us."

"Ah, Fjorvel, you are ever gentle yet to the point. You read my mood aright. And the wood berries you carry with you are a welcome gift. Let us sit upon the log beneath that tree and open our hearts."

With that the singers settled as best they could on a nearby log, taking advantage of a spot of dappled shade. Fjorvel passed the basket of sweet berries she had brought to Thomdar and he began to eat.

"You saved the ripest ones for me, didn't you?"

"Yes, Uncle. We always do."

"My dear children. I do not think my journey to the Dark Queen is particularly near, but when my rest comes I will know the singers of Vorthall will care well for the people, as you have cared for me."

"Are those the thoughts that distract you?"

"No, not at all. Did you notice a cloud across the moon last night?"

"Indeed, I did not, but several have mentioned it."

"Did they find it in any way unusual?"

"I don't believe so. In the sharing of our watches this morning none remarked upon it beyond noting that a cloud came from the west and passed."

"Then either my mind played tricks on me or the heavens granted me a special sight. Or the dark demon toyed with me. I simply cannot tell which."

"What did you see, Thomdar?" As Fjorvel dropped the respectful term for a near elder, she revealed her closeness to the chief singer.

"The Silver Queen seemed to grow as though she would fill the sky, but that was after the cloud arrived. Let me begin again."

Thomdar recounted his vision, concluding with his complete inability to make any sense of it. "If Hranild had anything to contribute to this puzzle, I am sure she would have announced it to us by now," he added.

"True enough," Fjorvel replied, "but that would probably only confuse us more. She is a cryptic one, bless her farseeing soul."

"Have you any idea what it might mean?"

"None, but I suggest we call a fast among the singers that our vision may be purified."

Thomdar agreed, and so the singers of Vorthall refrained from food that evening and through the next day, watching the skies together intently, singing through the night. No message came, however, at least not at that time.

CHAPTER 24

A message did come to someone else the following day. As Hranild sat on her "sunning stone" (as she called the spot where she enjoyed soaking up the daystar's warmth), her ebony companion began to croak. It was not the raven's common announcement of an approaching visitor nor any of the usual patterns of its harsh cries. The agitated bird flew from an ancient cedar to a nearby fir and resumed the alarm briefly, then skipped over to a tall pine to cry some more. The disturbed "aarck, aarck" was sometimes followed by a "tock" sound, then repeated as the raven flew withershins from one tree to another in a circle about the seer.

"Oh dear," said Hranild. When the raven had finished she focused on the rhythm of her breath and entered a deep meditative state. There she remained, still as a seated corpse and oblivious to the outer world, for nigh on to an hour. At last she inhaled deeply, stretched her limbs, and took up her staff. The seer rose and walked over to her cottage. There she prepared an infusion of mint and other herbs to freshen herself. She had work to do.

Njothir, fond of the old woman as he was, never rejoiced when she came to the chief's hall. Her messages were always cryptic and usually brought more foreboding than hope. So it was that a low-grade dread mingled with affectionate amusement when he shook his head and grimaced at her entrance.

"Daughter of Eghran," he saluted, using not her father's name but that of the God of Chaos and Change. "To what does Vorthall owe the pleasure of this visit?"

Hranild chuckled and feigned shushing the chieftain. "Son of Rathdar, you must be more discreet. I had thought it a well guarded secret that a god sired me. If you noise it abroad my neighbors will start bowing to me and making offerings. It would be scandalous; I cannot allow it."

Njothir replied conspiratorially, "You are correct as ever, grandmother. This sudden knowledge would upset the society of all Vorthall and I would face no end of troubles. I will guard your secret and treat you as a common old woman."

"Ah!" she responded in mock umbrage, "Common. Now you go too far the other way, grandson. Should I then publicly treat my chief as the young rascal I remember from earlier days? Would that not also shame our people?"

By now both of them were laughing. In a low voice Njothir said, "Well then, old woman, I am still a young rascal beneath the golden torc. Shall we declare a truce?"

"By the stars, yes, Njothir. You know, I am getting too old for these games, but the memories are pleasant. Many of your escapades added to these gray hairs, you know, and I have to admit I enjoyed scolding you and Ivor's children. What a lot of trouble you were. I did my best to terrify you."

"We lived in mortal terror that you would cast a spell on us and turn us into food for your raven. Or worse."

"Bah! There are no wizards in my family. And you weren't worth that much trouble. I wager you have grown into a handsome man, and I know you are a good one, though it pains me to admit it to your face. But how you have turned out so well after all that mischief, I cannot say. Had I been a sorceress you probably would have been flayed alive with a wave of my staff. And were you as wicked as you seemed back then, you would have me flayed alive for insulting my chief in his own hall today."

"And well within my rights."

"The power I did have—to see what my useless eyes cannot—told me you would some day lead us, though I kept that secret. Such knowledge may have salvaged your irksome ass from many a blow with this staff, for I can sense what I may not see."

"Then I thank you for your mercy. But tell me, grandmother, what brings you here today? I know it was not to banter with a troublemaker and you have been avoiding my initial question."

"True enough, my lord, though I trust you shall not deny me this word play while I have days left." At that point she paused, uttered a low "mmm," as though releasing with regret the memories they had just shared. She continued.

"Something dark is afoot. Actually, much in this poor world, but I speak of something close at hand and something to do with the companions we sent with Ian. I know, I know. My visions are muddled and unclear. You have said as much and I know it all too well. What I have to tell you may be utterly useless, yet as I serve you, son of Rathdar, just as I serve the truth, I am honor-bound to share what I see.

"From here we can do nothing for those we sent toward the setting of the daystar, save hold them in our hearts. Darkness gathers about them this day but it will not prevail. I see danger and blood spurting wildly, but I do not think it flows from any Norrung, the stranger included. Alas, that is about as clear as it gets. I told you this was useless, lord.

"For yourself, however, I have a warning. There is evil that threatens our people. Not that this is anything new, evil is always at hand to lead us astray or to attack us. Such is the nature of life under the stars. But something new, or old but not seen for some time, silently eats at the Norrungs like a wasting disease. You will soon face it and must act. I have no idea what you must do or how to do it. All I can say, grandson, is this: be careful. I am fond of certain scamps, even when they come into power, and I hope to haunt you until the Dark Queen calls me."

Njothir took the old woman's hand, twisted with age, and held it to his chest. "Grandmother, I thank you for this visit. You are always a source of trouble, causing me to wonder if I was so much trouble to you in earlier times. Probably so. Today I thank you for letting me know that amid our little games there has been a fondness on your side as well as mine. So long as you keep seeing things I have no doubt you will haunt me. If your inner vision fails, I beseech Weltar of the Long Years to keep our games alive.

"You have shared troubling things. Is there more?"

"If you ask me, I must say yes, but not for your ears. Be strong, grandson."

With that the young lord kissed Hranild's hand and she withdrew to pursue her other business. Njothir gazed at the unbraided gray tresses of the old woman as her sightless steps took her from him, wondering about her ways of knowing and the layers of confusion and error in all ways of knowing, especially his own.

CHAPTER 25

While dark clouds troubled the mind of Thomdar and Hranild pondered what evil threatened Vorthall, a fresh darkness arrived two days following the singers' fast. The daystar seemed as pale as the moon when dawn arrived, faintly shining through a dusky curtain. Most inhabitants of Vorthall assumed the heavens were merely overcast on a spring morning as they rose to their daily tasks but dread began to worm its way into their hearts as they stepped outside and realized things were not as they should be.

Murmurs of the demon spread from tongue to tongue and fear of returning plague caused each to eye neighbors as potential victims. The hope not to be touched by it often implied the hope that it would take another. This, in turn, led to guilt at wishing so awful a thing upon a fellow Norrung. Edginess rose from troubled minds and seemed to fill the air, unable to rise above the gray shroud cast above the village and dissipate in the heavens.

Amid this tension shouts erupted, and a clash of weapons. Curiosity struggled with fear only to be resolved when the clang of colliding blades and metal striking the hardened leather surface of shield lessened and the cries and scuffling moved toward the assembly stone and a swift neighbor girl hastened to summon Njothir.

The young chief strode toward the gathering place, wondering what had caused such alarm so early in the day. As he neared the clearing where Norrungs were already forming a loose circle of witnesses, Njothir beheld his foster brother Rutnir along with Hron holding fast to Hordal's grandson

Turstil. The latter's obsidian eyes glared in defiance but he bore no arms. The demi-giant Hron seemed on the brink of exploding with fury and had one of his immense hairy arms wrapped about Turstil's neck. Rutnir held his sword at the ready and a dagger poised against Turstil's ribs. Though sweat dripped from the faces of all three, Rutnir appeared relatively calm but tense. Njothir thought of Hranild's warning and realized this might be his first challenge to mete out mortal justice. His heart sank.

"What is the meaning of this disturbance among the people of Vorthall?" the young chief challenged aloud, silently offering a prayer to Wigdor for justice and Weltar for wisdom.

"These fools have misread me, Lord," Turstil managed to croak as Hron tightened his grip.

"I think not," Hron grunted.

"What is the meaning of this, grandson?" interrupted the honored elder Hordal. "Hron, why do you hold him so? There must be some mistake."

"Let us pray that it is only a misunderstanding, Uncle," said Njothir, seeking to calm the passions of all parties lest the situation worsen. "Brother?"

Rutnir answered his foster brother and chief without moving his dagger from Turstil's ribs, "The truth, Lord, must still be determined, may Hjelgi lead us to it. As I read it, there is evidence that Turstil may be involved with some of the raiders to the northeast."

"That is a lie!" spat Turstil.

"I did not say you were involved, cousin, only that there are signs of that possibility. In that I do not lie."

Hordal protested, "It cannot be true. I know my grandson."

Njothir drew a deep breath and asserted his command. "Let the council be summoned and let us consider the evidence. Let Turstil stand as a Norrung."

Rutnir withdrew the blade that had threatened the accused and Hron reluctantly released his hold. Turstil stretched his neck and looked at his immediate captors with disgust, yet remained where he stood. Njothir's formal wording signaled armed warriors and warmaidens to guard the council circle and any attempt to escape would be an admission of guilt and lead to instant death with no further deliberation. Turstil did not care for that option. Hron and Rutnir continued to stand by him, though Rutnir called a singer and two warmaidens to him and gave them instructions. These three then left the gathering.

By now most of Vorthall had congregated beneath the darkened sky of that vile morning. All but two council members had come without summons and youths soon brought these to the place of assembly.

Though Rutnir had not actually charged Turstil with betrayal, the possibility of such an accusation was shocking, for the bonds of the tribe were strong. While waiting for the formal opening of the council, the people could not contain speculation and a muted buzz of wondering and horror filled the air like a swarm of bees moving to form a new hive. The sky seemed to darken as the morning progressed.

Thomdar, meanwhile, approached Njothir and spoke in a low voice, asking that another singer might serve in his place as he was weakened by lack of sleep, anxiety, and fasting. The chief consented to this and Fjorvel came forward.

Njothir checked to see that all members of the council, save those on journeys, were present, then stepped forward and proclaimed: "The Norrungs of Vorthall have assembled. The Council of Vorthall is here. Let truth be spoken and heard. Let wisdom be known. Let justice be done and mercy not forgotten. Let the stars guide us."

The assembled Norrungs were finally quiet, their eagerness to learn what had happened overcoming the urge to speculate aloud. Respect for the Council also demanded attention. Fjorvel then raised her voice toward the obscured heavens and offered a hymn to the deities of wisdom, justice, and truth while an acolyte smudged the council members, the accused and his accusers with cedar smoke.

"What charge is brought before us?" Njothir demanded.

"Wigdor weigh my heart," began Rutnir, uttering the standard phrase that the Sky Lord who guarded oaths would examine his soul and find his words to be true. "I am Rutnir son of Ivor, a captain of those servants of the Fierce Mother charged with protecting the people from the lawless, especially brigands and raiders. Such have attacked our people to the east, the south, and the north ever since the fiery death came to our land and reduced our numbers. The vile Chegjan has also sapped the will of survivors, making entire villages weak—easy prey for those who recognize neither law nor custom.

"Those who fight with me have traveled eight days east of Vorthall where the farthest Norrungs dwell in Vulth by the Upper Tilçar below Mount Nigh and we have seen most of the lands between here and there. Halfway to Vulth lies Dinth below the peak where Mirfann Stream arises to flow south. Six moons ago, as Veshnel the Reaper journeyed across the heavens and just before the snows came to Dinth, we passed through the village and found that raiders had been there. They had attacked stealthily by night, killing the men folk of three outlying households. Their women and children were taken along with all of value."

Rutnir continued in the formal narrative style of Norrungs gathered for judgment. Children who had joined the assembly soon faded to the fringes to entertain themselves and a few teenagers and younger women were sent by their elders to begin preparing for a midday meal., their protests at being sent from the trial overcome by familial authority. Once dismissed, they hastened in hopes of returning to hear the conclusion. Rutnir proceeded to unfold the tale as the sky continued to darken, adding to a sense of dread about the entire proceeding.

"We followed the path of the outlaws as they fled north toward Çorn Stream and their own star-cursed lands. We caught up with a portion of their party that had paused to rest in the rearguard and the noise of the encounter did not bring the aid of their fellows, as would be the custom among our people, but only warned those ahead to flee in haste. Thus we overcame and slew those we found, for they were not skilled in warfare, only in treachery, and the rest escaped.

"Bratha of Dinth we rescued, widow of Rendor, and her children Rendathel and Brithir. One family alone were we able to save. Having lost their husband and father and their near neighbors, the family of Rendor chose to return to Vorthall with us and Bratha now stands near this day."

Rutnir indicated the direction in which Bratha stood with a movement of his chin and the lady lowered her eyes, pained by memories still fresh. Those near her stepped aside that Njothir and the elders might see her. She had dismissed her children at the first hint of the charges likely to be brought. The warrior continued, noticing that those he had sent on an errand had returned and nodded affirmatively in his direction.

"In the gathering of her few remaining possessions, Bratha recounted to us what had been lost, busying herself to mask the grief betokened by the ashes she had hastily applied to her face. She described the weavings she and her mother and her grandmother before her had woven, showing us the pattern on her scarf, a design unique to her family. I am not skilled in the weaver's art as my sister Ringskild is, and thus I cannot describe the pattern to you but I noted it for its skill and beauty. Bratha also spoke of the rings her husband had given her."

At mention of her rings, Turstil's face betrayed a hint of alarm and Njothir noted this.

"Bratha of Dinth," said Rutnir, "would you please stand before Lord Njothir with your back to Turstil."

In spite of her dread of being singled out before the people of Vorthall, the lady did so. These were her fellow Norrungs and they had taken her in. Whatever Rutnir asked, she surely owed him.

"Would you describe those rings to our chief and to this council?"

Her eyes still downcast with innate shyness, Bratha told of three rings she had received from Rendor. The first was one his grandmother had worn, a simple silver ring with a green stone of no great value but still of beauty. It had been the chiefest token of his love. The second, also of silver, framed a polished piece of shell that carried in its heart a pale rainbow of hues. The third was gold with three small pieces of amber.

Njothir had gently encouraged Bratha to speak up so that all the council might hear her words. When she had finished telling of the rings that had been taken from her, he asked if she might sketch the design of her weaving pattern on the ground before him with a stick. This she did, patiently and carefully.

Murmurs at the outer edge of the crowd resumed quietly while this took place, for Bratha required time to etch the intricate work into the soil. As she did so, Njothir also observed that Turstil had begun shifting his weight from one foot to another, as though anxious, though his defiant expression had been maintained.

It was a beautiful design of two birds in flight, each an echo of the other, head to tail in an endless circle. The balance and proportion of these feathered forms was impressive and there could be no doubt that Bratha was a skilled artisan.

"I thank you, cousin," said Njothir, "your skill is great and Vorthall is blessed to have you among us. Let us now recognize you as Bratha of Vorthall from the village of Dinth and not simply as Bratha of Dinth, for you are now one of us."

At the chieftain's words Bratha blushed and managed to stammer a thank-you before returning to her former place among the assembly.

Njothir nodded toward Rutnir who picked up his narrative.

"This morning, while passing through the streets of Vorthall, I spotted Turstil, who stands before us, and I noticed two rings upon his hand."

"Grandson, no," interjected Hordal.

"These appeared similar," continued Rutnir, "to the amber and green stone rings that Bratha has just described."

Njothir approached the accused and demanded to see the rings. Turstil presented his left hand on which he bore three rings. The man had long slender fingers that could easily enough bear rings made for a woman. Two of these matched Bratha's description, though the third was completely different from the shell ring she had mentioned. Turstil offered a defense.

"No doubt Bratha has seen me wearing these rings in Vorthall. Perhaps she desires them for herself and thus describes them to you."

"No!" shouted the aggrieved lady. "I have only seen this man at a distance and never noticed my rings."

"Peace, lady," said Njothir. "The accused may speak but judgment will not be made in haste. All must be presented and weighed.

"Rutnir, I have known you too long. Turstil would not stand before us if that were all you knew. You have more to say; please say it."

"Indeed, lord. Having noticed the rings, I asked Turstil where he acquired them. He replied churlishly, strengthening my suspicions. I asked to search his home and he drew on me. I cannot say no innocent man would act thus for an innocent man may be moved to great passions when falsely accused. Given my charge to pursue and punish those who attack our people and to reclaim our people and goods when possible, I could not let the matter rest. We struggled even as I insisted and Hron came to my aid. We subdued Turstil and brought him here to seek the truth of the matter.

"Because I seek the truth and acknowledge that, though I have strong suspicions, I do not know it, I maintain that I have only laid the question before the council. I cannot lodge a formal accusation against our cousin Turstil without further proof."

"Hah!" spat Turstil, "you have brought me here without a charge? What justice is that, 'cousin Rutnir'?"

Rutnir stared silently into Turstil's eyes before responding, the latter glaring back in return.

"I have sent a singer and two warmaidens to seek your lodgings and search for what you would not show us. Let them now come forward."

At this Turstil's defiance diminished. The three stepped into the place of judgment and were censed by the same acolyte who had done so at the beginning of judgment.

"What have you found?" Rutnir asked.

The elder of the two warmaidens began. "By Vrotni whom I serve and Wigdor who guards oaths, we sought out the home of Turstil and were guided to it. On behalf of the people we entered and searched for certain items mentioned by Rutnir. We found them."

Njothir took over the examination at this point. "What did you find?"

"Though Turstil is a bachelor, we found several items of women's adornment. This could be of no importance for they might have been treasures of his family or gifts he hoped to bestow upon some maiden. One was this ring of silver adorned with a piece of shell, as Rutnir had described it to us."

At this she presented the ring to Njothir, who called Bratha forward again.

"Is this your ring, Bratha of Vorthall?"

Tears began to fill her eyes before she answered softly, "Yes."

Njothir continued to hold the ring as he turned again to the warmaidens. "Did you find anything else?"

"We did, lord." At this the second warmaiden took from the bag she carried a linen blouse embroidered with pairs of birds. It was clearly Bratha's family design, exactly as she had sketched it in the dirt, though much more elegantly executed. Bratha began to sob uncontrollably as Njothir showed the blouse and the ring to members of the council. When the widow began to calm she turned to face Turstil, but the elder warmaiden restrained her.

"That blouse was made by my mother. What is it doing in your possession?!" she shouted.

"Please, lady," Njothir spoke calmingly, "the question will be asked. I pray you, step back."

Bratha was in no mood to step back but the strong maiden led her out of the circle lest the aggrieved woman act rashly. The second maiden brought another item from the bag.

"And there was this," she added, unfolding a hanging in which the bird pattern was woven skillfully.

Njothir turned to the star singer who had gone with the warmaidens. "All they have said took place as told to this council?"

"Yes, lord."

With those two words, Turstil's fate was all but sealed. By involving a singer, Rutnir guaranteed the testimony for star singers were forbidden to utter falsehood and none in Vorthall would now question what was said.

Rutnir, for his part, demonstrated no delight in his vindication. To him the day seemed darker than the deep shadow above Vorthall, for one of the people had evidently betrayed them all. He looked with sadness upon Turstil's face, clouded now with hatred.

Njothir did not stop the proceedings there. "Turstil, before Wigdor and this council, have you anything to say in your defense?"

"Yes, son of Rathdar. I came upon these items while trading and knew nothing of their history before I saw them."

Hordal added, "It is true that he traveled last fall. Surely that explains everything."

"Anything else?" queried Njothir.

"How can there be more? I bartered with a stranger from beyond Norgardh. How could I know these had once belonged to this poor lady? Of course they should be restored to her."

As Turstil offered this alternative explanation, Njothir watched his face closely. Turstil was now all innocence and reason. A slight chuckle at the beginning of each sentence betrayed a deceitful purpose.

With a final silent prayer to Wigdor, Njothir took a deep breath before speaking.

"Had you come by these things through honest trade, you would have said so at the beginning instead of accusing Bratha of lying to us. Nor would you have taken arms against Rutnir when he reasonably asked to see if you had other items from Dinth, unless you are an extremely quarrelsome man, and I have never known rumors to that effect.

"That you traveled last autumn is undoubtedly true, but that you were about honest trade is most certainly false. Whatever transpired beyond Norgardh or elsewhere when you came into possession of these things, and I hope before all the stars you did not yourself take part in the raid on Dinth, you are guilty of betraying the people.

"Does the council judge otherwise?"

Turstil blanched and silence hung in the air. Even Hordal could not defend his grandson and those who looked to him could detect the breaking of his heart in that moment.

Njothir could hear Hranild's words from the day before: "You will soon face it and must act." After a moment that seemed to stretch into many, Njothir spoke again.

"Had you betrayed me, cousin, I would have had power to forgive you. For betrayal of the people there is no wergild and no mercy.

"Let it be done."

As the judgment was delivered, Hron and three others took charge of Turstil, tearing his tunic to expose him from neck to waist and stretching his arms out. Knowing there was no escape, Turstil stood silently as a portrait of fierce hatred, awaiting his fate.

Though he had not formally brought accusation, Rutnir assumed he would have to take the role of Bratha's family and carry out the sentence. He stepped forward, hand upon his sword. Njothir stopped him.

"I cannot order what I will not do, brother. I am the people's chief and I have named Bratha as a woman of Vorthall. I will do it."

With that, Njothir took his own sword and faced Turstil. "Turstil, born at Vorthall and once my cousin, may Hjelgi lead you safely home." Having said this, Njothir thrust his sword under the traitor's ribs into his heart and drew down, spilling his guts. Turstil's eyes bulged with the shock then fainted with pain before he expired. In all this he did not cry out. The warriors carried his body from the place of judgment, their faces stern.

The sentence was in accord with the justice of the Norrungs and none could fault it.

While Turstil's body had been thrown out for wild animals, Njothir and Rutnir watched over it that night and allowed Hordal to reclaim his grandson the following morning. Custom was observed and mercy was shown. The venerable Hordal died not long thereafter, shaken by his grandson's treachery and the shame brought to the family, though none blamed the honorable elder. Njothir alone reproached himself, not for a just sentence but for the sorrow he felt that any Norrung could turn against his own. From that day forward he knew the full burden of serving as chief. Though he was known as Njothir the Righteous, it was a title he would gladly resign.

For the young ruler, the evil veil over Norrast that day had descended into the very hearts of all the people. He prayed that Ian and his companions were safe and would soon return successful. The darkness had prevailed too long.

CHAPTER 26

While all these things were taking place along the Nurgen Stream, Ian and his companions had come to Denev, where Wilda was rescued by Vladje, and eagerly moved on to Nimmoth. The following day the companions took advantage of the great market town and Hildir and Ian met Kirlat of the easy smile. Ian's thoughts at bedtime had been of Njothila, far to the east.

The daughter of Rathdar, for her part, was thinking of Ian as she combed her long chestnut hair. She had heard the deer hoof rattles two days before. Her brother would tell her nothing of what Hranild had said and this led her to worry about the stranger who had been a frequent companion after his arrival at Vorthall. Had the seer brought news of the Norrungs? Had something happened to them: an accident, a hostile attack, an illness?

Waiting without knowing was especially hard on the maiden. She had spoken on occasion with Rutnir. They both missed Ringskild, his sister and her foster-sister. The others were all friends as well. She missed the cry of Nordil's falcon Fjurthil and the sight of him swooping on his prey. Mostly she missed the stranger, the mysterious Ian from another world.

He made her feel at ease when most other people made her somehow more conscious of being the daughter and sister of a chief, marriageable, with all that implied. Njothila could be playful child, a curious maid, or a serious woman with Ian and not feel uncomfortable. He, in turn, seemed freer to discuss the world he came from with her than with any other Norrung, even Njothir who had more or less adopted him as a brother.

As Ian was learning the craft of a woodcarver, Njothila praised or mocked his creations as the whim took her. She cherished a few of his earliest humble efforts, shyly given to her, and looked at them often in his absence. Sometimes he had simply stared in her eyes without a word while she gazed back into the blue pools that were his.

"What does he feel for me?" she wondered. The only words they never seemed to share were those about their relationship. Beyond calling each other "sister" and "brother," of course, but that was not what she meant. Njothila did not feel ready to be any Norrung's wife and resisted the thought, which left her struggling for words to frame her feelings.

Sendhor, son of Geredh and Gwenda, had paid Njothila a great deal of attention but she was not interested in him. He was a good hunter and a decent enough man, for all she knew, but to the daughter of Rathdar he was only another refugee come to Vorthall. One of her cousins had praised him to Njothila and she was surprised to observe that she had never thought of him in such terms. Sendhor was tall. Sendhor was strong. Sendhor was handsome, with curls the color of straw and good teeth. Sendhor came from a good family. Hunters make good providers. Sendhor filled his trousers nicely and could surely make a woman happy.

"Why haven't you asked him to marry you?" Njothila exploded after one of these panegyrics.

"I would," the startled cousin replied, "but he fancies you. I cannot compete with a chief's daughter."

"Muck," exclaimed Njothila, "you are the niece and the granddaughter of chiefs and certainly as fine a woman as I or any Norrung walking beneath the stars. Seek him out, but please stop singing his praises to me."

After this outburst they made up but Njothila was glad not to hear Sendhor's name mentioned as frequently as it had been.

Glancing down at a crude wooden wolf carved by Ian and illumined by the flicker of a candle, Njothila acknowledged that if Ian would think of her as a woman and not merely as a sister, he certainly had her heart already. Like most men, he seemed clueless and she bit her lip wondering once again what he thought of her. She had no idea that, though his own thoughts were confused, Ian was thinking of her at that moment and wondering what she thought of him.

The following morning Njothila heard the rattles of Hranild's staff, though the sound was muffled. This was unusual. The seer did not visit the chief all that often. Twice within a few days was highly suspicious. Njothila wanted to know what Hranild was up to, especially since Njothir would not tell her what he and Hranild discussed on the last visit.

That last visit, which she had feared was about the Norrungs sent after the demon, preceded the horrible Turstil affair. Njothila had never seen anyone slain in cold blood and to see her own brother do it was unspeakable. It was lawful justice and right, but still awful. She knew her brother well enough to know he had been shaken by it also, no matter how many he had slain on battlefields. Was Hranild here to signal some other dreadful event?

Njothila glanced out a window in passing to see if they sky were darkened with an evil presence but the day was bright with occasional puffs of cloud. Following the sound of the deer hooves, Njothila turned a corner and collided with Njothir. He seemed startled and that was suspicious too. Good warriors are always alert and few things surprised her brother.

"What is Hranild doing here?" Njothila asked.

"She won't tell me, sister, so I can't possibly tell you."

"Don't fence with me, brother."

"May Iltir strike me with his silver shafts if I speak falsely," he protested.

Njothila screwed her mouth into a knot of unconvinced deliberation. For all the times they had quarreled or teased over the years, Njothir took oaths very seriously.

"If she won't tell you, then what is she doing here?"

"She said she was here to visit our Auntie Gethalen. I have no idea what to make of it. They have known each other for decades and are friends, but why Hranild would tell me no more is puzzling. She clearly thinks her visit is none of my business, and since she is as honest as a singer—at least insofar as I can tell—it must at least be true that she is visiting our aunt. What else she may be up to, and I am certain she is up to something, I have to leave to the stars and those two contrary crones."

"They can be difficult, can't they?" Njothila smiled. "But don't try to convince me you are not fond of them both."

"I wouldn't even try, sister. Though you know what I call Hranild."

"Yes, daughter of Eghran. She is a daughter of chaos, typically tossing everything upside down whenever she speaks, at least in her capacity as a seer. You named her well."

"She upbraided me the other day for letting her secret slip."

At mention of a secret, Njothila was suddenly all attention. "Oh?"

"Yes, she did not want me revealing that she is the offspring of a deity lest her neighbors make too much of a fuss over her or bring her offerings."

At that the siblings laughed, happy to have some focus other than judicial execution or their concern for Ringskild and Ian and the others.

"When she is not speaking for the stars, she is rather fun," Njothila observed. "Remember how she used to threaten you with all manner of curses?"

"Indeed, and the stars know I deserved them, as did the children of Ivor with whom I was always misbehaving."

"You tormented your little sister too, as I recall. Pity I did not have Hranild's store of curses."

"Well, as we grew up we realized the strange woman did not have the power of curses and we outgrew our pranks as well."

"Hranild did not speak to you of me, did she? The other day, I mean."

"No, sister, why should she?"

"No reason really. I just wanted to be sure I was not part of her chaos."

Njothir chuckled. "Well, at least not for now."

What neither of them knew was that Hranild's business with Gethalen concerned them both.

CHAPTER 27

There were no peace poles or similar signs on the two swift warships that escorted Gleth and the Norrungs into the port of Vothnell. They docked near the mouth of the River Fiona near more warships and a good number of warriors. The commander who first hailed them, Djutar son of Fræk, led them from the ship to Vothnell Castle, accompanied by guards. The Norrungs did not relinquish their weapons but they carried their peace poles prominently. The Vothneli had not anticipated that a wolf would also bound from the ship and walk between Ian and Wilda with no evidence of human command. It was a party of more than passing interest to the townsfolk of Vothnell.

The Castle was modest but solid, its walls of pale golden sandstone thick but not especially high. Defenses were based more on the thirty-foot cliff upon which Vothnell Castle squatted and the defensible road that began at the upper end of the town and wound to the left, gradually circling to the entrance. As the Norrungs neared the base of the Castle promontory, glancing anxiously at the fortress above them, a cry rang out from among the onlookers, a child's voice screaming harshly.

> Aiiiiiii! Darkness! Darkness!
> Who would go there? Not I!
> Hope! Silly, stupid hope!
> It will save you, seekers!
> Where the fir grows you began,

and came by a treeless road.
Ha! Try to find a tree where the one goes!
Watch for the dark where the two stand.
Will you believe me? Will you believe?
Whom will you love?
The blind can see where the young lord leads.
Do not despair beneath the crushing weight,
nor spurn the three that would help you.
I am the dancer, will you sing for me?
Sing with all your might,
but do not sing alone,
the dancer dances.

Djutar paid little attention, merely saying, "It is only Zhodor the Fool. He rants."

The Norrungs, however, had paused in their tracks to look beyond the warriors and townsfolk about them and see a young boy, perhaps eight or nine years old, with flaming red hair and tattered garments that scarcely covered his underfed body. Long thin arms flailed the air with a jerky, rhythmic motion, as he threw himself about. The boy's blue eyes were wide, his brows raised and forehead wrinkled with anxiety. The voice that came from his throat was that of a human child but it was chilling to hear, shot through with urgency and desperation. At mention of the dancer, the boy whirled about before falling to the ground, convulsing.

A couple of older children standing nearby knelt to watch over him but darted back into the crowd when Vladje broke from the midst of the escorted Norrungs and trotted over to the twitching Zhodor. The wolf sniffed at the boy, then licked his face and gave a short bark. At that, the boy's limbs stilled and his eyes focused. Gazing at the gray wolf, Zhodor smiled and giggled. Vladje returned to his place between Ian and Wilda and Zhodor's companions rejoined the laughing boy, whose eyes soon began to dart about wildly once again, though he said no more.

"The boy is no fool," Pjortan said, "he is a seer, and his words are true."

"Perhaps, singer," Djutar rejoined, "though most of what he says is nonsense, I have heard that some of his words come true. For the life of me, I make no sense of it. Stars bless you if you can untangle his words. Come along."

With that the party resumed their dusty ascent, rough stone to their right and a sharp drop to their left. Ian stayed close to the right and noticed his companions did the same. The Vothneli seemed less nervous but this was their everyday territory, not that of the visiting forest-dwellers.

As they worked their way up the broad hill the Norrungs pondered what Zhodor's strange words meant. Was the darkness an obvious reference to the Chegjan or some portent about Vothnell Castle? Who were the one, the two, and the three in this riddle of numbers? Was the dance a reference to the goddess Senjir or some mortal, or merely a symbolic action by Zhodor? Their thoughts were interrupted when they crossed the stone span bridging the fosse that set off the entrance to the Castle. Helmeted guards in chain mail snapped to attention and held pikes vertical as Djutar led the group within. Wilda nudged her husband and glanced down, drawing Nordil's attention to the hackles on Vladje's neck rising as they entered the seat of Furk's power. Ian had also noticed and they exchanged uneasy glances.

Within the courtyard life seemed perfectly ordinary. Vothneli crisscrossed the space on sundry errands, conveying supplies and engaging in conversation. The ring of a blacksmith's hammer came from somewhere out of sight. Functionaries could be spotted in white and black livery, an unusual combination in a world where white is the color of death and mourning.

The strangers had barely arrived in the courtyard when a great barrel-chested man came bouncing down the stairs from the ramparts. His complexion was florid, his hair and beard great curled tangles of black shot through with silver. His eyes peeked out from the mass of his face, cheeks and brow trying to join as though the upper half of his face had been mashed, though such was not the case. Some adventure in his past, however, had marked him with a crooked nose and scars were visible on his right forearm. Closer inspection revealed his right index finger had gone missing as well. He was clad in rough trousers and a white tunic with a black battleaxe on his chest. The man's ease and the deference of others marked him as Furk of Vothnell before any introduction could be made.

"What have we here?" he boomed over the din of the courtyard as he approached the Norrungs. "Guests? Splendid! Djutar, whom have you brought me?"

"A party of Norrungs, Lord Furk, heading west."

"Norrungs? And where would you hail from?"

Ringskild responded. "We are from the Forest of Norrast some distance east of here. Our lord, Njothir son of Rathdar, has sent us on a westward journey. I am Ringskild, daughter of Ivor, warmaiden of the Norrungs and captain of this company. May the stars bless you, Lord Furk."

Furk paid little heed to this diplomacy and seemed taken aback that the warmaiden was the designated speaker for the Norrungs, though women spoke freely and served widely among the peoples of the northern regions.

"You are far from your home, forest dwellers, and that piques my curiosity. What is the purpose of such a long journey toward the west?"

Wary of saying too much yet certain that dissembling would not work with this crude but alert lord, the daughter of Ivor decided to speak simply and truthfully.

"We come to seek the destruction of the Chegjan."

This led to a variety of expressions among the guards and bystanders, some with eyes widening in amazement and others smirking or emitting a low chuckle. Furk himself let out a great roar of a laugh.

"Oh! Hah! Indeed! That is quite an undertaking! Ah, ha, ha. Whew. And where will you find the formless darkness that haunts our lands? Have you been tracking it all this way? Was it moving upon the waters from which we have rescued you?"

In spite of his youth, Pjortan chose to answer at this point, from the perspective of his sacred calling. "You rightly marvel, Lord Furk, that anyone should seek to track the shapeless horror, and you may be assured that none of us sought to do so. We have come as bidden by seers and commanded by our Lord Njothir, and though our path upon the Mere was only convenience, there are tracks of a sort that we have followed. Where the plague has gone the Chegjan has visited, and increasing terrors have accompanied it. We have witnessed the savaging of animals and the abandonment of villages. We have heard accounts of sudden madness overtaking a crowd and leading to violence. These are the signs we have taken for guideposts."

The lord of Vothnell, noticing the star tattooed on Pjortan's neck, had focused his attention on the singer's words, knowing that star singers are forbidden to speak false.

"Hmm. Indeed, singer, I have heard rumors of all this from various parts. The demon does seem to leave behind a wake of destruction; though it seems unlikely one can track such a thing down. How do you propose to destroy such a mighty power with so small a company, Captain Ringskild?"

"That, cousin," she began, remaining polite but avoiding florid diplomatic address, "is an excellent question. If we were facing a human foe there would be no question but that we should need an army, which we clearly are not. Under the guidance of prophecy we bring weapons only to protect those of our party who are not warriors, for how could a lance or sword or arrow defeat a thing without a form? Our weapons against a demon are hope in spite of all we know, simple human love, and faith that the darkness will not prevail."

"Frail things," said Furk, "for I have known each of these to fail in less challenging circumstances. And yet, you pursue this errand?"

"We do, Lord Furk," Pjortan replied.

"There is no glory in sitting by while evil thrives," added Hildir. Fjurthil spread his wings as though assenting to the warrior's words.

"The humblest among us can take a stand." This from Wilda, who rarely spoke to strangers.

Wulfdar rounded out this clump of bravado: "How else shall we heal the world?"

Furk let a smile form and raised his brows. "Bravely spoken, all of you, but why is your lord not at your head?"

The Norrungs bristled at this insult to Njothir, who had wanted to lead the quest. Ringskild especially resented this slight. "He was the most eager of us all to answer the call but the prophecy forbade him to do so. The entire council and several elders had trouble convincing him to remain with his people. We came close to binding him lest his will override what the stars had proclaimed."

"I would dissolve any council that opposed me," said the proud lord.

"No doubt you would, Lord Furk," replied Ringskild, "but such is not the custom among our people. The world, it seems, is a varied place and its inhabitants follow many paths."

"More's the pity," Furk said. "In all of this, not one of you has mentioned or explained the large wolf in your midst, staring intently at me. Surely that calls for some comment."

"Hranild the Seer has told me that Vladje has been sent by the stars to watch over me," said Ian.

"And why would the stars take such an interest in you, lad?"

"I have no idea, Lord Furk, yet he has served as a guide and a guardian. We are not certain whether he has come from Morvladh, but this is clearly no ordinary wolf."

"Clearly not, if he walks as a member of your party." At this point, Djutar whispered a message in Furk's ear.

"It seems your wolf is a friend of Zhodor the Fool. Perhaps Morvladh is not particular about those whom he blesses. Is this wolf tamed?"

"No," said Nordil, "and I nearly lost my fingers learning it."

"This, my brother," said Ian, nodding toward Vladje, "takes orders from no mortal, though he has befriended two of us. He has allowed no others to touch him except for a few children."

"I have never seen a company quite like this, Norrungs. Nor can I imagine glory to be achieved in such an undertaking without noble leadership." Furk paused, as if considering his next course of action. "You shall be my guests this night. We depart in the morning."

"We, cousin?" Ringskild's hand clasped her sword more firmly as she asked this and there was challenge in her voice. The hair on Vladje's neck rose with the tension in the courtyard.

"Yes, cousin Norrung, we. You cannot dream I would miss such an adventure. Sleep well, we have a quest to pursue."

And with that he nodded to a couple of lackeys, turned, and strode into the castle.

CHAPTER 28

Djutar relinquished the Norrungs and Gleth to the guards and servants of Vothnell Castle. Seeing no legitimate cause for battle, Ringskild nodded a signal of silent assent to the rest of the companions and they all followed the servants of Furk. These led them to two rooms, one for the women and one for the men, showed them the location of the garderobes, and informed them they would be called for supper.

Once they were as settled as they were likely to be, they gathered in one of the rooms and conferred. The first task, before memories faded, was to recall and record the words of Zhodor, the child who spoke in fits. Given Vladje's behavior and Pjortan's instincts, all felt the boy was a prophet, tormented by the voices to which he gave utterance, and they wanted to compare what he said to the messages of Hranild. Among them, each contributing a fragment that stood out according to the hearer, they pieced together most of it. More challenging was the task of unraveling the meaning of such vatic utterance.

"Well," began Mechdar, "the darkness could obviously refer to the Chegjan, but was there a warning about this place, Vothnell Castle?"

Wilda responded, "Seers are always ambiguous, you can never be sure. I am fond of our Hranild, but my head gets turned round backwards whenever I try to unravel her riddles."

"Their words often have many meanings at once," added Ringskild, "and we could be looking at many kinds of darkness. My guess would be that the boy meant where we are headed, toward the heart of the demon."

"And none would choose to go there on their own," said Wulfdar. "We go in obedience to the stars and our Lord Njothir, and do so willingly. But we would not have considered this journey otherwise."

Ian, who was at the heart of this quest, often listened more than he spoke, hoping others would help him understand his role. He spoke up now.

"Zhodor mentioned hope and that is why we journey. The world must have hope or we all despair and die. Hranild said this Chegjan would be undone and this is the hope that sustains us. Of course hope seems foolish because no one knows yet how it can be done, what I must do when I face the darkness and meet the demon. But hope is a virtue of my people's faith and among you it is the gift of the stars. I think this is why the boy said it could save us."

"You speak like a singer, Ian," said Pjortan, adding, "and with wisdom beyond your years."

Volthir spoke next: "You would think that tree talk would make sense to us forest dwellers, and I understand where the poor lad spoke of our beginning where the fir grows. But what treeless road was he talking about?"

"That is the road I travel," Gleth answered, "the rivers and the Mere."

"Of course, Cousin Gleth, how could I have missed that?"

"Probably because it is a road you are not accustomed to travel, friend Volthir."

"True enough," the warrior agreed.

Meldreth, the heart-melting warmaiden, spoke next. "What is the riddle of the one, the two, and the three? How do we untangle these numbers?"

"I have no idea, cousin," responded Ringskild. "Where does the one go, and who is the one? Who are the two and where do they stand?"

"Who are the three helpers?" Vunskridh added.

Nordil wondered aloud, "If there is no tree where the one goes, does this mean somewhere in the waters, or a desert, or the highest peaks beyond the trees?"

Pjortan recalled Zhodor's question—"Will you believe me?"—and affirmed, "I certainly believe the boy, but I don't know what he is trying to tell us. Vladje honored the child and I take that as a sign from the gods. Hranild spoke of love, hope, and faith in her prophecy and Zhodor touched on them as well, if belief and faith are equated. I wonder what he means by 'Whom will you love?' though I suppose each of us wonders where to bestow our heart."

"Wherever you wish to, my fleet fellow," Meldreth said, tousling Pjortan's hair and causing the young singer's ruddy cheeks to turn several shades darker.

"I found hope when the boy said not to despair beneath the crushing weight," said Mechdar. "That line stood out for me because of the nightmare I had and this gives me hope. On the troubled night when I dreamed of such a weight, I feared it was a portent of my death by crushing."

"Hmm...You may well face some kind of weight, though it might be a weight upon the mind or heart as easily of the body, but if Zhodor addressed that line to you, then I doubt it means your death. So let us not despair," responded the healer, adding, "I would sorely miss you."

Ringskild assumed the tone more of a captain than a colleague as she said, "We have been fortunate so far in facing only minor perils and I fear far greater dangers lie ahead. I pray the stars we may lose none of our company, both because you are all dear friends and because I would return to our lord with every one accounted for. We must be cautious. I cannot discern Furk's motives, whether they be evil or merely foolish. Since there seems to be no clue regarding him in the prophecies we have heard, I see no reason for him to join us. Perhaps it is only his whim, but as we are in his lands and essentially his captives, though treated as guests, we cannot reasonably oppose him. Perhaps the stars and the journey itself will sort it all out."

"I think I understand another line," Ian interrupted. "The one about the blind can see where the young lord leads. Our Lord Njothir is very young for a chieftain among our people and Hranild cannot see with her eyes, yet she sees many things the rest of us cannot. Maybe Zhodor is telling us to trust Hranild."

"Indeed," said Wulfdar, "I would trust her into the very jaws of death, for she has never spoken false." He then added in a muttering voice, "Though I'm starless if I know what she means most of the time."

Pjortan spoke next. "What I cannot understand is the part about not singing alone. I do not doubt I shall have to sing with all my might when the time comes, and I always try to put all of myself into my song. Who will sing with me?"

"Perhaps we shall find out, young singer, when the time comes," said Jannir.

"I think I could see something of Senjir in the boy as he whirled about," the star singer replied. "Poor lad, to be given a voice by the stars but to suffer such torment. His friends seem to care for him, but it is a hard life he must live."

At that point the conversation fell into silence, each one puzzling out the trials and mysteries of life and the strange quest to which they had been called. To every soul there appeared the memory of all that could be lost and the frail hope of regaining a world where life and joy might flourish.

Ian's heart suddenly felt like lead within him, as though a great heaviness within was pulling him down. He had already lost one world and was not prepared to lose a second one.

"I know that I am afraid," he said. "Never in my short life have I faced anything so terrible as the power we chase. But for the sake of the people I now know as my own and for the world into which I have been cast, I refuse to give up. Let us follow where the stars call us, and Christ have mercy on us all."

"Who is this Christ?" asked Vunskridh.

"He is the one my people worship, the one who gave his life so others might live."

Wilda's forehead pursed into lines of anxiety. Breathing shallowly she asked, "Do you expect to give your life, Ian?"

"I really don't know," the youth replied. "That is certainly not my plan, though it may come to pass. But what is the point of living in a world that darkens every day and not fighting for the light? Besides, after Christ died he was raised again. So perhaps there is always more to the story."

"An interesting faith," Pjortan commented, "And I, for one, believe there is always more to every story than we can ever guess."

At that point a knock came on the door. A serving maid entered and bade the company follow her to supper.

CHAPTER 29

Gleth and the Norrungs followed the serving maid through the corridors of Vothnell Castle. Wilda continued to fret at the idea of Ian dying in battle with the Chegjan and Nordil did his best to put her mind at ease, reminding her that Hranild indicated that Ian would defeat the demon. "But at what price?" she queried in a whisper.

Nordil responded soberly, "I do not think his life will be the price, though I doubt this journey will not cost us dearly."

At that feeble reassurance, Wilda clutched her husband's arm and worried in silence.

The party soon came to a room with a large table set with food. A second server joined the one who had led them to dinner and together they served drink and cleaned up after the Norrungs had eaten. The food was simple but decent. Furk was not seen.

As the meal concluded a soldier entered and informed the Norrungs that Lord Furk would see them at breakfast. He led them back to their rooms and bade them good rest.

Throughout their discussion in the room before supper and their meal, the sound of great activity persisted in the background. The courtyard saw a great deal of traffic that afternoon and evening as preparations were made for Furk and his companions to set out on a journey. Orders were shouted by captains and stewards as others hastened to complete many tasks. Near collisions were common with so many coming and going in multiple directions, packing and making last-minute repairs. Goods were then sent down to the port and loaded on ships, leaving both staff and soldiers exhausted from working into the night.

The rooms of the Norrungs, however, faced on a small garden and not the main courtyard, so they could not observe and discern what they might from this hubbub. All they caught was the ambient noise of preparation, leading to speculative debate. Other than the clear message that Furk was intent on heading their quest from this point, nothing seemed certain. Pjortan urged trust in the stars and those signals they could understand, reminding all that their journey had been undertaken with faith and no certainties whatsoever. He sang an evening hymn and, with questions still chasing one another in each person's mind, they attempted to sleep.

Moderately, though briefly, rested and still anxiously weighing all manner of possibilities, the companions joined Furk and numerous others for a predawn breakfast. The forceful ruler seemed in excellent spirits in spite of having spent most of the night making plans and issuing orders. He hailed the Norrungs with a hearty shout as they entered and introduced them to some of his party, beginning with a man of olive complexion and lively, intelligent dark eyes that appeared to miss nothing.

"These good folks will be joining us. Here is my vassal, Baron Torthan of Valcor, an excellent strategist." Torthan smiled and nodded, looking directly at Ringskild whom he recognized wordlessly as the military leader of the Norrungs. His tunic bore the baron's arms, black with a gold falcon displayed and descending with talons ready to grasp its prey. Ringskild nodded in return, viewing the man with the neat chin strap beard as a formidable chap, preferring him to be an ally rather than an opponent.

Furk continued, gesturing toward a familiar figure. "Djutar you already know. He will be organizing our troops. And we will have a colleague of yours, singer," he said, glancing at Pjortan. "This is Baroness Athnel of Laoghar, whom I have invited to join her forces with yours, since you have indicated that we go into a spiritual battle. I want my troops to carry the blessing of the stars."

"Is this what 'not singing alone' is about?" the young man wondered silently as he beheld a woman of courtly bearing with green eyes and red hair. She had a star tattooed on her neck to mark her as a singer. Her cream-colored gown was elegant in line and delicate in fabric. She bore no baronial ornaments or heraldic insignia, though the air around her seemed to vibrate. Pjortan thought her much too beautiful to be going on a quest, but finally managed to stammer a simple, "My lady."

Athnel, who appeared no more than a few years older than her colleague, smiled and nodded graciously at the blushing lad before her.

Furk went on to name a few others then turned to the Norrungs, asking Ringskild to introduce her company to the Vothneli. This she did, beginning with Wulfdar, Gleth, Nordil, Wilda, Jannir, Pjortan, and Ian. She then presented her fellow warriors and warmaidens, finally concluding with Vladje.

"This, very special member of our company, came to us on his own and is known as Vladje. We suspect he may be sent by Morvladh, the Great Wolf of the stars, for he behaves like no other wolf. We do not command him for he is not tame. Two alone of our company may touch him. I would pray that all your followers be apprised of his sacred status lest someone seek to harm him in ignorance."

As this introduction drew to a close, Vladje trotted toward Lady Athnel, sat at her feet, and raised his paw. She laughed, lightly and musically, and took the wolf's paw in her own hand. "Lord Wolf, I am honored to meet you," she said. Vladje returned to Ian's side.

At this, Furk acknowledged, "Stars bless me. It is even as you say, daughter of Ivor. Hmmph. Much has passed before my eyes over the years, but nothing like this. My, my. Did you not say only two had been allowed to touch him?"

"Evidently the number is now three, Lord Furk."

"Then I shall give the order that none are to harm this wolf. Most extraordinary. Hmmph."

By now it had become evident that Furk had a number of vocal tics, including various noises and asides possibly addressed to himself. He continued to chat throughout breakfast in his usual expansive manner, full of bravado and good cheer, as though setting out on a hunting trip in good weather. No one would have suspected he was launching an expedition to battle a demon with powers of unknown extent.

Lady Athnel, who was seated next to Mechdar, observed that most mortals would approach dark forces with caution. "My Lord Furk is known for his willingness to face anything, not for his prudence. May the stars continue to protect him."

"And all of us," added Mechdar.

"Indeed," the lady singer responded with a smile that made Mechdar feel ten years younger.

Ian deemed the new singer a beauty, though it was not desire that told him so. He was smitten as a schoolboy is smitten with an older woman who is unattainable, perhaps the stunning wife of another man. Others may have fantasized bedding her but the English youth simply wished to be near her. She was a priest in this world, and might have been a madonna in his. Indeed, he had no idea if she were married or a maid. Most singers were not titled Lord or Lady. Vladje's lupine homage to her placed her in a category separate from most mortals. With Wilda and Vladje it had seemed different. She had been a substitute mother to Ian during this journey and it was in that way that he cherished her. For Vladje to watch over her seemed less extraordinary. All the Norrungs in their company seemed to grant Wilda filial respect and affection. This more exotic creature, who seemed to command everyone's attention, was different.

"Stop staring, lad, you'll embarrass yourself," said Nordil, who sat on Ian's right.

"She is just lovely," Ian replied.

"True enough," the older man said, "but I would be wary of her if I were you."

"Because she serves Furk?"

"Because your brother honored her. I believe she is good, not evil, but that does not equate to her being other than dangerous."

"I was only observing her, Nordil, not entertaining fantasies," Ian objected.

"Good. I expect others have fantasies enough."

"Knowing Wilda, cousin, I hope you are not one of them."

"Hah," Nordil responded, "a man may have his fantasies so long as he does not act on them. Or get caught glancing in the wrong direction once too often." The last remark came as he recalled an especially nasty blow from one of Wilda's cooking pots. And with that, the groom kept his eyes trained in any direction except that of Lady Athnel.

Ringskild and Torthan sat next to each other and close to Furk, sharing thoughts about approaching a demon. Torthan was intrigued by the thought of a battle without conventional weapons and rather loved the challenge. Ringskild was surprised that a battle strategist such as Torthan would take seriously her comments about the unusual nature of this conflict. Perhaps this western baron had other surprises. She hoped he did, and that they would benefit the quest, not harm it.

The sundry social, military, and political sparring kept breakfast lively, but not for long. It was soon time to be on the way. Furk gave a few more orders and his people responded efficiently. Soldiers not already at the ships lined up behind various ensigns, mostly white pennons that were smaller versions of Furk's silk banner with the black battleaxe.

Ian marveled afresh at this world of story as he surveyed the assembled ranks of medieval fighting men. He was accustomed to the warriors of Norrast but these bore armor with more metal and less leather. They looked more like the knights and foot soldiers he had seen in books, perhaps as much because of their sober mien as their armor and weapons. They were surely no fiercer than his companions but he had no way of knowing the humorous or tender sides of these strangers.

This was no vast battalion of Her Majesty's troops. Ian guessed there were maybe four dozen horsemen and a couple hundred on foot but that was vastly larger than the dozen who set forth from Vorthall no so very long ago. Life had become much more complicated, as if it had not been confusing enough already.

Ian was fascinated by their armaments: swords, spears, pikes, huge bows and quivers bristling with arrows. He had not seen the great quantity of other weapons already loaded on supply wagons and stowed on shipboard before dawn, along with stores of food, barrels of water, and provender for the horses. The massive war horses snorted, eager for action. There were not yet caparisoned for battle, their armor also having been stowed in the two maneuverable vessels in Vothnell harbor.

Ian noticed that Furk invited Ringskild to stay close to him and Torthan. Ian wondered if this were to reinforce their strategic resources or to keep an eye on the Norrung captain. Ian and most of the Norrungs went with Djutar. Lady Athnel moved to Pjortan's side and asked if she might travel with him so they could learn from each other and discuss this venture. Their first task, upon exiting the gates of the castle at daybreak was to stand before the entire host and sing together the Hymn to the Dawn, which they did.

Her voice blended in unison with Pjortan's clear tenor and he was pleased to note that, like him, she sang with fervent devotion. The hymn had barely finished when a trumpet sounded and all headed to the port to board ship. The entire town turned out to watch the procession from the castle. Ian spotted Zhodor and his mates at the edge of the crowd when Vladje barked in their direction. Zhodor waved frantically toward the wolf as if sending his adored older brother off on a campaign. Ian smiled, understanding the effect the wolf had on others. Athnel commented to Pjortan that Zhodor was a "holy child," and Pjortan was inclined to agree. It was the first kind comment about the boy from a Vothneli and the lady rose in Pjortan's estimation.

Down the circling path from the castle the long procession moved, stirring dust and driving all Vothnell to emerge, fervid with speculation. Every mouth relayed a different speculation on where Lord Furk was leading this force and why he did so. Some praised their lord's bravery while others muttered about the folly of going forth against the darkness. Women stood at the edge of the crowd, many with children clinging to them, as fathers, husbands, and lovers passed by. Unlike the forest dwellers, Vothneli warriors were almost entirely male. Four warmaidens rode in a cluster, evoking in Ian the image of Valkyries since they and some of their male comrades had beaten silver wings on the sides of their helmets.

The earthling observed the banners and blazons that identified various minor lords, captains, knights, and horse soldiers, wondering where each came from and what fealty they owed Count Furk. Mingled with them were some ten score foot soldiers, usually marked by some badge indicating which leader they followed. Furk's own troops stood out with the distinctive black and white combination repeated in their clothing. Ian realized he had just shivered, thinking that white was the color of death in Mídhris and black its color in England.

"It's not what we planned, lad," said Mechdar, riding just behind him. "But it looks as though it's what the stars are giving us."

"I do not understand the ways of the stars," Ian replied.

Mechdar grunted. "Even singers struggle to untangle their mysteries, Hjelgi guide us."

"So shine," said Ian, using a phrase he had learned from Pjortan: something roughly equivalent to "Amen."

At length the parade reached the docks and all clambered aboard. Three ships set out that morning, two of Furk's fleet closely flanking Gleth's merchant vessel. Together they sailed along the coast of the Mere to the port of Fimmoth at the mouth of the River Fiona.

For all her courtly manners, Lady Athnel seemed perfectly at home among the Norrungs and the sailors, devoid of pretension and totally relaxed. Vladje kept a close eye on her and Pjortan in addition to Wilda and Ian. The wolf clearly had his favorites.

Some of the forest dwellers found themselves ensorcelled by the waves and the thrill of riding upon the Mere. The rhythm of the swells was a new experience, as was the cry of gulls and the breeze that played with the peace feathers in their hair and filled the sails. The shimmering dance of fish beneath the water's surface and the flash of sunlight upon the waves lightened the journey toward Fimmoth. Cormorants poised on rocky outcrops, their wings outspread to dry in the wind and sun, amused the travelers as well. It was Wilda's turn to be ill on this leg of the journey and Nordil stayed solicitously by her side until her innards becalmed themselves. Like any fussy cook, Wilda blamed it all on the food in Vothnell, but not where Furk or any of the Vothneli could hear.

Hildir, Wulfdar, and Volthir chatted with the mariners, when those busy chaps could spare a moment to talk, and learned something of the rudiments of sailing. Meldreth chatted with sailors too, but her banter was in her usual flirtatious style. Few suspected she was gathering knowledge from them under the guise of salacious chat. Mechdar and Vunskridh joined Ringskild and Torthan. The Norrungs eyed the coastline, studying this new terrain and analyzing it in offensive and defensive terms, while Torthan added his own observations and experience with a terrain more familiar to him than to the others.

Ian caught himself staring again at his new-found object of adoration, the Lady Athnel, standing in the breeze, her dress clinging to her body under the influence of the wind, her red hair flying wild and causing her to laugh. Other eyes noted the lovely young woman also, but none so thoroughly as Pjortan, whose eyes followed the curves of her back, buttocks, and legs as the fine wind-blown fabric defined them. Just so his thoughts also followed her elaborate religious speculations. She seemed to love life as she loved the stars, with delight and abandoned devotion. Pjortan was scarcely aware of the passage of time.

That afternoon the miniature fleet of this unprecedented crusade sighted the small bay where the River Fiona debouched at Fimmoth. They docked only to be met by soldiers and officials at the quay, wondering what their business was. Furk stood forth, flanked by servants with peace poles, and announced that he was Lord Furk of Vothnell on the Mere, their neighboring port to the east. He continued to declare that in spite of this being an armed party they came with peaceful intentions toward their neighbors and only sought to pursue the Chegjan. All this was delivered in his most commanding voice, mitigated somewhat by his occasional, characteristic "Hmmph."

When Furk's declaration, augmented by a few haranguing asides, concluded, a tall slender man wearing a great silver chain of office over deep blue robes stepped forward. This was Peveç, Steward of Fimmoth, a man with his own sense of authority. His hair and beard were the color of iron with a few flecks of silver, his eyes a pale gray, his nose long and aquiline, his lips thin. The steward did not appear impressed with the lord of Vothnell, nor especially happy to see him. Soldiers and minor officials had stepped aside when Peveç came forward and there was a period of silence that made Furk a trifle uneasy. At last the steward spoke.

"Indeed, Lord Furk, our cousin and neighbor to the east, we have observed your approach and recognized your ships. The presence of so many armed warriors combined with obvious peace poles can only spark curiosity, but that pales in comparison with your intent to pursue the demon that haunts these lands. Those less aware of your prowess in battle and your iron will might be amused that anyone would seek to oppose a force beyond the understanding of mortals, but we have followed your exploits and can only marvel at the valor of those who would take up such a challenge.

"We acknowledge your declaration of peace to this city and its people and trust that it extends to all the people of the lands that serve Thioth and the Lady Rushvin, for were it otherwise we know you would have so informed us. We therefore bid you enter our port, cousin, as our friend and ally."

The Norrungs noted that Peveç had clearly set forth the terms upon which they were allowed to disembark, terms in accordance with Furk's declarations but Thiothi terms nonetheless. Peveç's lack of bombast signaled that Furk may have met his match in diplomacy if not in military prowess. The day, strange enough from its beginning, was getting more intriguing.

CHAPTER 30

Disembarkation took place in stages, since horses and considerable baggage were involved in addition to three shiploads of people. Peveç and Furk, flanked by the Fimmothi entourage, led the way into the heart of the city. A portion of Vothneli soldiers joined the Norrungs and Furk's personal party in this official vanguard. Combined with their local escort, this made for a sizable group threading its way through the narrow streets of Fimmoth, a town that had stood at the mouth of the Fiona River for centuries. Soldiers proved handy as the townspeople and merchants who normally filled the streets, augmented by the merely curious, competed for space. Surrounded by guards, the steward and the visiting lord were the only ones who escaped jostling. Otherwise the situation created opportunity for cutpurses, at least for those not next to the wary wolf. Vladje's occasional growls kept strangers at a distance.

Vunskridh sensed a sudden tension in Hildir, who walked next to her in the middle of the procession. She glanced left and caught the jerk of his chin pointing forward toward a vaguely familiar form in the crowd ahead of them.

"Isn't that the copperhead who fancies you?" he asked.

Taking advantage of her height, the blonde warmaiden looked over the heads surrounding her and caught a flash of profile in the distance before Vishgar disappeared into a side street. With people pressing on every side, there was little opportunity to pursue the sighting but Vunskridh knew her man.

"It is the fellow we met that horrible night, though I doubt he fancies me," she demurred.

"That much courtesy from a stranger had to be more than manners. I suspect they were partly for show, as he is quite the performer, but surely he was trying to make an impression on you, lovely lady," Hildir countered.

"Pfah!" said the maid, "he was speaking to Ringskild and tossing flowery words her way, not mine." She thus dismissed that line of speculation, ignoring the looks the man had given her before Djort's death and the discussion with Ringskild. "It is interesting that we have now spotted him twice since meeting him in Denev. Can you think of any reason he might follow us?"

"Eghran knows," Hildir retorted, invoking the trickster god, "but he would have to be twice as clever as I supposed to arrive here just ahead of us, with us at Furk's mercy and our plans overtaken by another."

"Yet if this seeming gentleman knows the direction in which we journey and was not waylaid by Furk, he could well have been lying here in wait."

"True enough, but for what purpose? His disgust with that filthy Djort fellow did not seem feigned, so I doubt he seeks revenge for the knave's death. Beyond that, I can imagine no design. I thought the adventuresome Lord Furk and the duty-bound companions of Vorthall were the only souls under the stars insane enough to seek out this demon on purpose."

"And until recently, cousin, we supposed that we alone pursued this path. I should never have suspected another might join us, much less seek to lead us to the halls of the Dark Queen, where all are received yet none return. Now there is Furk. Perhaps there will be more."

"You are a suspicious woman, daughter of Jornandir."

"Many have said so. And perhaps our paths simply overlap. We have seen no evidence that this Vishgar fellow so much as thinks of us." She paused, then added, "I mistrust coincidence nonetheless, cousin Hildir."

Hildir noticed the warmaiden recalled the red haired man's name but made no comment.

The coterie of nobles, warriors, and odd bits finally emerged from the crooked streets into the broad expanse of the Grand Square, where they promptly spread out into a more orderly formation before crossing the square to the Town Hall that lay opposite. Mature alders lined the edge of the square, giving Fimmoth both shade and a stately feel. Saffron and green banners hung from the upper floors of the Town Hall, adding a touch of brightness to the solemn matter of the journey toward the dark. Guards liveried in the same colors snapped to attention as the Steward passed, though their formality wavered when they watched a wolf stride into this seat of civic rule.

The courtyard was dominated by a fountain at the center. Low hedges and evenly spaced rhododendrons, backed by simple stone arches, defined the perimeter. As the easterners passed the fountain, Vladje paused to drink from it, startling a number of sparrows who considered it their exclusive territory, then darted back to Ian's side.

Ian patted Vladje distractedly, lost in speculation about Peveç's motivation. Why had he brought the whole party here instead of merely allowing them to arrange for lodging and the next stage of the journey? Was it to curb Furk's sense of self-importance or were there other political considerations at play? Vishgar the stranger, Furk the noble, and now Peveç the steward were human riddles and neither Ian nor any of the Norrungs had yet to find their meaning.

The dignified Peveç, quietly imperious and possibly as conceited as Furk though not given to embarrassing outbursts, led the party into a large room and bade the visitors take seats. Furk sat near the Steward and several Fimmothi dignitaries joined the group. Servants quickly brought drink for all and when this nod to hospitality was handled, Peveç began.

"My cousins, I am certain you have asked yourselves why I brought you here and I assure you the reason is simple. I wish to apprise you of developments north of here that might not have come to your attention. Whatever your quest may be, it is none of my business provided the interests of Lady Rushvin of Thioth and her realms are not compromised. If your intent is to labor against the vile demon that has afflicted so many then I am certain my lady will wish you well.

"We have other forces, however, working against Thioth and its territories. Beyond Thioth lies Fjorn, a region once friendly to our people. Currently it lies beneath the iron fist of Bulçar, a man of blood and treachery. Lady Rushvin daily receives Fjorni fleeing the villain's rule but our lands cannot sustain so many souls arriving with such suddenness.

"It is true that our numbers have been diminished even as the plague wanes. Survivors from other regions can help rebuild our life together, but the tide of life is not always easily channeled. To say we need to restore our population is one thing; to organize life with a sudden influx is quite another. Integrating those raised with slightly different customs and different expectations is no easy task. The traumas of sundry wars and acts of vile injustice take their toll. Those whose minds and hearts are scarred by these, not to mention their bodies, are often unpredictable. We thus have chaos following close upon the heels of plague.

"You who would journey north may find the dark fiend, but before you do I suspect you must first confront the dark heart of Bulçar. I could not allow you to proceed with no warning, nor did I wish to dishearten our people by speaking of this outside our Council."

As the words of Peveç ended, their meaning quietly sank into the hearts of his listeners. Even Furk was momentarily at a loss for words, though that moment passed. Torthan leaned near and whispered in his suzerain's ear, Furk thought about what he had heard, then opened his mouth to speak. The Norrungs, having witnessed his rashness, braced themselves for whatever might come out. They did not expect magnanimity.

"You are gracious, cousin, to inform us of the dangers to the north. I lament your lady's plight. Dear, dear, terrible. We too need more hearts, minds, and bodies to build again, yet I can see that a gift of the stars may also be problematic. Hmmph. Yes, yes. Perhaps if our territory of Vothnell received some of the Fjorni refugees it could benefit us both. It would relieve your stress and assist us. The chance of either being overwhelmed would be reduced. What do you say?"

"My lady will be honored by your suggestion, cousin," the Steward replied.

"Most excellent! Is there anything else we should know?"

"That was my message. Please greet our cousin Vjendar of Hlfin as you pass on your way to our Lady Rushvin. To her I bid you give our warmest greetings and expressions of loyalty."

"But of course, happy to," said Furk. Peveç smiled and nodded with great dignity. In all of this the Steward made no acknowledgement of a wolf in the Council Chamber, acting as though this were an everyday occurrence. The councilors were less self-contained. They did not inquire, but their stares were obvious. Vladje ignored all this but gratefully accepted a basin of water proffered by one of the servants.

"Cousin of Fimmoth," Ringskild interjected, "we are strangers to this part of the world. I am Ringskild, daughter of Ivor, serving Njothir, son of Rathdar, chieftain of the Norrungs and Lord of Vorthall. We come from the great forest of the east and have journeyed more than a moon in coming hither. Cousin Furk is your neighbor and knows this region. I pray you, can you explain the relations among the cities and rulers here?"

"Most gladly, lady," the Steward replied, enjoying the thought of diplomatic discussion with the commanding and beautiful warmaiden. Her manners were excellent yet her dress and weapons seemed somewhat barbarian to the urban dignitary. Peveç did not disdain that aspect of his guests at all. It made them interesting, and Ringskild more attractive. He reminded himself that this was not the setting in which his thoughts were all free to express themselves.

"Fimmoth is an ancient town, as you could see, built to take advantage of our location at the river's mouth. By virtue of our location we are the primary link between the lands along the Fiona and the rest of the world. North of here you will find Hlfin, a town and region under Baron Vjendar. You will undoubtedly meet him. Hlfin and Fimmoth both serve the House of Thioth, whose rule is currently vested in the Duchess Rushvin. She has wisely guided our lands for some forty years now and is beloved of her subjects."

At this flourish Ringskild wondered if Peveç spoke from the heart or was merely being a diplomat. Her suspicion evaporated as he continued.

"My parents fostered me with her and Lord Thjun, now with the stars. She is as dear to me as any mother could be."

The note of sincerity in the Steward's voice was evident.

"Thioth is a day's journey upriver from Hlfin. Fjorn is a hard day's journey further north. To the west of Fjorn is the Forest of Fjorn, an ancient place. The Fiona River continues northwest to the slopes of Mount Vjat. West of Fjorn are other lands subject to Thioth and beyond the Ulava River you will find Bjupazh and Westwaste. I do not know where your journey takes you but, given the identity of your foe, I suspect only the stars know that. In any case, I wish you well in the venture."

"Thank you, Cousin Steward. Is there anything more we should know of this Bulçar?"

Vladje growled at this mention of the man. Peveç paid no heed as he answered.

"Only that he is a savage and treacherous man. There is no crime or vice I would not suspect in him. He seeks quarrels with everyone, terrorizes his subjects, is free in the use of torture, plunders wherever he can, ignores treaties, and has raised two brutes as sons. I should avoid him were I on your path."

"Well counseled, and I thank you on behalf of my fellows and our people."

"Gracious lady," Peveç nodded, his narrow lips forming a half smile and his gray eyes twinkling.

"Well then. Hmmph. Let us be going," Furk said in his best diplomatic tone, seeking to reassert his headship of the expedition. "Thank you, cousin, for your warnings. I shall take them into account. And give your greetings to your lady, of course. Yes."

Peveç finally conceded his guest's title as he nodded again and said, "Lord Furk."

With that the party left the Council Chamber, passed through the courtyard, and reentered the Great Square. One of Furk's captains conferred with a couple of Fimmothi and reported on where lodging could be found, given that the day was now far advanced.

As Vunskridh emerged from the Town Hall she spotted Vishgar standing next to a square pillar at the far end of the colonnade on their right. As before, she did not need to see the snake tattoo on his forearm to identify him; she had studied his face well in Denev. A slight man with a narrow face and short-trimmed beard had just parted from him. The warmaiden immediately pointed them out to Ringskild, then strode in the copperhead's direction accompanied by Meldreth. Vunskridh noted the split-second expression of alertness in Vishgar's eyes when he spotted them, followed by a broad grin. He pushed off from the aged and pitted stone of the column on which he had been leaning, assumed his full stature, and inclined his head.

"Lovely ladies, what might a foolish fellow such as I have done to be blessed by the stars with your presence this afternoon?"

Vunskridh looked him full in his dark, playful eyes and wanted to slap him for the impudent assumption that she could possibly be beguiled by his smooth tongue.

"Iljelgi seems to have placed us repeatedly in the same place, saucy fellow. The Shepherd of the Stars has not explained why this is so and I wondered if you might make it clear to me."

Meldreth, who reveled in banter between women and men, was mildly surprised and greatly amused at her companion's bluntness.

"Alas, my lady, the God has not enlightened me either. Have you followed me all this way?"

The self-centered nature of this question caused Vunskridh's eyes to blaze. Her less intense colleague cleared her throat in a warning not to explode, at least not in this place and at this time. Vunskridh collected herself before retorting, "I doubt I should travel a furlong for you, Vishgar, son of Ioreth. And you may put away your dubious honey; its sweetness will not sway me. I assumed you were following us."

"My lady is exceeding blunt today. How could I have possibly offended you so?"

"You do not deny that you follow us?"

"The Dark Queen take me now if I have followed you here, my lady," he swore, raising his arms in an exaggerated gesture of innocence.

"I am not your lady, Ushtethi charmer, nor shall I be. Where are your companions?"

Meldreth's eyes widened with amazement. Vunskridh sounded like an accuser questioning an alleged evildoer before the council. Vishgar raised one copper brow in surprise but made no answer to the warmaiden's question.

"I would call you by your name, warmaiden, if I but knew it. There you have the advantage of me. You recall my name and that of my father, even the name of the village where I was born. Before you I am, to all purposes, unarmed."

"You speak with Vunskridh daughter of Jornandir of the Norrungs. Beside me stands Meldreth daughter of Njuthar. Now, where are your companions?"

"Thank you, my...Cousin Vunskridh. What companions do you speak of?"

"The small fellow who scurried away from you just before this fencing match disguised as a conversation and the large blond chap you were with in Nimmoth."

A questioning look flickered across Vishgar's face before he responded. "The little fellow just now was some nuisance trying to sell me an item that appeared stolen. I sent him on his way. I don't recall this large chap, as you call him."

"You walked beside him in Nimmoth. He had curly blond hair. Volthir and I both saw you."

"Indeed, one walks beside many strangers in cities. I much prefer the countryside where one is free to breathe without being poked and jostled by strangers."

At this point in the interrogation Meldreth tugged at Vunskridh's arm. Hildir and Mechdar were waiting for them, the rest of the party having crossed the square and headed for lodging. Vishgar glanced in their direction, smiled, and said, "I see your companions await you. How fortunate they are to enjoy your company. I hope we shall have the pleasure to cross paths again, daughter of Jornandir."

"I am sure we will meet again, son of Ioreth. I am not sure it will be a pleasure."

With that Vunskridh turned and strode toward the warriors who were keeping an eye on the entire interchange and Meldreth hastened alongside her. Vunni noted Mechdar's inquiring expression. He often called her "daughter" because his daughter married Vunskridh's brother Vagnir. Vunskridh knew she would have to retell the conversation that had just taken place before having a chance to digest it herself. Before Mechdar could ask, she began.

"I am not yet sure, my brother's father, what the truth of this fellow is. I doubt I shall like it when it is revealed."

CHAPTER 31

Rather than hire lodgings the Norrungs chose to stop at a tavern where they dined on a peppery boar stew and bread far finer than any Ian had encountered since he was torn from his home. They then retired to Gleth's ship for the night. This guaranteed a level of privacy no inn of Fimmoth could provide as they discussed the day's events. Most of the Vothneli did the same, though Furk and his closer entourage sought out lodgings to his liking.

Vunskridh and Meldreth reported their encounter with Vishgar, Vunskridh asserting that he was clearly up to no good and Meldreth acknowledging his evasiveness but also noting his good looks. Mechdar added that he did not care for the looks of the man: "He may be fair on the outside but his manners are a bit too slick. There is something crooked about the fellow." All agreed that he needed watching, especially if he continued to cross their path.

Of greater concern for the group was the level of threat posed by Bulçar of Fjorn. The Norrung tradition of electing a chieftain had generally proven a barrier to evil leaders, though competence was occasionally misjudged. Rule determined by inheritance seemed to the forest dwellers almost a guarantee that corruption would develop and evil ensue.

Ringskild, who had spent hours conferring with Baron Torthan, informed the group that the fastest way north of Fimmoth was along the River Road that ran roughly parallel to the Fiona River. Based on reports of the plague's path and various spreading evils, the Chegjan appeared to be traveling north and west. If they took the River Road it would lead them to Hlfin, Thioth, and Fjorn, as Peveç had indicated. They could choose to head westward before leaving the realms of Thioth. This would avoid the Forest of Fjorn, though the idea of being in a forest again had a strong appeal, even if it meant risking an encounter with Bulçar.

"I love living among great trees," said Wulfdar, "and an ancient forest may hold riches in the form of herbs I should like to have. But I prefer not to enter the realm of Fjorn. It would seem there is little evil this Bulçar would not do." By this point the Norrungs had all noticed Vladje's habit of baring his teeth at every mention of Bulçar. That in itself was ample evidence that the wicked man should be avoided.

Others joined in the discussion, yet most seemed of Wulfdar's mind. Ringskild added that in spite of her love of adventure, she did not wish to risk their mission. "It's bad enough that Furk has joined us. We do not need the complications of Fjorn."

So it was decided among the Norrungs to head west after visiting the Lady Rushvin. There Furk could convey his generous offer to accept some of the refugees, the greetings of Peveç could be conveyed, and the journey could proceed toward the setting sun. Provided, of course, that Furk could follow a reasonable course. The presence of Torthan and Athnel gave the Norrungs more hope than they would have had dealing with Furk alone.

The next day dawned clear. As the beams of the daystar touched the top of Mount Twij on the west side of Fimmoth, Pjortan and Athnel, who were now rarely apart, sang the hymn to the dawn. Captain Gleth bade the demon chasers farewell and returned to his ship, eager to return to a life with neither demons nor wolves. The company then assembled, bade the Steward of the City farewell, filed out through the massive stonework of the North Gate, and set out on the River Road.

"Sweet starry skies," Jannir swore mildly as the augmented company moved north. "What has become of our little band? We must be three hundred and more by now!"

Hildir smirked and joined the merchant as they shook their heads from side to side, looking at "that pompous battleaxe" in the vanguard, his banner hanging limp in the still air. Six of Peveç's men flanked him, forming an "honor escort" through the territory of Fimmoth. Furk's own bodyguards mingled with them. The proud baron rankled at the presence of the Fimmothi. Despite the alleged honor, they were clearly verifying the path and behavior of their visitors.

Norrungs were partly dispersed with Ringskild and Volthir riding near the front with Djutar and Torthan. Hildir, Jannir, Meldreth, and Wulfdar were two-thirds from the front, giving them an excellent view of most of the procession as it descended from the gate toward the river.

Somewhere in between these two groupings rode Ian, Nordil, Wilda, Vunskridh, Mechdar, Pjortan, and Athnel. Vladje, whether desiring a rest or sensing the chaos he would cause among strangers, especially among horses unaccustomed to him, rode in his favorite spot on Wilda's baggage cart. The choice scraps that the large-hearted woman often saved for him may have influenced the wolf's choice as well. The regular wagons, freighted with provisions and extra weapons, trailed with the rear guard and Wilda enjoyed her obvious status as one of the original demon chasers.

As a merchant, Jannir was decidedly a man of peace. He could not, however, deny the sight of so many riding forth to battle made the pulse quicken. The presence of Vrotni was almost palpable in the morning air. At one point a drum began sounding a steady beat and Vothneli soldiers gradually took up a battle song. Soon the lower Fiona Valley rang with the sound of warriors. The Chegjan may have been waiting many miles thence but the Vothneli seemed eager to meet it.

Though the surrounding battle lust increased the energy and alertness in her body also, Vunskridh said, to no particular audience, "They do not understand the Fierce Mother. They call her here, heedless of consequence."

"You speak rightly, cousin Vunskridh," said Athnel. "I would have her at my side when the time comes but we do not yet face our foe. These are good warriors but they have learned too well from our master to act before thinking."

Fjurthil seemed restless on his perch, agitated ever since the drumbeats began. Nordil, watching the falcon's unease, joined the conversation, observing that "those star-cursed fools of Furk have unleashed the goddess too soon." The song, however, died down and, though several small arguments punctuated the air, the morning passed without major incident.

Ian asked to learn more of Vrotni. "I know she is called on in battle but not much else."

Speaking for the company of warriors and warmaidens, Mechdar responded. "She gives us strength and valor for fighting. For that we honor her and her gifts are dear to us. But she shows no mercy and one must worship her cautiously."

Vunskridh stretched out her forearm, revealing to Ian the sword tattooed on the inner side of her wrist. "This is one of her symbols and shows me to be her votary."

"Of course," said Ian. "Mechdar has the same symbol on his shoulder. I remember seeing it the day we bathed in the stream."

"I do, lad," the warrior replied, "and so do we all in one spot or another, much as singers wear stars on their necks."

"Vrotni is wonderful and terrible," added Pjortan. "She is invoked at childbirth to protect the newborn. She gives mothers the ferocious love that would fight to the death to keep her child safe."

Athnel continued the lesson. "She is sometimes depicted as a lioness watching over cubs or as a mother eagle hovering above her fledglings. I would not choose to cross either mother, I assure you."

"Nor any mother," added Nordil.

"You are wise, husband," Wilda teased. "The goddess has many faces."

Here Athnel rounded out the lesson. "Vrotni is most commonly shown in battle madness, her skirt made of swords, her fingers and toes ending in talons. She wears a crown of nine skulls with flames dancing in their empty eye sockets. A lance is in her left hand and her right wields a sword. Blood drips from the long tongue that hangs between her fangs."

At this last remark Athnel smiled at Vladje, whose tongue had been lolling to one side. He promptly emitted a brief growl as though taking umbrage.

"My apologies, Lord Wolf," said Athnel, while all around the wolf laughed. Vladje seemed to accept the apology and returned to his more relaxed manner. Vunskridh added one final note.

"Some have claimed they catch glimpses of the fire in the goddess' crown during the heat of battle. I cannot vouch whether this be true or merely the fevered remembrance of sunlight flashing off blades and dancing in drops of battle sweat. In any case, it is called Vrotni's Fire."

The companions lapsed into silence, having covered most common aspects of the Fierce Mother. Ian said quietly, "I shall call upon her sparingly and carefully."

Mechdar approved. "You may well prove to be a wise warrior."

At midday the entire company paused for a brief rest and simple meal of bread, hard cheese, and mead. The Norrungs gathered by Wilda's cart, hoping she might have some extra treat. She allotted each a scrap of dried apple from the previous year's harvest and a few berries acquired in Fimmoth. Wulfdar insisted that each companion chew a few sour leaves he had gathered that morning, informing them of the leaf's power to preserve health. The flavor was not at all unpleasant but the tartness surprised those who had never tasted it before.

Furk rode through the assembly, keeping in touch with his forces. On the way back to the front he paused among the Norrungs.

"Lady Athnel, have you become a forest dweller?"

A flush rose briefly in her face then subsided as she replied, "I have always sought to learn the ways of strangers, my lord. These Norrungs live in a region very different from our coastal lands."

"Those strangers are especially strange who journey with a wolf. I see he has taken a liking to you."

"And I to him, lord."

Vladje, who had been lying with his head on the lady's knee, made no sound but Furk could see the fur on the wolf's neck rise. The baron rightly saw this as a lupine suggestion that he return to the front, which he did.

"By the stars," Wilda said, "I swear our friend will take a bite out of that man some day."

Athnel laughed and stroked Vladje's fur. "Darling wolf, I am sure it would poison you. That or turn you foolhardy. I pray you, abstain."

Not long after resuming the journey, the party came to a crude pillar beside the road. Peveç's men informed Furk that this marked the boundary between Fimmoth and Hlfin. They bade the Baron of Vothnell a good day, saluted Hlfini border scouts on a nearby hillock, and rode south with a relieved expression on their faces.

As the day wore on the sky slowly filled with clouds, puffs of white evoking a flock of sheep herded across the blue sky by Hjelgi, Shepherd of the heavens. The flock increased and its wool grew darker until the star vault assumed the hues of slate and the threat of rain was heavy in the air.

By late afternoon the adventurers reached the gates of Hlfin where it seemed they were expected. In spite of the weather the curious had gathered along the last mile or so before the Mere Gate, as the southern entrance to Hlfin was called because it faced the direction of the Mere. Baron Vjendar had ridden out that far with a company of soldiers to meet the visitors. He was well-fed and appeared shapeless beneath his fine garments. He had pale brown eyes, hair of a faded brown, including his wispy beard, and an easily forgettable face. He bore numerous jewels set in rings on most of his fingers.

As physically unimpressive as the young baron appeared, his eyes showed an alertness that warned viewers not to underestimate him.

Whereas the banners in Fimmoth were saffron and green, here they were saffron with a wavy blue pale that represented the Fiona flowing from north to south. The growing breeze caused them to snap as the river's sinuous symbol rippled frenetically. A trumpet sounded as Vjendar and Furk rode with their heralds to meet each other.

Formal greetings were exchanged and all then entered the city. Peveç had evidently been surprisingly effective in getting news to Hlfin before the party arrived, for Vjendar appeared to know all about them. "An enemy of the demon should be a friend of Lady Rushvin," the dissipated-looking young baron declared.

CHAPTER 32

Hlfin sat on the western side of the Fiona in a gentle valley between Mt. Twij to the southwest and Mts. Finthan and Hlinnat across the river to the northeast. It was not one of the major western towns. Within its perimeter the baronial castle sat at the highest point, a simple but solid block of mostly uninterrupted pinkish stone. With the sky so darkly overcast, the stone appeared a dull gray as the demon hunters approached. A very few openings gave vantage over the town and the ramparts formed a clean horizontal line with a few vertical slits for archers but no regular crenellation.

Watchmen perched on those ramparts observed as Vjendar led the whole entourage within the castle walls. The Baron of Hlfin urged a rapid stabling of the horses as Iltir the Archer sent his first arrow of silver fire across the heavens. All could see its flash but the storm was still far away and no rumble could be heard above the rising wind. More arrows followed and Dorgal took up her weeping as Iltir found his prey, for drops began to fall from the heavy clouds. The god's silver shafts began to follow one another in rapid succession, causing objects to form silhouettes framed by the flashing sky. Ivra the Drummer left off accompanying Senjir the Dancer to make the heavens shake with the beating of her bodhran. By the time all were indoors Dorgal's tears came in torrents.

The storm, however, was a brief shower of the early summer. The Archer tired, the Drummer ceased, and the Weeper was comforted. Within an hour all was calm and Hjelgi ushered the cloud flock to pastures further up the valley. The earth and all green things drank what they could and allowed the rest to pool or form runnels and rivulets draining toward the now swollen and muddy Fiona.

Vjendar appeared as gracious a host as Peveç had been a cautious one. He saw to the housing and feeding of the entire host, with the rain-soaked servants and peasants of Hlfin bustling about to see that it was done. In spite of the ostentation of his dress—for his silks and leathers were of the finest and the baronial jewelry quite overdone by most standards—he seemed lacking in the interpersonal vanity of both Furk and Peveç. Even Vladje showed no animosity toward him and Vjendar, for his part, must have been informed of the forest creature as well as of the overall mission, for he behaved as though a wolf and demon hunters in his household were the most normal things in the world.

The household dogs were not so relaxed about the unusual newcomer but their hostility ceased when Vladje's ice-blue eyes fixed upon them, thus enhancing his reputation among humans as an avatar of the Great Wolf of the heavens. Ian may have been the only skeptic on this matter, seeing the wolf as simply the essence of earthly "wolfness" and his best friend. Divinity seemed irrelevant, though Ian thanked his own Christian God and all the stars of Mídhris for sending Vladje to him.

Vjendar and his closest advisers met with Furk, Ringskild, and Torthan to share information and counsel. It became immediately apparent that the baron, no matter how bland his countenance and lax his body, was quite intelligent and paid close attention to his responsibilities. Maps were laid upon the table and lamps brought closer. Vjendar described the territory of Bulçar and the activities of Bulçar's troops in neighboring realms. It seems the lord of Fjorn was careless of boundaries and enjoyed asserting himself and his power. His elder son Njlvac led most of the sorties on the borders with Thioth and showed signs of being the true heir of his father's villainies. Thiothi spies gathered information where they could, though at great risk. Fjorni spies were likewise at work, possibly as far south as the key port city of Fimmoth.

Vjendar himself was careful to reveal his own knowledge and plans to very few and only dared share this information with strangers because his own spies had witnessed the testimony of Zhodor the Fool and the behavior of Vladje.

"What!" exclaimed Furk. "In my own city? You have spies? This is outrageous, sir! Have you no honor?"

"Cousin Furk, I assure you my agents and I have no intentions against you, your people, or your realm. But we look far and wide to understand what is happening in the world around us that we may better serve and protect our own lands and people. Rumors of strangers from the east on some improbable quest led me to seek further knowledge. At that time I had no idea they would be my guests and I desirous of aiding them. Nor that you would join in the quest, illustrious cousin."

Ringskild restrained her smirk, disguising repressed laughter with a mild fit of coughing. She assumed this flattery would calm Furk's ruffled feathers, as indeed it did.

"May the Stars send you ill if you speak false in this," Furk responded, "but, so long as you never work ill against me and you inform me in the future when your people are in my county, we shall be at peace…Hmmph. Cousin."

"It shall be as you say, Cousin."

"By any chance," Ringskild interrupted, "is one of your men a copper-haired fellow with a smooth tongue and a snake tattoo?"

"No, Cousin, though my men use many sources. Why do you ask?"

"We have crossed paths with such a man three times now in our journey. He speaks fair yet we mistrust him."

Vjendar replied that he would give orders to keep an eye out for the fellow the warmaiden proceeded to describe in more detail. He then went on to explain what he wished to share with the chasers of darkness.

"As I said when we met, foes of the dark demon should be friends of Lady Rushvin, and of Hlfin for which I answer to my Lady Aunt."

"You are nephew, then, to the Duchess of Thioth?" Torthan queried.

"Yes, Cousin. She is dear to her people and to her family, including my foster cousin to the south, the Steward of Fimmoth. But these are evil times. As you journey toward Thioth you will see people fleeing toward the south. Some abandon the only homes they have known when plague has left too few for a village to survive. Others flee the marauding of Prince Njlvac and men like him, preferring loss of homeland to the fate of those who fall into the hands of Fjorn. You will see the haggard faces of survivors, their countenance etched with anxiety, their eyes hollow with grief. Some start at the slightest unexpected sound or movement, some will cringe at your approach, especially with so many warriors. Keep your peace poles evident at all times for the sake of these piteous souls. I believe my cousin of Fimmoth has told you that all the lands of Lady Rushvin have been overrun by these unfortunates."

Ringskild, rising to the opportunity to say something nice about the lord of Vothnell, said, "Lord Furk has offered to take some of the refugees into his own territory, giving them a place to begin again and strengthening the numbers of Vothnell as they rebuild after the losses of the fiery death."

"Hmmph," responded Furk, attempting a balance between modesty and pride at his own magnanimity.

"Most generous of you, Cousin. Your place among the stars should be assured," said Vjendar.

Torthan, who suggested the idea to Furk, smiled and remained silent. He was pleased the idea had been accepted by his lord and grateful that something could be done for the afflicted population. A quick glance toward Ringskild told him she knew it was his idea and he was relieved she played along.

A sudden rapping on the heavy wooden door broke the course of diplomacy. Vjendar responded with a simple "Yes?" and a page timidly peeked around the door.

"Lady Athnel, my lords."

"Send her in, please."

"Yes, my lord."

The gracious singer entered the room and acknowledged those present.

"My apologies for breaking in to your counsels. Following the storm I have been watching the heavens. It is early yet for the season of raining stars but I beheld one in the region of Wigdor the Chieftain.

"Wiser singers than I have more precision in their readings of the heavenly messengers. My science and instinct combine to see in this a warning but I cannot descry to whom the warning is addressed. Perhaps the pattern of the Dancer's steps is shifting, and with it our fate. My hope is to alert you and wish you all well."

My gracious cousin," Vjendar began, "I thank you for this warning, though I am sure we all wish it were clearer and more favorable. Do you think it is for all, for some, or for one of us?"

"There certainty fails me and I must feel my way cautiously. My heart believes this warning is for one, yet my mind finds no proof of this. Whether it be for one of the mighty or one of the least, I have no clue. I only know it is my duty to pass this information to those who lead us."

"The Baroness of Laoghar," said Furk, explaining the lady's credentials, "is the wisest singer in my realms, not to mention her ancient and noble blood. I would not have set forth without her prayers and guidance. Indeed. Yes. She is also, as you may see, Cousin, a lady of great beauty."

The singer, uncertain whether she had been praised or demeaned or both, responded, "My lord is kind. I will now leave you to your work, cousins."

"We thank you, lady," said Vjendar to her already retreating back.

The Baron of Hlfin then returned to the maps in more detail, pointing out the extent of the Duchy of Thioth, its northern border running from Mount Finthan on the east to the border town of Othen, then along Othen Stream whose path rose from its join with the Fiona toward the southern ridge of Mount Uvjor. From there the border extended west to the banks of the Ulava River opposite the Bjupazhi town of Vorç. Beyond this border lay the lands of Count Bulçar of Fjorn toward the east and Duke Vaondir of Aonghe toward the west. Aonghe was at peace with Thioth and posed no known threat, nor was it threatened much by Fjorn, being separated by the dense Forest of Fjorn and Mount Uvjor. Most of Bulçar's outrages were perpetrated on his own people or his neighbors to the south and east.

Furk had little patience with geography lessons, relying on his strategist Torthan. The latter paid close attention to every detail on the maps before him, committing them to memory. Ringskild, more accustomed to lands she knew and less familiar with maps, paid as much attention as she could, knowing that minor details can save lives and win battles. When Vjendar had finished explaining the territories inked on the vellum stretched out on the table, Ringskild spoke.

"It is the desire of the Norrungs to turn west at Othen and cross the plain toward the Ulava River, thus avoiding encounters with any whose allegiance is to Bulçar."

Before Furk could counter such wisdom, Torthan agreed that such a course was desirable on at least two levels. The Ulava Plain offered the easiest terrain for heading west and any clash with Bulçar was likely to be costly. Furk accepted the proposal, even though it was not his own, silently reminding himself that chasing a demon was more exciting than dealing with some star-cursed villain who clearly had neither honor nor scruples.

Vjendar did not resist the temptation to inform the warmaiden of the far forest that the Forest of Fjorn was famous here in the western lands, known for its dense and ancient woods. There were traditions of both several holy groves deep within and not a few haunted sections where strange beings and lost souls who failed to ascend the star path still wandered. As the baron suspected, Ringskild drank in all he had to tell her of the woodlands, for she dearly missed her beloved Norrast. She imagined the lands along the Uvja River and ascending the slopes of Mount Uvjor as covered with lofty firs, pines, cedars, and oaks with willows and alders along the streams. Woodland beasts would shelter in the thickets and birds nest in the trees. For her the open skies that spanned the expanse of plains possessed a discomfiting vastness. She wondered if she would ever see Vorthall and her chieftain again.

"My lady," Torthan called her back to the present. "Does something trouble you?"

"No strategy, my lords," she reassured them. "At mention of a great forest my heart longed for home. I pray you, forgive me."

The men spoke over each other, assuring her such feelings were noble and there was nothing to forgive. Still, she reproached herself for being distracted, an often fatal error in battle.

Vjendar suggested they rest for the night, adding that he desired to accompany them to Thioth that he might visit with his lady aunt. Furk was inclined to take this as another manifestation of distrust but Ringskild felt the lord of Hlfin, though capable of far more subtlety than she had supposed at first, was sincere in this. Torthan wondered what else was going on behind the lively eyes in the bland face.

CHAPTER 33

Clouds smudged the northern horizon in three dark streaks the next morning but in all other directions the sky was clear as dawn approached. Pjortan and Athnel mounted the ramparts with the singers of Hlfin to greet the daystar as it rose above the eastern horizon. The Norrung singer had watched with Athnel the night before and shared her concern. Some of his companions noted that the usually peaceful youth now betrayed anxiety in his expression. Wulfdar would have approached to help Pjortan relax but saw that Athnel touched her colleague's temples as a healer might, spoke a few words, and dispelled the wrinkles in his brow. Wulfdar wondered: Was she a healer as well as a singer? What other surprises might the Vothneli lady have in store?

There was little time for pondering such questions or engaging in speculative gossip as the further enlarged company set forth once again on the River Road, with Vjendar, Furk, Ringskild, Hildir, and Ian at the forefront. Vunskridh, Nordil, and the two singers followed closely, with the other six travelers from Vorthall toward the middle. The Norrungs had worn eagle feathers and carried peace poles throughout their journey and others now made a special point of expressing signs of peace, as Vjendar had urged the night before, lest nervous refugees from the north be further terrorized.

The plague had begun to diminish along the upper Fiona and was now spreading further west and north. In light of this, plague alone would not explain why the irregular trickle of those fleeing toward haven in the south had grown into a steady stream. The northward procession did not encounter hordes, yet the reality of some significant movement of population was evident.

A few of those heading south appeared matter-of-fact about their journey but others manifested the traumas they were now fleeing. Some moved with blank stares as though not seeing where they went and others were observed nervously looking left, right, and occasionally behind them as though alert to imminent danger. Ian remarked that folks with such haggard faces and dark, hollow eyes seemed more dead than alive.

"Indeed, lad," responded Vjendar, "this sometimes happens following the fiery death but I suspect some of these have witnessed human wickedness as well." Furk added that he had seen such looks following terrible battles and Hildir noted, sadly, that these were not warriors but ordinary folk.

And so the morning passed. Once again Hjelgi seemed to be driving clouds from the Mere toward higher pasture but these were not as thick and dark as those of the day before. Still, a mild breeze held steady, causing the white and saffron pennons borne by the heralds of Vothnell and Hlfin to wave in the direction of Thioth.

An hour past midday some of Vjendar's men rode ahead without a signal. The procession was approaching a narrow point where the road passed a rocky outcrop on the left and a short but steep drop to the river on the right. Any manner of ambush might be staged there and the Baron of Hlfin took no chances when traveling in either direction.

As the scouts returned to signal a safe way ahead, Nordil, who rivaled Vunskridh for keen vision pointed out a figure seated on a ledge of the outcrop before them. Athnel and Pjortan moved ahead and drew beside Ian without explaining why, which caused Hildir and Ringskild to shift to a state of high alert, their hands resting on the hilt of their swords. Ian felt uneasy about all this. Pjortan quietly informed Ian that he could see a faint aura of stars about the figure.

It was a man with uncut and untamed hair that flew in all directions in the breeze, which seemed to blow stronger in the narrowing. He was seated on a ledge just above the heads of the riders. His beard was a wild tangle, his skin darkened to leather by the sun, and he was clothed in only a loincloth. A lightning fork was tattooed across his forehead and a small spike of bone pierced his nasal septum. Vjendar identified him as a hermit who lodged near the River Road.

"Dyrn has come!" the man cried several times, each cry feeling like ice down Ian's spine. As the Norrungs drew abreast, the hermit picked up a staff that had lain beside him, stood, and pointed the polished shaft toward Ian. "There he is! That's the Stranger. Do not fear the darkness; the light is within you."

Furk was on the verge of sputtering some protest but Vjendar silently restrained him. Before Ian or any of his companions could respond the wild-eyed man continued.

> No weapon of this world
> Singers, do not part
> We must be who we are
> Lady, hide no longer
> Beasts, remind humans
> To stay in truth
> Walking humbly
> We carry the light

At mention of the light, the hermit's tattoo flashed silver like the arrows of Iltir. At least it seemed to have done so, but the strange man turned and walked around the rocks and out of sight so quickly he seemed almost to vanish.

Those riding further back claimed to have seen a flash of lightning in the sky when all this happened but those near the hermit only wondered about what they had seen on his brow. Multiple conversations seemed to erupt at once, disputing the man's identity, message, and significance.

"Is your land filled with more of these madmen?" asked Furk in his most undiplomatic manner.

"We have never known him to be mad," Vjendar responded evenly, "though few can understand the man. Some say he is only a fool, others a holy man. He has never seemed threatening before today."

"He is like our Hranild," said Pjortan. "She is a seer among our people and her messages are always a puzzle yet never false."

Athnel added, "The stars are with him. I saw them shining within him."

"You are certain of this?" Furk challenged. "I saw no stars."

Pjortan immediately defended her. "I saw them too."

Furk backed down, muttering, "Well, I am no singer. Hmmph. And singers are not allowed to speak false. Indeed. Strange."

Ringskild ignored the nobles and looked to Ian, who seemed to be at the center of the hermit's message and whose face had gone quite pale. "Ian, are you all right?"

"I don't know. He said not to fear the darkness, but he terrified me. I don't know what I am afraid of and I want to be brave. You all have put your hopes in me and have given me so much of your very selves. I don't want to let you down. I don't think I mind giving my life for the Norrungs but I have no idea how to face the unknown and carry you all in my heart at the same time."

Hildir, one of the strongest of the Norrungs, spoke to Ian with an unwonted tenderness. "My brother, you cannot carry the whole world on your shoulders. We, who have journeyed with you, are not just sent to be your protectors. We carry you in our hearts and all our people do the same. Do not make us into a burden; we are here to uphold you. The bravest warrior knows fear and none of us knows what the next moment may bring.

"Ever since Hranild spoke, we have known a Stranger could bring hope. This hermit did not send us a message of fear. He reminds us the light is within us, and within you. We must not yield to the darkness. If the stars shine within our hearts, we must never forget they are there."

Ringskild, who had always known Hildir as a bit of a wild man himself, fierce and mighty in conflict, and reputedly quite a force with women as well, looked at her colleague in amazement.

"What?" he said, noticing her expression.

"You have spoken wisely, cousin," she replied. "Listen to him, Ian. We all know this journey has its dangers but Hranild, and Zhodor, and this hermit have all called us to hope, not fear. The singers and your brother wolf have assured us they speak for the stars, so let us trust their encouragement."

Ian heard his companions and felt a great fondness for them. Their words were strengthening. Still, at that moment just to be hugged by his mother back in Yorkshire seemed to be all he wanted. Or, perhaps Njothila. Why did she come to mind? Perhaps the scarf she had given him that he put about his neck when the clouds covered the blue vault of sky and cooled the land. The lad sighed deeply then assumed a smile.

"I was chilled by the hermit's words, but you are right, my friends. I shall try to keep the light in mind."

As the several discussions prompted by the hermit's actions continued, Vjendar urged the party to continue forward that they might reach Thioth.

Pjortan, who always kept an eye on Athnel, now asked her, "What, my lady, might the words mean: 'We must be who we are. Lady, hide no longer'?" He watched her thoughtful visage, waiting for a response, curious yet also delighting as always in the beauty of her many moods.

"What makes you think he spoke of me?" she challenged.

"Lady, do not mock me."

"I do not mock you, Pjortan. And I pray you, call me Athnel. We are alike singers and both serve the stars. Let there be no titles among us. It is in walking humbly that we carry the light."

Pjortan's heart faltered slightly at this new invitation. She had always been recognized as a most noble woman and seemed so far above the life of his forest home. Though Athnel had always spoken to him as an equal, still it was jarring to be invited into a new intimacy—an intimacy he had to admit he had come to long for.

"Athnel," he stuttered, accustoming his tongue to saying her name aloud. "I suppose he spoke of you because you were the lady next to Ian when he spoke. Do you hide who you are?"

"We are all hidden from one another, Pjortan, even from ourselves. Each of us is a great mystery known only to the stars. But yes, and I can see by your expression that you know I am skirting your question, I have not shown all of myself."

The Norrung seemed troubled and she hastened to continue. "Dear Pjortan, it is not that I would conceal myself from you, of all people. I am not sure whom I could trust more than you. But in matters as weighty and dangerous as the journey we are on it is not always wise to reveal everything at once, and certainly not to everyone."

Suddenly unguarded himself, Pjortan burst out, "I want to know everything about you."

Athnel's musical laugh was like water to one dying of thirst, so Pjortan took no offense. "I thought it was now obvious that even I do not know everything about myself. But fear not, I shall keep nothing from you. It seems…that sometimes…I have special gifts. Or powers. You could see the stars shining in the hermit just now, so you obviously have some special gifts yourself.

"Upon occasion, so long as I seek not to change the course of the world or do harm, I can call and things happen. There is some force that flows in the blood of my family. Frankly, I do not fully understand this, but perhaps the stars have spoken through this wild-haired man to let me know that these powers may be called upon soon."

"And that is all?"

"Is that not quite enough?"

"It is, my...Athnel."

She smiled at the lanky youth who rode beside her. Was it because he cared so much about her? Because he was so pure as to be easily satisfied? Because, in his hesitation, he called her "my Athnel"? She wondered if he had any realization of how much she had become his in the short time they had known each other, for no other person in her life had made her feel so free and so understood as this pious, large-hearted youth, Pjortan of Vorthall.

Though the western side of the River Road had widened after the narrows where the hermit had spoken, the Fiona still ran below and to the right. Vunskridh let out a shout, drawing the attention of those nearby to the flowing water. On its surface floated scores of fish, their bellies pale and shining in the wan afternoon light.

"What is this?" asked Vjendar, alarmed.

"It is death," replied Hildir. "First humans, then sheep, and now fish."

"Shorall save us," Pjortan muttered, invoking the Father of Life embodied in the constellation of the Fish.

Vjendar wondered aloud, "How shall people eat if the animals perish?"

Ringskild noticed a troubled look on Athnel's face, her usual pleasant demeanor now tightened with anxiety and frozen with tension. The singer stared intently at the dead fish flashing in the water as they flowed south with the current and her visage darkened.

"Enough!" she cried as though exploding in fury. Pjortan jerked in surprise and consternation and all nearby turned to look at her. Ringskild, who had witnessed the outer sign of the lady's struggle, was now filled with curiosity. Athnel, ignoring all around her and continuing to fix the waters with her gaze, raised one hand toward the Fiona and a golden glow seemed to envelope all her being. "Arise," she said, as though urging a vassal to cease kneeling. No vassal stood, however, only a fish suddenly flipped right side up. Vunskridh gasped. Another did the same, then more began to move and wiggle. The surface of the river roiled with action as the fish returned to life and began to swim about.

Pjortan was nearly oblivious to the fish, having kept his eyes on Athnel as she appeared, to his eyes, nearly transparent with a cloud of stars shining in the golden aura that enveloped her. Only as it faded did he turn toward the water to notice the transformation that had taken place.

Furk alone was unsurprised. He leaned toward Vjendar and muttered, "Our Lady Athnel is not just a singer but also an Usjeva, a Person of Power. Indeed. She travels with me for more than one reason, you see. Ahem."

"My lords," Athnel said with an edge of command still in her voice, "I believe we have someplace to be. Shall we resume our journey?"

"Indeed, my lady," replied Vjendar, signaling the company to resume its march northward.

Pjortan, his mind reeling from what he had just witnessed, said, "My lady hides no longer."

"Your Athnel," she corrected, "is who she is: no more, no less. And very mortal, I assure you, dear Pjortan."

With that the Norrung turned red from the tips of his ears to the soles of his feet. She smiled.

CHAPTER 34

Information is vitally important to any fighting force. The slightest change in enemy position, any shift in weather or diplomatic alignment, the odd stroke of fortune for good or ill—these traveled rapidly by word of mouth, along with endless rumors and idle speculation. News, gossip, and superstition were as much a part of warfare as weapons, training, strategy, and supplies. Furk's troops were thus all aware that a sorceress rode in their midst, though few had actually seen her powers manifested.

Lady Athnel's action on the River Road was accordingly noted by the Vothneli but caused little discussion. Vjendar's troops and the Norrungs, however, were filled with questions and all manner of theorizing flew in the afternoon air, though not among those riding within earshot of the Lady herself. Aware that she had become a center of attention, Athnel focused her own thoughts on the wonder of life, the horror of unnatural death, and thanksgiving to Shorall that she had been able to restore the fish and, she fervently hoped, those dependent upon them.

The River Road continued northward, winding its way through alternately rocky and forested terrain, eventually opening on a small plain surrounding the city of Thioth. Though the late afternoon sky was overcast, shafts of golden light broke through to highlight the walls and catch the flash of saffron and purple pennons flying in the breeze.

As before in Hlfin, a company rode out to greet and escort the expected force that approached the ancient town. Marshal Shlevor led the party of some two score, his unusual height evident as he rode toward Vjendar, Furk, Ringskild, and those who followed them. The Lord of Hlfin recognized Shlevor and explained to the others who he was. The man was of Tessian descent, his people coming from the southwestern lands beyond Hlv, Bjupazh, and the Westwaste. His skin was the color of dull reddish clay, his eyes black as obsidian and his hair dark as coal, long and straight. Today the marshal's impressive hair flowed free, hanging below his shoulder blades. A ritual scar marked each cheek in honor of his ancestors. In garb and practice he had become Thiothi, however. His tunic was parti-colored, the right side saffron and the left purple, typical of the livery of Lady Rushvin, his personal badge of crossed silver pikes on a field of black sewed over his heart. Shlevor's personal dignity stood out above the dignity of his office, the man's presence being more impressive than the gold chain about his neck and the gold mace in his right hand. He rode a handsome sorrel warhorse and was flanked by two heralds, one bearing the banner of Thioth, the other a peace pole.

The three leaders of the southern company advanced to meet him, similarly accompanied.

"In the name of Her Grace, the Lady Rushvin of Thioth, Star-blessed Lady of the Lands from here to the Mere, I greet you. May your coming be to the good of the people under her sway." With a slight pause the marshal continued. "My Lady, wishing no slight to all her worthy visitors, extends special greeting to her beloved nephew, my Lord of Hlfin."

Vjendar replied first, having been singled out and as the vassal of Thioth. "May peace, health, and prosperity attend my Lady Aunt and all her people." He then smiled warmly and added, "It is good to see you, Cousin." Shlevor nodded in acknowledgment. The respectful salutation "cousin," widespread in all the northern lands, implied a relatedness not defined by blood or marriage, as there was no such relationship between Shlevor and Vjendar.

The young lord of Hlfin continued, "It is my honor to present to you Lord Furk of Vothnell, our eastern neighbor, and Lady Ringskild of Vorthall from the people of the Norrungs who dwell far to the east in the Forest of Norrast. They come to Thioth in peace and in hopes of doing great good for all the peoples of our various lands.

"My Lord, my Lady, I am pleased to present to you the illustrious Shlevor, Lord Marshal of Thioth."

Ringskild, coming from a far less courtly society, was both intrigued and amused by the more florid diplomacy of the western lands. She was grateful for the discipline of a warmaiden when she heard herself introduced as a lady, a title rare among the Norrungs and usually reserved for the chieftain's wife. Even then it was not often used. Free-spirited forest folk preferred to call each other by name, appending patronymics for formality or using honor titles such as "grandmother," "uncle," or "cousin." The daughter of Ivor bore neither hostility nor disdain toward women titled lady, in fact she was quite fond of Athnel, but, if she herself were to be honored by a title, her preference would be "the mighty warmaiden" or "the skillful weaver."

Formalities and pleasantries ensued and the enlarged party then entered Thioth. Ian's eyes grew wide when he beheld the thickness of the outer walls and the immensity of the wooden gates reinforced with iron bars and huge bosses. His respect for the city's defenses grew when the circuitous path they followed led them through two more rings of defensive walls. Torthan was especially interested in all of this, never missing an opportunity to study both offensive and defensive strategy. He explained to Ian that Thioth was undoubtedly a very ancient city, having built new walls as it expanded and taking advantage of such expansion to create a triple defense of the inner city.

As the vanguard of the company reached the main square of Thioth, newcomers expected the party to halt. Next to a star watching tower stood an elegant castle, evidently of recent construction as the stones showed little weathering. The carvings were highly skilled and the saffron and purple banners of Thioth hung from its façade in abundance. Shlevor only led them past it as Vjendar explained.

"My Uncle, Lord Thjun, oversaw the final phases of the new Castle Thioth that you now see. My Lady, however, for all that she held him dear, has always preferred the Old Castle where her forebears ruled. I suspected that might be where we are headed and our path now confirms this."

Furk's bushy brows went up as his mouth went down in amazement. "Two castles, eh? My, my. Quite a luxury. Keeping one up is damned expensive. Hmmph. Amazing woman, no doubt. Ahem. Indeed."

The long file of the mixed company divided at this point. Shlevor's men directed Furk's and Vjendar's soldiers into the new castle while the principal members of those groups and all the Norrungs continued along a broad but winding way for a few more minutes before reaching the smaller square in front of the Old Castle. Far less elegant in style, this fortress stood (or loomed), a mass of stone, darkened and pitted by weather yet solid and honest.

The two singers had continued to flank Ian since the encounter with the hermit, perhaps to comfort him after his fright. The Anglo-Norrung lad suspected they might be protecting him with spells, though he noticed no unusual chants when they occasionally broke into song, nor had Athnel glowed with a golden light or done anything strange since raising fish from the dead. That was more than enough strangeness for any day. In any case, as Ian passed beneath the portcullis of the Old Castle he noticed Athnel stiffening in her saddle as though she had been startled or struck. At about the same time Vladje let out a single bark.

"What is it?" Ian and Pjortan queried in unison as Athnel glanced about the courtyard.

"I sensed something," she replied, "and now I am sure I have spotted it. We will talk of it soon enough." Athnel said no more and the two youths knew better than to ask further. Once inside the fortified entrance, Ian noted that some of its doorways had common barrel arches but others bore straight lintels hewn of large timbers or great slabs of rough-hewn rock. Everything about the fortress spoke of great age.

As soon as the riders had dismounted, Shlevor gestured toward a squire awaiting them near the entrance to the great hall. Nordil would have seen to the Norrung horses but the marshal assured him they would be well treated and that Lady Rushvin wished to meet all the forest dwellers. The visitors followed the squire through an antechamber and into the hall.

Though the hall was long and its clerestory windows admitted only a portion of the early evening light, the room was brightly lit by many well-placed torches and candles. At the far end Lady Rushvin sat in a great stone chair, softened by several velvet and goose-down cushions. Behind her hung a great tapestry with intricate designs of plants, trees, fruits, flowers, birds, and other animals illustrating the changing seasons. Gold and silver threads provided highlights, though the silver was dulled by age. In the center was a great shield with the arms of Thioth: a purple field with a saffron tressure, a silver wolf rampant regardant in the center and, upon the tressure, twelve silver stars. Guards and attendants stood on either side of the lady whose presence dominated the room.

She was a slight woman: small-boned, slender, and spry. Her hair was a blend of iron and silver, braided and coiled atop her head. A simple circle of silver sat on her brow, studded with garnets. Deep lines etched her face but the energy of her personality kept her from seeming old. Her gown was rich, its color matching the garnets of her diadem, its trim worked in silver threads. Rings bearing various precious and semi-precious stoned adorned bony fingers, the joints of which had swollen with the passage of seven decades. Softest leather formed her slippers.

A herald had barely struck the stone floor with his staff to announce the visitors when Rushvin leapt from her seat and rushed forward crying, "Nephew! How good it is to see you."

The lack of decorum startled the strangers. Even at Vorthall a chieftain would be more formal when visitors arrived. For his part, Vjendar hastened into his aunt's embrace. They exchanged hugs and kisses, then the old woman looked intently at her nephew's face. Satisfied, she turned to the others as Vjendar sought to restore propriety.

"My Lady Aunt, may I present to you Count Furk of Vothnell, Baron Torthan of Valcor, Baroness Athnel of Laoghar, Captain Djutar son of Fraek, and the company from Vorthall, chief city of the Norrungs who dwell in the Forest of Norrast far to the east.

"The captain of their quest is Lady Ringskild daughter of Ivor and foster-sister of their chieftain, Njothir son of Rathdar. I am told that few are called

Lord or Lady among the Norrungs, yet I am compelled to title her as such for she is surely a lady among her people or she would not be charged with such a perilous task. Her fellow servants of Vrotni are the warmaidens Meldreth daughter of Njuthar, Vunskridh daughter of Jornandir, and the warriors Volthir son of Brethir, Mechdar son of Thumnar, and Hildir son of Voltar. Jannir son of Stejni has acted as their guide, seeing that he is a widely traveled merchant, though we have now led him beyond regions known to him. Pjortan son of Drethor, like the Lady Athnel, is a star singer and Wulfdar son of Daghna is a healer wise in herb lore. Wilda daughter of Tjuva has handled mending, cooking, and general good nurture for their company and her husband Nordil son of Kendan serves as groom and falconer. You see Fjurthil the Fleet, his falcon, with him."

Here Vjendar drew a breath before continuing. The Norrungs meanwhile marveled that he could recite not only their names but the names of all their fathers. Respect for the young baron continued to grow at this demonstration of his thorough knowledge.

"Ian son of William from beyond the wood is the youngest among them though the center of their quest. He has evidently come to our lands from some other world, the stars only know how. From various prophecies it seems he is the one not of this world whose doom it is to destroy the dark fiend and all these others have gathered to help him do so. From his first appearance in our world he has been companioned by the most unusual member of their party. May I present to you one whom we suspect may be Morvladh himself returned to earth, Lord Vladje."

While each person introduced had nodded, bowed, or curtsied upon presentation, Vladje came forward, emitted a short bark, then returned to Ian's side.

"My friends and companions," Vjendar concluded, "I present to you Her Grace, Duchess Rushvin of Thioth, beloved of the people."

"Beloved of you, at any rate, Nephew," she retorted, then switched instantly into courtly speech. "My lords and ladies, friends and champions, cousins of feather and fur, you are most welcome here.

"These are dark days, as you all know. I have ruled here in this house of my ancestors since I was scarcely older than the young ladies of your company. That is a long time but, for the most part, it has been a happy time. This is a good land, along the Fiona River, and its people are good people. I was blessed in the companionship of my Lord Thjun for most of that time. Though I miss him sorely and long to join him on the star path, yet for my people I remain here.

"We are challenged on many fronts. The fiery death has passed through, as it has in your lands as well, taking a heavy toll. I would guess that a fourth to a third of my people have fallen to it, though in a few villages it has taken them all." At this, she seemed to withdraw for a few seconds into a private vision of such total loss, but soon resumed. "It is difficult to pick up life again after such devastation. Therein lies the second challenge.

"Though our lands are fertile and we have been spared both drought and flood of late, the will of the people is sapped. After so much loss, we find it hard to pick up the threads of daily existence and perform the necessary tasks of life. A collective malaise seizes us all. Even I have been tempted to stay abed more than once. Fortunately, I am too old and set in my ways to do so.

"The third obstacle in the way of resuming a happy life is the star-cursed demon. I have never confused it with our lack of will. To me it seems to feed on that, yet operates on a darker level. Strange curses have seemed to fall across the land. First there was sheep's death, as we call it, though it has been happening to people as well. I have seen the results of both and hope never to see the like again. This very morning our fishers and river folk reported a mass death of the fish in the Fiona, though there was no evidence of poison in the waters. Dogs have lapped at it with no ill effect, though I have ordered the people to drink from wells and cisterns rather than draw water from the river, just to be safer.

"This Chegjan also seems to eat at human minds, driving all reason and order from them. Riots, murders, jealousies, suicides, and all manner of wretchedness have seemed to spring up at random. The chronicles tell of such things, of course, but not so often as we see them now. Terror strikes at the heart of every dwelling. Who will fall victim next? Who will go mad?

Who will suffer because of the madness? Whom can one trust anymore? And I have heard even worse things but prefer not to speak of them.

"The fourth challenge is similar to the third but it is no demon, unless demons take human form. That would be Bulçar of Fjorn, my neighbor to the north. Every imaginable corruption is his. Wherever the power of Bulçar or his sons—may none of them behold the stars again—wherever, as I was saying, their power is felt, there too hearts quake with terror. I almost feel that it is easier to accept the horrors wrought by a demon, for that is beyond all reason, but when such monstrous evils are done through the wickedness of a human heart, if Bulçar and his spawn even have one among them—that is simply too awful to contemplate. And because we are weakened by the first three challenges, the Bastard of Fjorn (and I use the term advisedly) is now reaching into my lands and harming my people. As if it were not bad enough that we receive those who flee from him, most of them damaged beyond any use in rebuilding human society.

"So, there you have it. A weary ruler's or, if you prefer, an old lady's, list of woes. Lastly, I share in confidence that I fear that one or more in my court are in Bulçar's employ, and that, above all, breaks my heart.

"Having said all that, my friends, you must know that I am glad to see you. Any who would stand against the world's evils are people I rejoice to call friends. Be welcome. Let us refresh ourselves and talk some more."

At that signal several pages came forward to lead the visitors to their rooms and a short nap before supper.

The meal that evening was like the castle: solid, unremarkable, and reassuring. In the course of conversation Torthan complimented Rushvin on her choice of castle, noting that, though the new castle was indeed beautiful to behold, the older structure was more solid and easier to defend.

"You have a good eye, Baron," the lady replied. "Innovation is a good thing and I admire those with new ideas and the courage to pursue them. My Thjun was one of those, working closely with everyone from master masons and carpenters to every manner of artisan in bringing that lovely work into being. How it delighted him! I think there was not a single laborer in the entire work that he did not talk to. It is a work of beauty and I feel some guilt since he meant it as a tribute to the beauty he saw in me.

"Alas, it reminds me too much of him when he is no longer walking beneath the stars to share it with me. We mortals are strange beings who can endure many things, yet the pain of love can be too much for us. But that is neither here nor there. I choose to live where my people have lived for centuries now. There is wonder in the new and often great good but there is often great good in the old as well, and comfort. I am happy in these halls. And you are correct in noting that they are well built and easy to defend. I know more ways in and out of here than someone a fourth my age could ever guess. Perhaps the times we know, dark as they may be, cannot compare to the troubles our forebears faced. It seems my beloved Thioth was built for defense more than anything, a sad commentary on our history but a reality for a city on a plain."

Torthan responded to the lady's analysis by adding that though the need for defense was unfortunate the work of her ancestors was thoughtful and thorough, a tribute to their intelligence and engineering. She smiled and said, "You are gracious. I am beyond flattery whether directed at me or my ancestors, but your words are true and your eyes sincere. I thank you."

If Torthan's eyes were sincere, Rushvin's were keen and her mind quite alert. All could see that link between the elder and her nephew Vjendar. Her age and his bland features could easily lead someone to underestimate them, which sometimes worked to their advantage. Neither seemed to miss a thing. Just as the young baron of Hlfin was thorough in his knowledge of everything and everyone to come to his attention, so the duchess of Thioth stayed well informed. Peveç and Vjendar had both done their work, perhaps along with others, and she was fairly familiar with the demon chasers and their quest before they had arrived.

"Healer," Lady Rushvin addressed Wulfdar with her usual lack of formality, "I am very glad to see that you are among the party from Vorthall. I pray you spend some time with the servants of Vuchtall in my service following our meal. There is much wisdom and art in your craft and I hope you will be able to learn from one another. I have instructed them to do whatever we can to provide you with resources for the trials that lie ahead. My heart tells me that if you succeed in facing the Foul Thing then you and your companions will see much suffering and horror. May the Great Bear, Healer of the Stars, guide you in those moments."

"I thank your Grace," Wulfdar replied.

Rushvin inquired of Furk concerning the lands around Vothnell, asking details of some of the battles in which he garnered fame, and thanking him for offering to accept excess refugees that her lands could not adequately accommodate. Gratified by such attention, he took a liking to the Lady of Thioth and, in his mind, forgave her for not addressing him first.

The meal was a leisurely one as Rushvin had many questions for members of the party. She was especially curious about the tribal society of the eastern forest, so unlike the feudal world she knew, and managed to elicit a few Norrung songs from the group. Meldreth was delighted but surprised that the old woman wanted to hear one of the bawdy songs so dear to the warmaiden's heart and Rushvin laughed warmly at the suggestive verses.

Before the especially ribald conclusion, a deep growl interrupted the song. All eyes turned to Vladje, who had hitherto been quietly seated between Ian and Wilda, contentedly dining on meat scraps the two had been sharing with him, as had one of the Thiothi servants. Now the wolf was fixedly staring at a man who had entered the room to bring a message to Lady Rushvin. It was Vorn, the lady's steward, a man of many years service. Vorn was of average height and build, easily spotted by his shoulder-length blond hair, now mixed with gray. He had become a steward rather than a fighting man because of a minor birth defect; his left hand was misshapen.

At the sound of the wolf, Vorn turned his attention from his lady toward the muscular bundle of dark mottled fur now bristling with hostility. Evidently Vorn was not so well informed as Rushvin herself and quite unprepared to encounter a hostile wolf in the castle dining hall. His expression gradually changed from startled to curious to anxious.

"The Lord Wolf seems unhappy, Vorn," said the duchess, watching her steward closely.

"Indeed, your Grace, his unhappiness is most evident. I cannot say I am altogether happy to see your Grace in the presence of a wild beast. Are you sure you are safe? There appears to be no tether on him."

"I feel quite safe with him around. He is no ordinary wolf."

"As you wish, my Lady. I was merely about to confirm some of the provisions for tomorrow morning, but perhaps this is an inopportune time."

"This is an excellent time. Did you have questions about requirements to support this company on their quest?"

"Yes, your Grace, and what they might need depending on the path they take."

Vladje took a few steps in Vorn's direction, an action that may have given rise to the sweat appearing on the steward's brow. The sight of bared fangs approaching could hardly have given the impression that things were going well.

"What is this wolf doing here?" he asked nervously.

"What are you doing inquiring about my guests' path?" retorted Rushvin. "That should be of no interest to you." Vladje's growl deepened as she continued. "Unless you wish to report it to others, perhaps. How long have you been with me, Vorn?"

"Twenty-three years, your Grace, in faithful service."

"A long time indeed, time to build mutual trust. I have trusted you to manage things according to my wishes. You, in turn, have trusted my wishes. Yet, I have of late noticed you asking more questions than usual. This raises questions in my mind."

"Surely your Grace does not doubt my loyalty?" said Vorn, now visibly shaken.

"Possibly not, but loyalty to whom? Do you still trust me, Vorn?"

"Of course, your Grace!"

"Then would you please approach the Lord Wolf and extend your right hand toward him."

"Your Grace, this is madness. He appears ready to eat me alive."

"I will presume not to take that as a slander against my sanity, Vorn, but if you trust me you will do as I ask."

All blood seemed to drain from the steward's face. With eyes widened in terror he took the first step toward Vladje. Norrungs and Thiothi were all on full alert as the quaking man took a second and third step. Vladje matched him pace for pace until they were six feet apart. The wolf had stopped growling but his lips were still retracted to reveal ready fangs. As he attempted the fourth step, Vorn turned and bolted, crying, "I can't." Vladje leapt upon the fleeing man's back as Rushvin stood and shouted, "Vladje! Down."

To the amazement of all, with the possible exception of Rushvin herself, the wolf backed off before drawing blood, and stood alert. Vorn's retreat had been cut short as he faced a wall of drawn daggers.

"Did you think I could not protect you?" Rushvin accused, "or that this unusual creature, who is neither tame nor wild, would harm you without reason? What did you fear, Vorn? The judgment of nature? Or mine?"

"I could not trust a beast, your Grace," the miserable man said even as a stain of fear spread down his trouser leg.

"And yet I did trust him, Vorn, with no prior proof. I was proven right, for he obeyed me while you did not. How foolish we are to think we are superior to our fellow creatures. I fear you may have made a great mistake, Vorn. After so many years with me, you have, I suspect, trusted yourself to a far more dangerous beast, the Bastard of Fjorn. Perhaps I am wrong, but if you are not in league with him then you have allied with one of his sons. They are all less than human and worse than beasts. You should have trusted me. And the wolf who is a guest in my home." She then spoke to the Thiothi guards who surrounded the hapless Vorn.

"Send him to Master Brindar. I will know all." With that command the Lady of Thioth consigned her steward to the dungeon master for interrogation by torture. Her suspicions were confirmed within the hour and two accomplices were also apprehended.

In the meantime conversation resumed, though with an added tension. Rushvin thanked Vladje for his outstanding and faithful service to her people. "Young Ian," she added, "the stars have clearly blessed you to send such a guide and protector. I am likewise impressed by your human companions. May faithfulness be rewarded. I pray that Hjelgi will lead you to your destination and Weltar grant you wisdom in the time of trial. The stars keep you all."

The Thiothi joined their lady in this blessing by raising their cups and drinking to success.

Rushvin continued, "Speaking of the blessed stars, how is it that your company is blessed with two singers?"

"The Council of Vorthall, deeming this dangerous quest to be more spiritual than military in nature," Pjortan began, "felt that a singer might offer some guidance and protection. As our chief singer is my Uncle Thomdar, he suggested my name and I was sent."

Furk bristled and hmmphed at this lessening of military import. Mechdar added that Pjortan was not only young but modest. "Pjortan here was not named because of avuncular favoritism, my Lady, but because he is highly learned and devout in spite of his tender years. We are very glad to have him watching over our souls and bodies."

At the words of the seasoned warrior Pjortan blushed.

Furk seized the moment to speak on his own behalf. "Lady Athnel of Laoghar is likewise young but is also devout and possessed of a gifted mind. Indeed. She is also, as was demonstrated this afternoon, a lady of power and has served me and my troops on several occasions. Ahem. This most unusual wolf," he could not bring himself to use the affectionate name Vladje, "has so far allowed only three people to touch him and Lady Athnel is one of these. Yes. I would not be surprised if she spoke in the tongue of wolves as she seems to communicate with animals."

Rushvin responded, "I have never been blessed with such interesting guests as tonight. Vladje has spent most of the meal between Ian and Wilda. Am I to assume they are the other two?"

"We are, your Grace," said Wilda. "And he saved me once from a fate worse than death. I owe him more than the scraps I feed him." As she said this she ruffled the fur of the wolf's shoulders, then leaned over to kiss him on the forehead.

Volthir observed that had he attempted what Wilda just did he would withdraw without half his face. "For all that I am fond of our brother wolf, he never lets us forget that he is his own creature. Several of us almost lost fingers for attempted friendliness."

"I shall not press my luck," said Rushvin. "I am most grateful that in the moment of trial he served me faithfully and will ask no more of this noble animal. Thanks to his intervention, I believe it is now safe to discuss your plans for I trust my people still in this room. I believe you intend to head west after leaving Thioth."

"We do, your Grace," replied Ringskild, speaking for the Norrungs. "The route we discussed with your most helpful nephew would take us north only so far as Othen and then west toward the Ulava River."

"That, indeed, is the easiest path west, though I would spare you another step closer to Fjorn if it made sense turn west from here," Rushvin confirmed. "Othen, however, remains under our control and you should be all right. Do be cautious, my children, for you are near the border."

The fond address was accepted by the company as the noble lady was old enough to be the mother or grandmother of almost everyone in the room.

Athnel spoke next. "Your Grace, I noticed a most unusual architectural feature at the entrance to your hall."

"Do you mean the star stone, dear?"

"I believe so. It is the stone above the entrance?"

"Yes. They say it fell from the heavens in my great-grandfather's days, though I have never noted anything unusual about it except its source in the sky."

"Appearances are so often deceiving. I felt its presence before I spotted it, so my guess is that it comes from the stars with great power."

"What might this power be?" Rushvin queried.

"That is precisely the question I ask myself. Perhaps it has protected your family and this castle, perhaps it bears some message from the stars. I have no idea yet but with your permission I should like to examine it first thing in the morning."

"Of course, dear Athnel. I am sure a scaling ladder or something could be arranged, though it might not be seemly for a lady to climb it."

Taking no offense, Athnel replied with a smirk, "I think I can find some men to do the mounting." At this Meldreth's hearty laugh relieved a moment of tension as not a few men and women had blushed at Athnel's remark.

"I am sure you can," chuckled Rushvin.

Reassured by very earthy and familiar thoughts, the diners concluded their meal and retired for the night.

CHAPTER 35

Before retiring, Athnel took advantage of the moon, one night past full, and walked about, accompanied by Mechdar. She appreciated the older warrior's ability to keep company with little conversation and she preferred not to have Pjortan along this time. While Athnel enjoyed and delighted in the company of her fellow singer, she was also aware that her feelings for him could distract her from careful observation and clear thought.

Wigdor the Chieftain was in full prominence as the zodiac made its annual procession. Humming part of a hymn to Wigdor, the singer offered a prayer to the god of justice that affairs would be sorted aright and truth prevail in this world of confusing appearances and uncertain loyalties. As she did so Athnel found herself grieving that someone who had served Rushvin for many years could turn against his liege lady.

After noting what she could of the patterns of the stars, Athnel spent almost an hour looking at the star stone in the cool light of the moon. Honoring both Athnel's calling and mood, Mechdar kept watch silently as the singer seemed to drift into a trance. What she saw or heard or felt during this time he had no idea and when her vigil ended they retired without discussing it.

The Old Castle of Thioth buzzed with activity well before dawn the next morning. A ladder had been found for Athnel's purpose and she wasted no time deciding who should climb to observe the star stone up close. Pjortan exulted to be her choice, unaware that it was only in his role as a star singer that he had been selected and not because of any special feelings she might, and did, have for him.

Having ascended some sixteen rungs, he looked closely at the stone and almost lost his balance as the world faded and he found himself drawn into the depths of the stone. This was not so much a matter of natural transparency, as might be the case with a crystalline structure, but more a mysterious quality possessed by this strange "chunk of sky" embedded over the portal. Pjortan had felt himself drawn both into the stone and into the depths of the heavens, his spirit rushing past stars and into an endless void. His neck began to move as though he might be dizzy and shouts from below pulled him back into the solid immediacy of the present place and moment.

Athnel had intended to ask him to do more but felt it would be risky. "Thank you, Pjortan. Come down and share what happened."

Reluctant and relieved, Pjortan descended and tried to put into words what he had just seen and sensed. "It is both marvelous and terrible, I wanted to go on forever," he said.

"Was there any message in the stone?" Athnel asked.

"None that I discerned," he replied with a feeling that he had disappointed her. "Only a sense of great power."

"That may be all we learn, dear Pjortan, but I could not keep from investigating. Ian, would you give it a try?" At these words, Pjortan's heart sank and Athnel's calling him "dear" lost its effect. He had failed.

Athnel continued addressing her words to Ian. "Since you are the chosen stranger, there might be a message for you. But it may be wise not to look too closely at the stone."

Ian climbed the ladder, trying to ignore the chuckles of warriors who observed that Lady Athnel seemed to choose the pretty young boys to do the "mounting." For her part, Athnel regretted her wit the night before while Ian and Pjortan both blushed.

"Now what do I do?" the youth asked upon reaching the stone, distinguishable from its surroundings by its strange shiny texture and unusual coloring.

"Try putting your ear to it and see if it speaks. It would not be ordinary words, you must listen with the ears of your heart," Athnel instructed.

Ian leaned closer, turning his head to the side and pressing his ear to the stone. Those below fell silent as though listening with him. A full minute passed with Ian willing his breath to slow lest it drown out any message. Still he heard nothing and so reported to those below.

"Perhaps a different contact, Ian," said Athnel. "Place a hand on it and close your eyes, but don't get dizzy."

The lad gave this a try, but still nothing happened.

"One last thing," the lady singer shouted up to the waiting youth. "Place your forehead against the stone and in your mind let yourself be one with the stone."

Ian did as she said. This sort of mystical practice was all very strange to him. Nothing in his life on earth came close to this and his life in Vorthall was aimed toward the very practical trade of woodworking. He would have felt far more comfortable with a mallet and chisel in his hands, shaping a table leg. Still, he gave it his best effort. Allowing his forehead to touch the cold stone lightly, he inhaled deeply then imagined releasing his being to the stone as he exhaled.

A couple of breaths later Ian sensed a vibration, yet it was not a bodily perception. His eyes were closed and the sun had not risen, but it was as though he had been lying in a field and the sun had come from behind a cloud, light flooding his being through closed lids. This went beyond sunlight, however, and seemed to grow in brightness moment by moment.

Had he been seeing this with his bodily eyes the young man would have been blinded for life, he was sure of it. Instead it seemed to keep growing and he was becoming one with it. Everything else melted away. Ian lost all sense of time and place. There was no ladder holding him up, no cold stone against his brow, no companions observing him from below. There was no dark demon awaiting him, no England and family lost in his past. His skin no longer defined his physical boundary in the world. There was no world yet all worlds seemed present. There was everything and nothing. Ian and the Light were all that existed. He was floating in the Light. He was the Light and the Light was Ian. Ian and the Light were all things.

As he floated beyond all time and place, Ian lost consciousness and control. Fortunately, those below were watching him closely and the strong arms of the Norrungs caught him as he plummeted from the ladder toward the courtyard below. They laid him on a nearby bed of straw and Wulfdar and Athnel crowded in, the one to assist and the other to question.

The expression on Ian's face was one of pure bliss. As his eyelids parted, the eyes within seemed to drift out of focus at first, gradually coming to rest on Wulfdar's concerned face. Ian's mouth formed a silly grin as though he were quite drunk and he muttered, "Beautiful."

"Ian," Wulfdar called gently.

"Lovely," said the youth, rolling his head to smile at Athnel this time.

"Yes, she is lovely," said the healer, "but I am nobody's idea of beautiful. What happened?"

The dazed Ian replied, "No. You are all beautiful. Everything is beautiful. Light is beautiful. I am beautiful. The world is beautiful."

Athnel cut this litany short. "What did you see, Ian?"

"Light. Lots of light. Wonderful light. Everything light."

"And how do you feel now?" the healer questioned.

"All light," Ian replied, "wonderful." The intoxicated grin returned and Ian resembled nothing so much as a lad who cannot hold his mead.

Wulfdar persisted. "What were you doing when you saw the light?"

Ian looked puzzled for a moment. "Don't know. Just light. No, cold." At that he put a hand on his forehead. "Rock. Star stone. I was one with the star stone."

"That's right, Ian," said Athnel. "You were trying to see what the star stone might tell you."

"It told me I am Light," he answered, "there was nothing but Light. We are all Light. Everything is Light."

Athnel smiled. "Yes, Ian, that's right. That is why we sing to the stars. Let's get some breakfast into you. Do you think you can get up?"

"Of course," he said with all the confidence of youth.

"Just be careful as you do so," cautioned Wulfdar. "And I am going to give you a draught of something to go with your breakfast, just to help you get your feet solidly back on the ground."

"Whatever you say, Wulfdar, you are the healer."

"Good. I wish more patients followed my orders. I am relieved you know who I am."

"Silly, wise old man," Ian said, still sounding woozy, "Of course I know you."

They then ate heartily and prepared to depart.

Lady Rushvin was not altogether through with the demon chasers, however. Having lost her two sons, a daughter-in-law, and two grandchildren to the plague, she had no one in sight upon whom to bequeath her jewelry.

"My beloved heir, young nephew Vjendar here, will have fine things to give his wife," said the elder ruler then added, after a stern glance and a pause, "when he gets around to finding one. For now, I beg the ladies among you give joy to an old woman's heart."

With that she proceeded to give gifts worthy of a princess. Pjortan beamed when Rushvin gave Athnel a necklace with multiple strands of gold beads and pearls. To Vunskridh she gave a silver ring set with a great amethyst and to Meldreth a carved amber brooch. Wilda received earrings of carnelian and silver and Nordil kissed her after she put them on, swearing she was the prettiest wife in all the lands about the Mere. She then poked her husband in the ribs and reminded him he was supposed to say the prettiest woman in the entire world, then the two laughed.

Last among the women, but obviously not least, was Ringskild. She was given a tiara of gold set with stones of green jade. When the warmaiden protested that she was not the noble sort of lady to wear such a thing, Rushvin reproached her. "My dear, you lead a brave company on a dangerous quest on behalf of your people and all the people of these lands. I cannot imagine a nobler woman. Besides that, I wager that if you cannot become the chief of the Norrungs you may well become a chief's wife. I pray you remember me when you have occasion to wear this and wear it proudly."

At mention of becoming a chief's wife Ringskild was not the only Norrung to think of her foster-brother and chieftain, Njothir. Rushvin's scenario seemed plausible enough and there was general chuckling among the forest folk.

To all the men among the nobles and the Norrungs Rushvin gave fine silver daggers in skillfully tooled leather sheaths. Two of the men received something other than a dagger. To Furk the lady gave a noble cape of mink trimmed with ermine. "This," she said, "belonged to my dear Thjun, a fine husband and warrior. I am sure he would be proud to see you wear it."

Furk stammered and sputtered in his usual manner but showed his gratitude quite diplomatically.

"Ian," the lady concluded, "you have been sent on a very different mission than any warrior I have ever heard of. It seems to be important that you are not a warrior. Because of this, I felt a dagger would not be the proper gift. I know you are aware of how dangerous your quest is and how important to all of us. If I were in your place I should wonder if I had a future after all this. For that reason I want you to ride from here with hope and with and old woman's blessing. Here is something for your future bride, whoever she may be, when you return home."

With that she pressed into the youth's hand a beautifully wrought gold ring with three garnets nestled among small gold leaves.

"It is beautiful, my lady."

"And so shall your wife be," Rushvin replied, then kissed his forehead before he could even utter his thanks, which he did upon recovering from the gift and the kiss.

There was one darker matter to attend to. It had been established the night before that the family of the traitorous steward Vorn was innocent of his betrayal and had no knowledge of it. Given all that had transpired, Rushvin dared not allow a potential for conflicted feelings to grow in her court so she decided that Vorn's wife, now widow, Mirdel and her three children be sent with Vjendar to be placed under the charge of Peveç in Fimmoth. There they will be treated well but under virtual house arrest. Marshal Shlevor handed the weeping woman, her son who was reaching adolescence and her two younger daughters over to Vjendar's troops. Rushvin embraced Mirdel before her departure, saying simply, "It is for your own safety."

"Now, off with all of you," she concluded, "and Hjelgi guide you!"

Saving time after such extensive farewells, Pjortan and Athnel sang the Hymn to the Dawn from their saddles, and the demon chasers headed north.

If one asked the stars they might tell of vast masses of ice moving with the slowness of geologic time across portions of the land, dragging and tumbling immense rocks with them. Peoples along the Fiona River only knew their terrain varied from place to place and the River Road became stony more often as one journeyed north.

Travelers from Thioth to Othen thus crossed a mixture of grassy meadows, riparian woodlands, rocky terrain, and occasional barren stretches, all within a few hours. As the habitat varied often, so did the music of birds near the road and the activities of small diurnal animals. When Vladje took exercise he might find himself snacking on a mouse darting among grasses or a lizard basking a bit too long on a warm boulder.

The morning seemed lazy enough and the scattered clouds indicated no storm yet all were on alert as they drew closer to Fjorn. There was time for idle chatter and ponderous discussion, however, and so the early hours passed.

Wulfdar revealed that the healers of Thioth opened to him their great store of herbs and remedies and that he found himself impressed. His saddlebags now contained several new herbs, ointments, and potions, most for the body but also a couple for the mind. The Thiothi had also taught him a new set of touch points on the body to ease headache and a simple chant for harvesting gnordwort. After so much late-night learning, Wulfdar caught several naps in the saddle as they rode, as did Athnel whose energy was low from her moonlit vigil.

Feathers in the hair of the armed party and prominent peace poles did little to diminish the apprehension of the locals as the company neared Othen. This was border territory at the northern limit of Lady Rushvin's sway and the threat from Fjorn was very real. Easily extended trust was a luxury for other regions; here it could be a fatal error. Scouts on loan from Thioth were able to reassure Thiothi soldiers posted in that area and bear their lady's greetings to Baron Raftor of Othen.

Othen was close to Thioth, not the usual day's journey from the last city. The travelers thus reached it by late morning. They exchanged courtesies and news with Raftor, a pleasant but anxious man weighed down by great responsibility. Black ringlets surrounded his bald spot and continued down to form a thick beard. He gratefully accepted a sealed message from Lady Rushvin, then warned the strangers that Bulçar's forces had been making frequent sorties across the Othen Stream border. It was impossible to make any border impervious, so Raftor and his forces did the best they could, working with loyal Thiothi to prevent incursions when possible and deal with the ones that happened. Skirmishes were frequent and bloody.

"If I were you, I should avoid the roads near the stream and take the Drush Pass. It is not so easy a path but one less likely to be riddled with the

225

Bastard's minions," Raftor advised. He quickly sketched a map showing them how to find the pass and continue west toward the Ulava River.

By noon the company had thus turned west and slightly toward the south, lunching on food they had brought from Thioth. They found themselves headed into a valley of stone and scrub with gradually narrowing walls. Scouts had gone ahead as the passage would eventually be quite narrow and no one wanted to take chances. Lunch was forgotten when the scouts returned in haste.

"My Lords, we think you should see this," was all that was said before the general company. Furk and Torthan, Ringskild and Hildir rode in front, following the scouts beyond where the path curved about a rocky spur. This vanguard drew to a halt where the scouts indicated a log by the road. The buzz of flies revealed it was not a thick branch on the ground but a man's leg, cut off at the groin and left lying there.

"The flies have come but it is still moist," Hildir observed.

"What butchery is this?" the horrified Torthan mused as Furk spluttered into a rage.

"By Wigdor and Vrotni, hmmph, some blackguard will pay for this," he swore.

"If we find who did it," Ringskild added pessimistically.

"There is more," a scout interjected, to be met by Torthan's quiet, "Gracious stars, no."

The scout spoke truly, however, and not far beyond the severed leg was a hand, the hand of a young man already hardened by labor and marked by calluses. By now the company had caught up with the leaders and all proceeded paying special attention to what might be lying along the way. The other hand soon appeared and some carrion crows had to be chased from the arm further along. The deliberate scattering of body parts and the sheer act of imagining what the victim may have gone through roused tempers among a force now eager to remove their peace feathers and do battle against such villainy. The second leg and other arm were a little farther to the side of the road but still visible as though an obvious taunt or dare were being made. At last the man's headless torso was seen propped up on a boulder as though watching the road without eyes, the bloodied tunic so dirty and stained one could scarce tell it had once been a dull green.

"I have no remedies for this evil," said Wulfdar, his heart sinking and all his new medicines from Thioth seeming worthless.

Wilda reproached the look of despair she saw on the healer's face. "My cousin healer, the only remedy we have is to do as much good as we can in this short life. You have sworn your life to do what you can, no mortal can do more."

Her words were cut short when a great string of oaths erupted at the head of the procession. The final fleshy part of what had recently been a man gaped with mouth and eyes swarming with black flies as it stood no longer on a neck but a rude stick. It seemed as though every deity in the heavens was named and profaned as seasoned warriors expressed their outrage at such treatment. There was no honor in treating a human in such a manner. A beast may kill and eat with no feeling for the creature it fed on but no beast performed this sort of wanton cruelty.

Hoping to see no further butchery, the party moved on. Somewhat more than a mile later they found a dead tree on the slope above the dusty road. In one piece, as near as could be seen, a woman was tied to it, whether alive or dead none yet knew. The warmaidens urged their horses toward her and were relieved when she stirred slightly at the sound of their approach. Vunskridh gave the woman some water from her water skin, noting the many bruises on the woman's face and arms and the torn gray dress that left her breasts bare before the elements and any who might pass by. Meldreth cut the rude ties that held the battered woman and helped Ringskild hold her up. As the poor lady regained consciousness, her eyes glanced about her in panic and she began to scream, then gradually calmed when she saw the anxious but kind faces of women before her.

"It's all right, sister," said Vunskridh, using an especially intimate form of address. "Your attackers are not here. We are friends."

"Have you seen my husband?" the woman asked frantically.

"We cannot say," Ringskild replied cautiously. "Should we have seen him?"

"We had visited my mother and were returning to Othen by this way. Suddenly we found ourselves surrounded by horrible men. I think they were from Fjorn but we believe anything bad about them these days. They kept my husband behind and brought me here. Then...."

Meldreth held the traumatized woman and stroked her back. "There, there, we know what evil men will do."

"They...they said they would come back for me!"

"They shall not have you, sister," Ringskild proclaimed. "You are with us now."

"But what have they done to my husband? He is such a good man."

"We will look for him," Torthan replied, having drawn nigh. "What does he look like?"

"He is an ordinary man to others but not to me. Of medium size, with strong hands, a scant beard, and a wonderful head of long brown hair. His trousers are a dun color, like most folks, and his tunic was a sort of mossy green."

"Yes," said Ringskild, choosing forthrightness, "we have seen him. He is not in the hands of those evil men but he journeys now to the halls of the Dark Queen."

At news of her husband's death the new widow let out a frightful wail and began to sob uncontrollably. The warmaidens led her gently toward Wilda's cart and helped her settle in. Before she would mount the cart, however, the woman flung herself to the earth and smeared handfuls of dirt upon her moist cheeks to proclaim her loss. Vladje had anticipated her presence and vacated his place near Wilda. Wulfdar was brought to assist the woman and he managed to have her swallow a tincture mixed in mead. Meldreth tied her horse to the cart and rode beside the grieving woman.

"They can't have gone far," thundered Furk, "I say we punish the wretches. Forward!"

And upon that order the company proceeded toward the narrows of the Drush Pass.

Filled with righteous indignation and a fresh blood-lust, Furk and other leaders spurred their horses as they pursued the westward road into the narrows of Drush Pass. Vladje advanced with them, dashing up the slope as the warriors rode through the twisting canyon where they had to pass single file. The vanguard had just made it through when all were alerted by the sound of rocks falling. From the middle of the company and still east of the narrowest passage, Wilda watched helplessly as what proved to be a large rockslide descended and blocked the pass, burying some of those riding just before her. The frantic woman barely calmed the horse pulling her wagon amid the rearing and neighing of war steeds all around her. As the panic of the sudden halt and ensuing collisions subsided, warriors dismounted and strong hands turned to the work of digging out those caught in the slide. A couple of riders who caught the least of it were saved, but the third was no longer breathing. It was Jannir, who had been the Norrungs' guide through so much of this journey. For all the gifts he had with him, Wulfdar could only shake his head in acknowledgment that there was no medicine to call back from the star path.

As Wilda recognized the battered and broken form of the merchant, covered in dirt and blood, it felt as though time had stopped and even her heart had paused its beating. He who had traveled so far and so often pursuing his trade would not return this time to his loving family. Wilda thought of Jannir's wife, Vellen, who spent so many months of every year waiting for her man's return. Remembering to breathe again, Wilda drew a deep breath and returned to the rush of time. At first she mouthed an almost silent, "No," then cried in protest, "No!" She had scarcely begun to lament Jannir when her thoughts turned to her beloved Nordil who had entered the pass. Had he made it through or perished like Jannir? She had now way of knowing. And then her cries rose to the stars, inviting Dorgal the Weeper to join her laments.

Meldreth, who had sought to comfort the woman whose husband had been butchered now embraced Wilda and joined her keening, even as Volthir assisted Wulfdar in straightening and cleaning the mangled body of their comrade. Athnel, knowing the limits of her powers, was present as a singer and not a sorceress. She began to chant Ushni's Lullaby, the hymn that welcomes the Dark Queen's children home. Pjortan joined in the second line as they sang Jannir's way on the first steps of his final journey.

> Come, my children, and do not fear
>
> The journey home, the path of peace....

Lacking ashes, the Norrungs used dust to smear their cheeks in mourning. The companions of Vorthall had become close during their travels and they would now do the family's part for their fallen guide. As soldiers went around them, seeking a way above or around the impasse that had only recently been their door to the west, the forest dwellers did what they could until Jannir's pyre could be prepared.

A dozen of the vanguard made it through the narrows. As the stony cascade was falling, Vunskridh wheeled and gave the alert. With dust still flying she levered rocks aside with her lance and others joined in. They were able to free Nordil and Furk's sergeant Miglac who were bruised but not badly harmed. Baron Grath, another of Furk's vassals, had a badly damaged shoulder but was pulled out alive. It was soon evident that anyone deeper in the rocky torrent had no hope. Two excellent war steeds had to be put down, an act of mercy that always pained Nordil, who loved horses only slightly less than he loved his wife, who even now was keening over the death of Jannir at the other end of the narrows. Nordil asked the stars to watch over her, trusting his memory that she would be far enough back to have missed the landslide.

Caught up in the urgency of the situation, the small party that had made it through to the far side of the slide was not prepared for the sudden arrival of others from the west. The keen ears of the Vothneli sergeant Trno first noticed approaching hoof beats. Swords were drawn and all were on alert as the first riders appeared.

Beneath their armor they wore red tunics, marking them as warriors of Fjorn. They wore no feathers and bore no peace pole. Ringskild and Furk assessed the approaching enemy, noting that they approached at a leisurely pace and were not charging. Were they that confident?

Indeed they were, for the western end of the narrows widened quickly into a broad canyon and it quickly became evident that more than three dozen Fjorni faced them and they had no retreat. Was this the place to make a brave and suicidal stand? In most circumstances that would be Ringskild's choice, taking as many of the foe with her as possible. Her duty now was to a larger quest and she held her fighters back while Furk blustered but made no move to attack.

At the head of the Fjorni rode a large young man on a black mount. He had an outer tunic of blood red with the black head of a lion emblazoned upon it surrounded by a golden orle. This would be Bulçar's eldest son, Njlvac, of whom the demon chasers had heard much, none of it good.

Ringskild took the initiative when Njlvac was within hailing distance.

"Firstborn of Fjorn, what brings you to the lands of Thioth?"

"I might ask the same of you, strangers, for you are no more Thiothi than I."

"We travel here with the blessing of Lady Rushvin, which I am certain you do not."

"I doubt the old lady's blessing means much out here, warmaiden. This increasingly looks like Fjorni land, or haven't you heard?"

"I have heard things I would prefer not to believe, but nothing to diminish the rights of Thioth."

"We are often reluctant to believe the truth, lady. The power of Thioth is waning while that of Fjorn grows, whether you will or no."

"Power is a volatile thing, Njlvac, and I am speaking of rights."

"You have the advantage of me, stranger, for I do not know your name though I suspect you are one of the wandering easterners I have heard about. Even so, you must know that rights without power are no rights at all."

"By Wigdor," Ringskild swore, "power without right is power misused."

"You are a fascinating philosopher, lady. Perhaps you would care to continue this debate at leisure? I have come to escort you from this barren place."

"We don't require an escort from here to the Ulava."

"But that is not where you are headed. My task is to lead you safely to Fjorn."

"Safely!" snorted Furk. "About as safely as that poor blighter you carved up back there?"

"Ah," Njlvac smiled coldly, "I see you admired my work."

Vunskridh pointed to the wall of rubble behind her and asked, "May we assume this was also your work?"

"Indeed, lady, how kind of you to notice. I could not take your entire company to my father, so decided to bring him the most daring, which, surely, you are."

Throughout these pointed exchanges the Fjorni drew closer until the hapless dozen were essentially encircled, with a few archers above and behind them. Choosing to fight another day, if possible, Ringskild silently signaled acceptance to her companions and turned to question Furk. "My Lord, we can die nobly here, though I see no advantage to our purpose in it, or we can hope to fight again. What say you?"

"I say this cheeky bastard should be butchered without mercy, hmmph, but I admit we cannot do it in these circumstances. We have raced into his trap like bloody fools. Indeed. And there you have it."

With this eloquent summation from the Count of Vothnell, the Norrung captain informed Njlvac they would go with him, though she would dearly have loved to sever his smirking head from his shoulders.

CHAPTER 36

Beside the Mither River a very different trap held in its tangles a captive who struggled to decide between resistance and acceptance. To fight the forces that ensnared her made all the sense in the world. To yield could lead to failure and shame, though it held the faintest hope of a better possibility. She faced no timeline enforced at sword point but knew the decision had to be made soon.

Torn between hope and fear, the hapless woman felt herself to be a plaything of the stars. Two of the mightiest deities were known as tricksters: Eghran, the god of chaos, who overturns the known and casts all into confusion, and Desh, the goddess of love. The latter promised sweet bonds yet often teased and left her victims with broken hearts, while the former created opportunity for new possibilities and new pitfalls but with no certain path forward.

In her small room in the craftworkers' section of Nimmoth, Kirlat battled the two tricksters nightly as she continued to wrestle with the dreams awakened by her brief meeting with Hildir. Reaching to undo the sash at her slender waist, she glanced at the raven feather tattooed on the back of her right hand. Like most tattoos it proclaimed her calling and told all who met her that she was a feather woman. There was no disgrace in such a trade but one had to be wary of the occasional jealous wife. Kirlat had done well enough and had for years convinced herself that the married life was not for her.

How could so few minutes on a thirsty afternoon change all that? she wondered, fumbling with the scarlet silk. It seemed that as she unbound her dress the invisible binding of her heart became tighter. The feather on her now trembling hand troubled her for it was the sign of Desh the Raven, the playful goddess. Kirlat's tattoo honored the Queen of Delights but it also reminded her that the goddess brought couples together in marriage.

This was the difficult time of day, when work and simple socializing were done and Kirlat was alone, preparing for the night. Her troubled thoughts made sleeping difficult and she was exhausted at each day's end. While undoing her hair and combing the long brown tresses, she told herself for the hundredth time that she had to make a choice.

Kirlat was still young enough to be beautiful and old enough to be skilled in her work, one of the most desirable women working the meeting places of Nimmoth. She could reasonably assume an adequate future for a couple more decades. By then she would have friends enough and the social skills to work at trades not based on beauty and would have savings for her elder years. This was the path of the known, the reasonable, the expected.

The other path was one of great risk. She had inquired around and knew that Hildir was one of the group now known as the demon chasers and that they had headed downriver to Mimmoth, presumably there to turn west. It would be foolish to assume the Norrungs would return home by the same path and that Hildir would cross her path again. If she were to see him again, she would have to seek him out and there was every reason to believe this was doomed to failure from the beginning, not least because the demon chasers might meet some horrible fate and Hildir perish.

If she left Nimmoth, she would have to forsake both friends and customers and all she knew and start life again somewhere else, perhaps in many locales. It would take a while to become established in her current trade and what else might she do?

If the quest succeeded and Hildir survived and she found him, would it matter to him? Was their meeting a casual flirtation? Would he want her for a night, perhaps more, then move on? Then where would she be? A stranger among strangers. The risk was immense.

Amid her heartache, Kirlat knew that as the risk was great, so was the cost of staying where she was and longing for the passing warrior. With a great sigh she threw herself onto her bed, muttered aloud, "Hildir," and fell into a troubled sleep.

The following morning Kirlat visited a star singer who had just finished the Hymn to the Dawn.

"Cousin," she addressed the older woman, who turned toward the feather woman with a look of peaceful compassion. "I come for your blessing."

Kirlat unfolded her struggle and the decision she had reached. The singer placed her hands on the younger woman's shoulders and sang:

> Weltar of many years
> Bestow her wisdom on you
> That your steps may go aright
> And your journey end well.
>
> Wigdor judge of oaths
> Keep your heart true
> And see that others
> Deal with you honestly.
>
> The Fierce Mother give you strength
> To do what you must do
> And the Bright Mother bless you
> With happy issue to your quest.
>
> Desh play with you fairly
> And not mistreat your heart.
> Hjelgi keep you on a true path
> And may the stars shine upon you.

At the last line, the singer traced a star on Kirlat's brow then smiled at her. Kirlat wiped tears from her eyes, desperately hoping the singer's prayer would be heeded and the stars watch over her. She gave the singer a silver coin and one of her own bracelets by way of thanks, then headed quickly to the alehouse where most of her customers gathered. She told the ale mistress of her plan to move on lest anyone worry in her absence, gave the woman a kiss, and rushed back to her room.

There Kirlat finished packing all her belongings into a trunk, wrapped herself in a traveling cloak, and hired someone to carry her trunk to the docks and load it on a downstream vessel. That evening she was in the great port of Mimmoth. Neither sightseeing nor work was on her mind. Kirlat used her winning ways this time to seek information. For once in her life she blessed tiresome functionaries, for the records of the Mimmothi toll collectors were thorough and their tongues given to petty gossip. With many smiles and a few cups of wine, she soon confirmed her suspicion that the demon chasers had sailed west toward Fimmoth.

For all the excitement of her daring adventure, Kirlat fell asleep with a smile that night, no longer haunted by her struggle. By dawn the next morning she was aboard a merchant vessel headed toward the Thiothi region of the Fiona River.

That day was unusually clear and Kirlat caught glimpses of the morning sun on the peaks of Mount Hiovith far in the distance. Light danced upon the waves, birds wheeled overhead, and life seemed new and exciting as the boat sailed past Nimos, Tugdal, and Vothnell. With Furk far away and the Vothneli less aggressive, Kirlat's voyage went smoothly and by the next evening she had landed in Fimmoth and found a room for the night.

The next day she set about locating a new home, eventually finding one not as nice as the one she had before yet clean and adequate. A tour of shops and alehouses allowed her to orient herself to new surroundings and potential customers. Kirlat expended more charm on her fellow feather women than on the men of Fimmoth at first, knowing that one needs friends and territory is not easily shared. She had begun life anew.

For all the superficial ease of starting over, Kirlat found the next day to be difficult. All her fears and doubts resurfaced and she felt as though the Chegjan had sent one of its dark tendrils specifically to her own heart and mind. What sort of new life was it to do the same old thing in a new setting? How far had the demon chasers journeyed at this point and would they return? It was difficult to imagine them not stopping at Fimmoth on their way back yet nothing guaranteed that this would be the case.

By midafternoon Kirlat found herself seeking out midwives for the location of a non-military shrine to Vrotni. Having done so, she hastened to one of the town's markets, purchased a hen, and headed to the mothers' temple. Motherhood was not the issue that brought her there that day, though most visitors to the shrine were new mothers. What Kirlat sought that day was courage. She entered the building of aged stone and was met by an attendant, clothed in a wine-colored robe, her hair hidden by a yellow scarf and her hands dyed blood-red. Kirlat followed the woman into the heart of the shrine where a huge statue of Vrotni presided.

It was carved of dark stone and portrayed a lioness, immense and fierce, her forepaws placed on the heads of her two cubs in a gesture of either protection or benediction. The tall pedestal was made of local sandstone and was inscribed with prayers that Kirlat could not decipher. A few other women were about their private prayers in the torch-lit sanctuary and their murmuring created a buzz that mingled with the smoky scent of resin and precious gums.

Kirlat handed the hen and the customary three copper coins to the attendant, who nodded and left the room briefly. Kirlat stood at a respectful distance from the fierce goddess whose huge paws were at eye level. She was not especially pious yet felt that at this point in her life she needed to call upon the stars, so she did what she had learned, in the distracted manner of a child, from her mother long ago. No easy and comfortable prayers came to mind so she waited and simply absorbed the sacred atmosphere.

The attendant returned, this time wearing a mask of the goddess, the face of a lioness captured in a stylized snarl, the whole painted red for the blood of life and death. In one hand she bore the sacrificial bird that Kirlat had offered and in the other a stone knife. Standing before the Fierce Mother the priestess cleanly slew the hen, allowing the gore to drain into a pit in the earth in front of the goddess. She then took the bloody knife and touched it to Kirlat's forehead, leaving a vertical streak of red in the center. Having thus united the worshipper and the deity, she withdrew, leaving Kirlat to offer her prayers.

Lost in a ritual with which she was not familiar, Kirlat stood for a while in a daze, then began to pour out her heart.

"Mother, you are the soul of courage. You would do anything to protect your children. I come today as one of your stray cubs, lost in uncertainty and seeking your help. Give me your courage, I beseech you. Steel my heart and strengthen my resolve. You are untroubled by doubt and I am full of questioning. I feel fear but you do not hesitate. Make me strong and fierce for the future. May your stars shine forever."

Having said all she needed to say, she stood transfixed as though waiting for a nod or a slowly winking eye but the great stone remained unmoving. Even without a miraculous sign, Kirlat felt a renewal of her inner courage, a reawakening of her inner lioness, and left the shrine feeling her prayer had been answered.

Rapidly blinking in the sudden brightness of daylight, Kirlat found herself looking at another woman struggling with emotions. Mirdel rode through the streets of Fimmoth, followed by her son and daughters and surrounded by soldiers, as she headed toward the Steward's Palace that was to serve as her prison.

The proud woman refused to display grief or dread before the Fimmothi, though her white garb and ash-smeared cheeks marked her as mourning for her late husband. Vjendar had granted her and her children every dignity, as though Vorn had perished in an accident rather than been executed as a traitor. The terrible news and its consequences had led to much weeping during the journey from Thioth, but Mirdel now rode with her body erect and her expression composed. Unaware of their father's actions, the children took their cue from their mother's behavior and passed among strangers as though nothing unusual had taken place.

The new widow and the feather lady thus both drew on all their courage to face a new life in the port city while locals passing through the streets around them spared little more than a glance at either the widow's garb or the bloody mark of Vrotni.

CHAPTER 37

Prince Njlvac ordered the disarming of the new captives. His captains Zoldar, Viço, and Ulniç took delight in doing so. Zoldar's alert green eyes missed nothing and his pleasure in disarming nobles such as Torthan, Furk, and Baron Grath showed in a broad grin lacking one tooth. When Furk's sergeant Miglac protested, Zoldar struck him with the broad side of his sword, quieting objections and leaving a painful bruise.

The warmaidens braced themselves for the unwelcome searching of the shortest of the three captains, Viço. His stubby fingers seemed determined to check every inch of the fierce young women. It was all Vunskridh could do to quell her reflexes and not fillet the man before he could touch her. Ringskild maintained as much dignity as possible when her turn came, as did Ian and the dusty but alive Nordil. Hildir and Mechdar, along with the Vothneli captain Brona and sergeant Trno were disarmed by Ulniç, an older warrior with cropped gray hair and the right side of his face discolored by the scars of some ancient fire.

When his underlings had bound the captives' hands and were satisfied, Njlvac signaled for all to move out toward Fjorn. They proceeded west until a trail rose off to the right. They mounted this path to work their way toward the upper Othen Stream where Thiothi forces were few and allies, whether by bribery or terror, were plentiful.

The path was rocky and had many switchbacks, the afternoon was humid and the daystar heavy upon the riders. Having spoken for her people, Ringskild was clearly a leader and thus rode near the front where Njlvac could keep an eye on her. He pondered the steely demeanor and measured decisions of this warmaiden, so very unlike himself. She, in turn, compared what she had heard of "the Bastard's Spawn" with what she observed. The prince had his father's coloring, his face pale as milk and his hair coarse and dark as iron. Njlvac's brows were thick and nearly joined in the middle, his lips were full, and his face and hands showed many scars, both fresh and old. In spite of the heat, he did not seem to sweat. In the course of the sweltering ride toward the southern slopes of Mount Uvjor, Ivor's daughter noted that the prince was easily irritated and acted hastily. She hoped this might work to her advantage at some point. Her chief fear was that something might happen to Ian, undermining the entire mission. Ringskild vowed anew to die, if necessary, to prevent such a disaster.

Baron Torthan was intrigued by another, General Çrdna, Njlvac's second-in-command. A large fierce-looking man, Çrdna wore a patch over his missing left eye and had a carved bone crescent inserted in his nose. Somewhat taciturn, the experienced warrior did not easily share information. Still, Torthan the strategist gently queried about the topography of the land and how the Fjorni planned and executed the effective landslide. Since it was a *fait accompli*, Çrdna told some of the details with an admixture of pride, leading Torthan to conclude that it had been the general's tactic and not the prince's. The Baron of Valcor did not inquire about the butchered young husband and the violated woman used as bait, preferring not to ponder those details. He held no doubts that for all their titles, organization, and tactics, the Fjorni rulers were savages.

The moisture hanging in the air grew more oppressive as the spring day drew to a close. Thick clouds that had been building all afternoon finally released their burden just as the travelers forded the Othen and entered the territory of Fjorn. A flash flood turned the Othen's waters brown as they rose higher and the last of the Fjorni crossed, cursing but without incident.

An hour's rain-soaked ride beyond the border took them to Njlvac's base camp on the eastern side of Mount Uvjor, deep amid oaks just below the pine belt. There other forces awaited and gave shouts of glee at the sight of captives. This gradually gave way to murmurs when it was learned that the prisoners were not Thiothi. Still, some looked to be noble and worth possible ransom.

The storm did not let up and Mechdar swore that Dorgal the Weeper must have lost her firstborn that night for so many tears to fall from the heavens. Whatever she lamented, the skies continued to shower into the next morning. It was a miserable night and a spirit of gloom prevailed among the prisoners. Even Ian, who had only that morning had such an overpowering vision of light, seemed to waver. Njlvac, however, was pleased and the Chegjan, if it noticed, might have mocked its would-be foes.

The dawn was bleak and gray, the rain calmed only to a steady light shower. General Çrdna's harsh countenance and gruff voice interrupted any hope of prolonged dreaming as he announced it was time to move on. Having traveled in the company of star singers for so long, the Norrungs missed the dawn hymn and wondered how their companions on the other side of the landslide fared. Some unfortunate souls had clearly perished. They knew this much from their experience on the far end of the mass of rubble, but how many in all? And who? What was the damage on the near end among those who were just reaching the narrows? Nordil was chiefly concerned with his beloved Wilda but all wondered and feared the worst. There was no shortage of silent curses invoking the wrath of the stars on Njlvac and his ilk as the now enlarged contingent proceeded northeast toward Grudhor on the banks of the Fiona.

The descent from Mount Uvjor's lower slopes was through rocky terrain where the oaks thinned and scrub took over: buck brush, greasewood, whitethorn, with willows and horse chestnut near streams, the latter's clustered white spikes dripping, like all else, with the relentless rain. Rivulets formed everywhere and the muddy footing was often treacherous. At one point a horse was lost and its Fjorni rider injured. The Vothneli and Norrungs expected a healer to attend to the man but, at a nod from Njlvac, Viço simply dispatched both soldier and horse and all rode on.

Midday brought them within sight of a minor hamlet. A horrific stench assailed the passersby, mitigated only by rain and gradual drop in temperature. Alongside the road gallows had been hastily erected, the waterlogged planks forming a harsh silhouette. From them hung eight or nine bodies, sodden and bloating, women and children as well as men. When the living prisoners glanced with distaste at the sight, Zoldar announced without emotion, "We had a minor insurrection. The village has now calmed down."

Ringskild reproached herself for not fighting to the death, fearing that in her bid for time she may have doomed them all to some unspeakable fate. If they were being taken to Bulçar, his reputation could not encourage hope for better treatment than what his son meted out. She heaved a sigh as they rode beyond the suspended victims of Fjorni "justice," knowing she never considered facing a demon would be easy but wishing their quest had omitted demons disguised as human.

Hildir, riding beside her, heard the sigh and guessed some of its cause for he had entertained similar thoughts. "This tale is not yet told," he said gently. "I pray my cousin recall old Hranild's words, 'Who forsakes victory shall have it.' You and I enjoy the battle and, I dare say, we do not disdain the glory that comes from it. But we did not set out this time to seek glory or military triumph. We seek to preserve the life of one young man on whom our hopes are pinned. Had we defied the scum-dwelling lion's whelp, Ian would have perished with us."

"You are right, cousin Hildir. And Zhodor told us stupid hope would save us. None could say that hope right now seems anything but utter folly, so let us hope and be saved." The discouraged captain gave her fellow a wry grin and they rode on, lost in the endless patter of the rain and many uncomfortable thoughts.

They came to the plains without further incident and reached Grudhor. The town stood on the west side of the river a short ways below the point where the Uvja River ended its rushing descent from the peak of Mount Uvjor and joined the Fiona. Grudhor was governed at the time by Njlvac's younger brother, Prince Stjor, and the entire party advanced toward the stout-walled castle to meet him.

The cadet princeling could be recognized by his tunic with the same black lion's head on red that Njlvac wore only differenced by a silver annulet instead of a golden orle. Unlike his older brother, Stjor bore no obvious scars though his nose was crooked. His green eyes sparkled with delight at the sight of prisoners.

"Ah, brother, what presents do you bear our father today?"

"None of the old woman's, I fear, but interesting nobles and warriors nonetheless. May I present to you the vanguard of the demon chasers we have heard so much about."

"Demon chasers! Ha, father should find them most amusing. Where do they hail from?"

"Some from a forest far to the east and others from the coast. We lured them into Drush Pass and cut them off from the rest of their party with the most wonderful landslide. I believe their intent was to wreak some awful punishment on me. You know how noble southerners consider themselves."

"Brother Njlvac, you probably deserve whatever they had in mind yet, once again, you outsmarted your foe, undoubtedly to their great sorrow. Speaking of punishment, perhaps you would care to join me in dealing with some treason?"

"It would be a pleasure, brother. Who's the villain?"

"A cobbler, would you believe it? He had plied his trade here in Grudhor for years but it turns out he has been passing information to our neighbor in the south." With that, Stjor turned to one of his guards and asked that the man be brought forth.

Ian, who had witnessed Lady Rushvin's swift judgment of Vorn in Thioth, did not expect to see mercy shown to anyone in Grudhor who served her. Even so he was not prepared for what he was about to witness.

The hapless cobbler entered the hall, his feet hobbled with iron shackles and his hands manacled, a stout guard on each side holding the chain for the corresponding hand and four other guards surrounding him with halberds. Bruises and bloodied abrasions gave evidence of his treatment up to this point.

Furk hmmphed and cleared his throat with distaste at the evil smiles on the faces of the sons of Bulçar. Stjor addressed the prisoner. "You have been the eyes and ears of Thioth in our city, a terrible betrayal of the people of Grudhor and our noble father."

At mention of their father, the cobbler, knowing he would not survive much longer, spat.

Njlvac commented, "You see how vile his soul has become, insulting his lord like that."

"Well," Stjor responded, "he has certainly forfeited all claims to mercy. But he shall no longer be eyes and ears for the enemy." With that he drew a dagger, stepped forth, and sliced off the cobbler's ears, tossing them to a couple of large hounds that had been lounging at the edge of the crowd. Having tasted fresh morsels, they now watched their master with alert eyes.

"Brother?" Stjor invited and Njlvac then did the honors in putting out the man's eyes. The cobbler had tried to remain silent and give the villains no pleasure in his cries but roared in agony as his orbs were gouged out. The hounds snacked again and drew nearer.

By this point Furk was a bundle of fury, making all manner of odd noises in lieu of exploding with outrage. Torthan and Grath each laid a hand on him, reminding their liege silently that nothing would be gained by speaking out under such circumstances. Having never been in battle, much less present to see alleged humans take pleasure in torture, Ian had difficulty believing what he now witnessed. Lady Rushvin had allowed torture to obtain a confession and followed it with prompt execution, but this could not be any form of justice. It was nothing more than blood lust.

"I think this villain has told his last tale to our foes," Stjor proclaimed as guards forced the man's mouth open and one extended his tongue with pliers. Stjor then sliced off the victim's tongue as his brother commented, "Well done."

"Do you think he might yet send notes?" asked Stjor, nodding to yet other guards.

"Who knows, my prince," Njlvac replied with a mock look of concern.

A great block of wood was brought forward and the man's right arm placed upon it. Stjor unsheathed his sword and sliced off the hand. The hounds pounced on it and began to quarrel.

"I so hate to see brothers quarrel," Stjor said with a wink, then gave a nod. The left hand joined the right and each hound had its treat.

By this time the cobbler's arms were free though his feet were still in chains. No resistance was left in him and he was faint from loss of blood.

"Well, we have other things to attend to," Stjor said, wiping his blade on his victim's tunic. He completed his judgment with a final dagger plunge under the ribs and into the heart. The expiring cobbler was then tossed by the guards to the side of the room where the hounds began a serious feast on fresh human meat.

Nordil and Ian, neither of them warriors, had become ill at this point, though neither reached the point of self-embarrassment by emptying his stomach. Ringskild had been noting the expressions on the members of Stjor's court. None seemed surprised, amazed, or disturbed by what had just taken place. They may have felt inner revulsion but none revealed it. "What manner of creatures are these?" she wondered silently.

There was no leisure for pondering. The two princes gave orders and the captives were taken to spend the night in the dungeon. Sitting in the straw of the dank room they wryly observed that at least they were not chained, only locked inside the foul space. A few prisoners were chained to the wall. Despair and exhaustion had already drained them of most life. One side of the room was moist from seepage as the rain continued to fall outside. The previous night had been bad enough.

"I am sorry you are all in this mess," said Ian.

"You are in it too, cousin," said Mechdar.

"But if it weren't for me, we would not be here," the lad countered.

"True enough," Torthan added, "but these villains and their father would still be perpetrating their savagery, the world would still have more sorrow than we can comprehend, and the Chegjan would grow without challenge. So long as we live we can carry the light. If the stars have foretold our duty, then we must carry it out. Amid all the bestial deeds we have witnessed today, and I apologize to all beasts for using the term, yet we can still be revulsed. That alone is a sign that the stars have not abandoned us, for only the starforsaken could look on today and not be sickened. Young Ian, we are here because the stars have brought us here. No blame attaches to you."

There were murmurs of assent though it was difficult not to feel starforsaken that night, lying on the filthy straw and cold stone. No starlight penetrated there and Ian struggled to remember the Light.

CHAPTER 38

Completing proper burial rites as best they could in restricted circumstances, the Norrungs kindled the fire of Jannir's pyre and commended his body to the elements and his soul to the stars. Lacking mourning garments, Wilda tore a spare shift into strips so the mourners could at least wear white headbands. The respected and widely-beloved merchant's departure led to many a track in the ashes on his friends' cheeks.

With anguish enough from this one loss, the Norrungs made impassioned pleas to the stars that the other members of their party may have made it through safely to the other side of the massive slide that had sent tons of boulders, rubble, and dirt to block the Drush Pass. As yet it had not occurred to them that worse things may have been on the far side, nor that the disaster had been the act of mortals rather than the simple course of nature.

The Vothneli, meanwhile, had similarly carried out minimal obsequies for their fallen comrades, commending them to the star path and watching the columns of black smoke rise even as the first sprinkling of rain came. Though Athnel could not reverse the course of human death, Pjortan wondered if she had any part in keeping the rains to a light mist until the pyres had done their work. No one wanted tragedy to be followed by the ill omen of bodies half burnt. They were spared this but only barely.

Dorgal's tears went rapidly from an aspersion to a downpour shortly after the funeral flames had died down. Scouts returned from their searching to help the company of soldiers set up tents before all were sodden. The night was spent in fear that flash floods would overcome them in the narrows. By morning the horses were standing in a foot of water but the humans were not completely drenched.

A muddy detour was made to the south around the narrows of Drush as the company slogged through wet clay and clambered over rocks. Wilda's cart and other vehicles had to be left behind and as much baggage as possible loaded on the pack horses. Wilda saw no problem in riding on horseback but she was loath to let her cart go. Still, necessity forces hard choices and there was no other way forward. The rain lessened somewhat from time to time but did not cease for more than a few minutes at a time as the bedraggled travelers clambered on an irregular path that made it clear why the Drush Pass was preferred, no matter how narrow.

It was not until late afternoon of the second day that they finally worked their way around and entered the Pass from its western side. No companions were to be found and rain had long since washed away any tracks they might have left. Two messengers were dispatched to return by any way possible to Thioth, to let Lady Rushvin know what had transpired. Disappointed and concerned, the rest of the company camped in the natural bowl where their leaders had been captured two days earlier, avoiding the ruddy cascades that flowed from small side canyons.

The following day they glanced at leaden skies, from which the Weeper's tears still came, and guessed at the timing of dawn. Pjortan and Athnel sang the Hymn to the Dawn with as much feeling as they could muster, trusting Shach to still be in the heavens whether they beheld him or not. At last, following the original plan, they continued westward to Uvanor, hoping to find the rest of their party there.

Uvanor stood on the edge of the Ulava Plain, due south of the peak of Mount Uvjor. The mountainside boasted a yellow pine forest while to the west and south lay broad, fertile fields. Journeying with a bit of caution on wet ground, the travelers reached it by midafternoon and promptly began inquiring about their lost fellows. Neither their companions nor any word of them was to be had. Further dispirited, the Norrung-Vothneli contingent gathered on the Street of Inns and found lodging for the night. Officers and other leaders gathered to discuss what they should do next. For the sake of command, the Norrungs chose Volthir to lead them and the Vothneli acclaimed Djutar as their captain. The two men accepted the responsibility laid upon them but led all the party in a toast beseeching the stars for the safety of Furk and Ringskild and those who followed them.

That night's rest may have been uneasy with concerns for those missing yet it was also in dry shelter. Djutar and Volthir gave all permission to sleep in the next morning. By mid-morning the company turned to a day of exercise at arms, general repairs, and restocking of supplies. Since Uvanor was a city within the rule of Thioth there were no problems with these arrangements. Though no less concerned for their companions, those in Uvanor felt better for a day not spent marching through the rain and slept the sound sleep of the exhausted that evening.

Volthir found himself praying to Weltar each day, beseeching the goddess to grant him wisdom now that the companions were split and he had no idea where Ian, their champion, or the others might be. Captain Djutar, himself once the "captor" of the Norrungs, made similar prayers as he felt the weight of leadership now that Furk, Barons Grath and Torthan, and Captain Brona were gone. Both new leaders laughed when informed by the singers that each had made offering to the goddess for the same thing and both of them tended to utter, "Where do we go from here?"

CHAPTER 39

The Norrung captives huddled close for comfort that cold, dank night in a room with no rugs or tapestries, nor bed nor blankets. Stone and straw were not enough for warmth. The Vothneli also tried to conserve heat by sleeping close to each other with the exception of Furk. The Lord of Vothnell felt it beneath his dignity to curl up with those who were not his peers. Unfortunately for him, the great fur robe so recently bestowed upon him was among the baggage on a pack horse and not with him in the Grudhor prison.

It did not help anyone's mood that Njlvac seemed rested and alert the next morning when he arrived with the gray light of dawn, accompanied by his general and captains to retrieve the hapless captives.

The ride that day was easier since they could take the River Road north to Fjorn. For most of the journey no more than a mist fell from the heavens though the winds from the distant Mere blew chilly. The Fjorni captors appeared no less wet and miserable than the demon hunters from the south yet the prince's chipper manner grated throughout the day. Mechdar observed the cruel foe's smiles and wondered what paternal praises might fill his imagination with anticipation. They were cold smiles, not the type that spoke of warm affection or delight, and they were marred by the white scars that not only marked the prince's face but also disfigured his lips near the middle and at one edge. There could be no comfort in Njlvac's good mood.

As disciplined warriors, the prisoners knew to turn their thoughts from any seeds of resignation or despair and to spend their journeying hours in observation and calculation. With innocuous questions they learned as much as possible about the Fjorni, their land, and their ruling family. They were careful to ask in a relaxed manner, probing neither too forcefully nor too often, mingling their talk with inconsequential banter. Being especially mindful of the cobbler's fate, each questioner gleaned only a little bit. Collectively they spent most of their time digesting what they learned and pondering the potential implications of each tidbit.

Terrain took on greater importance than it had before. If there were any chance of escape there would be no friendly guide, no Thiothi scout, no Jannir, no cooperative local lord, only the need to flee through hostile land with vicious pursuers. Landmarks and their sequence were silently memorized, even in so clear a path as the River Road.

Early morning saw them cross the Uvja River on an old stone bridge, not far from where the Uvja joined the Fiona. Captor and captive alike were grateful for the rocky span that spared them from fording even a minor river, now swollen with two days' worth of late spring rain and full of rushing debris.

As the day wore on, Njlvac pursued his own inquiries, quizzing Furk, Ringskild, Torthan, and Ian on the matter of chasing a demon and what political ties might be involved in such a venture. He shared with Furk a sense that military might and strategy were the primary components of conquest and found the whole matter of prophecies puzzling. Torthan was particularly interesting in that he served Furk yet did not discount the Norrung propensity for viewing this as a spiritual struggle. What sort of man might the Baron of Valcor be? Clearly a cleverer adversary than his overlord, though possibly more of a thinker than a warrior. For fierceness, Njlvac was betting on the Norrung warmaiden who spoke for their group. In her he saw a banked fire and an iron will. It would be interesting to face her on a battlefield.

Ian had never cared for being the center of attention as it usually spelled trouble. That had certainly been true with his brother Steven. So long as Steven caught their father's eye, Ian was typically safe. Likewise if William Dyrnedon were doting on Annabelle, the youngest, or rolling his eyes over cousin Harry. All the confusing utterances of the seers implying that Ian was "the chosen one" made the youth uncomfortable. The hermit crying "Dyrn has come!" and pointing his staff at Ian was completely terrifying.

The outland lad was thus relieved that his companions were fairly tight-lipped about his role when Njlvac was asking questions. Torthan interrupted a couple of times when Furk seemed on the verge of saying too much. To Ian it was obvious they were all protecting him and he was glad to limit his own admission to saying that a Norrung seer had insisted that he go along but he had not the least idea what he was supposed to do. That much was true, which was a good thing, as Ian had never developed the art of lying beyond blaming mishaps on his cousin or brother.

Thoughts of his family thus distracted Ian that afternoon and he found himself tossed about by many emotions. Each passing day in this new world made it harder for him to remember the world from which he came. Faces grew somewhat vague and he found himself recalling family members more in terms of characteristic gestures or tone of voice. Harry was encapsulated in his tiresome snore. Annabelle reminded Ian of buttercups though he had forgotten why. Mother was best known in the warm embrace of her ample bosom and in her cheery voice. Aunt Susan came through as nervously bustling about, always in a bit of a dither, and Father was remembered as a no-nonsense manner and the distinctive fragrance of his pipe. All in all, it was not a lot to hold on to in a world where he had no family portraits.

"Your mind seems far away, cousin," Nordil said.

"It is. I was thinking of my family and it seems I keep forgetting more and more about them."

"Distance and time will do that to us all, lad," said the older man. "And the details do not really matter. Perhaps you can take comfort in the fact that you do remember them. That is the connection of heart to heart. Even the gap between worlds cannot sever that."

"Do you really believe that, Nordil?"

"Ha. You would question your elders, boy? Yes, I really do believe that. If we come from the stars and return to them, we are all connected forever. It is neither long ago nor far away that I was severed from my dear wife. I think she is well, but I have no way of knowing, no way to tell her what has befallen me. We are trapped in the misery of not knowing but I trust she knows my love for her will always be there. I am confident in her love for me, stars bless her. For you the gap is far greater. Still, yes, I believe in love."

"Thank you, cousin," Ian replied. "I hope I grow into your strong faith."

"We never stop growing," the groom answered.

As the daystar prepared to descend behind the northern slope of Mount Uvjor, the riders came to Fjorn, the Fjorni prince filled with anticipation and his prisoners with dread. Were they to become food for dogs, held for ransom, or merely acts as toys in a deadly political game?

Red and black banners hung wet and dark at the Princely Gate into the capital city of Fjorn, swaying now and again as the wind continued to blow upriver. To the captives it seemed that all was wet and dark, bleak and bedraggled. Guards posted at the entrance had an expression of misery on their faces as though they had been promised a bright spring day and then been doused in cold water and kept in the dark. Only a few streaks of lighter gray broke the monotony of the rain-dark sky. The rose-colored sandstone of the city walls had turned the shade of drying blood. Citizens glanced briefly as the riders passed through the city but no great stir of excitement greeted the returning prince. As the company drew near the castle entrance a great flock of geese honked in alarm and every head in the courtyard turned toward the newly arrived.

Ringskild's heart tightened in revulsion when Njlvac assumed the role of noble host and offered to help her from her horse. He was enjoying whatever game he played far too much and she managed to give him a good thump as she executed an exaggerated dismount on her own.

"I beg your pardon, Son of Fjorn," she said in mock apology.

"Think nothing of it," the prince replied in mock courtesy. "Please, follow me."

He led the entire party past the great iron-barred doors, though a short corridor, and into a smaller courtyard. They circumambulated its enclosed garden to enter the central part of the castle and shortly came to the chamber where His Magnificence, known by his foes as the Bastard, awaited them.

The setting was no great hall but more of a meeting room. Prince Bulçar of Fjorn sat in a chair of carved oak decorated with iron bosses and padded leather on the back and seat. His scarlet tunic bore the black lion's head of his house wrought in fine embroidery, its eyes and tongue stitched in gold thread. A simple coronet of slightly tarnished silver sat on a head of coarse black hair, flashing occasionally when light from the clerestory or the room's torches reflected from polished pieces of jasper and hematite. He had great bushy black brows that contrasted with his pale skin and the ivory of his excellent teeth. Fleshy lips sat beneath his plump nose and his trimmed beard was of the same thick dark hair as above. He was clearly a strong man, firm of body and will, though his body had begun to soften with age and with allowing his sons and soldiers to do much of the fighting for him while he attended to matters of state.

On a smaller but similarly decorated chair sat his wife, Princess Gizli of Hlv. It was obvious that Njlvac had his father's coloring for Gizli had the copper hue of her people and lustrous black hair as straight as her husband's was wavy. Her tresses hung over her shoulders in two long braids, intertwined with deep blue satin ribbons. A similar ribbon held a veil the yellow of sunflowers upon her head as it trailed behind her. Her bracelets and earrings were of silver set with opals and a great collar of small gold coins rested about her throat and descended almost as a breastplate. Her gown was a deep green like moss growing in shadows on a cloudy day. One trait she had passed on to her firstborn was the alert look in her eyes, eyes of jet that seemed to miss nothing. High cheeks and a straight nose added to Gizli's beauty. She was clearly a person of great presence and dignity, making the captive guests wonder how she ever was matched with the Bastard of Fjorn.

That, of course, was a tale of dynastic relations, a mixture of political and economic interests that paid little heed to the individuals who had to live out such an arrangement.

"Ah, my son, what have you brought to us today?" Bulçar greeted.

"You have heard tales of demon chasers, Sire, who hope to track down the Chegjan. We have managed to bring you their leaders."

"Indeed? I cannot imagine what one would do with a demon if one found it, unless one wishes to perish in some unspeakable end."

Ian had trouble picturing a more unspeakable end than that given the cobbler in Grudhor the day before at the hand of the two princes, yet he kept his peace.

"Nonetheless, my Lord, here they are. Some have come from the far eastern side of the Mere and some from the coast to the south, all pursuing the tracks of the demon."

"From the south, you say? Are they loyal to Thioth, then? Old Rushvin's people?"

"No, Sire. From the territory of Vothnell between Fimmoth and Mimmoth. They have come through the old woman's lands and no doubt have her blessing, but they have their own allegiances, so far as I can tell."

"Well, if they have her blessing they can be no friends of ours. Where did you take them?"

Njlvac smirked as he replied, "They thought they were in pursuit of us and rushed into Drush Pass where we cut them off with a convenient landslide. Instead of overtaking us, they found themselves overtaken."

Bulçar frowned. "So, there are more of them?"

"Many more, Sire, but they will waste a great deal of time either going back or finding a way forward. Nor, with the rains, will they find any tracks to pursue us. As their destination was to the west, they are not likely to follow us north. The mere fact that they took the Pass rather than the common road closer to our border indicates their reluctance to be anywhere near us."

"Bah, cowards most likely," the Black Lion grunted. This caused a surge of indignation to pass through the captives but they held their tongues. Bulçar noticed that they did not take his bait.

"So," he continued, "you have been searching for this demon. Have you spotted it yet?"

"Ringskild spoke up. "We have only seen the results of its presence. Its path seems for the most part to follow the plague and thus we go where it has been."

"If you only go where it has been you shall never find yourselves where it is now," Bulçar asserted.

"It seems we travel a bit faster than the plague has done," replied Mechdar, "and so we hope to catch up."

"That," observed the Prince, "is a strange hope. Are you so fond of death?"

"No, sir," Mechdar continued, choosing not to address Bulçar by either title or as cousin, "we have no fondness for death, though as warriors we see enough of it. We seek the demon's destruction."

"Ah. Hah! Oh," Bulçar chortled and the Fjorni in the room snickered, "stars bless me. What weapons do you use on a demon? Do you have some magic amulet? Will you draw it into a game of riddles and overcome it like some folk tale? How can you aim a spear or thrust a sword at something that has no body?"

"There are prophecies that indicate no bodily weapon will destroy it, Your Magnificence," Torthan said, using Bulçar's diplomatic title. "We can only hope that when the time comes we will know how to attack."

"Hope? Again, that slippery word. And if the time comes and you still have no clue? What then? Just stand there while your bones melt? Sweet stars, you must all be mad!"

"Perhaps," Ringskild replied, "but we obey the prophecies and the wishes of our lord."

"And who is your lord?"

"Njothir son of Rathdar, lord of Vorthall and chieftain of the Norrungs. Our land is to the east in the great Forest of Norrast that we left over a moon ago."

"And this," added Torthan, "is Lord Furk of Vothnell on the Mere, who has joined this risky but very noble cause."

Furk hmmphed in acknowledgment of his introduction as Bulçar continued his own musings.

"Noble causes rarely win anything save mention in a song perhaps. I would rather win a duchy in my own cause." And with that Bulçar confirmed his intention to conquer the lands of Thioth and take them from Lady Rushvin, though this had been suspected and surprised no one.

Bulçar concluded this phase of interview by turning to his son. "What do you suppose we should do with them, Njlvac?"

"We could hand them over to the demon if that were a simple thing to do. I should enjoy seeing the Chegjan make sport of them. But I doubt such a course is realistic, so I am guessing their people would pay ransom for them."

"We can hope that is the case. Additional monies are ever useful, especially when preparing for war. Let the letters be drawn up, making our demands known."

"Yes, Sire," his son replied in the tone of a courtier.

"In the meantime, chains," Bulçar ordered. And so the twelve were led away to spend another night in prison, only this time in chains.

"My son curries my favor," thought Bulçar to himself, *"perhaps a bit too eagerly. I wonder if he hopes to succeed me sooner rather than later."*

Njlvac did not have to wonder. If the opportunity came, sooner was preferable. But for now he only wished to stay on his father's good side.

In the night of despair there was still light
Stars shining beyond the black clouds
The beam of love between faithful friends
A stranger's candle a ray of hope

--The Deed of Ian

CHAPTER 40

As Ian listened to the endless rain outside the high barred windows of the cell, his thoughts turned to images recalled from home. The stories in glass of his parish church told how Jesus' triumphal entry into Jerusalem on Palm Sunday was followed by his betrayal, beating, and ugly death. Jesus knew what it was like to be treated as a messiah and then become a prisoner and object of scorn. Ian did not feel like anybody's savior. He had been treated as the fulfillment of prophecy and now his right leg was shackled to a stone wall in a barred room with other unfortunates. Was death next? Sighing deeply to release the tension, Ian closed his eyes and tried to recall the vision of Light.

Vunskridh watched the lad's troubled face. She too had concerns about the whims of Bulçar and her own fate but her mission was to protect the outlander at all costs. Her belief system had no messianic imagery so she did not think of Ian as a savior, yet he was a promised one and she dearly hoped the visions of Hranild were true and Ian would deliver the world from the power of the Chegjan.

Ian's face slowly relaxed, anxious wrinkles fading as his breathing became deep and steady. Wherever he had gone in his mind had to be better than this prison, Vunskridh assumed. She did not envy the responsibility they had all thrust upon him—or that the stars had thrust upon him. The warmaiden would not trade places with the youth; it was easier to watch over him and possibly die than to face the demon herself.

When Ian found himself at last in the presence of the Light he had experienced with the star stone of the Old Castle at Thioth—could it be only three days ago?—his countenance assumed a different look. Vunskridh observed a faint half smile forming and watched his entire body relax. She sensed, but did not see with her eyes, a golden glow emanating from his face. She blinked and shook her head to make sure she was not hallucinating, then looked again. As before she saw no new light in the room yet she felt the presence of light. "Holy Stars, watch over us," she prayed silently, glancing at the windows that admitted the light of Ruanel, the Pale Goddess, just four days past full. It was a comforting and unusual sight since clouds had been blocking most light and this was a rare moment when an opening allowed the moon to shine on the prison windows.

Compared to the dungeon of Grudhor this chamber was an improvement on a purely physical level. The straw was fresher and the room was larger and less chilled. While their shackles limited movement, the prisoners had some freedom of movement because of long chains. Bloodstains on a couple of the walls made it clear, however, that the room existed for dark purposes.

Minutes passed slowly. Whispered comparisons of what the various companions had observed in the past few days could not fill up the hours. It already seemed as though they had been captives for far longer than actual count would allow.

A comradeship had begun to emerge between Norrungs and Vothneli that was not evident prior to captivity. Trno, Miglac, and Torthan joined in sharing the nighttime watch over Ian, though they did so discreetly when Furk was asleep lest his vision of military glory be offended by their support of a mystical mission.

Midnight had passed when Miglac nudged Ringskild. A sound of approach in the dead of night hardly inspires confidence and within moments all were awake. Fresh torchlight could be seen through the grille of the fortified door and murmured voices on the other side inspired a surge of alertness through all the prisoners. Unable to discern the words of the conversation, the chained companions could only tell by its tone that there was some dispute before the wooden bar outside was lifted and keys turned.

Two guards entered the room, each holding a torch aloft in one hand and a sword at the ready in the other. The sudden light overwhelmed the captives' eyes briefly but new shapes in the room soon became more distinct. No prince had come to taunt them, neither father nor son. The visitors were women, three of them, veiled in great hooded cloaks and bearing baskets.

One could be recognized when torchlight flashed off her golden pectoral. The Princess Gizli had come to the prison. Ever the gentleman, Torthan addressed her: "My lady."

"Hush," she cut him off. "I prefer quiet voices, little discussion, and no courtesies. You have done no wrong to my husband or the people of this land. I see no reason for you to suffer. My ladies and I have brought you some food and drink to sustain you better."

The baskets were presented, each filled with bread, cheeses, meat pies, and one wineskin to be shared by all. As the food was being distributed, Gizli leaned close to Ringskild and whispered, "My cousin, if you will take my daughter with you, I shall help you all to escape this place. Say nothing, just nod if you will or no."

The warmaiden was taken aback by the sudden offer but she nodded in the affirmative while reaching for a small pie. Maintaining the charade, she whispered, "I thank your Highness for this kindness."

Speaking a little louder for the benefit of the guards, Gizli replied, "You are welcome. It is my duty to see that guests in this place are fed. Please say nothing of this to my husband or son."

"You have our word, Princess," Furk affirmed.

"Until later then," said Gizli as she and her women retrieved their baskets and departed.

Refreshed with food and at least a little to drink, the companions conferred when all was once more dark and quiet. Ringskild shared the princess' offer and all felt a spark of hope.

"Can she be trusted?" Grath asked.

"We have no way of knowing," Hildir responded. "I would never trust her husband or sons. Yet she seems quite unlike them."

Vunskridh added her observations. "We only saw her briefly this afternoon yet I would not say hers was a happy marriage, for all her stately position and formal propriety."

"It's true," said Ringskild. "There was nothing amiss in her behavior, though all she had to do was sit and be silent, but I saw her reactions to Njlvac and suspect she despises her own son. Not a very maternal attitude, but then, with a son like that...."

Furk broke in, "I will take the word of women on this. Yes. With the blighters she's stuck with it was all I could do not to call them out, unarmed as I was. Hmmph. Didn't pay much attention to her. Nice enough lady, bringing us food. Indeed."

"Assuming we do not perish in the night from poisoning," Mechdar said, articulating a nasty possibility, "I say we take her at her word. Unless this is a truly devilish plot by Bulçar, she had to take risks even coming to us. And what better hope have we?"

"None that I can see," Baron Grath agreed.

There was more assent to Gizli's proposal, then Torthan injected an unpleasant thought. "Why does she ask us to take her daughter with us and not herself?"

The group mulled this over and Trno spoke. "I do not think she expects to leave here alive."

Ringskild said, "I agree. But next time we see her I shall urge her to go with us."

And to that they all agreed.

Many thoughts made sleeping difficult that night but at least the vile princeling and his bone-pierced general did not intrude at dawn. A meager breakfast of stale bread and water was provided and gratitude to Gizli increased by the contrast in victuals.

The waiting hours went by slowly, as they had done the night before. Just before midday a captain and six guards came for Furk and Ringskild and led them away. With no explanation for this action the other captives remained in a state of anxious suspense.

The Lord of Vothnell and the Norrung Captain had not been hauled off for torture, however. They were brought into the great hall where Bulçar informed them that the letters for ransom had been drawn up. In spite of their captor's reputation they were not required to forfeit an ear or ring finger to verify that they were held. Bulçar simply insisted that each of them sign their respective letters after verifying the list of captives.

As they did so, Ringskild noted that once again Princess Gizli sat beside Bulçar only this time a third sat next to her. This had to be Gizli's daughter, the Princess Çirazel, a young woman of about Ian's age with straight dark hair like her mother and similar facial structure. Her complexion was between that of her parents, a light brown complimented by a wealth of gold jewelry accented by amber and lapis. Her eyes were hazel, her lids shadowed with a green pigment. Çirazel's gown was a pale yellow and her scarf a deep purple. The princess was indeed lovely and ripe for marriage. Perhaps this was why Gizli wanted her removed from Bulçar's power.

When the ransom letters were completed and the two leaders returned to their chains, those who awaited them exhaled with relief as they entered. They shared what they had signed and Furk then added, "My, my, my. The young princess is a lovely morsel."

"Lord Furk is right," added Ringskild, "though he might have put it more delicately." With that she provided a detailed description of the young woman who had to be Gizli's daughter.

"If she is as lovely as you say and marriageable, I would volunteer as husband," said Hildir, the notorious womanizer.

"It would take more than a young girl like the princess to tie you down, Cousin," Ringskild replied.

"And what about the Nimmothi woman you were sighing about not so long ago?" jibed Vunskridh.

"Yes," Mechdar chimed in, "what was her name? Curly something?"

"Kirlat," Hildir said simply.

Vunskridh shrieked with delight, "I believe our Hildir is blushing!"

"I don't think we need to draw the attention of our guards by loud voices," Torthan admonished.

After that discussion was somewhat muted and more serious, though the Norrungs all smirked when looking at Hildir, a habit he found most annoying. At one point he grumbled, "I don't see why I shouldn't be worthy of a princess," but the condescension in their agreement rankled even more and he said no more all day.

Dorgal never left off her weeping as the heavens alternated among sprinklings, showers, and cloudbursts, an endless succession of rain upon rain. At least the captives were indoors, though that was small consolation.

Who would trust a dishonest man?
Place faith in a known thief?
Strange the paths we sometimes travel
Senjir whirls and we must follow
--The Deed of Ian

CHAPTER 41

In the middle of the second night in Fjorn the Princess Gizli returned to feed the prisoners. Ian was intrigued at how quickly something can feel like a regular ritual, this being only the second time. Once more she arrived after midnight, though no arguments took place before the door was unbarred and she entered. Two women accompanied her and all bore baskets of food. This time she had managed to bring a second wineskin, some dried apples from the previous autumn, and carrots along with bread and cheese.

She had another treat besides the additional wineskin: her daughter. Ian caught his breath when he noticed that one of the supposed serving women wore jewelry similar to Gizli's. When Çirazel proffered her basket toward him, Ian stammered a whispered "Thank you" then added, "Your Highness."

"Shush," the princess said and the youth was silent. Gizli did the talking. She whispered to Furk and Ringskild a fragment of her story.

"I am a Princess of Hlv, from the islands south of Ulnor. If you can take my daughter back to my people there will be great rejoicing. I know my people and they will honor her and welcome and reward you.

"You may fulfill your quest but you must take my daughter Çirazel away from this place."

Ringskild responded, also in whispers, "We are happy to take her with us, but why do you not leave also?"

"I do not fear for myself," the princess answered, "but every day that passes threatens her. You must help me."

"We will, Princess," said Furk in his most chivalrous tone.

Gizli expressed her thanks and informed them escape would not be that night but would be soon.

As the Fjorni departed, Brona nudged Mechdar and nodded toward Hildir. The look in Hildir's eyes made clear that he had caught a glimpse of the young princess. Mechdar said, "Steady on, Hildir," in a loud whisper meant for all present.

Hildir mouthed, "What?" with a look of mock innocence as all around him snickered quietly. The Fjorni did not need to be privy to humor about their princess.

Vunskridh began teasing Hildir further, whispering the names Çirazel and Kirlat in alternation until he finally said, "Why couldn't I have a princess AND a feather woman? I know I'm man enough for both of them."

Ringskild snorted then asked him, "And how are you going to feel when one of your two women suddenly dies of poison? Count on it, they won't settle for half of you."

Nordil added, "You could interpret that as a compliment, meaning any woman who didn't want all of you doesn't deserve you, but in any case I would drop it, if I were you. Before you ever enjoy any other two women, these two," he nodded toward Ringskild and Vunskridh, "will drive you to an early grave." It was the warmaidens' turn to look all innocence. For his part, Hildir knew when he was outnumbered and was silent.

Talk then turned to the serious matter of reviewing what the captives knew of the castle's layout and analyzing potential escape routes. What they knew was not encouraging and they took their sleep, hoping new possibilities might occur to them by the morrow.

The next day did not begin with fresh insights but with a watery, lukewarm soup accompanied by more stale bread and a continuing drizzle outside the barred windows. Baron Grath encouraged all present to exercise as much as they could with shackled feet in order to maintain their strength and flexibility. All but Ian and Nordil executed mock battles without weapons and Ian fingered the scarf Njothila had given him, using the rosary design she had woven into it instead of beads, recalling the sacred mysteries he had been raised with.

With these and other means they fought the boredom of captivity and the incessant sound of rain. Norrungs and Vothneli traded stories of their lands and occupations, learning more about how their customs differed or were the same. The Norrungs missed the storytelling gifts and humor of Meldreth but would not wish their captivity on her. Sergeant Trno surprised them all by occasionally singing snatches of star hymns. "My mother was a singer," he explained. "I am a soldier. I try not to forget the stars lest they forget me."

That afternoon Furk muttered, "I say. Hah." Thus alerted, all turned toward the windows and caught glimpses of blue sky. The clouds scattered for a couple of hours and indirect sunlight provided a period of cheer. A fresh wind then brought in some heavy clouds and the unusually long storm resumed with cracks of lightning and rolling thunder. Any concept of time had, by then, blurred.

Something outside the daily round of sameness brought a shift in dynamics that evening when three new prisoners were added to the cell. They were all rain-soaked and had been roughed up and bloodied but at least showed no signs of Njlvac's exquisite cruelty. The first was an immense bearded man, his blond curls plastered to his head. Whatever he may have done, three guards attended to him alone. The second to enter the cell was as slender and quick moving as the first was huge and deliberate. His beard was trim and he seemed to be checking out every aspect of his new residence at once.

Before the third could enter, Vunskridh quietly swore, "Holy stars, not again!" This puzzled everyone until the Norrungs spotted the third man and recognized him by his gold earrings and snake tattoo. It was Vishgar, the smooth-talking chap whom Vunskridh had distrusted since they first met in

Denev. The warmaiden did not wait for the Fjorni jailers to finish chaining the newcomers before she launched her verbal assault.

"So, son of Ioreth, we meet again! You swore you were not following us, yet here you are. What am I to believe?"

"Ah, Cousin Vunskridh," the tall man replied, "The stars smile even in this vile place. The Dark Queen has not taken me, so my oath must have been true. Why under heaven would I follow you? One could as easily conclude that you have laid a trap for me, lovely lady."

Vunskridh easily fell into the prosecutorial mode she used whenever he was around.

"Oh, stop the fancy talk. What are you doing here?"

Vishgar replied simply, "Accusations have been brought against me. What are YOU doing here?"

"What sort of accusations?"

"Hold on, daughter of Jornandir, first you must tell me why you are here before I answer."

"We are held for ransom. Of what are you accused?"

"Thievery, my lady."

Vunskridh was actually surprised that the copper-haired man was speaking plainly. She was not convinced that he was speaking truthfully, but at least he had dropped his flowery style.

"By Wigdor," she swore, "that would not surprise me."

"I am sure you are ready to believe any evil of me," he replied.

"That is sadly true. Now that you have laid aside flattery and fancy talk, can you tell me why we keep encountering each other?"

"No, I truly cannot. I have been journeying toward my father's home which is north of here. Your path is your own, but we have been traveling in the same direction to this point. When the Prince of Fjorn is finished with me I pray that either Vuchtall or Ushni will be kind."

Vunskridh had no idea what Vishgar's personal piety might be and was inclined to believe he had none. Yet it was interesting that he invoked the Great Bear, the god of healing, and the Queen of the Dead. These were certainly apt enough in Bulçar's territory. The warmaiden allowed herself an expression of human concern.

"Is you father well?"

"So far as I know but age takes its toll. I have hoped to see him again while I still may, perhaps even return to his honest trade, carving wood in my home town."

"Since you speak of returning to an honest trade, may I assume there is some truth, then, to the accusation against you?"

"So long as you are not my judge or agent of punishment, fair lady, you may."

Throughout this exchange the other prisoners were paying close attention. At this admission, the quick little fellow protested, "He speaks for himself."

Furk, as senior lord among the company and one who had often sat in judgment, interjected, "Your turn will come, man, and I'll wager she has questions for you too."

At that the ferret-faced chap was quiet.

Vunskridh added, "I only asked concerning Vishgar, at least thus far." She then turned her attention back to the handsome man who towered over her. "Why would you steal from honest people?"

He paused before answering. "I suppose because one can. I rather like the game of it all. And most are not as sharp-eyed and swift to react as you that evening in Denev."

"Was that cutpurse associated with you then?" she inquired.

"No, sweet lady, I never saw him before or since."

"How often must I remind you not to flatter me with fancy words, Vishgar?"

"Until you are no longer fair nor sweet nor a lady, cousin. It is not flattery to speak true."

"Hah," she replied feebly, then turned on Hildir who was silently smirking. "Don't start, cousin, or Bulçar will be the least of your worries."

Vishgar resumed, "The Bastard of Fjorn is the chiefest of my concerns, though you are not far behind."

Vunskridh wheeled back toward Vishgar and announced, "If I were your judge, you should fare ill."

"A pity," said the confessed thief. "Of all who walk the earth, you are one I might submit to."

"By all the fires of heaven," she swore again, "what is this? A courtship in chains? Are you mad, you lying...?"

Ringskild cut off the exchange. "Enough, Vunskridh. We may all have our opinions but Wigdor will judge and Bulçar may do worse. It seems you have answers to some of your questions. If this fellow, for all his wickedness, fancies you then I am certain you are more than capable of discouraging him. For now we are captives together in this wretched place. I would not have our energies distracted from the situation."

With this warning about the need to work with Gizli and focus on escape, Vunskridh waved a hand dismissively at Vishgar. She was not done, however.

Motioning toward the large blond, she announced, "I saw this man walking next to Vishgar in Nimmoth, though Vishgar later denied any connection. And this fellow," here she nodded toward the small chap, "spoke with Vishgar in the courtyard after we met with Steward Peveç. Again, Vishgar claimed he was a stranger. For all that you considered me highly suspicious, tonight you see that I was right not to trust him. I will say no more."

"Good," rejoined Ringskild. "We can see that this fellow had spoken deceptively. He may or may not be journeying toward his father's home. He certainly is a scofflaw and he now faces the judgment of someone far more evil than he could ever be. If we can agree to so much, we may yet get some sleep this night."

Grath spoke next, "I believe, ladies, that all of us are irritable from our confinement, the ceaseless rain, and our anxieties about what each day in the hands of the prince might bring. I join in counseling peace among us. So long as these fellows take nothing from us in goods or honor, they are not our foes."

"Well spoken," added Torthan. "I confess that my own temper grows shorter every day, as does my eagerness to be away from here, should that come to pass." He turned to Vishgar's companions. "I assume you have names."

"Hnaç," said the large one listlessly.

"Fliç, my lords and ladies," said the nervous little one with a mock bow.

There seemed no need to inquire of their patronymics or places of origin, they were clearly baser chaps than the intelligent Vishgar who probably coordinated their efforts.

"See that you do no evil in here," Furk warned.

Hnaç seemed indifferent to this threat but Fliç glanced toward Vishgar, who said, "My companions and I have no wicked intentions toward our fellow prisoners. May there be peace among us."

"Indeed," Furk replied. "I am certain you are no gentleman, yet you have the airs of one. Hmmph. I pray you live up to your better seeming and I shall treat you accordingly."

Several eyebrows were raised at this most eloquent and diplomatic utterance of the rash lord of Vothnell. A truce prevailed in the confined space.

The troubling question, of course, was what to tell Gizli and what to tell the three thieves. This was a major complication and led to occasional whispers and much silent pondering.

Ian, who had been either an observer or a compliant center of attention throughout the mission, now took the initiative. He gathered the other Norrungs to remind them of the messages of Zhodor and the nameless hermit.

"We know that we must always remain in hope, right? What if our paths have crossed in accordance with the stars?" At this Vunskridh snorted, but Ian persisted. "The hermit said we must be who we are. I don't think that applied only to Lady Athnel revealing her powers. It is true for all of us. This Vishgar is finally revealed for who he is: a thief with fancy manners. Not very admirable but now we know him as he is, or at least much more than we did before.

"What if they were sent to help us? I may be wrong, but Zhodor told us not to spurn the three who would help us. Perhaps he meant some others, but we have encountered Vishgar four times now. I just wonder what you think."

Mechdar responded, "I do not know if they would help or hinder us and the Princess Gizli in our plans. But if she returns again tonight we must either soon include them or figure out how to keep them out of it."

Nordil asked, "What skills might thieves bring us?

"Unless my instincts err," answered Hildir, "that Fliç fellow is a cutpurse. He is too alert and quick and nervous to make me comfortable but I wager he could lift a key or a weapon easily enough."

Vunskridh reluctantly acknowledged that if Vishgar could strategize as nimbly as he talked, he could join forces with Ringskild and Torthan. "But that's all I grant him," she added.

Ian wondered aloud, "What about the big thug?"

Ringskild had an answer for that. "Large strong brutes have their purposes. He could probably dispense a guard or three with his bare hands. Though I must admit, I care not for Vishgar's accomplices."

"What?" Vunskridh protested, "Does this mean you think Master Snake On His Arm is an acceptable sort?"

"Smooth tongues and pretty faces have their purposes," Ringskild said, smiling. With that she conferred with Furk, Torthan, and Grath to sound them out. Grath opined that it was a huge risk to include them, but also a dicey matter to cut them out and risk having them hinder the escape. Furk placed no stock in prophecies, as usual, but Torthan reminded him that none of them would be there if prophecies had been ignored. The entire venture was based on them.

Ringskild and Torthan wanted to sound Vishgar out and did so.

"Son of Ioreth," Torthan began, "we are all in a precarious position, given the Black Lion's reputation."

"You mean the Bastard?" Vishgar retorted.

"I use a more formal title, but yes. There is a possibility of escape but I dare say no more unless you vouchsafe to behave honorably by Wigdor's judgment and your mother's womb."

The invocation of one of the more serious curses in all the lands about the Mere was never a casual matter. Whatever Vishgar's personal faith or lack thereof, his response now could bless or curse his life on earth and his future hereafter. An agnostic would be cautious in such matters and one would have to be as low as Bulçar to dismiss the curse.

Vishgar paused a moment, weighing his response.

"I value my life and my freedom. I have no quarrel with any of you, a certain warmaiden excepted, and I mean her no harm. I can command Fliç and

Hnaç but there is no guarantee on earth that they will always do as I say. But for myself, yes. By the judgment of Wigdor and my mother's womb, I shall deal honestly and honorably with you."

Ringskild watched Vishgar's eyes as he spoke and saw no mark of deceit. She nodded to Torthan, who nodded in silent agreement.

"Do all you can to convince your fellows to work with us," urged Ringskild, "for we need to join all our forces if we would succeed."

They then explained Gizli's request and offer, including the prophecy that inspired taking Vishgar into their confidence. He then said he would inform his colleagues of the nightly visits of the princess but share no more until he had met her himself. With this agreement all settled down so far as the anxiety in the prison allowed.

CHAPTER 42

Aunt Susan was awakened instantly when Annabelle first began to toss and turn in the bed they shared. "Poor dear," she thought then tried to fall asleep again. It was in vain. Annabelle Dyrnedon, like her aunt, awoke at the slightest disturbance, but when she slept it was usually quite peaceful. This time she began to make small groans of distress, finally shouting, "No!"

"Wake up, dear," Susan said, shaking the girl. "You're having a bad dream. Wake up."

Annabelle's eyes flew wide but her face was still contorted with anxiety. "Oh, Auntie, it was horrible." Then she began to cry while Susan tried to rock and comfort her.

"There, there, dear, it was just a dream. Nothing to be frightened of," she reassured her niece.

As Annabelle's sobs subsided she began to describe the dream. "It was Ian. He was in a dark place with a bunch of fierce looking people. And then there were screams and fighting and blood everywhere. I saw a big man snap another man's neck as easily as you wring a chicken's neck. And there was a woman in a lovely gown and lots of jewels who got stabbed. And Ian was running but there was blood on his face. Oh, I hope he's all right, wherever he is."

"Let's just assume he's fine, Annie. I can't imagine that he could ever be in the thick of something like this nightmare. You know he's not that kind of boy. And he has our prayers every night to watch over him."

"But it was so real, Auntie. I could hear the sounds and the awful smells."

"Shush, dear. You'll just relive it if you keep on talking. Let's think about that nice park we visited last Sunday. Didn't we have a lovely picnic? You were playing with that French boy, weren't you?"

"Jean-Louis?" the girl replied. "Not especially. There were lots of us there."

"Just be careful. It seemed to me he had his eyes on you. He is a handsome lad, though, I will admit."

Annabelle responded with indignation, "Aunt Susan, I didn't notice. And I don't know if you are trying to discourage me or draw my attention to him."

"I'm not sure myself, dear," said Susan, grateful that the girl's thoughts had turned from the nightmare.

In another world altogether a nightmare was beginning to end. Kirlat, who struggled daily amid the tension of her dreams of Hildir and the task of earning her living in the way she knew best, was walking toward one of the market squares of Fimmoth when her path crossed with that of the Lord Steward.

Peveç noticed the attractive young woman in spite of her shopping attire, chosen to avoid notice unlike her working gowns. A homespun scarf covered her hair and the brown dress was loose and unremarkable. The steward, however, liked to be aware of all that happened in the port city and was not blind to a pretty new face. Nor did he miss the raven feather tattoo on her hand proclaiming her occupation.

"Are you new in Fimmoth?" he asked.

Kirlat looked up at the nobleman, his chain of office obvious, as were the guards who flanked him. She pondered what crimes she might be accused of and could think of none.

"Yes, my lord," she replied, bowing her head in respect..

"Might I ask why you have come here to ply your trade?"

"My lord, I am an honest woman and my occupation is evident. I have traveled this far in hope of finding someone. And I hope some day to have a better trade than my current one."

"Have you found this person?" Peveç persisted.

"No, lord. He has gone far to the north. I do not know if I shall ever see him again."

The steward was intrigued by the feather woman who stood before him, her basket half full of foodstuffs. He spoke gently lest his office terrify her any more than it already seemed to.

"May I ask, Cousin, if you met him before or after you became a working woman?"

"Only recently, Sir. He comes from the eastern forests and, from what I hear, journeyed north from here."

At this the steward's brows shot up in surprise. "Do you mean he was one of the demon chasers?"

Kirlat did not know if the magistrate's knowledge bade good or ill, but she answered honestly.

"I believe so, lord. He was with a lad. They were both rather handsome," she admitted, blushing.

"You must mean the bundle of energy with the large muscles," Peveç said, laughing mildly.

"I suspect you are right, Sir," Kirlat acknowledged, thoroughly flustered.

"He is part of a noble company and I pray they succeed in their quest. How is it you come to seek him?"

"To speak truth, my lord, we hardly met. It was a thirsty afternoon in an alehouse in Nimmoth. They must have come from the Street of the Woodcarvers as bits of sawdust and shavings clung to them. We spoke briefly, then their friends called them away. But there was promise in his eyes."

Feeling foolish as she spoke her dreams aloud, she babbled on. "Oh, I know men can be false, Sir. And women can be foolish. For that matter, it can work the other way as well. We mortals are frail creatures. Still, I esteem him worth the seeking. You might say I follow a dream. Yet for now, I do what I know to do, for I would not be a parasite or idler in your city."

Peveç was amazed at her tale, naïve and bold at the same time yet told simply and without self-justification. Whatever tales she might spin for her customers, she seemed at the moment to be what she claimed, an honest woman.

"As you can tell, young woman, I have met the man and his companions. They have indeed journeyed north and all good people wish them success. If you hope to find a better trade, perhaps we can be of mutual service."

His phrasing made her uneasy, for she was not interested in becoming the mistress of a nobleman, not even one as distinguished and, for his age, good-looking, as this one. Kirlat frowned slightly and waited to hear what he had to say.

"A lady and her children have been given into my care. Her husband recently went to the Halls of Ushni. I seek a woman to wait upon her and would prefer an honest stranger for the task rather than someone already involved in the life of the court. Would you be interested?"

"My lord, you honor me," said Kirlat, "seeing we have only just met. Your faith would not be misplaced, I assure you, but I do not know anything about waiting on a lady. Or about children. My cousin's babes have not seen me for several years now."

The steward looked at her, wondering himself if he knew what he was doing.

"You know what it is to be a woman. You know how to beguile and entertain, and that would be useful in the life of someone who will feel trapped at court. If there are ladylike skills to be learned, I suspect you are a quick study, and your demeanor today can match that of any baroness, though I have not met any with the Raven's mark.

"As for the children, they would be a challenge no matter who waited on Lady Mirdel. They all lost their father and feel bereft. They have been taken from all that is familiar and are stuck with me at the orders of the Lady Rushvin of Thioth. The boy is on the verge of becoming a man, and if you serve you are not to beguile him. Is that clear?"

"Perfectly, my lord. I tire of beguiling men and I can keep a trust."

"Good. The other two are younger girls who cling to their mother. You would help with the children and wait upon Lady Mirdel. You would not share secrets with others of my household nor entertain their gossip. I will also expect you to keep me informed of the lady's wellbeing and the behavior of her children."

"I would be your spy, then?" asked Kirlat.

"Effectively, yes, but not with evil intent. There is more to the story and I will share what you need to know. My concern is that they be well cared for and, so much as possible, not feel imprisoned in court. I need the help of a woman I can trust. Are you that woman?"

Peveç looked at her intently, as if scrutinizing her soul. Kirlat recalled the singer's words before she left Nimmoth:

> Wigdor judge of oaths
> Keep your heart true
> And see that others

Deal with you honestly.

She knew her heart was true and prayed that Wigdor would make certain the steward was not dealing falsely with her.

"With the help of the stars, my lord, I am."

The Lord Steward then took note of where Kirlat was staying and bade her be ready within the hour. She rushed to her room, changed into the most dignified dress she owned, and once again stuffed all she owned into her trunk. Soldiers came to escort her to the palace and carry her belongings.

Kirlat had trouble convincing herself this was not a dream.

CHAPTER 43

The last thing Baron Raftor of Othen expected to see coming from Fjorni lands was a rider bearing an ash pole crowned with evergreens, feathers, and a yellow strip of cloth. A peace pole was also the last thing Raftor would trust if it came from Bulçar, which it did. Even so the lone rider was granted safe passage across the border and, escorted at great speed, to Raftor's presence.

Bulçar had counted on the southerners to honor a peace pole, though he himself recognized them only according to whim. "The simple fools," he said to his son Njlvac, "will behave 'honorably' to the end, and that is our advantage. The future belongs to the ruthless, my boy. We turn their supposed strengths into weaknesses, using their foolhardy courage and honesty against them. When their lands are under our control, then they can make up pretty songs about 'loyalty unto death' while they send their goods and taxes in our direction. Hah! The stars favor the clear-sighted."

Raftor, having lived close to the border and listened to sadder tales than anyone should ever hear, was very clear-sighted when it came to Bulçar. The exhausted and rain-soaked stranger that was led to his courtyard that night was received with extreme caution.

"Lord of Othen," the panting man said, "I bring letters to be conveyed far from here. One is for your Lady Rushvin, one is for the Council of Vothnell, and one is for Lord Njothir of Vorthall. I am told they will be of great interest but that is all I know. Will you speed them on their way?"

"Messenger of Fjorn," Raftor replied, "am I to assume they come from the Black Lion himself?"

"They do, Sir. You can see his seal." The herald handed a leather pouch to Raftor, who glanced inside as a torch was brought near, and saw what appeared to be Bulçar's seal.

"Let us go within, herald, we are in the rain. Your horse will be well cared for."

At that the man dismounted and wearily followed the baron inside, lugging the peace pole. Several guards flanked him. As they crossed the threshold, Raftor said, "You may entrust the pole to any of my guards. I acknowledge it and the feathers in your hair and recognize your exhaustion. Even so, be advised to make no sudden moves, for I know more than enough of your master."

Before the messenger could protest, Raftor added, "You need not defend him. I would not quarrel with one who carries on behalf of another."

Wrapped in a blanket that was brought forth and seated near a fire, the Fjorni rider sipped a cup of mulled wine and watched Raftor examine the contents of the pouch. There were, indeed, three letters, each tied and sealed with a large blob of red wax bearing a lion's head encircled by a serpent and abbreviations for the words: BY THE STARS' GIFT, BULÇAR PRINCE OF FJORN. One was addressed to Her Grace Lady Rushvin of Thioth, one to Lord Njothir son of Rathdar of Vorthall, and one to the Regency Council of Vothnell. A fourth letter bore the same seal but was not tied shut. It read as follows:

> By the Stars' Gift, His Magnificence Bulçar son of Grdna, Prince of Fjorn, to All who read This, Greeting. Be it known that certain Persons have come into our Lands and their Well-being is in the Hands of their respective Peoples. It is therefore in the Interest of the Rulers and Citizens of

Thioth, of Vothnell-on-the-Mere, and of Vorthall-of-the-Norrungs to read the Letters sent herewith and to respond most promptly and prudently. The genuineness of these Messages is well attested therein. May All Those who bear Good Will to Those addressed speed these Letters to Them.

A large illegible flourish beneath the text had to be Bulçar's signature as his seal was next to it. Although no other seals were attached, Raftor's attention was caught by two smaller signatures, those of Furk (including a rough sketch of a battleaxe) and of Ringskild daughter of Ivor with a sword symbol. It was not the sword of Vrotni, worn as a tattoo by those who go into battle, but that of Wigdor the Chieftain, the Judge and Guarantor of Truth.

Whether the symbols and signatures were forged or authentic, the message was alarming. Bulçar was claiming to have captured some or all of the demon chasers and these appeared to be letters demanding ransom. Raftor could see no course but to forward the letters to Lady Rushvin. She might then speed the others to their addressees, though by all accounts the Norrungs lived far to the east. A prompt reply on behalf of the Norrungs would be difficult. Was there some deadline in Bulçar's mind?

"You have completed your task, messenger," the baron uttered with a heavy sigh. "You will be fed and may return to Fjorn in peace."

"Sir," the herald replied, "my task will not be completed until I report to Prince Bulçar. May I tell him you will speed his missives to their recipients?"

"You may, man."

The following afternoon, many hours before both princesses visited the captives, Lady Rushvin received the pouch bearing the dire news. Overcome with distress the noble lady swore, "Grandmother Weltar, by Your Sacred Shell, what am I to do?" The starry Tortoise, goddess of wisdom, would be evident in the sky before long, but the season was not yet. Even Rushvin, for all her years, could not comprehend the ancient wisdom of Weltar, compassionate grandmother of the heavens who listened to the woes and dilemmas of all her children's children.

The court of Thioth continued to ring with Rushvin's outrage well into the evening. "The bloody star-cursed Bastard could not have found them trespassing on Fjorni lands! 'Have come into our lands' indeed! Hog-tied and hauled, if anything. Vrotni's fire take him! How that poor girl ever got promised to him I will never understand. Stars help extra daughters. If my Thjun had not restrained me, I might have gone to war with the old king of Hlv when he let his sixth daughter be given to that viper. Sweet starry skies! And now he wants ransom! The nerve of the villain. If he were before me I would flay him alive."

The household of the Old Castle, like all the Thiothi, held their lady in great esteem and affection, but this night even those closest to her tried to keep a certain distance. The fury of the passionate old lady was not unprecedented but it had reached a new height. None disagreed with her assessment or feelings but all considered her a bit too volatile for the first couple of hours.

At last she calmed down enough for reasoned discussion. The prior morning she learned of the mishap at Drush Pass and that the vanguard had not been found. Now she had reasons to understand why they were missing. "This is Njlvac's work," she concluded, guessing accurately. "By the Stars, they will pay for this."

At dawn the following day, Vjendar led all the troops he could muster on practically no notice and rode north upon the orders of his aunt.

Raftor had sent messengers not only to Lady Rushvin but toward Uvanor. That had been the intended destination of the demon chasers. If any had not been captured, they should know what had allegedly transpired. For all his suspicions concerning Bulçar's gifts for treachery, Raftor could not imagine the Bastard or his sons ever invoking Wigdor. If Ringskild's signature were forged, the forger would have used the sword of Vrotni to represent a warmaiden. His intuition told him the beautiful and fierce woman was signaling that they were indeed prisoners of Fjorn.

The rains and muddy roads had calmed the Fjorni raids south of Othen Stream. The messengers thus took the ordinary and easier route to Uvanor in spite of the weather and reached it at sunset, even as Rushvin ranted in

Thioth to the east. It was easy enough to locate the large body of strangers in the town.

Scouts had been sent in several directions looking for the missing parties but most had returned from their fruitless search by the time Raftor's men arrived. Djutar and Volthir were informed of Bulçar's assertions and Raftor's sense that they were true. Even as that night approached, the company rode forth, heading northeast toward the border. With the guidance of the messengers from Othen, they traveled as hard as they could, having rested the previous two nights.

Pjortan's suspicion about Athnel diminishing the rain for Jannir's funeral was confirmed as he watched her mouthing a spell when they set out. The night journey entailed no more than descending mists, a true blessing and sign of Athnel's power. By dawn they were at the border, ready to ford.

This time no peace poles were being carried for all to see and no warriors had feathers in their hair. Streaks of red paint in honor of the Fierce Mother appeared on most cheeks, mimicking the blood mark that Kirlat wore on her brow the day of her sacrifice at Vrotni's shrine.

Even as they prepared to ford the stream, fresh scouts arrived to inform them that troops from Thioth were about to join them. They waited a brief while for their comrades, taking advantage of the pause to eat something. There was no telling when there would be another pause once the border was crossed.

When the Thiothi forces arrived, Volthir and Djutar recognized the Tessian Marshal Shlevor at their head, his expression stern and his eyes ablaze with blood lust. The great warhorse he rode seemed to sense the excitement of riding to battle. The two parties greeted each other and exchanged information.

They acknowledged that the life of the captives was clearly at risk. Djutar was bound to defend the life of Lord Furk and Volthir and all the Norrungs were sworn to defend Ian. They would fail if their attack led Bulçar to slay the prisoners. Against this path lay the option of waiting for ransom to be made, but a ransom from Norrast would take months and the Prince of Fjorn was too volatile to trust that long. Shlevor's duty was to Lady Rushvin and she, frankly, wanted Bulçar and his sons to pay for their cumulative villainies with their lives. Nonetheless, she did not want to endanger the demon chasers.

As the three leaders debated their course of action, Wulfdar's voice rang out with a single word, "Look!" All within earshot turned toward the healer, who pointed overhead. Flying through the misty dawn three great eagles were headed in the direction of Fjorn. Gelje, the Eagle, was goddess of seers and their visions, so all who beheld the unusual formation viewed it as a sign. As with all visions, however, interpretation was the key. The three war leaders turned toward the star singers with questioning expressions.

Pjortan immediately linked the leaders with the eagles. "I believe you three are figured in the flight of the eagles. Perhaps we should go ahead."

"Lady Athnel," Djutar said, "is this your opinion as well?"

Athnel pondered the question then replied. "I prefer to have some seer give words to a vision, though I admit that often makes things no clearer. If Gelje has sent us these messengers then I believe Pjortan is right. The most obvious interpretation is that the eagles correspond to you, Cousins Shlevor, Djutar, and Volthir."

Volthir, more accustomed to following orders than giving them, looked to his fellows and said, "Well then, shall we?" Even as they nodded concurrence, a second unusual thing occurred. Just across the fording spot a howl arose. It grew as more voices joined it. A wolf appeared on the opposite bank and others could be spotted in the bushes and woods beyond.

"Vladje?" shouted Pjortan. The wolf barked as if in answer, then headed off on the path toward Grudhor.

"I believe we have our confirmation," said Athnel.

Volthir spurred his horse into the stream and some four hundred riders followed into Fjorni territory. As they rode toward Grudhor they could hear the goddess Ivra beating her great sky drum and once in a while they caught glimpses of Iltir's silver shafts in the distance. Still the heavens held to no more than a steady mist.

There was no need to raise a hymn to Vrotni that morning; she was present in every heart.

CHAPTER 44

Vishgar told his colleagues so little that when the prison door opened in the middle of the night he had to restrain Hnaç with his arm and Fliç with a glance. Anyone unfamiliar with them would never guess the various instructions Vishgar could give Fliç with a few facial expressions. Hnaç, however, was not a man for subtleties and he was quite miffed at refraining from what he considered an opportunity, if not for escape then at least for some good bashing of heads.

Princess Gizli knew about the three thieves who had joined the company of captives and had given them some thought. If they were not included in her plans, they might undercut them and betray her. When Ringskild asked if they might be incorporated, Gizli quickly agreed, merely asking the warmaiden if she thought they could be trusted.

"Within limits," Ringskild replied. "They heartily desire to leave this place, as do we, and I doubt they mean us any harm, though I would not trust anything of value within a league of them. They will not betray our efforts tonight."

"Good. My serving lady will unlock all the leg irons, but you are to remain in them, just in case, until it is time to flee. My daughter will curl up under her cloak in that far corner. Cover her with straw."

"I have brought you some weapons now. There were difficulties in gaining access to your arms but I have mostly succeeded. Here are your daggers for any initial encounters, which the stars and the deep waters forbid.

"Fortunately, my husband and sons are aware of my habit of feeding prisoners behind their backs. They disapprove but I have been doing it for years, unless I deem a particular prisoner worthy of suffering. My heart cannot bear to see folks tormented by starvation while enduring the anxiety of bondage in this place. Imagining what my husband might do is enough to unnerve the most valiant. Only the dull and foolish enter these cells without terror."

The great-hearted princess then outlined the most effective escape route plus a couple of alternates in case circumstances should shift. She then repeated the primary route to reinforce it.

"When the candle stub I leave you now runs out, it will be time to act. Silently throw off your chains, unlock the door, head to your right and down the steps. Grab a torch from any wall. Take the second passage on the left that runs under the oldest section of Fjorn Castle. When two ways present themselves, choose the left. It is a small passage but it leads to freedom. Should guards be posted there, they cannot be heard. Slay them and keep moving. You will come to an unused door. It is barred on both sides, but the outer bar will be removed and your shields and weapons will be lying outside under a dark blanket. The Pale Queen is now nine days past full and the bundle of arms will be in deep shadows.

"Before you open that outer door, however, extinguish any light you have with you and proceed cautiously. Stay to the left of the open court and you will come to a gate toward the stables. You will find your horses in a pen on the far side. Your tack is in the adjoining shed. My daughter can help you with all this as she and I have spent many evenings practicing this in our minds."

"What will your husband and son do when they discover us gone, Princess?" Furk asked gently.

"By the time the candle burns out, the Lord of Fjorn will be journeying among the stars. That is why you must wait a bit longer."

The Vothneli ruler persisted, "Won't you come with us, Highness?"

She smiled wistfully and replied, "I cannot arrange your escape and flee myself at the same time. I do what I must for my daughter's sake."

Çirazel distributed food and daggers as the servant unlocked the iron shackles at the prisoners' feet. When that was done, she headed for the darkest corner of the room and lay down, covering herself with the great black homespun cloak she wore that night. When the lovely and nervous young woman succeeded in disappearing in the shadows, Vunskridh and Grath scattered straw over the dark bundle that was a Princess of Hlv.

Gizli watched all this, then turned to the larcenous trio.

"You fellows may or may not be guilty of the crimes I have heard mentioned, but it is of no matter to me. You shall benefit from what I have done this night and I pray you remember it. I ask only that you deal loyally with my daughter and with your companions here. If you incline to any higher gratitude, I urge you to make an honest living.

"Lord Furk, I now entrust the key of this prison to you." Gizli fumbled in the flickering torchlight for a moment.

"Fliç," Vishgar said simply.

The slight man handed the key to Princess Gizli.

Vishgar explained. "My companion is gifted in obtaining things and I had not explained the situation to him. I doubt he realized from whom he acquired the key. Please accept my apologies for his effrontery, Your Highness."

This time Furk was not the only one to let out a somewhat indignant, "Hmmph."

The Lady of Fjorn handed the key to Furk, stood tall, and surveyed the room one more time.

"My daughter, the blood of Hlv flows in you. Be proud of it. May your life be long and happy. Never forget how much your mother loves you and may Tjiweth, the Bright Mother, watch over you.

"You others, remember: do not leave until the candle burns out. There is not much wax to consume. May the stars speed us all on our way."

She picked up the torch with which she had entered, turned, and left the room with empty baskets and only one serving lady.

Whispers erupted in the sudden darkness as the escape plan was rehearsed, speculations grew, and tension escalated. Ringskild spoke to the huddled shadow, "Princess, will you be all right thus?"

"Yes, lady warrior, but until we are far from here I bid you call me Nintel. It is a common name among the girls of Fjorn."

"As you wish, Nintel."

With "Nintel" huddled in the darkness, thirty eyes watched the lone candle as it burned down. Intakes of breath and anxious rustling accompanied its guttering. At last the flame died and the deep darkness was filled with activity.

Nordil and Grath assisted Nintel as she arose and shook the straw from her cloak. The lords and warriors instinctively formed a line by which they were in physical contact and protected the outlander and the princess from the three thieves. The demon chasers now had a double mission.

Furk fitted the key into he lock and a collective sigh of relief greeted the noise of its turning. A touch of fresher air wafted into the room as the door swung wide open. Vishgar ordered his fellows to follow and "behave for once" as they all exited the prison cell.

Sergeant Miglac and Nordil took torches from the wall outside the cell and the captives headed to the right. Ringskild and Brona led the way and Vishgar suggested that Hnaç stay near them as his strength could dispatch guards easily. The first guard was no problem, however, as he lay passed out, perhaps from whatever Gizli may have put in his mead. Hnaç made certain the guard would not waken to give an alarm.

While the candle in the prison had been burning down, Gizli returned to her quarters and her loyal serving ladies carried out various orders. The princess took a few minutes to compose herself, then took some wine to her husband's room.

She found Bulçar in a pleasant mood. One of his feather women was massaging his shoulders as he contemplated several items on a table next to where he sat. Gizli looked at the source of the prince's amusement and spied an array of iron hooks and a freshly sharpened flaying knife.

"Ah, wife, you have discovered the excellent way I plan to teach the thieves of Fjorn to mend their ways. Those chaps we caught today will pay dearly in the main square tomorrow morning. I'll wager every cutpurse in town will flee the city like rats from a burning building. For a while at least."

The almost hungry smile he displayed as he said this sickened the princess who was all too aware of her husband's delight in inflicting pain and fear on others. Nonetheless, she retained her composure.

"I realize you hate these events," he continued, "but as Lady of Fjorn you will sit beside me in the morning while judgment is executed."

"As you wish," Gizli responded, lowering her eyes. "I brought you some wine with Tessian stag's horn powder, husband."

"Do you think I need it, woman?" he retorted.

"Not with the young woman who kneads your shoulders, husband, but I confess to thinking of my own needs," Gizli pretended to the flustered coyness of a middle-aged wife wishing to encourage her husband without enraging him. "Perhaps later."

"Perhaps," Bulçar uttered ambiguously as he took a sip of the wine. "Maybe even now," he added with a threatening tone. Gizli recognized it, a prelude to fierce and occasionally brutal lovemaking. Was she going to be forced to witness him with the feather woman?

"Leave us," the prince said to the young servant of Desh and turned toward his wife. "So, you hunger for me, do you?"

"I hunger with the passion of the starving for food," Gizli answered. In her heart she finished the thought, hungering to see her husband's death.

"So, my Hlvi vixen, why don't you come here and remember what a real Fjorni stag's horn can do."

His arousal was evident but Gizli knew it was from the woman who had just left, not from a Tessian potion and certainly not from his wife. The princess put on a false smile and added extra movement to her approach, causing her full skirt to sway.

"This horn, my Lord?" she said, grasping his manhood through his trousers and fixing him with her dark eyes.

Before he could say yes, Bulçar's bushy eyebrows shot up and his eyes widened with recognition as his body twitched. A sudden fear seized and held him even as the fierce heat of anger rose in his chest. The prince known widely as the Bastard now tried to say something but all he could do was drool profusely. Panic spread across his features as saliva flooded his mouth and his eyes began to water. Gizli continued to hold his gaze as though she would, with a look, pierce his twisted soul and understand how anyone could become so unfeeling and cruel as the man she had been forced to marry.

Her dark eyes flashed and a smile crept across her face as she observed his helplessness.

"Do you need assistance, my Lord?" she asked in mock concern when his body began to tremble. "How shall I hold you up?"

Gizli reached for a couple of the flaying hooks as her husband collapsed in a convulsing heap at her feet. Realizing even the cold hatred that had accumulated in her heart over the years could not justify becoming like him, she tossed the hooks on the floor and simply leaned over Bulçar.

The Lord of Fjorn's last sight under the stars was his wife watching with satisfaction as his body failed him and the light faded. The only woman to embrace him that night would be the Dark Queen waiting at the end of the star path.

Freed of the man who had made her life an endless nightmare, Gizli of Hlv left him on the floor and returned to her own bedroom. By then the beneficiaries of her plans were leaving another nightmare behind.

Not far beyond the sleeping guard outside the prison were stone stairs descending further into the depth of the castle. With one torch near the front and the other near the rear, fugitives in the middle relied more on touch than sight as they descended the nineteen steps. Their groping hands encountered a crystallized deposit from many years of seepage and a dank smell reminded them where they were. The floor at the lower level was wet and slippery but not flooded. The fugitives groped their way and stepped carefully, trying to quell their sense of urgency lest haste give rise to error.

Whispered reminders guided those in front past the first passage on the left and on to the second. Here they turned. It was not long before the taller among them hit their heads on stone. The passage ceiling gradually lowered until only Fliç could avoid crouching in order to advance. At a few points it narrowed as well and Hildir, Hnaç, and a few others were forced to turn sideways.

The sense of enclosure and confinement was sufficiently intense for a few to consider, for just a moment, whether the prison cell were not preferable. This momentary inconvenience, however, led to potential freedom and Bulçar's dungeon usually led only to a horrible death.

When they reached the barred door, Hnaç lifted the large wooden shaft himself. Torches were extinguished and all braced for whatever might wait on the other side. Were the young princess herself not with them, the fugitives would have anticipated a trap. What they found was only silence and fresh air.

Silence did not prevail everywhere in Castle Fjorn that night. Gizli was climbing into her bed when the carved doors of her room swung open with a bang and Njlvac entered, screaming, "What have you done?"

"Mighty stars, Njlvac, what do you mean?" she replied.

"What have you done to father?" demanded the furious prince.

"Is something wrong with my husband?" Gizli asked, assuming an air of innocent distress. "He was well when I left him."

"You lying Hlvi bitch," Njlvac spat. "He was well when his favorite wench left the two of you together. Now he lies in a puddle of his own drool, reeking of shit. He is dead and you killed him!"

All the revulsion she had ever felt for the ill-begotten fruit of her own body came together as she stood proudly before the Bastard's son.

"Why would I kill Bulçar?" she protested. "I would gain nothing and you would gain everything. Don't be a fool."

"My father was a fool for indulging you. Where is my sister?"

"Why do you ask? Are you calling a regency council?"

"There is no need for a council, mother. I am now Lord of Fjorn! Where is Çirazel?"

"Asleep, I should hope, though if your father is dead she will be awakened soon enough."

"She is not asleep, nor in her room. Where have you hidden her?"

Gizli recoiled, partly feigning shock and partly stunned to hear Njlvac's near-admission. "Have you gone mad, boy? Where else would she be? And what were you doing in her room?"

"Don't pretend with me, mother. You know as well as the stars how I feel about my sister and you are innocent of nothing," he snarled, the scars on his face throbbing.

"And you are guilty of everything, you vile princeling." Gizli hurled the accusation at the vicious creature standing before her. All disguises had fallen by the wayside.

"Vile, am I? Your own son?"

"Every day I reproach myself and curse my own womb for having brought you into this world. There is no evil of which you are not capable. You are worse than your father and I pray that Wigdor will render terrible judgment upon you both."

Quaking with fury, Njlvac drew his sword and spoke with venom in every word. "Then I honor your curse, Mother!" With that he thrust the blade into Gizli's belly and gave it a mighty wrench.

The princess had expected no less and made no attempt to escape or deflect the blow. Through her last agony she voiced a hope and a curse. "You shall not have her, star-forsaken…"

The new ruler of Fjorn stood over the bleeding woman who had nursed him years ago in hope that he might be a good Hlvi son untainted by his father's vices. Such dreams faded over the years until all she could feel for the once-cherished babe was fear and loathing. Fear for her own safety faded as she became aware that the feelings he bore his young sister were unhealthy. Thereafter Gizli put great effort into precluding any opportunity for him to act, even encouraging his violent scouring of border lands to keep him away from the castle. She died trusting Çirazel would never live in dread of her brother again.

Having violated one of humanity's oldest taboos, even Njlvac felt a moment of horror as he stood over his mother's body amid spatters of blood like red carnations adorning her bier. Pulse thundering in his ears, he drew air in great heaving breaths, this particular death having surpassed anything he might have seen or done on a battlefield.

Taboos, however, were not for him. He was now the Black Lion of Fjorn. His newly established Magnificence wiped the princely blade on Gizli's skirt as though he had just slain a person of no consequence. After slipping in a puddle of blood, Njlvac re-established his balance and roused the nearest guards to search the castle for Çirazel.

Chaos worked against the sudden heir to the Lion Throne as word of Bulçar's death filtered through the household, followed almost immediately by news that Gizli had also perished violently. Njlvac's personal force and reputation for savagery compelled obedience to his orders yet the legitimacy of his new status was called into question by the manner of his parents' death. Servants rushed to tend to the noble dead, colliding with soldiers dashing in search of the young princess.

Moving swiftly but much more carefully, the newly freed captives emerged into the late night air and found the hoard of arms as Gizli had promised them. The skilled warriors could distinguish their own shields and weapons even in darkness and were soon armed.

Nintel led them along the shadows of the courtyard and was unlatching the gate toward the stables when cries of alarm reached their ears. "Quickly!" she urged as they moved noiselessly toward the pen where their horses awaited them. While crossing the muddy stable grounds the party realized the seemingly interminable rains had ended at last and a faint hint of dawn could be seen.

"Who's there?" a stable hand challenged just before Miglac clamped a hand over his mouth and slit his throat. An occasional whinny from the horses was the only alarm as they neared the enclosure where they would find their rides to freedom.

Torthan softly called his horse and felt the excitement of confirmation when the great warhorse came to him. Nintel showed the party where they might find their saddles and all acted efficiently in the dim gray light.

A couple had already mounted when beams of torchlight approached. "Hurry!" Grath urged just as a dozen soldiers rounded a corner and came between the escaping party and liberty. At their head was Njlvac.

"So this is what my bitch mother was up to!" he exclaimed into the early morning air. "I might have known Princess Tender Heart would do something like this eventually. But why now?

"I believe I see the answer. Dear Sister, what are you doing among these criminals and enemy forces? You belong with your family. Come to me now and the rest of these may go their way."

Ringskild's voice was never so cold as it was that morning, slicing through pre-dawn mist like a sword of pure ice. "She goes with us, Njlvac. You may go with Ushni."

As if in fulfillment of Ringskild's words a dagger flew through the air and lodged in the young prince's heart. "A gift from Lady Rushvin," said Mechdar with satisfaction as Njlvac swayed and fell.

With three members of the royal house dead and one intent on fleeing, the Fjorni were not certain what they were fighting for. Honor, habit, perhaps a nagging fear that the rumors were false and Bulçar might be alive and waiting to see how things played out. In any case, they engaged but were no match for the determined party of experienced fighters. The Fjorni soon dissolved in chaos and the former prisoners rode toward the Forest of Fjorn and freedom.

CHAPTER 45

Unaware of the disasters that had just occurred to his family, Stjor was occupied with other matters that morning. That heavenly trickster, Eghran, seemed to be at work wherever the prince turned. Lightning had struck an outbuilding adjacent to Grudhor Castle and the populace was babbling about Iltir's wrath even as people were scrambling to keep the fire from spreading. The heavy soaking of the week before worked in their favor but this was only the beginning of the day's chaos.

Messengers from Ytsraf on the east side of the Fiona arrived with news that peasants in the hamlets south of there were revolting against the suzerainty of Fjorn and Count Frednar sought help from Grudhor and Fjorn. An uprising would complicate Bulçar's plans to gradually seize lands south of the territory of Fjorn. At the moment Fjorni troops were scattered to harass and plunder, thus engendering in border folk a state of fear that could be manipulated. This meant no centralized army was ready for immediate action. The prince was reluctant to make a major commitment without consulting his father. Displeasing the Lion could be a fatal mistake, even for a son, especially a second son.

Stjor rather wished Njlvac would take on this task. His elder brother was excellent at mobile strikes and was currently unburdened by the responsibilities of administration. Stjor, on the other hand, was expected to govern Grudhor and its surrounding lands, including the border with Thioth. Thiothi antipathy to military action had spared him too many worries but one never knew what might change or when.

As Stjor pondered how many men he could spare in such a venture, loud shouting in the main square distracted him. With a curse aimed at the racket, the prince dispatched a page to see what it was.

When the rains had finally relented that morning there were a few buzzards in the sky, nothing unusual. As the day wore on, more joined them. Gradually the sky became dominated by the great black birds circling the city of Grudhor. To see them soar and hover over the countryside was merely the course of nature, the feathered scavengers helping to cleanse the land. Buzzards circling a city in any number—this was unheard of. People were gathering to watch them and beginning to panic.

Stjor thought this foolish but a guard ran in and urged him to see for himself. Annoyed, and expecting to see a dozen silhouettes against the sky, the prince gasped to see scores, perhaps as many as a hundred birds gliding in updrafts with the occasional waver typical of their kind. Together they created a constantly shifting black cloud. At sight of the prince at a balcony above them, the crowd in the square began to murmur.

Following the fiery shaft of Iltir at dawn, this new omen could not bode well. Stjor wondered silently: *Peasants, lightning, buzzards—what in Eghran's name was going on?*

Not daring to do more at the moment, Stjor ordered a contingent of thirty knights to go with the messengers from Ystraf and do what they could to help put down whatever insurrection was brooding. He hoped that would at least buy time.

These had only been gone an hour when news came from the southwest that a force rode against Grudhor and even now approached through the outskirts of the forest.

Djutar and Volthir had followed the wolf pack, generally avoiding roads and taking advantage of tree cover to mask their approach. Marshal Shlevor consented to this approach, both tactically and because he had seen Vladje's interactions with Lady Rushvin. By midafternoon they had emerged from the shadows of ancient stands and descended into younger growth mingled with fruit trees.

The three "warrior eagles" hovered at the edge of the woods nearest Grudhor. Having seen farmer folk flee at sight of them, they suspected that word of hundreds of mounted warriors would have reached Stjor, no matter how much they had avoided roads. The southern allies might have seen the dust of the assembling forces then exiting Grudhor Castle had the week of rain not turned the earth into mud.

It had been so long since the Fiona River Valley had seen bright sunlight, even late afternoon appeared dazzling. Red and black banners stood out as Fjorni troops approached the woods. Vladje and his companions had paused at the edge of the woods and it seemed he had become the general for this operation. When the wolves finally sprang forth it was the signal for the southern allies to advance. Even lacking sleep from their night journey, the southern host felt high energy.

"For Njothir and Vorthall!" shouted Volthir as he rode forth with his few Norrungs and a hundred Thiothi.

Djutar proclaimed, "Furk and Vothnell!"

"Rushvin and Thioth!" Shlevor screamed above the din.

Their close followers heard and echoed the battle cries as pulses quickened with the sudden shift into action. Prince Stjor viewed the advance from his midnight black charger, glancing nervously at the buzzards still circling. *Had they anticipated this battle?* He wondered if the day could possibly be stranger than it had been so far, then prayed for Viotni to guide him. Stjor assessed the forces arrayed against him and rapidly deployed his own troops on both horse and foot. They charged toward the invaders crying, "Bulçar and Fjorn!"

The battle cry he had not expected came from inhuman throats. As the two small armies neared, the Fjorni noticed a pack of wolves circling them and howling. Nor, in keeping with the other strange events of the day, was this any ordinary pack of wolves. There may have been as many as three or four dozen of them. Some approached the horses to snap at them, causing disarray among the troops. Wary of the wolves, foot soldiers suffered from divided attention. The only thing approaching normalcy in this incipient battle was the hail of arrows loosed by archers on both sides. Bodies began to fall.

Then the opposing forces collided. Djutar led the Vothneli down the middle of the slope toward the city, clashing head-on with Stjor's troops. Shlevor arced to the right and Volthir to the left in a pincers attack on the Fjorni.

With foreigners on three sides and wolves attacking on his rear flank, Stjor felt his heart sinking. Was this to be his last day under the stars? Even as he tasted his mortality one more portent appeared. Three golden eagles came flying toward him, one from directly ahead and one from either side. Their cries pierced the air above the conflict as they swooped toward him, climbing at the last possible moment. Stjor could feel the rush of wind and the sound of air in their feathers, they passed so close over his head. He had no idea whether their flight was a blessing or a curse but he was certain he was their focus.

All around the confused princeling the unanticipated battle raged. Clanging and grunting and the screams of the dying filled the air. Amid all this chaos one rider managed to get through to the prince. It was not a foe but one of his father's most loyal guards. The news he brought was not good.

"Your Magnificence," the man began, addressing Stjor as though he were more than a second son. "Your father and brother are slain. You are now our sovereign prince and Black Lion. May I be the first to swear allegiance to you?"

"It can't be," was all Stjor could manage at first.

"I assure you, Sire, it is true," the messenger affirmed.

"How are my mother and sister?" the prince asked.

"Your lady mother also journeys among the stars, Sire. Your sister has evidently fled with the prisoners toward the depths of the Great Forest."

"How came they to perish?"

"We cannot be certain. It seems your father fell to poison at the hand of your mother. Prince Njlvac wreaked vengeance upon her and he fell to one of the demon chasers. I believe your mother arranged the prisoners' escape and sent your sister with them."

Stjor considered his situation. Rule was now thrust upon him unexpectedly. He had certainly been jealous of his brother's position as heir to the principality but he had never expected himself to succeed to the Lion Throne. Even as he did so, he was surrounded by enemies on a day of signs and wonders. Unfortunately, they were not auspicious. Even the golden eagles seemed, after this news, to be attacking him rather than anointing him as sovereign.

"Sound retreat!" the prince shouted when he reached his decision. "And fetch a damned peace pole!"

The southern forces continued to attack and harass the retreating Fjorni as they worked their way toward the city gates, only relenting when a peace pole was brought from Grudhor and raised next to the prince.

As much as they mistrusted anything having to do with Bulçar's family, the allies would not, themselves, dishonor a peace pole. The three leaders rode back and forth, calling off their troops, and even the wolves withdrew. When the front line finally held, they waited to see what Stjor intended.

Before approaching the southerners, Stjor had his face smeared with ashes of mourning to honor his slain father, mother, and brother. He then rode forward with a handful of captains and two heralds, one bearing the lion banner and one raising the peace pole. Volthir, Shlevor, and Djutar rode to meet him, accompanied by Vladje and several large wolves. Close enough to hear each other yet far enough that neither side could attack, the parties spoke. Vladje growled as Stjor approached but was silent when the parlay began.

Stjor spoke. "Noble foes, the House of Fjorn has this day suffered heavy losses and the stars have fought against us. Birds and beasts have allied themselves with you and Iltir struck our city this very morning. My noble father now travels the star path, along with my brother and mother. You see before you the new Lord of Fjorn at a very dark hour. The few forces that have fought with me this day cannot stand against you at this time and I lack the stomach for needless slaughter. Will you accept a peace or no?"

Djutar and Volthir, recognizing that this was not their part of the world, turned to Shlevor. The Tessian marshal who served Lady Rushvin stared at the now humbled princeling who sued for terms. Stjor, aware of his deeds and the threat of being held to account, struggled to maintain a calm appearance. For all the treachery attached to him, he was behaving now according to civilized custom. But was he telling the truth?

At length, Shlevor responded. "Lord Stjor, if what you tell us is true, then it is up to my lady to agree upon terms of peace. What conditions she may require I cannot say. If you and your people are willing to renounce the evils you have visited upon the lands of Thioth and honor the borders long recognized between Fjorn and Thioth, there may be a chance of peace. Without that promise on your part, no agreement can be reached."

"By Wigdor, I swear to honor our borders and leave the lands of Thioth at peace," the prince replied. He would be busy enough trying to rule Fjorn.

Shlevor added that it would be expected that neighboring lands at peace with each other should also enjoy peaceful trade and Stjor agreed to that as well.

At that point Djutar spoke up. "Your reputation is known, Prince, and we have witnessed your own people fleeing the reign of your father and the depredations you and your brother have practiced. Are you willing to keep the ways of justice and learn mercy or do you intend to consume your own people with greed and the lust for power, glorying in the infliction of great suffering?"

Stjor was insulted at this intrusion into the domestic policies of Fjorn. Who was this foreigner to dictate conditions? The prince weighed his options, noting that if neighboring lands were to band together he would be at their mercy. Fjorn had been ruled by the iron will of his father and savagery of the young princes. On his own, Stjor was unlikely to control his own lands while resisting enemies on every side. He did not inherit many allies from his father but there were foes aplenty.

"Our justice is a matter internal to Fjorn," he asserted. "I can only assure you that I shall seek the prosperity of our people and not their destruction."

In this he was sincere. A ravaged and restless populace would spell disaster. If only for his own peace of mind and healthy revenues, the new Black Lion would be gentler than his father was or his brother might have been.

"That," Shlevor commented, "would be a step in the right direction. Until formal terms can be agreed upon I am willing, in the name of Lady Rushvin of Thioth and the Lower Fiona Valley, to recognize a truce between us, with the strictest proviso that our borders be honored. Additionally, and in this I speak with all the fury of my lady, if the Norrung and Vothneli captives your father held for ransom are anywhere within the lands of Fjorn, you must surrender them unhurt. I know my lady, and she will allow no compromise on this."

"They have escaped and taken my sister with them. I have been told they headed into the Great Forest, directly toward the regions where most fear to go. I will send word that you may have them, if any find them. They were merely pawns, to be exchanged for funds to launch a war that now will not take place. They are of no interest to me."

Great offense was taken at these words as those "pawns" were dear to the southerners and Ian was vital to hopes of destroying the Chegjan. Vladje and his fellows bared their teeth at the remark and emitted a low growl that made even Stjor's war horse skitter. Unaccustomed to wolves who understood the tongue of the two-leggeds, Stjor gave a puzzled look.

"You have offended more than a wolf, Prince," said Volthir. "These are Morvladh's people and your remarks just now trouble even the stars. We have all seen strange things today. You would do well to consider the judgment of the skies as you assume rule in Fjorn."

The Norrung warrior continued. "Will you grant us safe passage to seek our comrades?"

By now Stjor had settled firmly into his decision to make concessions today in order to live and rule tomorrow. "I shall order the letters drawn up."

"See that you do," Shlevor said with a clear edge of threat in his voice.

"Let us meet here in an hour," Stjor concluded. "My lords."

"Your Magnificence." The hint of mockery in Djutar's voice struck the orphaned prince to the quick but, though furious at the implied insult, he was a better master of his temper than his late brother had been. All parties nodded in mutual acknowledgment then rode back to their respective armies.

The intervening time was spent gathering the dead and wounded, healers working feverishly to save those they could. Mass pyres were hastily assembled, though dry matter was scarce. The few Norrungs had suffered bruises but no losses. They found some fallen wolves and carried them to the pyres with as much dignity as they would have given human warriors. Vladje howled as Pjortan and Athnel sang for all the dead, chanting Ushni's lullaby and the Star Path Song. Children from the city were seen chasing buzzards from the field until all the dead could be claimed.

The daystar was sinking behind Mount Uvjor and a few fires burned when Stjor rode forth again. This time he was dressed in mourning white, relieved by a black lion's head hastily appliquéd to his tunic. On his head was a princely crown and on his cheeks more ashes added to those applied before. He was accompanied once more by heralds bearing the peace pole and the banner of Fjorn, but this time also by selected members of his court. Lacking his father's coarseness, the new ruler assumed the mien of a dignified sovereign, or as much as his inexperience would allow. Those viewing him for the first time would not easily credit that he had recently fed a man to dogs. Those Fjorni who had witnessed that barbarity hoped he might yet become a decent prince.

The heads of the three factions of the southern alliance rode out to meet him, along with peace poles borne by their own heralds and, as before, a small contingent of wolves. They were also joined by a Thiothi baron, Meldreth, and Lady Athnel. Both parties met in the twilight. Stjor signaled an older man with ruddy hair turning gray and an untamed beard, a thick gold chain about his neck and a fine leather pouch in his lap. The man urged his horse toward Shlevor and proffered the pouch.

Stjor explained, "Lord Ardiç has the letter to Lady Rushvin suing for terms of peace. It incorporates our oath regarding the honoring of our shared borders and the promise to leave Thioth in peace during our lifetime, may the stars prolong it."

A second pouch was brought forward by a woman with a stern and serious face, her hair hidden beneath a scarf of fine purple linen. She presented the pouch to Volthir as Stjor went on.

"Mistress Ornathel is our chief scribe. She has had several copies of a letter of safe passage made for you and your companions, in all regions under the sway of Fjorn until the midsummer full moon. They bear our seal and the attestation of our councilors, including two lords who have just come from the capital and testify to the sad circumstances that force the rule upon us. In additional token of your free passage we give you this ring since we now wear the ring of our father."

Ornathel handed the ring to Volthir who replied simply, "I thank you, Prince."

Shlevor expressed the wish that all present and their children and children's children might now live in peace. "May Vuchtall heal our lands and the Bright Queen grant us increase."

"The stars grant your prayer," added Athnel. Vladje gave a short bark of agreement or blessing, none was sure which.

With that the parlay ended and all returned to the business following a battle. All slept as best they could that night. On the morrow the Thiothi would return south and the demon chasers ride north into the Great Forest. Both sides kept anxious watch lest the truce be broken. The skies remained clear and the stars looked down. The truce was kept.

CHAPTER 46

The former captives had hardly left the city when a lone rider approached. Nintel cried out, "It's Lady Zlida! Wait for her."

Though the name was unknown to the group, the face was not. It was the lady in waiting who had joined Princess Gizli in bringing food to them. Her copper skin and features indicated she was from the southwest and probably came with Gizli from Hlv.

"Talk later," she shouted, "we are pursued." With that she spurred her pale horse and the flight continued along the Forest Road with occasional detours to avoid encounters. Since the fugitives were not returning the way they came, the presence of Zlida and Nintel was most helpful. Zlida seemed especially familiar with the area.

"This way," she urged. "The Fjorni fear the Forest and I know of a sacred grove." With a jerk of her head she led the way and the strangers, reassured by a nod from Nintel, followed.

Zlida was not the only one who knew the region, however, and they had not gone far when a small group of soldiers ambushed them, breaking from thickets on either side of the path. The warriors quickly formed a ring about Nintel, Zlida, and Ian. It was the first time Ian had seen full battle close up. His heart pounded as he tried to retain control of his horse amid the chaos.

The attacking Fjorni were of roughly the same number as the company of demon chasers. None had encountered a Norrung warmaiden before, to their dismay. The lightning reflexes of Vunskridh were in full display but it was Ringskild who took Ian's breath away. Battle fury came upon her and she seemed another person altogether, as though Vrotni herself had come among them. Gone was the careful calculation the youth had seen in her so many times before. Ringskild gave the impression of turning in every direction at once, striking before, behind, and beside her with force and skill. Combating two or three at once appeared mere child's play to this woman berserker and Fjorni were ill-equipped to face her.

Ian's head whirled as he tried to be aware of all that happened about him. Amid the thudding of blade on hardened leather shield and the constant collision of horse and rider there was the sharp noise of colliding swords that sent shocks up his spine. The morning smell of muddy earth mingled with the scent of blood and the acrid sweat of battle fever. Cries of the wounded and dying rang in Ian's ears as he prayed to every saint of his world and all the stars of this one.

And then it was over.

As suddenly as it had begun, the conflict faded in the early dawn air. Half a dozen Fjorni lay dead in the muddy clearing. Amid them lay Trno, the Vothneli sergeant who had sung in prison to the stars. Meldreth, Torthan, Vishgar, and Furk had superficial wounds. The Fjorni had fared much worse and several moaned on the ground or leaned helpless against a nearby tree. The last few, tasting defeat, had fled. Once Grath and Miglac had laid Trno's body on his horse and lashed it in place, the party resumed its flight into the depths of the Forest of Fjorn.

This was not how the Norrungs had hoped to see the forest. Love of woodland life and respect for trees coursed in their veins and all had been disappointed that their planned course ran south of a great expanse of ancient trees. Fleeing for one's life, however, and trying to protect a princess and a chosen demon destroyer at the same time, cannot compare to journeying through stands of noble trees at leisure, experiencing the wonder of greenery never seen before.

Zlida led the battle-drained company deeper into the trackless forest, orienting herself by rare glimpses of Mount Uvjor and rock formations she appeared to recognize. As evening drew nigh they came to a line of stones, each about knee high and spaced a rod apart. It was the outer boundary of the grove sacred to Elithel, goddess of maidens and young girls.

As yet, the trees seemed no different, though the air seemed hushed and peaceful. At the second ring of stones, spaced somewhat nearer to each other and clearly curving in a great circle, Zlida called the party to a halt.

"We must ride no further this day," she announced. Tether your horses outside this bound. We may walk within the second circle and camp there. You men," she added with a stern glance and firm voice, "are not to enter the third circle under any circumstance lest you anger the goddess."

Nintel added, "We should be safe here. Few of the people of Fjorn dare come this far into the woods and we will be under the goddess's protection. My mother brought me here just before I became a woman."

At mention of her mother, the young princess was filled with emotion. She finally managed to ask, "Zlida, how fares my lady mother?"

The woman whose adult life had been spent caring for Gizli and, since birth, for the young princess, looked tenderly at the girl barely turned woman. "My child," she began, "your lady mother has this day done a great thing. She is free of your father."

Having lived all her life in court, Nintel recognized evasion. "Zlida, how does she fare?"

"She gave her life to free you, but not before ending the Lion's reign."

Nintel allowed the truth of what she had dreaded throughout all her mother's plotting and planning to sink in. Silent tears welled in the hazel eyes that, over the years, had seen too much and smiled too rarely. Virtually all her smiles had been when she was with her mother, laughing or sharing secrets. Gizli's laughter would now only ring in Nintel's memory. Her mother had kept one last secret from her, the final stages of her plan.

The young woman finally spoke. "So my father has also embarked toward the stars?"

"Yes, your Highness."

"I have thus lost mother, father, and brother in one night?"

"Yes, child, I'm afraid so."

"Njlvac is no loss to me, nor to the world of mortals. He was worse than father. But how shall I live without my mother, Zlida?"

"We shall miss her every day of our lives, dear. But you are the daughter of Gizli of Hlv and you will live and become a powerful and beautiful woman, as she was. I am sure of it."

"You love her as much as I do, don't you, Zlida?"

"I cannot claim the love of a daughter. But yes. Like you, my heart is now quietly breaking and I must learn to live without her."

The two held each other tightly in quiet sobbing until the first wave of grief had passed. Zlida then opened a saddlebag and fished out one of Gizli's necklaces. It was an intricate mesh of silver interwoven with beads of blue and green, its motion giving the effect of ripples on water.

"She wanted you to wear this when you meet your grandmother. She packed her jewels for you, dear, and ordered me to deliver them. She is…was… a proud woman and wanted her daughter to know she was a princess.

"I also brought these for us, little one," and with that endearment from Çirazel's childhood, Zlida drew out two large white headscarves woven of fine stuff. Wiping their tears, the sorrowing women donned the mourning white that nearly enveloped them. Wordlessly they then neared the sad little fire that had been started by the others.

Following so much rain the woods were soaked and only the driest branches in spots semi-sheltered from the rain had any chance of being kindled. Nintel and Zlida were not seeking physical warmth. They took the first ashes and smeared their cheeks to honor a woman to whom all present owed their lives.

Under the great oaks that circled that holy place the company sang Ushni's Lullaby, heedless of their lack of a star singer among them. They sang for Gizli and for Trno and for all the losses of their lives. The Dark Queen's embrace was loving and warm yet it could not fill the hollow places of the heart that night.

The men, meanwhile, had dared not risk smoke from a funeral pyre and dug, instead, a grave for Trno. They sang such snatches of death songs as they could remember, wishing his voice were still among them. Furk commended his faithful sergeant to Hjelgi and all the stars.

Preparations were made to get some rest and the night watches were divided up. The women entered the third circle, following Zlida's lead. Here the stones were taller and the evening air was filled with the music of a small stream. Elithel's Grove centered on an ancient spring that flowed amid the dark rocks of an outcrop, descending to nourish waterside plants, wild white azaleas and lilies that shone pale amid the shadows. Sacred starweed grew there as well and the goddess's own tree, virgin's willow. The melody of occasional birds added to the serenity of the place.

Near the center stood a large white stone, partly dressed, around which women would dance and sing at the new moon, now only four nights away. The four women silently gave thanks for surviving the events of the past few days, though part of Nintel's heart wanted to be journeying the stars with her mother.

Wishing to have some time to herself, the princess asked to remain in the center of the grove a bit longer. The others withdrew and the girl settled on a tussock, allowing herself to settle into a new solitude, the aloneness felt only by those whose parents were no longer upon the earth.

With her robes and great mourning scarf wrapped about her and her eyes shut, Nintel's thoughts were far away. Lost to this world, she did not register at first a rustling in the grass near her. When she did become aware of the sound it was only a split-second before she felt large arms grasp her and a hand clamp over her mouth. The horrified maiden first had visions of her brother, returned from the dead and determined at last to take what he had been desiring now for almost a year. Struggling wildly to fight against Njlvac's lust she flailed about, wanting to scream and weep and be ill all at once.

Remembering that her brother had joined the stars and this was not a nightmare, she realized it was another very real foe trying to throw her to the ground, someone much larger than the dead prince. Hnaç! It was the immense blond brute who was one of the three thieves.

Mumbling in protest beneath his great paw, Nintel managed to reach up and grab some of the ringlets on his head and yank for all she was worth. Hnaç only grunted and slammed her to the earth. She felt the weight of his body upon her, warm with lust and ready to violate her even near the altar of the Virgin goddess.

For all the shock Nintel felt at the impending fate, torn between the struggle to resist and a sense of interior withdrawal to lessen the agony, the villain felt a shock even greater. Just as his flesh touched her inviolate thigh, Hnaç experienced a sharp pain in his right leg, as though fire had shot through every nerve.

Vunskridh had taken advantage of a moment when his limb was extended away from the body of the princess and cleanly sliced off his foot. As he recoiled in pain and surprise, the warmaiden cried out, "Princess, get away. Now!"

Nintel used all her strength to crawl out from beneath her attacker as he sought to rise and face his assailant. She managed to slide to one side of him, just enough to give Vunskridh another opportunity. The shadow of Hnaç contrasted sharply with the white fabric of the sorrowing maid and Vunskridh aimed a sword blow at his shadowed torso. It was not a fatal strike but, like the first—now bleeding profusely—it threw the rapist off guard. Nintel clawed at the ground to free her legs of the man's weight as he was rolling in order to face the furious servant of Vrotni.

Before he could draw his own sword or make a dagger thrust, Hnaç felt the blow from which he would not recover, a strike between shoulder and neck that reached his carotid artery. Jets of his foul blood struck the stone altar. His sacrifice was almost complete. Vunskridh kicked his body over so he faced the sacred earth that he had defiled then tore open his ribs from the back with sword blows that terrified the princess nearly as much as the attack upon her. The warmaiden cried, "There! You have violated this holy place and now paid the price. If I did not fear the goddess I should leave you here for the animals."

Before she could do more, Zlida and Ringskild rushed into the clearing near the spring to see what the commotion was and Nintel became violently ill, retching until not even bile was left.

Few words were needed to describe what had taken place. Zlida promptly took charge. "Carry his body outside the first circle. There beasts may feast upon him. I will cleanse the grove and tend to the princess."

The warmaidens did as instructed, nor did they allow any of the men to help them when they were outside the second circle. When Hnaç was finally deposited outside the sacred perimeter, Vunskridh pulled out his lungs and arranged them like bloody wings then wiped her hands in tall grasses.

Ringskild had seen her fellow in battle several times but there was a new tension in Vunskridh. She appeared tight and withdrawn, her fury clearly not yet spent. No words were spoken as they returned past the curious men and into the Virgin's grove.

"Are you all right, little one?" Zlida asked Nintel as the women hauled off the corpse of the defiler. "How far did he succeed?"

It was a brutal question but one that mattered in the precincts of Elithel.

"Almost, Zlida, but not quite. He was just about to…when she struck. He had no warning. Oh, Stars! I thought at first it was Njl…" and at that point sobs replaced words.

"How awful. Yes, dear, your mother confided in me and I could see myself that your brother had unholy thoughts. You are a brave girl. I should say, a brave woman. Too much has happened to you in your short life, and far too much this day.

"Come, let me perform the rites of the goddess."

Zlida led Nintel away from the place of her attack and had her sit close to the spring. The noble lady who had spent so many years as a servant was in charge in this place, being a priestess of Elithel. She uttered some prayers before breaking off a branch of virgin's willow and dipped it into the spring. Singing a chant to the Virgin of the Sky, Zlida sprinkled Nintel, then the spot where Hnaç had attacked her and his body fallen in death, and finally she circled the altar.

When the cleansing ritual was completed, she sang again and gathered starweed. Crushing the leaves by rolling them between her palms, Zlida then massaged the young woman who had managed to escape still a maiden, letting the scent of the herb envelope her, its essence to become part of her. Inhaling the fragrance of the stars, Nintel found the first relief of this day of endless nightmare. The Virgin of heaven gradually inhabited the princess with the purity of her divine presence and graced her with the detached serenity of the stars.

The warmaidens watched, curious about rites of the goddess they had not witnessed before. Zlida's hymns worked a cleansing spell on them as well. When she was through she led the other three women back to their camp. A finger to her lips bade the men say nothing and ask nothing. Elithel's gift to all the women that night was sleep.

Sleep did not come so swiftly to the men. Fliç had begun to shake all over when he saw Hnaç's body carried out of the grove. When the warmaidens had returned to the circle of the goddess, he drew closer to his companion's remains and beheld the blood eagle. At that, he broke into a cold sweat and became violently ill.

"Will they do the same to us?" he asked Vishgar while wiping his mouth clean.

The elegant thief replied in a calm tone: "I doubt it, my swift-fingered friend. But now that you know what they are capable of, you would do well to honor the goddess, leave virgins untouched, and keep your talented hands in your own pockets."

"These warriors are savages," Fliç observed. "You see what they did to him."

"They are anything but savages. I believe what you have witnessed is the immediate carrying out of righteous judgment. Whatever Hnaç was up to in the Virgin's grove, I doubt his intentions were pure. Only a fool would anger a goddess...or a Norrung warmaiden."

Fliç marveled that anyone could be so calm amid multiple dangers. For his part, Vishgar simply went to sleep, not far from the redoubtable Vunskridh.

Ian was reeling from the violence of the day and his wide-ranging emotions. He was relieved to be free of Bulçar and Njlvac, sad that Gizli had not escaped. Trno's singing was sorely missed that night, as Ian longed for some comfort. The lad had feared the brutality of Hnaç and had no idea how he felt about the bloody corpse in the distance. He sought familiarity in conversation.

Knowing nothing of Elithel, Ian asked Mechdar about her.

"Ah, lad, she rules the sphere of young girls and maidens. I remember my daughters, Regnild and Dagnil, going off to celebrate her rites before they became women. It will not be long before little Vunnild, Dagnil's girl and the joy of my old heart, does the same. They grow up so fast.

"But you asked of Elithel. We men honor her but are not part of her worship. That belongs to the women. You should beware the goddess' wrath if you behave unwisely with a maiden, cousin. Myself, I hold the anger of a maiden on a par with that of the stars themselves, and that's a word to the wise. You are of the age to find yourself in trouble easily enough."

"I shall keep your advice in mind, cousin Mechdar," Ian replied with a smile before changing topic.

"Do you think we are in any danger from the other two thieves?"

Mechdar did not hesitate to say the worst danger was past. "That big fellow was good for only one thing: killing. His mind was as weak as his hands were strong and that is a dangerous combination. I would have feared him but our cousin Vunskridh has sent him on the star path.

"The nervous chap is good at lifting things but after watching him empty his guts at the sight of blood, he is probably no danger to our health. I would just keep a distance between him and myself or my possessions.

"Now our friend Vishgar is another matter altogether. I don't know what to make of him. He is as clever as the great lunk was stupid, and clever can be dangerous. You've listened to the man. He makes you want to believe whatever he says. I would wait to see if what he says is really true. Deeds make you, lad, not words. I don't know what this one is made of yet. But I wouldn't fear him physically, unless his own neck is at stake."

"He tries to impress Vunskridh, doesn't he?"

"Hah. Yes, Ian, I think he does. And she tries to discourage him but I'm not sure she wouldn't like to impress him right back."

With a chuckle—the humor of those desperate for relief—the two settled in for some rest while Torthan and Miglac kept the first watch.

CHAPTER 47

Forced to taste his father's bitter medicine, Prince Stjor surrendered ten noble hostages to guarantee his promises. These were chosen from several parts of Fjorn and were children and youth who would essentially be fostered to the Duchy of Thioth. They left Grudhor a few mornings later with Shlevor and the Thiothi, their families apprehensive and weeping for fear the prince might break his word and seal their doom. Were his power more secure, Stjor may well have renounced his promises at the first opportunity. What saved the hostages and preserved the peace was the prince's need for the very families from whom the captives had been chosen. Their support and practical assistance were vital to his own survival, given the chaos into which the principality of Fjorn had fallen within only a couple of days.

Consolidation of power, reorganization after upheaval, and restoring a semblance of normalcy were Stjor's immediate concerns. As the eldest surviving child of Bulçar, Stjor was the obvious heir to the Lion Throne and he counted on the people's need for an orderly succession. Even so, there was a weakness to his claim.

His father's nickname, the Bastard, was popular among foes and only whispered in Fjorn. Bulçar was the natural son of Prince Grdna and a merchant's wife. Grdna was succeeded by his legitimate son, Prince Revith.

Revith and his pregnant wife were killed on a tour of his realm shortly after being crowned. While the official story is that this was the work of bandits, most assumed it was an assassination orchestrated by Bulçar.

Stjor and his sister Çirazel were the only direct descendants of Prince Grdna, but the new Black Lion was only too aware of a couple of distant cousins he would have to deal with. In the meantime, he needed friends and allies. Concessions would be made for the sake of the throne and his own wellbeing. For that reason the new ruler made an effort to reassure the ten families that he would honor his word and their loved ones would be safe. To that end he enlisted them in securing the southern border and maintaining peace with Thioth.

Placing men he trusted in charge of Grudhor, Stjor rode north on the River Road toward the princely capital of Fjorn and the throne.

Before Stjor's entourage set out, a smaller party headed north. These were the Norrungs, accompanied by Athnel. They had all risen well before dawn and traveled with two guides. One was a Fjorni woodsman who had traveled widely in the Great Forest. He knew its landmarks, its legends, and some of its dangers. The Norrungs had found him and, in light of the truce and their letters from Prince Stjor, he was willing to accept some of their gold in return for assistance.

The other guide, and the one they trusted even more, was Vladje. Once the truce was in place his lupine companions returned to the woods and he resumed his place among the Norrungs. Wilda was overjoyed to have his company once again and ruffled his fur affectionately. At the head of the company, Vladje guided them through woodland roads and forest paths west of the River Road. His goal was not the city of Fjorn but the rest of the demon chasers.

One more group rode from Grudhor that day: the bulk of the Vothneli. In deliberations the night before it had been decided that Djutar would lead the Vothneli forces southwest toward the original westward route. Taking so many through the forest would only slow everyone down. The northern contingent, once reunited with Ian, Furk, and the others, would then also head west and the two groups could gather in Jorgil on the Ulava Plain.

The inhabitants of Grudhor, their town and outlying fields emptied of the various hosts, breathed a great sigh of relief and thanked the stars that yesterday's buzzards had returned to the countryside.

That same morning Furk, feeling strongly that decency needed to be observed, asked whether Hnaç might be buried before they moved on.

"Absolutely not!" Zlida replied. "The judgment of the goddess must be observed. Given our precarious situation, we dare not risk the loss of her favor."

"Quite. Yes. Understood. Terrible business. I, hmm, well…. You're right, of course."

One glance at "Nintel" in the early light told the men all they needed to know of Hnaç's behavior the night before. Owing their freedom to Gizli's desire to spare her daughter, they felt themselves culpable of failing her and prayed to the stars that the young princess had suffered no more than a failed attempt.

Risking his life, Vishgar approached Vunskridh. "Daughter of Jornandir," he began cautiously, "I am deeply sorry for whatever transpired."

Vunskridh's hazel eyes smoldered as she glared at the slippery man with the snake tattoo. Finally she replied. "You live this morning because I assume you had nothing to do with it."

"Believe me, lady, I admit to being a thief but I have never harmed a woman and I do fear the stars that witness all things. I only thought Hnaç had gone to relieve himself. My self-reproach is for bringing him into your midst. In that I am guilty, though I have never wished harm upon you or your companions."

"Keep that fear of the all-seeing fires of heaven in mind, then, son of Ioreth. I would not hesitate to punish you in like manner."

Vishgar held the warmaiden's gaze for a long moment then affirmed, "Woman of the Norrungs, I realize you mistrust me and have reason to do so. Your blades are swift as the shafts of Iltir, and your temper also. For several years I have lived by mingling pretty truths with lies. We both know this. If I would see my father before he journeys to the stars then I must survive your judgment. To that end, I pray you judge whether I now act honorably, nor hold the evil deeds of my past against me."

"I shall believe my eyes, Ushtethi," she replied.

"That is all I ask of you. There is one question I would put to you and I pray you hold it an honest and honorable inquiry. The mysteries of the goddess are none of my business, nor are the secrets that must be kept. Still, my heart compels me to ask. Will the princess be all right?"

"You dare a great deal, Vishgar, given all that has taken place. The princess has lost her parents and been set free of the brother who was her greatest terror. She has fled into the unknown with complete strangers. She has been attacked in the sacred precincts of the goddess. Mercifully the Virgin came to her rescue. I believe she will be all right but there is much healing yet to be done.

"You have sworn to her mother to help protect her, as have we all. All eyes will be upon you and your swift-fingered friend. You have more to fear than my judgment. Keep your companion in check. Behave as a gentleman. You may yet live to see your home."

Vishgar smiled at the earnest woman who stood before him. "I am relieved for the princess. Thank you, Vunskridh." He bowed and turned away to join in preparation for their departure.

Zlida informed the party that they had enjoyed the protection of the Virgin of Heaven that night, and probably the superstition of Fjorni who feared the deepest parts of the forest.

"We should put more distance between ourselves and Fjorn this day. We can head toward Mount Vjat and passage to the west. Before we do, the goddess should be thanked and honored. You men may finish packing while we women perform the rites"

Furk and his barons Grath and Torthan were more accustomed to giving orders than following them, yet they accepted Zlida's authority in this strange place, marveling at the authority she bore so comfortably. Their introduction to her had been in Bulçar's prison where she had unassumingly brought them food and quietly carried out her lady's orders. Here she acted as a priestess and spoke with the power of the stars in her, while they did what they were told.

Ian noticed this shift in roles and pondered the fluid nature of power. He wondered if he would have the strength he needed when the time came and prayed it might be so. For now he turned to readying himself for the next stage of the journey from Vorthall to the stars knew what.

Within the inner circle of the sacred grove, Zlida smudged the women with smoking herbs and sang a morning song to Elithel. Once more she crushed starweed in her hands and enveloped Nintel in its fragrance, uttering a chant of protection. With tears in her eyes—so powerful were her emotions after all that had taken place—Zlida then offered a prayer to Vuchtall the Healer.

The four women drank from the holy water of Elithel's spring. Refreshed, they returned to the men. Ringskild carried a gourd of the spring water and Zlida a fresh branch of virgin's willow. The priestess sprinkled the men that they might also be cleansed and protected by Elithel.

The rituals completed, the fourteen pilgrims mounted their horses and rode out. Trno remained in the earth, within the Virgin's sphere of blessing. Hnaç's remains corrupted under her curse. The water continued to gush and flow from the ancient rocks, mingling its music with the song of birds and the rustling morning breeze.

Reasons for the popular fear of the Forest of Fjorn emerged as they rode. From time to time the paths they took were overgrown with impenetrable tangles of vines. This was an annoyance but not especially fearful. What may well spook those unaccustomed to thick groves were the creaks and groans emitted when the limbs of close-growing trees rubbed against each other as they swayed with the wind. Such sounds came from high overhead and gave the impression that the forest was alive and the trees talking, warning intruders that they were unwelcome.

Forced to make several detours, the party found itself in a large and very dense grove by late morning. Here the thick columns of living wood dwarfed the riders. A thick canopy of dark green filtered out most of the sun's light, though the day was cloudless and bright. Traveling in deep shadow, the Norrung-Vothneli company felt very small and almost lost to the world of the living. An occasional tendril of mist added to the effect of powers beyond human understanding at work all about them.

Fliç, who could not shake the memory of the previous night's turn of events and the sight of his companion lying in a blood eagle, was completely unnerved by every sound and shadow of the deep woods. Vishgar, tiring of the nervous comments and sundry fearful shrieks, told the little man to shut up or risk being left tied to a tree. This threat put an end to the frightened chatter but did not altogether stifle startled squeals. Still, it was an improvement.

To Vishgar's dismay and the annoyance of all, Fliç fainted and fell from his horse when a sudden "Raak!" pierced the thick air of the shadowy grove. It was only the cry of a raven, soon answered by another. Brona and Vishgar helped Fliç back on his horse, pointing out the source of the noise and assuring him it was not some demon waiting to attack them all.

Though not presaging an attack, the two ravens did make themselves known. Calling back and forth at great volume, they then began a series of flights from tree to tree, with occasional acrobatics, darting about the travelers. None could ignore them and many comments were made. Some laughed at the display as though the birds were providing antics to entertain the riders. Others complained of the distraction and a few proclaimed them messengers of Desh, goddess of love.

The end result of the aerial display and its concomitant racket was a half hour of very slow progress through the forest. By the time the ravens flew off, the companions were barely emerging from the dark, majestic grove into a range of smaller trees. Here they were among stands of oaks or medleys of pine and fir. Whereas there had been a thick surface of duff from evergreen needles and stands of tall ferns in the groves of giant trees, here thickets of brush made passage a challenge. The one consolation was that any pursuers would also have to work their way through the trackless woods. Deer trails helped but riders on horseback preferred a wider passage.

What they did not know was that their only pursuers were not soldiers from Fjorn but their own companions, riding behind Vladje. Their passage from the south had been easier and they had even found an easy ford to cross the Uvja River. The wolf had shown consideration for Wilda and her wagon, guiding them around denser tree growth where a wagon would never pass and onto manageable trails. Even so the travelers had cut through brush at numerous points and occasionally put shoulders in service of moving the cart over uneven ground.

Shortly after noon they reached Elithel's Grove. Warned by the woodsman of its nature, none even crossed the outer circle, including Athnel and Wilda. A more gruesome warning was the partially consumed body of Vishgar's former companion. The ritual mutilation enacted upon him proclaimed some heinous misdeed. Refreshed by water from the spring, drawn at the point where it exited the outer circle of stones amid banks of cress and a backdrop of mountain azalea, the riders renewed the quest for their fellows.

Using a quicker track on the edge of the deep grove that was pointed out by their human guide, the pursuers gained on the fleeing companions. No ravens croaked and flew in distraction. Vladje resumed the role of scout when they reached the thick brush of the next section, locating passages that made travel easier. Once he picked up the scent of Ian and his companions he let out a cheerful yip and a few howls, then sped forward.

Lady Athnel let out a few howls of her own. This gave rise to a combination of laughter and puzzled looks. Pjortan realized she would probably never cease to surprise him.

The cries of the sorceress were matched by howls much further north as wolves began to pick up the cry. The daystar was not close to setting and, even if it had, there was but the slightest crescent remaining of the waning moon. The daytime cries of these nocturnal hunters sent a shiver up Ian's spine and his companions looked about them, puzzled.

"Do you suppose Vladje is near?" Ian asked Torthan who rode beside him.

"Nothing would surprise me, cousin," was the baron's reply.

As the northern half of the demon chasers rode over a rocky stretch, the singing of the wolves sounded nearer. The riders passed among shrubs fragrant with the spring flow of resins, their trousers dusted with pollens as they brushed against white and blue blooms. The afternoon seemed unreal, with mottled shadows tempering a bright sky while night howls encircled them.

When the entire party was in a small meadow, Ringskild gave a signal to halt. A large wolf faced them on the far side.

"Vladje?" Ian cried hopefully.

The wolf made no sound or move.

"I doubt it's your friend," said Furk, even as other wolves emerged from the shadows.

Having become accustomed to Vladje's presence, the company was at a loss to interpret such unusual behavior from what appeared to be ordinary wolves. Of course, "ordinary" was a difficult word to apply to the creatures after knowing Vladje.

Torthan observed that they were neither attacking nor drawing any closer. The riders formed a circle facing outward in case the wolves should charge them, but no move was made. Being the most accustomed to lupine company, Ian slowly rode toward the large wolf that first faced them. When he was about twelve feet away the wolf bared its teeth. Ian spoke to it but it only growled in response. Keeping an eye on the formidable creature, Ian carefully withdrew to the circle of his companions.

Ian tentatively began to sing a simple song that Pjortan had taught him. It was about Morvladh, the Great Wolf who ran through the skies with Athna the Hunter. Gradually the youth found his voice and sang as though chanting a lullaby to the wolves. They neither fell asleep nor lessened their guard but they appeared attentive. Ian had sung it many times to Vladje, who seemed to enjoy it. When he reached the end of the song a few of the wolves raised their voices as if adding a verse of their own. Ian sang the song again and the wolves listened.

This time he took no requests to repeat the song. Ian simply commented, "These are Morvladh's servants. We need not fear them but we should obey them. We are held here for a purpose."

"Have you become a seer now, or a singer?" Miglac teased.

Ian blushed. "No, cousin. I only know that Morvladh has befriended me. While I would never assume that all earthly wolves follow his orders, these respond to a song honoring him. It hardly seems likely they would do so while meaning us ill."

"Lord Furk," Ringskild began, "would you concur that the stars are holding us here for some reason or do you think we should break out and take our chances against these beasts?"

"Lady," he replied, "I was never especially fond of Ian's furry friend yet I am persuaded that he is sent from the stars. Indeed. As for those who stand all around us at this moment, I am not certain. Hmmph. How could one ever be certain? Yet I suspect the lad is right."

And so they came to tether their horses and wait in the clearing as the afternoon wore on. The wolves also seemed to relax, occasionally chasing a rodent snack or lying down with attentive eyes on the humans. When the rays of the daystar slanted low a distant howl came through the trees. The guardian wolves responded with a chorus that unnerved the horses and set Fliç shivering in terror.

Approaching hoof beats set the warriors on high alert. They swiftly remounted and armed, bracing for battle. The battle never happened as the first sighting of the assumed foe was when Vunskridh spotted a flash of gray. Vladje came bounding into the clearing and headed straight toward Ian with a happy "woof!"

"Vladje!" Ian shouted. "Is it really you?" He dismounted and the two exhilarated in reunion, the wolf licking Ian's face and Ian tousling Vladje's fur. As this took place the riders from the south came into view.

"My Lords," cried Athnel, saluting Furk and his companions.

"Dearest wife," was Nordil's relieved sigh.

Several uttered, "Thank the stars," and much embracing, shoulder clapping, laughter and tears followed.

Çirazel, Vishgar, and Fliç were introduced to those who had just arrived from the south. Wilda informed her husband and the others of Jannir's unfortunate death. Brief comparisons of losses and adventures were made. As humans talked the wolves dispersed until Vladje alone remained. Wulfdar looked at wounds from recent skirmishes. At last the reunited Norrungs and their new additions returned to the matter of journeying on.

They rode in the direction of Mount Vjat, continuing their many conversations as the day drew toward a close. Stjor's succession to the Lion Throne brought little comfort to Princess Çirazel, though she was pleased to hear that her brother was sufficiently overwhelmed to have chosen peace. "Perhaps the people of Fjorn will once again live without fear," she said.

"At least there is now a chance for that," Volthir responded. "I doubt he will last long without the support of several important families. An uprising in the east was taking place before your father's death. Barons are often ambitious. All these will have their own desires and grievances that your brother must contend with."

Grath interrupted. "Let us not speak ill of barons, cousin, especially while Torthan and I can hear you."

"My apologies, Lord Grath," said the warrior. "Your loyalty and that of Baron Torthan have never been in doubt."

"Hmmph," added Furk. "Indeed not. Good men. Yes."

Torthan chuckled, knowing Grath's sense of humor. Grath then broke into a roar and the entire company had a tension-releasing fit of laughter, some to the point of tears, though some had only been caught up in it and had no idea what was so funny.

CHAPTER 48

The reunited companions had no shortage of tales to share, in the telling of which they realized there had been more than enough adventures of late. All were grateful that things seemed to be calming down. Aside from their by-now-customary wolf, no more animals behaved strangely for the next twenty-four hours. The rustling of wind through the leaves of trees and the singing of birds fell well within the range of normality. The only excitement came when the woodsman warned them all to give wide berth to a patch of deadly bas vine he had spotted on the left side of their path.

"The slightest touch is instant death," he warned. No one wanted to test this pronouncement and all rode just to the opposite side of the trail at that point.

His other comments were merely wood lore that helped pass the time. The Norrungs delighted in this woodland journey, drawing energy from being among trees once more, while the Vothneli, more accustomed to fields and towns, looked forward to open spaces.

As they camped for the night, the entire company delighted in the expanse of stars twinkling through the trees. After the stretch of clouds and rain it was good to see the sky and everything seemed brighter now that the two halves of the group were restored. There was comfort in the thought of the stars looking down on them. Pjortan and Athnel offered several evening hymns and even Fliç seemed to relax.

Hoping to head west, the travelers were disappointed the next morning to encounter scattered patches of bas vine just close enough to make a passage through too perilous to risk. The deadly plant provided warnings in the skeletons of animals that had wandered too close.

"Perhaps," observed Hildir, "this is one of the reasons people fear the Forest of Fjorn."

"It would be a good reason," added Meldreth.

"I wish there were a safe way to gather some and study its properties," Wulfdar said with the detached air of one ever seeking knowledge.

"None that I know of," cautioned the woodsman. "And you, cousin," indicating Hildir, "are right that it is a major source of the superstitions that abound about this region. I lost a great uncle to it and have always kept my distance."

Ringskild and Furk conferred then announced they would ride further north until it was safe to head west. The demon chasers thus headed uphill toward the Tejth River and the Seven Giants. The Fjorni explained how they got their name.

"Before the children of Fjorn ever came to this land the earth was filled with monsters. Rachthors lurked in the woods and gnords flew overhead. Vurgals swam the Mere and the larger rivers, ready to devour creatures as large as a cow. Giants hunted these beasts and traces of them still remain. Have you ever seen a bridge carved from rock or immense caverns dug into the mountains? These marvels tell us where the giants once lived.

"As the time of giants drew near a close there were seven cousins, mighty among their kind, each claiming the blessing of their grandfather, Hrugdal the Landcarver. He was a great king among the giants and ruled at the height of their power. With his death came the decline of their race. His grandsons all wished to rule as he had ruled, though none were worthy to do so. Their struggle for sovereignty threw the land into chaos, causing destruction far and wide. It was here, near Mount Vjat, that they gathered for the final contest to determine the rule.

"The stars were so displeased with the evil done by the seven cousins that they decided to put an end to the struggle. Before the giants could join in combat they were turned to stone. With the great contenders eliminated, the race of giants diminished and eventually disappeared. But we shall see what remains of the seven before this day is over."

"Were there really giants?" Ian asked.

"According to the old stories, yes," Mechdar replied.

Ian continued his inquiries. "What are rachthors?"

Athnel responded, "I doubt that anyone really knows. Descriptions varied so much it would be hard to describe one. The one thing all the stories agree on is that rachthors had lots of sharp teeth. Some tales mention horns, some give the rachthors fur and others ascribe feathers to them. Their eyes are either as large as a chief's drinking cup or small and shine with a red light. They were monsters that lurked in deep woods or dark places like caverns, their favorite food was human flesh, and parents have terrified generations of children with threats of them."

"Something like, 'Behave or the rachthor will get you?'" Ian guessed.

"Exactly so," Athnel laughed.

Volthir said his uncle threatened to throw him to the rachthors when he was especially naughty.

"What a wicked thing to say," opined Wilda.

"Did you believe him?" asked Ian.

"Absolutely," Volthir replied.

"But did you behave any better?" mocked Brona.

Volthir chucked as he confessed, "Never for more than a minute or two."

The riders wound their way uphill through the fir forest, inhaling the pungent aroma of mountain misery as the hooves of their horses crushed it. At one turn in the road they caught sight of a stone outcrop above the trees. It was the first of the Seven Giants, huge bodies of stone scattered around the River Tejth. They stretched over a space of about eighteen miles, each rising high above its surroundings in solitary stubbornness, as though even in death the cousins could not come together.

As the travelers drew closer to the first "giant" they were able to spot a couple more, one across the river's south fork from them. They decided to follow the river's edge, riding between the rocky monument and the Tejth, working their way uphill yet turning toward the southwest and the Ulava Plain.

Mercifully, no bas vine was to be seen in the area and they were cheered to think they finally journeyed toward the rest of their company and their destination. This refreshing cheer shifted to apprehension when Vladje began to growl.

The companions were passing a section at the giant's base where great slabs of granite had split into roughly horizontal layers from centuries of water seeping into cracks and freezing. Decomposed granite had formed most of the earth beneath them and small clumps of grass and plants with wispy gray foliage and tiny white flowers managed to assert themselves here and there. The sun was shining brightly in a sky with few clouds and everything about the afternoon suggested a leisurely nap. The tension in the wolf had communicated itself to the horses and humans, however, and all were alert. It did not take long to discover why Vladje had given warning.

One section of stone served as a basking space for gorselsnakes. These were usually about three or four feet long with cream-colored bellies, their backs a pale tan with bands of light, dusty jade. In each green band is a black diamond with a spot the color of lapis at its heart. The snakes are not especially aggressive but their venom paralyzes and is strong enough to be fatal to humans.

The ledge next to the demon chasers was covered in a mass of such vipers, torpid at first but writhing to life at the presence of intruders. Others emerged from among the rocks into the path before the journeyers, slithering along the ground or coiling to raise their heads as if to strike.

"Sweet slithering sisters of Eslij!" Vishgar swore by the name of the goddess, Serpent of the Skies. His frequent practice in uttering oaths enabled the silver-tongued thief to pronounce this one without hesitation.

Vunskridh did not miss the chance to taunt him. "I should think by the tattoo on your forearm that you are her votary and a friend of serpents."

"In art, lady. I do not consort with them."

"My mother's snakes!" gasped the princess.

Athnel followed up on this, asking, "Was your lady mother a worshiper of Eslij?"

"Yes," Çirazel replied. "She kept gorselsnakes in her apartments to honor the goddess of weaving."

Zlida confirmed this, adding, "They are sacred to the goddess. Princess Gizli never feared them."

"Neither shall we, then," Athnel proclaimed. "All of you, move cautiously but be ready to follow me in single file. Make no sudden moves and you will be safe."

The singer and sorceress dismounted carefully, handing the reins to Pjortan, then moved to the head of the company. Once there she face the twisting mass of serpents and began to sing a song to Eslij. Çirazel and Zlida could be heard softly singing along as much as they could remember from hearing the late princess.

As she sang, Athnel began to sway, slowly taking on the fluid movements of a serpent herself. Her fellow singer, who could rarely take his eyes from this fascinating woman, gripped the reins of her horse so tightly his knuckles turned white, fearing she might fall victim to the deadly reptiles.

The ever fearful Fliç kept to the rear of the procession, watched over by Hildir and Miglac, and this may have prevented another fainting episode. Pjortan gasped when he saw Athnel bow down toward the snakes, her face bobbing left and right and well within striking distance. Eventually she reached out and took one snake in each hand, holding them behind the head and allowing their bodies to either dangle or wrap about her arms as they pleased. Standing erect once more, Athnel resembled a priestess of Eslij as she began to advance.

Athnel's usual golden aura when doing deeds of power was replaced this time by a nimbus of the same dusty green as the bands on the gorselsnakes. It seemed to shift and writhe with the movement of the vipers she carried, calmly moving through the poisonous mass. Snakes parted as she passed and the rest of the party went through. Evidently the song to Eslij had an effect on all who listened for the horses were calmed as well. With the exception of Fliç, all seemed confident of safe transit, at least during the passing.

Once all had made it safely through the venomous barrier, Athnel turned to face it. Concluding her song, she placed the two gorselsnakes on the ground and watched them slither back to their companions. She turned to behold the pale faces of her companions. Only Zlida and Çirazel seemed composed, though they were also wide-eyed. Athnel laughed.

"I am counting on all of you to show more courage before the Chegjan than you did with these snakes."

Vishgar, who had not gotten to know Lady Athnel, bowed with a flourish then said, with his characteristic smirk, "I should like to count on you nearby when facing either demons or vipers, gracious lady."

"Don't be taken in by the sweet words and fancy manners, cousin," Vunskridh interjected. "The man is a common thief and not to be believed."

The scoundrel's unkempt red facial hair undulated as his face assumed an expression of hurt and he laid his right hand on his chest in protest. "Daughter of Jornandir, will you always accuse me? And so falsely?" He then turned toward Athnel and continued, "A thief, I grant you, lady, but certainly not common. How many thieves have such sensibilities, such depth of feeling, or such complex stratagems as your humble servant?"

A second mock bow gained Vishgar a gentle kick from Meldreth riding beside him. She could always be counted on to stand by her sisters. He straightened himself to his full height, dusted his trousers, and said to the men, "My brothers, beware these women. They make gorselsnakes appear gentle."

"I thought I proved they are," teased Athnel.

"I should like to prove how far we can ride today," Ringskild intervened. "Thank you, Athnel, for protecting us just now. May we continue our journey? Cousins?"

And so they rode a bit further along the banks of the Tejth past the stone giant until they could look down toward the vast Ulava Plain and across toward the daystar descending through distant clouds toward the hills of Bjupazh. Relieved at surviving both bas vines and gorselsnakes, they descended into the woods that lay between them and the prairie below.

CHAPTER 49

Wild grasses and scrub once carpeted the vast plain extending a hundred miles along the east side of the Ulava River. When spring brought warmer weather, countless miniature blooms of white, purple, and pale yellow dusted the expanses of this prairie. Successive migrations of animals grazed here and humans also found its rich loam suited for grain and other foodstuffs. They defined its hitherto unbounded fertility with markers and low stone fences or hedges. Soil was turned, seed was planted, and water for mills was plentiful. Untroubled by scarcity, the realms of Aonghe and Thioth shared the plain and its wealth in peace.

The Norrungs and their companions surveyed as much of the plain as they could see, the Ulava itself lost in distant mists. The forest dwellers had never seen such an expanse with the exception of their brief time upon the Mere when the water seemed to go on forever. One's heart swelled to survey something of such immensity.

Even so a troubling feature unfolded amid this pleasant vista. It may have been low clouds, settling thick and mingling with smoke from hearth fires scattered across the plain, only it seemed unnaturally dark. The shadow expanded toward the river and hovered there.

Too far away to know for sure what it was, the demon chasers descended once more into the trees, following paths mostly trod by animals. Sooner or later such trails would lead to water. Before long they found a stream and camped for the night, assuming the rest of the Vothneli forces were somewhere to the south.

Captain Djutar and the host of Furk's troops were gathered in Uvanor where they had rested and exercised once before. Were they able to rise toward the heavens like eagles they would have a sight line toward the small band to the north and west of them, for they too were on the eastern edge of the plain. The lower slopes of Mount Uvjor stood between the two parties that evening as all took such rest as they could before the morrow when Djutar would lead the Vothneli north and Furk and Ringskild turned their party south.

Both groups set out as dawn approached, each contingent heading for Jorgil, Lady Rushvin's northernmost city on the Ulava Plain. Djutar roused the soldiers, noticing their restlessness. Was it the anticipation of soon meeting their lord or the hope of seeing fresh territory without riding into battle?

Djutar was eager to return command to his suzerain in spite of being an able commander in his own right. It was not the responsibility but a combination of two other factors that weighed on him. One was the vagueness of the mission. A concrete task such as attacking Stjor's forces before Grudhor was uncomplicated and gratifying. Chasing a demon was an uncertain venture with no clear precedent.

The captain's second misgiving arose from this being Furk's quest. Loyal to a fault, Djutar would serve his lord in any venture, no matter how dangerous or foolhardy. He would ably and readily marshal the men to respond as Furk commanded. Heading up the troops while Furk was elsewhere left him in an awkward position. Unlike his lord, Djutar was not driven to achieve battle glory and felt no need to pursue a demon. Still, he would command the troops and lead them toward Furk as best he could. He looked forward to seeing his brave, impetuous master again.

Flanked by the banner of Vothnell, its black battleaxe blazoned on a white field, and a peace pole with its yellow band—both hanging limp in the still air of the approaching day—Djutar rode forth. The pre-dawn racket of birds in every tree, proclaiming either their territory or their lust, began to fade as the daystar's rays touched the land. Djutar missed the presence of Athnel and

Pjortan chanting the Hymn to the Dawn. He heard their melody only inside his head.

> Disperser of the morning mist, giver of joy
> Upholder of truth and source of justice
> No deceit can stand before you

The captain, who abhorred all falsehood, prayed for truth and justice in his own heart. He felt the warmth of sunlight falling upon him as he traveled north on the Harvest Road, so named for the bounty of these lands. The scent of dew-moistened earth nourished Djutar's heart. Life would follow the plague as morning followed the night.

A touch stiffer and a bit less rested, the northern contingent rose from sleeping on the ground where they had camped for the night. The spot they had chosen was near a stream flowing into a large pond. Ducks emerged from the rushes and moved like shadows floating on the mirror-smooth surface, occasionally diving for morsels at the bottom. Ian held his breath when he saw a great egret gliding just above the water, a vision of reflected white elegance in the pale morning light.

Whereas Djutar could only imagine star singers greeting the dawn, Ian's companions heard Pjortan and Athnel's voices weave together as they all rode south through thinning woodland toward the chaparral. From there they descended to the fields of the plain by way of scattered hamlets.

As they approached one such cluster of modest homes, the sky seemed to darken. Perhaps it was only passing smoke from a cooking fire, yet such smoke as the riders could detect carried with it a strange scent. Roasting flesh, for certain, but something was different.

A vacant-eyed child, perhaps four or five years old, spotted the warriors and moved, slowly at first and then running, to notify others. From the lack of people and the child's behavior, the visitors assumed the plague had taken a severe toll on the tiny settlement. Having witnessed the horrors of both plague and war, the riders steeled themselves for whatever might come next. They still were not ready.

As they came round a hut and gained a view of the smoke's source, they saw a great spit being turned over a fire. The haggard woman who seemed barely to have strength to turn it did not even cast a glance at the approaching company, though the child tugged at her dress to alert her. The roasting flesh on the spit was human.

"Dorgal's tears!" Ringskild swore when she recognized what was happening.

Ian felt breakfast rise in his throat and Wilda let out an inarticulate shriek. More oaths exploded in the midmorning air.

"Tjiweth's heart!" "Shorall's eyes!" "Stars save us!"

Furk burst into action, spurring his horse and shouting, "By Wigdor, this shall not stand!" Before any reconsideration was possible he ran the hapless woman through. She fell into the fire herself and the now-screaming child clung to her, the rags it wore bursting into flame. Every heart seemed to stop, aghast at the sight.

There was no recovery at this point. The only mercy possible came from Athnel who raised her face toward the daystar and extended one arm toward the unintentional pyre. With a mighty rush the flames leapt as high as a mounted rider, giving rise to a blast of heat that forced the entire company to withdraw. Within minutes what had been a cook fire now performed funeral rites, consumed the three within its grasp, and subsided to a pile of greasy cinders, its tragic ashes flitting in updrafts like charcoal-colored moths.

Sickened by what she had to do, the Lady of Laoghar felt faint. She dismounted and leaned against her horse until the weakness passed. Meldreth and Pjortan came to her side to reassure themselves that she would be all right.

Mechdar, Volthir, and Miglac performed a quick search of the houses and confirmed there were no others in the settlement.

Wulfdar sprinkled the area where the grisly spectacle had taken place with dried leaves as he sang a cleansing chant, praying that the place might be healed. Since no other souls had been spotted among the handful of houses, he supposed they had witnessed the end of the last three inhabitants. The ritual he performed was on behalf of any who might some day come there, lest they be touched by evil. He also acted for those who had been part of it, hoping to lessen the terrors of memory.

Furk was not sure what he felt, now that the moment had passed. The burning indignation that ran through his entire body when he realized a fellow human was being cooked for eating had impelled him to action. That action had slain a woman who was evidently on the point of starvation and despair. Her fate entailed the death of a traumatized child. The Lord of Vothnell could point to no particular justice served, only the purging of his own fury. In this there was no honor. Even so, he could not say he felt true shame. Confusion and emptiness seemed to predominate.

Given all the passions experienced in the group, none dared judge his act and some wondered how one could rightly judge the situation they had encountered. How do the great taboos stand up to moments of great desperation? When does one say, "I cannot do this"? Is there a point beyond such protestation when one realizes one can, and might?

Not one for self-reflection, much less for philosophical speculation, Fliç could only focus on his own fears and muttered once more to Vishgar, "They will kill us. I am sure of it."

"Weltar's patience!" Vishgar cursed. "Will you just shut up? Your life might not be worth saving but if they haven't taken it yet they probably won't. If you whine about it one more time, I may send you to Ushni myself."

For once, Fliç knew when to be silent.

When those who needed to remount had done so, the travelers resumed their southward path, each lost in thought.

As conversation gradually resumed, the chief topic was the influence of the Chegjan. The devastation of the fiery death that swept across the lands north of the Mere was bad enough, striking all ages and stations, unraveling the fabric of families and villages, and robbing the land of vitality. To have such overwhelming loss followed by fits of collective madness, violence, and chronic fear placed too great a burden on the human spirit. Anxiety, desperation, lethargy—these had become the hallmarks of much of society. That pockets of resistance and endeavor still existed was testimony to an enduring spark within the human heart.

The demon chasers were a dedicated band, mutually nurturing that spark and acting upon it. When tempted to give up, they buoyed one another's spirit, yet today they felt the cumulative effect of all they had witnessed. Ian wished, not for the first time, that this new world with all its adventures would fade and he could find himself arguing with his brother Steven back in Dribley Parva once more. Even facing his father's wrath would be a safer venture than the mess in which we was now embroiled. How he longed to hear his mother's voice or feel her embrace again!

Wishing, however, did not make it so. Reality, for now, was the horse beneath him, the road before him, and the companions surrounding him. It was also, stars help him, the prophecies that set him on this journey and the darkness waiting for him. Ian felt cold on this spring afternoon, as though his heart had become ice. He shivered and turned his thoughts to the endless Light he experienced while in contact with the star stone.

CHAPTER 50

While Ian sought to lose himself once more in the overwhelming brightness of the Light, Prince Stjor's mind was also on light, though from a different perspective. The new ruler did not seek to lose himself in the Light beyond all light but to have more light shining on himself. It was the day of the royal funeral and he was dressed from head to toe in white silk, adorned with just enough gold to be recognized as His Magnificence, Prince of Fjorn. Considerable negotiation had taken place to arrive at the correct amount of jewelry to proclaim his office without seeming ostentatious, not to mention the adequate shading of ashes on his face to betoken his grief.

The daystar was not cooperating with the prince for the city of Fjorn was overcast with mist and light clouds. Stjor could not shake the image of the circling buzzards that had so recently darkened the sky and he kept glancing upward to verify that it was not happening again.

With his personal guard and the barons of the principality, Stjor followed the bodies of his father and brother in the journey to their pyres. Hired mourners preceded the deceased, wailing to the accompaniment of bone pipes. Most of the townsfolk had gathered, whether from curiosity or desire for spectacle. Few were there to mourn.

This was unlike the funeral that took place while Stjor was negotiating a peace with Thioth. Servants loyal to Princess Gizli made immediate arrangements for her rites, aware that she should would not want any association with her husband or either son, dead or alive. Gizli's beauty and generosity toward the people had made her beloved, all the more so because she contrasted with the capricious cruelty of the prince. Because the royal marriage had strengthened ties between Fjorn and Hlv, many Hlvi traded in Fjorn. At word of her death and of the sudden funeral, they spread the word throughout the city. By late afternoon the procession from the castle to the great plaza took place.

Gizli's household staff was in mourning white and had marked their faces with ash, as had all the Hlvi in Fjorn. What surprised them was that the people of Fjorn lined the streets in white garments as well, lamenting the late princess. Flower petals were thrown on the bier as her body passed and there was no need for hired mourners. Disconsolate shrieks rose spontaneously as she passed.

When the flames of her pyre had finally burned down, citizens gathered close to take ashes from the pyre and place them on their foreheads and tear-streaked cheeks. The city mourned as one.

Fearing reprisals from Stjor, the Hlvi left the city that night and headed for their homeland, avoiding the River Road they knew the Prince would take.

Flowers did not greet Bulçar and Njlvac, nor did any but Stjor and the barons wear white. It was later told that after the fires died down and the formal rites were concluded, a few young men flung horse droppings upon the ashes. They risked their lives to do so, for guards were posted. The soldiers, however, took no action and Stjor was not told of it.

A new and unexpected era had come with great suddenness. All of Fjorn waited to see what shape it might take.

The truce between Thioth and Fjorn held. Stjor dared not break it in early days and, as months became years, he realized there was little to gain and much to lose by following in the footsteps of his family. Vjendar and Shlevor maintained a careful watch at the border.

CHAPTER 51

The journey along the Harvest Road had renewed Djutar's spirits as he took in the sight of rich fields in the quiet morning. The recent rains had suppressed most signs of spring but now birds tweeted and chirruped amid the hum of bees, the latter hard at work gathering pollen and fertilizing fruits and flowers. Farmers too were busy tending their fields, whether tilling or weeding or sowing crops. The only bothersome factors were the reality of the Chegjan luring them onward and the irritability Djutar perceived among the troops.

Were they restless under his command? Weary of traveling far from home? Or was it something else? Djutar could not tell. Whatever it was, it seemed to communicate to their steeds as well for the horses seemed a bit skittish. The road was peaceful and open fields provided excellent vantage. No surprise attack could take place here. What was making man and beast alike edgy on so fine a morn?

Admitting the reality, Djutar broached the matter with the lieutenants beside him. "Cousins, have you noticed the restlessness among us this morning?"

Stavna the Stout, as he was called affectionately, grunted and gave a toss of his rapidly graying blond mane, before replying. "How could I not? The men are fidgeting and some have snapped at their fellows. I find no reason for it, but something is amiss. Of course, something always is. My charger of many years and more battles has a mind of its own today. There! Did you see him dance sideways as though he would leave the road just now? I tell you, Senjir is out of step today."

Djutar considered Stavna's reference to the Dancer, goddess of creation. Perhaps the entire created order was out of rhythm. Something was not right.

He could always count on an opposite opinion from Bluthni as he and Stavna never seemed to agree on anything. Bluthni was as tall as Stavna was short, as carefully mannered as Stavna was rough, and as cheerful as Stavna was grim. He laughed at his fellow's remarks but allowed some common ground.

"My cousin has never opined that the Dancer stepped aright, at least for so long as I have known him." Bluthni's grin drew a snort from Stavna. "Though I will grant you both that there is restlessness in the air. Perhaps it grows from the hope of reunion. If our comrades of the forest have found each other and the Fjorni are more honorable than the princes that have ruled them, well then, this may be the day we see our Lord Furk and all the others.

"Nor do I doubt that we have a slight excess of energy from that skirmish with Stjor the other day. The frightened fellow yielded so easily—and that alone would make even me suspicious—that we did not have the chance to show our fighting mettle. There has been much travel and little action, cousins. Servants of the Fierce Mother like to be challenged."

"You may both be right," Djutar responded diplomatically. "I shall be glad when all our forces are together and gladder still when this quest is concluded and we can return to our wives and homes."

"The stars grant it," Bluthni agreed.

"And Eghran not meddle with it," grumbled Stavna.

They continued along the road and passed a stream where women were washing clothes. The musical chatter was a pleasant sound in a world rebuilding after plague. Bluthni made a lewd observation about the way wet fabric clung to some of the women and the soldiers generally enjoyed the sight. At first glance, the women were apprehensive, but seeing peace poles and feathers in the soldiers' hair, they relaxed and a couple teased the men riding by. The older women rebuked this boldness then rolled their eyes knowing that youth and springtime can no more be held back than a spring flood. Much laughter followed the passing of the soldiers. Life seemed nearly normal again.

Just after this refreshing scene Stavna pointed ahead and said, "Captain, look!"

In the distance a black cloud, thick and low to the ground, seemed rapidly to recede and dissipate, yet there was no plume of smoke rising in the sky.

"I do not like this," said Djutar, spurring his horse to see what it was. The whole company of the Vothneli followed. No sign of the mysterious smoke remained when they reached the place where it was spotted. What the soldiers found was a flock of goats and two goatherds, an old man and a boy, likely the herder's grandson. Black and green flies were already gathering about them.

The goatherds and the entire herd lay by the side of the road, eviscerated, bleeding, their bones misshapen like spilled candle wax.

"Shorall's guts!" Stavna swore, matched by Bluthni's "Holy Athna!"

Djutar had heard of sheep's death but now he beheld it. "Cousins," he said quietly, "we have just seen the Chegjan at work."

Discipline was not quickly reestablished as rumors flew and every soldier felt compelled to get a look at the wretched sight. A few were ill, some were excited, none were indifferent. This would provide stories to tell back home around a winter fire, provided one made it safely to Vothnell again.

The thrill that mingles with horror eventually faded into the sober awareness of the great danger in which they stood. If this be the work of the dark demon, what might happen to those who march to oppose it? Many a soldier silently besought the starry heavens that Furk and the forest folk knew what they were doing.

Captain Djutar ordered the building of pyres for the goatherds. While this took place nearby villagers approached. When they saw the carnage and recognized its victims, Eghran erupted in their midst. Cries of desolation, imprecations, weeping and beating of breasts ensued. Clothing was torn and dirt rubbed on faces. Some ran back to the village and soon the goatherd's daughter and mother of the boy arrived. Dorgal, the Weeper whose tears are rain, could not have wept louder or more profusely.

The soldiers finished their work and stood aside for the mourners. Men of the village carried the goat carcasses into one spot for burning. None dared eat meat tainted by a demon.

Djutar expressed his condolences then gave the order to ride on. He had a sick feeling that none of them had a clue what they were up against.

CHAPTER 52

Shaken by what they had witnessed, both parties halted their converging travels early that day.

Djutar observed signs of fatigue in the Vothneli under his command, the sort of exhaustion caused not by exertion or lack of sleep but by emotional trauma. The edginess of the day had shifted, following the sight of "sheep's death" and the grief it occasioned, to a pensive lethargy.

Bluthni commented on the consequences for the herder's family. Beyond the loss of the goatherd and his grandson, they had lost an entire herd of goats, their presumed livelihood. No goat milk or cheese, nor meat. The price exacted by the Chegjan was high for that extended family.

Djutar felt the price was far too high for all the peoples who lived on the north side of the Mere. He wondered if the Chegjan, unchecked, would circle the entire sea and devastate all the lands of Mídhris. Prophecies notwithstanding, the captain questioned whether the demon could be defeated.

At the moment, he knew his men were shaken. He did not want to present the soldiers in his charge to Furk in this condition. Djutar halted the march and ordered them to make camp before reaching Jorgil. There was no objection.

For their part, the northern contingent under Ringskild and Furk, wrestled with its own demons that afternoon. The ebullient Lord of Vothnell had become withdrawn, uttering little more than the occasional "Hmmph." Volthir pointed out to Ringskild that Furk appeared both shaken by the slaying of the would-be cannibal and smoldering with an inner fire that seemed to build in intensity.

Furk had joined himself to the Norrungs' quest for his own reasons, military vainglory being an obvious one. Over the course of this journey with the forest folk, the mission had become more personal. The count's devotion to justice and the horrors he had seen together reinforced his passion to destroy the Chegjan and establish righteousness in the lands it had devastated.

As Ringskild took stock of the company as a whole she realized they were all somewhat withdrawn. The thought of anyone so desperate as to eat human flesh shook the basic values they all shared. The sudden death by sword and fire had seemed pointless yet gruesomely real. The Norrung captain conferred with Torthan and Grath. All agreed that the collective state of shock might best be countered by getting a good night's rest. They halted in a pleasant meadow and camped well before sunset.

Following an evening hymn, Pjortan lay awake, scanning the heavens for guidance or reassurance. Gelje the Eagle could be seen soaring amid the other fiery deities. The singer tried to soar with the stars, recalling the time he was taken into the heavens back in Thioth, though without the dizziness. The least little sliver of the Pale Queen had revealed her presence earlier, slipping behind a cloud just after midnight. Tomorrow would be the night of the new moon, a new month, a new beginning. Pjortan closed his eyes and settled into mingled thoughts of the stars and of Athnel.

It was not so quiet a night in Fimmoth. Lord Steward Peveç would dearly have loved to behold the stars in the quiet of the countryside. Instead he beheld Lady Mirdel crashing into his study with the heavy bang of the carved door and protests of guards in the background.

"I know what she is!" the lady exclaimed, her breathing heavy and her cheeks flushed with indignation.

Peveç initially recoiled from the accusatory tone and flashing eyes of Vorn's widow. Having wielded absolute rule in Fimmoth, subject only to the suzerainty of Lady Rushvin, he was rarely confronted by anyone. The Steward was known for his unruffled air of command. Faced with this feminine fury, Peveç was at a sudden loss.

Mirdel was of average height and seemed even shorter next to the slender height of the Lord Steward. She was pale with anger and her body shook in the rust-colored gown she wore. Strands of red hair escaped from the white scarf she still wore in sign of mourning and candlelight sparked in her topaz jewelry. She clearly expected some response from Peveç.

"What do you mean?" was all he managed.

"You have sent me a feather woman for a lady-in-waiting."

"Has she attended you poorly? Failed in her duties?" the steward countered.

"That, Lord Steward, is hardly the point!"

"I should think her performance is precisely the point," Peveç replied, his equanimity returning.

"I don't want her 'performing' with my son. He is coming of age." Peveç suspected the fire of Vrotni was flashing in a mother's eyes at that moment.

"No more do I," he responded. "She has been told that death awaits her if she tries. The safety of all your children is of concern to me, Lady Mirdel."

"Then why did you bring 'that woman' to me?" The disdain in her voice was evident as she nearly spat the words "that woman."

"Because she is quick-witted and skilled at entertaining in more ways than the one you presume. I thought she might lighten the burden of your stay here. And I chose her precisely because she is not part of the court. I would spare you the evils of gossip, Lady. Attendants are prone to that vice. Kirlat's independence of courtly life leaves her answerable only to you and me, devoid of other loyalties."

Mirdel snorted. "Hah! That shows how much you know, Lord Steward. The woman may serve here but her heart is out wandering with the demon chasers. Her loyalty is entangled in foolish dreams. Mere necessity binds her to us."

"Necessity is a powerful bond, my lady. I am not certain even the stars can compel the human heart, yet wherever our hearts may stray we all find ourselves where necessity places us."

"Necessity has placed you well, Lord Peveç. Not all are so fortunate."

"I am sorry for your loss, lady. We have each lost a spouse, though your circumstances were especially grievous. We have tried to lessen your burden."

"I grant you that. Still, you cannot deny that this palace is my prison?"

"Her Grace has set bounds, it is true, yet I prefer to consider you and your children as my guests."

"A pretty word for captives," Mirdel grunted.

"We are all captives here—captives to duties and protocol, slaves of our passions and bondservants of gossip. No one who is truly free lives in a palace, lady."

"Yet you are free to come and go, Peveç!"

The Steward stared into the widow's amber eyes before replying. "I travel the streets of this great port yet I can never lay responsibility aside. People do not see Peveç the man; they see only the Lord Steward. And who is he? A role, an office, a diplomatic fiction!"

"What then am I—" Mirdel responded, "a ghost, a traitor's wife—yes, I am not a blind fool—a prisoner, an object of rumor, something to be hidden away?"

"You are a lady, Mirdel, a nobly born woman of wit and beauty and more than enough fire to live fully for years to come."

"You mock me, Peveç."

"No, lady, I see who stands before me."

Mirdel pondered the steward's words then returned to her original topic.

"Then who waits upon me if not a servant of Desh?"

"A young woman who is capable of telling the truth, willing to earn her keep, open to learning, yearning for love."

"Do you have feelings for her?"

Peveç smiled. "No. She is pretty and all the things I just said about her, but she is young and not for me. I leave her to the Norrung warrior, if their paths ever cross again."

"Why did you send her to me?"

"Because she is free of the ways of the court. I thought she might provide you with a wider view of the world than the walls of this palace can afford. Perhaps I have made a mistake; it happens. Is she attentive to you?"

"She is."

"And to the children? By which I do not mean overly attentive to your son."

"She appears to have become fond of them already, much to my surprise."

"Has she displeased you or in any way behaved badly?"

"Only by being who she is."

"So you and the children are waited upon and Kirlat has not acted displeasingly."

Mirdel hesitated. The phrasing of Peveç's question precluded her complaint and they both knew it.

"You refuse to acknowledge a problem, Peveç."

"I had thought you insisted on seeing one where one didn't exist, Mirdel."

"Starfire!" she cursed, stamping her foot. "You are a stubborn man."

"Fortunately," Peveç smiled, "you are a sweet, reasonable woman." Mirdel glared as he continued. "We both know that noble blood is no guarantee of virtuous character, for many of the finest pedigree behave basely. It should also be widely recognized that lack of noble birth is no impediment to sterling character and noble living. Can you grant me that, lady?"

She was not inclined to grant anything yet.

"I have made inquiries in Nimmoth where she frequented an alehouse in the Craft Quarter. There are no ill reports of this woman. She was well-liked by all who knew her, and before you say it, I speak of more than customers.

"Kirlat behaves honorably. Her service of the goddess cannot be held against her. I see no reason to fret on account of her, unless you seek to protect your son."

"I do worry about him."

"Every parent has fears for children as they reach adulthood. We expect so much and they are often so unready. Folly beckons them at every turn. My one fear in sending Kirlat to you was that possibility. As I have already mentioned, I have told her that her life hinges on treating him as she would her own child or a brother. If you have any evidence that she encourages wrong thoughts in him, much less unseemly actions, you will tell me and she will face my judgment."

A fierceness in Peveç's voice touched Mirdel. Perhaps he did mean well. At last she spoke.

"I admit she has dressed more modestly than feather women do in all the time she has been with me. She has given my son no more nor less attention than the girls. Yet…"

"Yet what, my lady?"

"I saw him stare at her raven feather tattoo today. She wears unfashionably long sleeves most of the time but she cannot hide it without wearing gloves and I fear he knows all too well what it means."

"Would you have me explain to him that she is not available to him nor to any man while she serves here?"

"His father should teach him these things. I miss Vorn, no matter what he may have done," she said with a tone of defiance.

"I understand. And I cannot replace a father. But if you will, I shall speak with your young man. I will also remind Kirlat of our understanding."

"Thank you, Peveç." Mirdel paused. "You have been kind to us."

"You are welcome here, Mirdel."

The lady who entered in a rage now departed quietly. The Steward of Fimmoth listened to the swishing of her garments as she left his chambers, the long white scarf trailing almost to the hem of her gown. He remembered when he wore white after the untimely death of his wife. Tjiweth had not blessed them with children. Peveç snorted ruefully when he caught himself envying the "captive" widow.

CHAPTER 53

Kirlat was untroubled that night, unaware of the conflict swirling about her. She had adapted quickly to serving Lady Mirdel. The natural empathy she felt toward other people paid handsomely in her previous line of work; now it manifested as concern for the well-being of the widow and her children.

Never having had a husband to lose, Kirlat could not fathom the depths of Mirdel's loss. Still, she had lost loved ones and knew the pain faded but never went away. The children were especially vulnerable, losing both their father and all familiar surroundings. Accustomed to living at court, they were in a recognized atmosphere but the faces were all new. They had to find new playmates and new friends to trust. Kirlat tried to earn their trust for the simple reason that they needed her. The obligation to report to Peveç ceased to motivate her.

The two girls reminded Kirlat of her cousins in Crumbly, upriver from Nimmoth. She joined in their games as well as helping them groom and dress and learn to behave like ladies. The boy was a challenge. Caught in the awkward gap between childhood and manhood, he was constantly at sixes and sevens.

With his father gone, young Gavron wanted to be the man of the household. He assumed a gravity beyond his years, breaking occasionally into outbursts of childishness. Dealing with Gavron, Kirlat and Mirdel never knew when to expect responsibility and when to expect folly. Kirlat sometimes caught him playing with his sisters then, upon noticing her, switching into the shaky dignity of a youth striving to be grown up.

Gavron's eager, and occasionally haunted, deep blue eyes and dark red hair contrasted sharply with the pale ivory of his skin. With his father's height and his mother's wit, he would attract his share of young women very soon. Kirlat could see all this but she felt no temptation to violate her promise to Peveç. Her feelings towards Gavron were maternal, or perhaps those of a solicitous auntie. Kirlat saved her passions for the warrior from Vorthall, next to whom Gavron would always seem a child.

As Kirlat dreamed of Hildir and slept with a hint of smile creeping across her fair features, Ian and his friends slept only fitfully. A chill had crept into the ground even as anxiety teased its way into the minds of the companions. The insidious cold worked its way into the bones and seemed even to numb the heart. Sleep was difficult. Athnel's star watch was cut short by a dark cloud from the west obscuring the heavens. Furk brooded. Ringskild wondered how she could rally the spirits of the group when dawn arrived.

Ian woke as he had his first day in this world, with a lick from Vladje. An attitude held over from earlier days in Yorkshire asserted itself as he muttered, "Be gone, wolf." This drew a bark from Vladje and Ian concluded that he had offended the sacred animal. "I'm sorry, you just remind me of my brother in the morning. At least you don't kick me out of bed." Ian only erred in naming technique. Vladje grabbed a sleeve and began to tug at the youth.

"All right, I'm getting up. Pax?" The wolf relented.

The sky was dark and the air cold. Ian wondered what Vladje was on about, thinking it was still at least an hour before dawn. He gradually realized the darkness was from a thick overcast, like coal smoke, blocking the early morning rays of the daystar. Athnel and Pjortan began to sing the Hymn to the Dawn in spite of the lack of obvious light.

When they reached the line beseeching the Sun to "melt the ice of our hearts," Ian rather wished it would melt the ice in his bones as well. Then he thought of the sheep by the Ercoille and immediately regretted thinking of melting and bones together.

He also wondered if he had just blasphemed in his heart and prayed the Daystar to forgive him. It was awkward being caught between two faiths, though he realized that by now he accepted both as being true. Both worlds would probably consider that a heresy, he supposed. All he knew right now was that something evil was at work and he was cold and grumpy.

The companions finished their morning preparations, mounted, and resumed the journey toward Jorgil. Ringskild rode among the group, reminding them of the reason for their quest and of prophecies indicating success. She had some effect but words could not disperse the mist hanging in the air and preventing the morning from warming either body or spirit.

The tracks they followed led them through orchards of fruit and nut trees— plums, apricots, almonds—all mingled with sundry stands of oak, willow, and ash. Were the mood of the travelers brighter, they might have declared it lovely country. Trees gradually gave way to tilled fields as they worked their way west and south.

They had only ridden two hours when they reached the Harvest Road. In less than an hour they rode into Jorgil, a scattered town consisting of a cluster of villages with a central walled city. The hamlets lined a network of roads heading in all directions, evidence that Jorgil served as a nexus of trade. Situated centrally, it linked Uvanor, Vathil, Stjolvanor, and half a dozen lesser towns along the plain. Traders from the regions of Aonghe, Fjorn, Bjupazh, Hlv, and Ulnor, as well as Thioth, passed through. The only unusual personages in Jorgil that day were the Norrungs from so far to the east. Jannir had passed through once before years earlier. This morning he could only look down from the stars.

The travelers began inquiring about the Vothneli troops and it took no more than a few questions to learn that the armed contingent had just entered Jorgil from the south. Citizens and visitors to Jorgil alike were glad peace poles were evident when they heard the cries that went up as the Vothneli saw Furk and his companions. "Furk and Vothnell!" the soldiers shouted loudly, some beating on their shields.

Wulfdar saw Furk's expression light up at sight of his troops. Perhaps the moodiness of the prior day would pass. The healer had used a strong tincture to lift Furk's spirits but it had little effect. He hoped reunion with the count's followers would do what potions could not.

Indeed, a surge of relief flowed through the entire assembly now that the parties were rejoined. Djutar felt a great burden fall from his shoulders as he addressed Furk.

"My Lord, I rejoice to see you. Behold your forces."

"Ah. Yes. Thank you, Captain. Good to see the men again. Indeed."

Djutar wondered if his eyes misled him in spotting moisture in Furk's eyes as the count surveyed the troops and the banners of Vothnell. It was good to see his fellow captain, Brona, along with Miglac and Barons Grath and Torthan. He inquired after Trno only to learn that he had perished in battle. They traded stories of their losses, and Djutar also greeted the Norrungs who had once been his virtual prisoners.

The Vothneli were informed of the new members of the company: Princess Çirazel, Lady Zlida, Vishgar, and Fliç. Fliç was disappointed that Furk told the troops to keep an eye on their possessions when he was around, though he was hardly in a position to protest against the truth.

As the leaders went beyond social reconnection, discussion turned to the path of the Chegjan. Djutar told of the dark cloud and the fate of the goats and their herders. Torthan sketched the tragic encounter in the now-deserted village but spared Furk the full tale of cannibalism, knowing it would provoke his lord to an extreme reaction. Volthir recounted the sighting of the dark cloud on the plain and Lady Athnel added the darkness in the sky the previous night.

Concluding that they were at last close to the demon, these champions of light decided not to pause in Jorgil but to head west toward the Ulava River. A quick meal was taken in the town and they again set out, this time on the road toward the ford at Vorç.

The level road through endless fields could not have presented a more innocuous prospect. People of the land were busy tending their crops in hopes of harvests to come. Insects hummed in the spring afternoon.

Small shrines could be seen along the road, variously honoring the bountiful parents, Tjiweth the Bright Queen and Father Shorall. The former was sometimes depicted as mother goddess with great breasts and a body for bearing many children or as a crowned and seated queen. The latter was invariably pictured as a fish, though he was more associated with the riches of the waters. Along with these were statues of Veshnel the Reaper.

The bucolic panorama was marred by an awareness of what lay ahead at some unspecified place and moment. Nordil noticed a restlessness in Fjurthil, who nonetheless refused to fly forth. Wilda glanced at Vladje and saw the fur on his neck rise. She pointed this out to the others and Pjortan ominously told Ian to ride between him and Athnel. The Norrung fighters formed a ring around the singers and Ian without conferring.

Once again, Ian felt completely overwhelmed. Was this to be the final confrontation? No new prophecy had come, no fresh dream that he could recall. Where was the guidance he needed? What must he do? What could he do?

As he struggled with these and other questions the air ahead of them seemed to thicken, as though a thin cloud were forming in a blue sky. The condensation was not moisture, however, but the smoky darkness associated with the Chegjan.

"Remember the Light," Athnel counseled. Ian closed his eyes, inhaled deeply, and visualized uniting with the star stone. Though he had practiced this a number of times, the overwhelming sense of being lost in the heart of Light, of being one with it and with all things, never returned in such power as it had that one time. Still, it helped him recall the experience. What he usually took away from such an exercise of the imagination was a renewed sense of light and connectedness, but no fresh instructions. Concluding the meditation with another especially deep breath, Ian reopened his eyes.

The road had led to an untamed section of the plain, devoid of hedgerows and untouched by plows. A great grassy slope, dotted with shrubs and with stones that had lain there beyond human memory, stretched out before them. Near the far end the black mist appeared to gather, drawing itself into a cloud that floated inches above the ground. Like the billowing smoke of a fire it constantly shifted, rippling before the demon chasers with a dark energy.

Vladje growled and the horses became skittish. Hearts began to pound at the sight of this evil, facing them in challenge. Gradually the cloud seemed to grow in height as though it could overwhelm them all, dancing in a black column. Malevolence radiated from it like icy tendrils that reached out to touch the hearts and minds of those who dared to approach it.

The forces of Vorthall and Vothnell lined up on their side of the field, mortal warriors facing a foe unlike any they had known. Athnel began a hymn to Wigdor, god of truth and judgment. The troops of Vothnell raised the hymn to Vrotni that they had sung so prematurely the day they left Fimmoth. Ringskild asked Ian if he knew what to do.

The English youth shook his head and confessed that he hadn't a clue. From his left he heard Torthan's voice saying, "It's all right, lad. None of us knows how to fight a demon." The Vothneli tactician and the Norrung captain conferred and a small debate over the prophecies broke out among the other Norrungs.

That was when Furk erupted in all his warrior fury. "By all the stars, I shall fight it!" He spurred his horse and charged across the field. "Vothnell and the Light!" he cried. Wishing he could restrain his lord and refusing to let Furk go alone, Djutar charged with him and the Vothneli joined in the charge against the darkness.

The Chegjan's vaporous manifestation rose even higher, writhing with added energy. As Furk charged into the edge of the black cloud, the towering thing came down upon him and those closest to him. Their shouts were muffled and in an instant all was silence.

CHAPTER 54

Ian had forgotten to breathe as he tried to absorb what he had just seen. As his protesting lungs forced air back into his numbed body, the concentrated darkness on the plain began to dissipate as though blown lightly on the wind. Like clouds dissolving in sunlight without a trace in an azure sky, the Chegjan faded into tendrils that vanished as they drifted west. By the time the final wisp reached the Ulava nothing more could be seen. All this within the space of half a dozen breaths.

It was then, as air desperately inhaled by all whose breath had caught now turned to oaths and cries of horror, that Ian realized what stretched among the grasses before him.

Men and horses were scattered randomly, their bones reduced to puddles, all life sucked from them. Limp, motionless forms lay in mute testimony to the power of the darkness. Their silence roared in Ian's frantic mind as he sought to invoke the Light.

Everything about him swirled chaotically. Blurs of color, disjointed motion, faded sounds—nothing formed a whole. Then Ian realized these fragments were himself, galloping toward the fallen white banner marking the spot where Furk fell. Sound no longer retreated as though muffled in quilts; it vibrated throughout his body. It was his own voice screaming, "Noooooooooo!" above the rhythm of hooves pounding the earth.

Ian had secretly mocked the mannerisms of the pompous Lord of Vothnell. Like all the Norrungs, he considered Furk an intrusion in their quest. It was only now that Ian realized how much he also admired Furk's sense of justice and impulsive courage.

Ian leapt from his horse and threw himself on the hollowed remains of the dead warrior. Frenzied and weeping, the youth protested, "No. No! This wasn't supposed to happen. I was supposed to face the damned thing, not you! Not you. Uncle, Uncle! No!"

Hildir and Ringskild had joined him as the other Norrungs surveyed the disaster. They allowed the Chosen Stranger to pour out his grief and protest all the injustices of life. When Ian's weeping began to subside, Hildir gently clasped his shoulder. "He died with full honor, Ian, brave to the last moment of his life."

"But it's supposed to be me," Ian protested. "Too many have died."

Hildir continued, speaking with great tenderness. "We all must walk the star path, lad. And none of the prophecies say you must die to destroy the demon."

Before Ian responded, Ringskild extended a hand to help him up. "Come, Ian, we will honor Lord Furk. There is much to do."

Ian allowed himself to be led as he rose and they joined the others in taking stock. In their loyalty to Furk eight score Vothneli had perished in a moment. Those who were spared wandered in a daze among what remained of their comrades. The faithful Captain Djutar who had first captured the Norrungs—or, as he preferred to say, invited them to enjoy Furk's hospitality—lay beside his lord. Nearby were Miglac and Brona and Baron Grath who had shared captivity in Fjorn, and others the forest dwellers had come to know. Torthan had escaped the Chegjan simply because he was evaluating the situation with Ringskild and was delayed in joining the charge. He now spoke to the Norrungs.

"We must take action. The men are wandering in chaos."

"Let us gather the noble dead, Cousin," Ringskild replied. "Today they are all noble."

"I agree," said the Gold Falcon, Baron of Valcor, and heir presumptive of Vothnell. As recognized leaders, he and the warmaiden organized the living to gather the dead and begin assembling the pyres. Many, but not all, of the nearby residents overcame their dread of the demon and assisted in collecting firewood. Most would not touch those slain by the demon, yet all wanted their land cleansed as quickly as possible.

It was an immense task and lasted until after the appearance of the evening star and the singing of the vesper hymn. Wulfdar had enlisted Athnel and a few soldiers in the afternoon to help him use such remedies as he had with him to ease those who had come near the black cloud but not been consumed. They had sustained various injuries and a few were out of their wits. On the periphery of death were a few with no hope of survival. Wulfdar helped ease their passing. Pjortan and Athnel had sung Ushni's lullaby several times.

They joined in singing it one more time just as Furk's pyre was lit. His closest and most loyal companions had been laid around him that they might accompany their lord on the star journey. Furk's body had been wrapped in the magnificent robe given him by Lady Rushvin. The great white banner emblazoned with the black battleaxe was raised next to him. Athnel could barely choke out the words and Pjortan carried the hymn.

> The stars await you, their song is joy.
> All you leave behind is worry,
> All that is good will come to me.
> Feasting awaits you and reunion
> In my halls where all are welcomed
> And my face at last is seen.
>
> Come, my children, and do not fear
> The journey home, the path of peace.

Few faces lacked wet streaks among the ashes of mourning. Torthan knelt before his departing overlord, weeping silently yet maintaining a solemn expression.

> Hjelgi stands beside you now
> To guide your steps among the stars.
> Welcome awaits you at my table,
> There you will find love and laughter.
> Though my face is veiled to mortals
> You will find it gracious and loving.
>
> Come, my children, and do not fear
> The journey home, the path of peace.

Athnel had managed to rejoin Pjortan in this second stanza but halfway through she collapsed in grief. Pjortan forced himself to finish the hymn as Wilda and Meldreth held the Lady of Laoghar, whom they had come to view as having the strength of three warmaidens. Her affection for the nobleman whom she saw so clearly, in all his virtue and all his folly, revealed its depths as she poured out her grief.

Ian, having vented his own surprising feelings earlier, stood at the foot of the bier, stared into the rising flames, and added his own verse to the hymn, though spoken and not sung.

> Vothnell's Lord was ever fearless,
> Strong support of those who suffer,
> Riding into certain darkness,
> Now he journeys into starlight,
> Soon to see the Hooded Queen
> Who will greet him, Furk the Mighty.
> Djutar, Miglac, Grath go with him,
> Brona, many faithful warriors.
>
> Come, my children, and do not fear
> The journey home, the path of peace.

The night was filled with lament as the fires burned on the Plain of Ulava and the Servants of Vrotni named the brave deeds of comrades who had fallen before the darkness.

CHAPTER 55

Smoke still rose from the pyres but no veil of menace spread across the heavens that night. Ruanel, the Pale Queen, was just one day past new and formed the barest sliver to compete with the glittering deities that shone clear. For all their clarity, the astral glory could barely reach through the pall of grief that wound its way around the hearts of those who survived the tragedy enacted that day.

After all rites were completed, Ian reverted to the confused boy who entered this strange world. He was comforted by Wilda. Ever generous of heart, she was happy to serve as a surrogate mother to this lad and held him as he wept for every loss he ever knew. Hellebore Cottage and the Dyrnedon family seemed far away and he forever doomed to live here as an orphan. Even Vorthall was but a memory at this point and the prospect of seeing it again dim. His foster brother Njothir, the valiant young chieftain of the Norrungs, had been a stabilizing force in Ian's early days in Norrast, yet Njothir ruled far to the east. The news of Jannir's death and the memory of Trno's end in the Forest of Fjorn were still fresh, and the savagery of Bulçar and his sons had seared Ian's heart. Now the experience of so many dead, blasted by the foul creature that eluded them, including men who had become friends and heroes in his life—it was overwhelming and Ian sobbed until tears would come no longer and he was emotionally exhausted.

Many a brave man wept that night for fallen comrades and family members, even as the dead now walked among the stars in the company of Hjelgi. The living stayed up late, scouring the sky for a glimpse of their friends and pondering the fate of mortals.

Torthan and Ringskild declared the following day a time of mourning as well as a time to finish burning the carcasses of the horses that perished with their riders. A great deal of better wood available had been used for the pyres of the warriors and the people of the area were enlisted to find such added wood as possible to prevent the spread of disease. Given the heavy rains of late, this was a challenge and the task was imperfectly accomplished. Still, they did what they could.

As the fires were lit, Pjortan chanted a song of Torvu, the mighty war stallion of Wigdor the Great Chief. He had learned it form his uncle Thomdar as a little boy. The elder had used the song as a game with Pjortan when the latter was first learning to ride. It calmed the boy's apprehensions and Pjortan had always loved the song. It seemed fitting now as a tribute to the steeds that had fallen in service to the warriors who rode them.

White banners had been set up on the field to honor the dead and signal the sorrow of those still walking beneath the stars. Pungent herbs were burned to ease the smell and purify the land. With Lady Rushvin's letters in hand, the mourners were able to obtain food for a funeral feast and Torthan promised payment to the locals who provided the victuals. Great quantities of mead were consumed that day and many tales were told of the valiant and faithful who had perished the day before.

Messengers were sent to Thioth to inform Lady Rushvin of the events that had taken place. The remaining Vothneli reorganized the command structure until their return to Vothnell. The Lady of Laoghar and the Gold Falcon discussed the conflict between her duties and her wishes. She had sworn fealty to Furk; what was now her obligation toward his successor?

Furk had lost wife and children in the plague. His only sister, Agnar, had married Baron Relkar of Dhoret far to the south end of the Mere in Sendhial. She perished in childbirth. Fulkar, their sickly babe, would do well to survive to adulthood and could hardly assume rule at opposite ends of the sea. Furk's next nearest living relative was his second cousin, Baron Torthan of Valcor. Torthan had no ambitions to rule more than Valcor Manor and the few lands that served it. His joy in strategic planning was about meeting challenges, not acquiring and holding territories and power. Assuming Furk's mantle was not something he ever expected or desired, as Furk was still young enough to marry again and sire an heir.

"My lady," he said to Athnel, "I have no choice but to serve the people of Vothnell. You, however, do have a choice."

"How so, lord?"

"Your fealty was to Furk. When his heir is invested you could swear loyalty again. Unless there are a few natural offspring about whom I know nothing, that heir is likely to be me. Should Relkar claim Vothnell for his son, there would still be a regency as the babe has scarce left off his wet nurse. I doubt I should escape being regent, though. I assure you, I would not be reluctant to hand over the lands of Vothnell to young Fulkar.

"Whatever my capacity," Torthan concluded, "I value your service, and even more your friendship, but I make no claim upon either."

"You are a kind and generous man, Lord of Valcor. I do not envy your sudden burden and wish I could ease it. You are also a very astute man and fully aware that my heart draws me away from Vothnell and into the eastern woods. With your leave, I shall remain with the little band who would oppose this dark thing. If we prevail, then I would stay by Pjortan's side. We have not directly spoken of the future, but every indication tells me he would have it so."

"Trust me, Athnel, he would," Torthan chuckled. "You go with my thanks, my friendship, and my blessing, singer to the gods."

The lady smiled and replied, "And you, Torthan, go with my thanks and friendship as well. May the heavens bless you, friend of the stars."

This private discussion was followed by more public deliberations. In the light of Furk's death and the loss of Vothneli lives, Torthan and his captains decided it would be better to leave the quest and return home. The men of Vothnell greeted this news with joy, hoping the embrace of their loved ones would help ease the loss of their comrades. There was also a sense of relief that rule in Vothnell would be sorted out quickly.

It was not glad news for the Norrungs. They had all resented the unexpected addition when Furk decided to join the quest, and the entire host would be problematic as they moved further across the Ulava. Even so, some of the Vothneli had become familiar companions. Farewell succeeded farewell as the Norrungs realized they would say goodbye to Torthan, who had collaborated so closely with them.

For his part, Torthan was especially loathe to part company with Athnel and Ringskild. He and Athnel had joined forces to support, and sometimes protect, the irrepressible Furk, thus bonding as fellow conspirators. The baron had also enjoyed analyzing situations and evaluating strategies with the warmaiden, whose intelligence and beauty captured his attention the day they met. She gave indications her heart inclined toward another but Torthan was reluctant to leave the fiery and powerful woman.

Initial farewells were said that night. The mead from the funeral feast augmented the maudlin aspect of it all but the affection, admiration, and regret expressed that evening were sincere. The Baron of Valcor blushed when Wilda delivered an earnest lecture advising him to get a good wife and start making babies.

"Vothnell needs an heir for the next generation and I can tell you need a woman, young man. Falcons are great fliers, as my Nordil's feathered friend Fjurthil can prove, but they need someplace to return to. And don't be haphazard about choosing one, either. She should be as clever as you or you will soon be bored. Somewhere in these lands there are bound to be ladies who can strategize. And take my advice," Wilda concluded, "you don't want a pretty girl with no fire to her, or some skinny wench unfit for bearing children or for cuddling up to."

"That's enough, dear," Nordil interjected, hoping to cut this unsolicited rant short.

"Just giving the chap some good motherly advice, husband. Lucky for you that you got a good woman, though if it had been left to you stars only know what would have happened."

"Your advice is sound, Cousin," Torthan said smiling broadly at Wilda. "If you come across any such woman, be sure to send her to Vothnell."

Having recovered somewhat from the sudden grief that overwhelmed him the day before, Ian made the rounds of the Vothneli soldiers, thanking them personally for riding with the Norrungs and their service to Lord Furk. Mechdar and Vunskridh noticed this and spoke approvingly of the young outlander, rising above his loss and fear to think of others. Ringskild was doing the same as Ian, which drew the same approval though it was expected of her as captain of their company and, as Mechdar added, the likely future wife of a noble chief.

Noble and affectionate deeds and words thus concluded the day that followed unexpected and heart-rending loss. Pjortan and Athnel lay near each other, watching the stars as others drifted to sleep. One of the seasons of falling stars was just beginning and they witnessed a couple. Amid their holy discernment of the sky, Pjortan asked Athnel if she were certain of her desire to remain with the Norrungs.

"Tanje," she replied, using the most affectionate form of his name, "do you need to ask?"

All the young singer could do was blink and smile in the night.

CHAPTER 56

For all the fondness he felt for the wolf, Ian was happy to waken to birdsong rather than Vladje's tongue. The predawn racket in the trees surrounding the field formed an unavoidable presence that would not be ignored. Ian blinked his eyes open tentatively, hoping he would not be met with signs of too much mead the night before. Whether he had practiced moderation or was enjoying the resilience of youth, no ill effects blunted his experience of the morning.

Gray light was melting into hints of dawn, a faint glow on the horizon. Ian thought of Vorthall and Thomdar intoning the dawn hymn amid the stately trees of the forest far to the east. Soon Pjortan and Athnel would be singing it here, not far from the banks of the Ulava. With this incessant chirping of birds as a chorus, Ian thought, ruefully admitting to himself that the intrusive noise was actually a cheerful sound.

A gauzy stretch of thin clouds far to the south provided the only flaw in an uncluttered sky. Peals of laughter reinforced the brightness of the morning as Nordil and Wilda shared some private joke. Even Princess Çirazel could be seen smiling as Meldreth and Zlida exchanged pleasantries.

Grateful that the Chegjan had moved beyond their territory, the people of Jorgil and its surrounds supplied hearty fare for the warriors' breakfast and some provision for the next few days. The entire party saddled up and set out on the road toward Vorç, banners bright beneath a cloudless sky as they rippled in the breeze.

Having seen enough of battle in the past few days, Ian had carefully arranged the feathers Njothila had given him. His hair, now grown in the Norrung fashion, was now long enough for the full braids sported by his companions. Though not skilled in the art of war, he bore a sword for his defense and some body armor. Ian had come to resemble a Norrung warrior, though he lacked the warrior temperament and sported no tattoo of Vrotni's sword.

Taking advantage of the special status attached to him, Ian rode beside Torthan that morning. The youth asked many questions about Valcor and the other lands attached to Vothnell, about Furk and his family, and the challenges of ruling. The baron patiently answered the curious youth until Athnel distracted him by pointing out a lapis bird flying nearby.

The deep blue wings and body gave the bird its name. In outline it resembled a mockingbird and shared the mocker's dusty breast. Aside from the intense lapis color of its feathers, the bird's most striking features were the iridescent turquoise and emerald spots on its wingtips and its dramatic flight song, rising an octave and dropping to outline a major chord.

I suppose this is the day for birds, Ian mused as he observed the bright spot of blue flitting over the green fields.

Another distraction of the morning was the verbal sparring between Vunskridh and Vishgar. The eloquent criminal and the righteous warmaiden seemed incapable of leaving each other alone. The companions had reached a consensus that the deadly potential of these conflicts had passed and it was now more a battle of wits.

"If you twisted no more than the snake of your tattoo, I might believe a third of what you say," Vunskridh charged, "but the serpent on your arm is a straight line compared to you."

"You wrong me, cousin. I have forsaken my devious past and you give me no chance to shed that old skin and begin anew."

"At least you admit you are a snake, Vishgar. You should call the vipers "cousin" rather than pretend a relation to me."

Ian ceased to listen, suspecting they would continue in this vein until they tired of it, only to resume later in the day.

By noon the blue and green of the lapis bird was echoed in thick green stands of willows to the right of the road and blue sky mingling with sunlit sparkles in the river's riffles ahead of them. They had come to a ford between the meandering loops of the Ulava, allowing fairly easy passage across the fine gravel in the shallows.

The beauty of the day, the singing of birds, the rhythm of fields and trees, the refreshing air about the broad river—these had all been tinged with melancholy. The travelers shared the knowledge that with the crossing of the Ulava came a parting of ways. Hugs and hand clasping, blessings of the stars, and some misty eyes marked the end of the shared quest. The Vothneli, under Torthan and his captains, now took the Ulava Road downstream toward the Mere and home. Fliç, with Torthan's consent, joined them, eager to be as far from danger as possible. He may have underestimated the danger of being under Torthan's watchful eye, but the Norrungs shed no tears at his departure.

Lady Athnel and Vishgar had chosen to remain with the Norrungs. Vunskridh, predictably, objected to Vishgar's company. For his part, the copper-haired fellow said he was obliged to remain with those to whom he owed his freedom.

The most perplexing choice in this separation was that of the princess. Lady Zlida felt they should accept Torthan's offer to escort them to Ulnor, whence they could proceed to Hlv. Çirazel surprised everyone by opting to remain with the Norrungs.

"In the Grove of the Goddess, Vunskridh saved my life and my honor. I shall remain with her until her quest is finished and she can be thanked by my people."

The young woman was adamant about her decision and demonstrated the strong will of both her parents. When Zlida protested, Çirazel calmly commanded her obedience. The noble ladies of Hlv thus remained with Ian's companions as they turned north along the river.

Sadness at parting, combined with the lazy flow of the Ulava on such a beautiful afternoon, resulted in rather ambling progress toward the river town of Vorç. It was a minor trading center in the commercial network of the Ulava Basin.

No one in the party needed to ask whether the demon had passed through. The first clue was the sickly sweet smell of death in the air. It was followed by the sight of misshapen carcasses, both human and animal, scattered at irregular distances along the roadside.

Based on the dark cloud's direction toward the river, it seemed likely that Vorç would lie in its path. The shock rippling through the Norrungs came from the absence of any sign of survivors, or mourning, or attempted burial. If the Chegjan had come here immediately after the devastating attack on Furk and his companions, the corpses would now have lain in the open for two days. Who would leave their fellows or family members exposed like this? Or had the foul thing taken all the living?

No man nor woman nor child could be seen as they neared the town, only carrion birds and insects, performing their task of cleansing the land. Just as the riders reached hailing distance of dwellings along the perimeter of Vorç, Mechdar pointed out a child running from their approach. Ringskild verified that peace poles were clearly visible as the company entered the gate. A couple of guards were there but they gave no challenge, simply quailing as the riders passed. One even fainted upon spotting the wolf in their midst.

"I had not thought us quite so fearsome," Meldreth teased.

"They were overcome by your beauty," Volthir shot back.

"Or terrified by your ugliness," the warmaiden retorted.

"Hush, both of you," Ringskild ordered. "Something is terribly wrong here."

It would not be the first time they had encountered a place abandoned, or nearly so, by its inhabitants. Vorç, however, was not abandoned. The townspeople were there, but they were not milling about and doing their business. Heads would appear in windows and doorways then quickly disappear. Whispers floated in the air and unseen children could be heard crying. Whenever the riders came around a corner, people would scurry out of sight and doors would slam shut.

Tiring of this behavior, Ringskild gave a few signals and her warriors quickly captured a youth who had lingered longer than his fellows. He was nervous yet did not appear as frightened as the other inhabitants of Vorç. Ringskild eyed him as he stood between Volthir and Meldreth, wavering between defiance and fear. The lad was, perhaps, a bit younger than Ian though not as tall. He had fine black hair drawn back in a pony tail, unlike the braids of the Norrungs, and hints of a future mustache and goatee shadowed the clear olive skin of his face. Large, dark eyes darted about as he assessed his situation.

"You have nothing to fear from us," Ringskild assured him. "We come in peace but we cannot talk with people who run from us. What is your name?"

Sweat began to break out on the lad's upper lip as he answered with a thick Bjupazhi accent, "I am called Pushta."

"Thank you, Pushta. I am Ringskild daughter of Ivor, captain of this company. We have come from a great forest far to the east, following the path of the foul demon that has just been through your land. Those of us who serve Vrotni are here only to protect our people, not to harm others.

"Can you tell me, Pushta, why the people of Vorç are so frightened?"

"It is the demon you speak of, captain. Two days ago a black cloud gathered outside our town, large as a great swarm of blackbirds and active as a mass of gnats. I almost thought I could hear it buzz but it was silent. It had begun like a dark mist but then it drew itself together and became dark as scribe's ink, then descended to the earth and moved across the land.

"I was watching from a hill where I could look down upon its path. The feeling I had while watching it was like the one I had when the plague came to our town. I was afraid the fiery death had returned and began to shiver even with the daystar still shining. That thing moved toward the city gates but seemed to change its mind. Instead it went all around the walls.

"I wanted to shout an alarm but I was afraid that the thing would come toward me. Down by the road I could see things where before there had been people and cattle, some horses. They did not move but neither did they look like dead things. What would you call them? Puddles of skin? I don't know, only that I was very frightened and almost wet myself.

"The dark thing looked like black smoke, boiling all the time. It finished circling Vorç, and then it began to thin again into a dark mist. The mist hovered above the town for a few minutes, like a thin summer cloud only black. After that it headed up the river toward Gennor.

"That is all I know, but ever since this terrible thing all our people shake at every rustling leaf. A mouse could chase a dozen men, I think. Everyone is afraid it was threatening us, warning that it would come back to finish what it started outside the town.

"You are the first outsiders to come our way since all this happened. My companions wondered it you were in league with this 'demon' as you call it. They did not stay to find out, but I wanted to see who you were."

All this poured out of the youth as though he were relieved to unburden what he had witnessed and even confess his own terror. Vladje had paid attention and given no sign that the lad spoke false. Ringskild nodded her head in honor of his straightforward recital.

"You have done well, Pushta. Even the bravest warrior knows fear and is wary about the unknown, yet you delayed so you could know for yourself. That took courage, as did telling strangers what has happened. I think you will grow to be a good man.

"We have seen what happened here before, all across the lands north of the Mere. It happened first to sheep and we called it 'sheep's death,' but now it happens to other animals and to humans as well. Just before the demon, that we call the Chegjan, came to your land it destroyed many of our friends and companions. I am sorry that more have perished.

"That is why we follow the evil thing. Prophecies indicate that there is hope it may be destroyed. We will not terrify your people any further. We shall ride out of Vorç and camp to the north. Though we are here for good and not evil, I would not add to your fears. Please tell your people to take heart. The demon has moved always west or north and I think it will not come back this way."

The lad looked at the warmaiden, fierce and commanding yet also reassuring. He was of an age to find this stranger exceedingly beautiful. For a moment he felt he could follow her to face demons but the memory of what he had seen recalled him to reality.

"Thank you, lady captain," he said.

"The stars keep you, Pushta," Ringskild replied, then gestured to lead the company through the town and upriver to camp for the night. Pushta watched them go as his fellows gradually emerged to ask him who the strangers were and what had been said.

CHAPTER 57

Lulled by a soporific drone, the comrades might have enjoyed the countryside along the Ulava. The industrious yet seemingly random flight of bees, darting among spring flowers both large and small, wove a web of sound and motion luring observers into an altered state wherein past and future ceased to be. Gently swelling low hills contrasted with the flat plain on the other side of the river. The recent heavy rains had produced lush green vegetation and Tjiweth, the Bright Queen, seemed to proclaim her bounty wherever one looked.

Ian and the other adventurers would have been glad to let the day caress them with beauty and the promise of future harvest. Instead, their hearts dwelt on the strange atmosphere of Vorç. Their unease reminded them of a prior experience and it was Nordil who finally named it—the night they came to Lesser Vish, abandoned by the last survivors of plague. A haunting sense of desolation hovered about the hamlet and they could not bring themselves to sleep there, preferring instead to camp among the trees rather than in the vacant dwellings.

Vorç felt like that in spite of its inhabitants. The Chegjan had so terrorized the people that they seemed to vanish in obscurity. Even with furtive sounds and glimpses of motion, Vorç felt empty. Moving bodies populated the place but the very sense of their presence had fled. The Chegjan had spared their lives but somehow stripped the force of their personhood, turning them into living shadows. Pushta alone seemed real.

Consideration for the population of Vorç may thus have counted for less than the demon chasers' discomfort when Ringskild announced they would camp to the north. She did not want to pause among the frightened and spend the night surrounded by their timorous anxiety. Better to lie beneath the stars and enjoy their blessing.

Vishgar, whether to impress Vunskridh or simply to prove he could be more than an impediment, busied himself helping set up camp between the road and the river. The sometime thief wielded an ax skillfully, quickly providing a supply of reasonably dried wood for a fire.

After supper Vishgar could be seen sitting on a nearby log, chatting with Vladje as though reminiscing with an old friend. The wolf appeared relaxed and attentive. Hildir, Meldreth, and Nordil watched this one-way conversation, wondering what it all meant. Nordil named what all of them were pondering.

"I have never seen Vladje relax in the presence of evil."

"Hmm, true. If she doesn't want him, I might be available," Meldreth commented in a lewd tone. "Vunskridh really should see this; I think she needs to reconsider her opinion of Vishgar."

The three were unaware that Vunskridh had glimpsed the interchange from across the fire, though she could not gather her feelings about it into any clear evaluation.

Later that night Ringskild observed the velvet sky as the Eagle rose above silhouetted trees, flying after the Chieftain. She thought of the young chieftain of the Norrungs, her foster-brother and lord, Njothir. Being so far from him was something like riding through Vorç. The warmaiden ached with the lack of his presence. Since childhood she had fed on his eagerness and energy, and he on her fierce spirit and strong will. If only she could hear the warm tones of his voice speaking common sense with his characteristic frankness…. Then she could lead this company again without the doubts and second guessing that had begun to trouble her.

Torthan had been a welcome companion in the quest but he was not her soul mate, playfellow and co-conspirator. The Baron of Valcor was brilliant and handsome. Ringskild enjoyed his company and they were well matched for leading fighters as a team. When each day ended, however, her thoughts were of the Norrungs' finest warrior, his laughter, his reddish-gold mane, and the muscled arms in which the deadliest warmaiden of Vorthall would joyously surrender.

Ian, for his part, was happy to snuggle next to Vladje when the wolf returned from Vishgar's chat. Soft music came to his ears from the gentle rippling of the nearby Ulava. The campfire yielded warmth and the scent of resinous smoke. The Yorkshire lad chose not to entertain his fears that evening, allowing his senses to lead him into the night's embrace.

Invar, deity of dreams, set to work, drawing Ian into the depths of sleep, then spinning her magic. As the aroma of burning wood lingered in his nostrils, Ian saw the hearth fire in Vorthall as he and the children of Rathdar talked easily in the night. Yellow flames danced above the deep red glow of embers, emitting a golden glow that shifted over the room. When his gaze was not lost in the sinuous movement of the fire, Ian found himself repeatedly looking toward Njothila, whose eyes flashed with the fire's reflection. It seemed the less she spoke, the more she said, speaking in the silent language of a maiden's glance.

Njothir's words brought Ian back to the conversation. "If people lose hope they will not survive. This thing must be destroyed. I cannot stand idly by as the life of the Norrungs is slowly drawn from them. We who have survived the fiery death must not now yield ourselves to the deadly cold seeping into the hearts of mortals."

As the chief's words echoed in his mind, Ian imagined frost forming within, encircling their hearts and gradually turning them into lumps of ice. He watched the flesh of Njothila turning a pale blue as all her warmth faded. She collapsed to the floor and Ian leaped to her aid. It was too late. The maiden was cold as the worst snows of winter. Ian turned to Njothir who had likewise perished.

The tears he wrung from the despair that seized him fell as ice drops. Ian could feel the deadly cold invading his own body as he tried to form the word, *No!*

Just as Ian felt the last remnants of life trailing from his body, the floor beneath him shook with a loud thump followed by endless rattling. It was Hranild's staff slammed on the pavement, its deer hooves shaken with indignation, as the blind woman imperiously called him back to life.

"You shall not yield to this thing, young Ian! It is terrible but it is not omnipotent. It is only darkness. It cannot give light, though the smallest reed can burn. It has no true life in itself, it only feeds on our fears. It cannot love, though every mortal heart can do so. You are more powerful than it can possibly be. You can hope, and you must."

She pounded her staff on the floor once more.

"You now see what is at stake. All that is precious can fall prey to darkness, but it does not have to be so. If you love, and I believe you do, you must never give in. Trust the Light, Ian. Trust..."

As Hranild's voice faded, Ian found himself floating in darkness. Yet the darkness was not total. Faint clouds of gold and violet glowed in the distance. Pinpricks of light gradually emerged, some brighter than others. Ian felt himself soaring among the stars, joining in their great wheeling pattern across the heavens. A warm sensation grew within him, a comfortable peace suffusing his whole being. When he felt he could stand no more of such goodness, it sharply faded.

Ian now felt himself cloaked in darkness, this time a complete lack of light. The air he took into his lungs was a hot, foul smoke. Instead of floating in the sky, he now lay upon hard stones, cold as Njothila's lifeless body, their rough edges bruising him. Sheer terror forced a panicked cry from him as he woke, gulping the night air as he sought what was real.

Athnel's voice was firm but gentle. "It's all right, Ian. Invar has woven dreams for you and drawn you into her web." The singer touched his shoulder in reassurance.

"You are awake now, here beside the Ulava River. Feel, Vladje is here with you, and your friends surround you."

"Oh, Athnel, it was awful. And some of it was wonderful. And...Njothila! And Njothir! Are they all right? How can we know?"

At that point Vladje licked Ian's ear and Athnel was grateful for the lupine reassurance. "We cannot know, but we have no reason to believe anything is amiss at Vorthall. Lord Wolf here seems untroubled. I take that as a good sign. Whatever visions came to you this night, dreams do not always tell us what is or what will be. Sometimes they tell us what might be, for good or for ill. If your dream was wonderful and awful then perhaps it gave you several possibilities, or different views of the same reality. Let your dream give you clues. Only time will tell us what Invar has spun in the night."

"Hranild told me I must always hope. And I must act because I love."

"Was that the dream or when you were in Vorthall?" Athnel inquired.

"In the dream just now, but I think she said things very like this back home."

Ian realized he had just called Vorthall home, but said no more about it. Athnel noticed the word choice also.

"Do you think you can go back to sleep now?" she asked.

"I am... afraid to, I think," Ian replied.

"Perhaps our cousin Wulfdar might help," she suggested.

Ian protested. "I don't want to wake him."

Athnel chuckled. "Although I was keeping watch over you, rest assured. You just woke the entire camp."

"Oh dear. I'm sorry."

"Don't worry, Ian. Between Volthir's snores, the cries of wild animals, other people's dreams, those who keep watch, and simply relieving oneself in the night, the camp is never completely quiet. Not to mention when Wilda and Nordil are feeling romantic, but we are politely supposed to ignore that. I know Wulfdar is concerned about you."

Precluding further protestation, Athnel signaled the healer, who approached.

"Was it a nightmare, lad?" Wulfdar asked.

"Yes," Ian answered simply, then added, "I am reluctant to go back to sleep."

"I understand," the elder said. "Let me give you something for dreamless sleep. You might be a bit groggy in the morning, but Invar should leave you alone."

Ian was happy to avoid Invar the Spider, the goddess of dreams. He may wake up to see new webs glisten with dew but at least he can avoid her snares for the rest of the night. He chewed a leaf that Wulfdar proffered and followed it with a draft of fresh water. The healer reminded him of the meditation technique for relaxing and Ian was soon asleep.

Wulfdar and Athnel watched the lad on whom so many hopes had been pinned.

"Thank you, Wulfdar," she whispered. "Sometimes I feel so helpless."

"I cannot imagine you helpless, lady," he replied. "Anything but that."

"You know what I mean. None of us knows how to fight a demon. None of us can completely protect this young man. Indeed, we don't really know what we are doing."

Wulfdar looked at the beautiful young sorceress and singer in the starlight and smiled. "We may not know exactly what to do with a demon, dear lady, but we do know what we are doing. We stand by each other, and we love, and we hope. This lad has the gift of a great heart and though I have known him to play tricks, he lacks the guile to work true evil. I would put an honest and loving heart against the greatest evil the world has known. Frankly, with the possible exception of that Vishgar fellow, I believe our entire company, Lord Wolf here included, is blessed by the stars with such a heart. Even if we perish, we shall perish loving. That, in itself, spells the Chegjan's defeat."

"I had not realized, healer, that you use words as much as medicines. Thank you."

Wulfdar returned to his sleep and Athnel watched Weltar the Tortoise rise in the night sky before her turn to sleep came. Drifting toward slumber, she invoked that goddess of wisdom for guidance. The camp lay in peace until just before dawn.

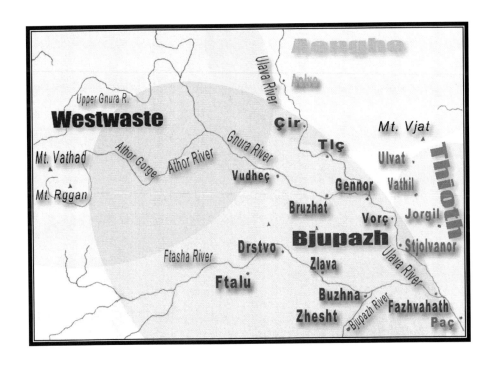

Bjupazh and Westwaste

CHAPTER 58

An unseasonable cold gripped the Ulava Valley. Wulfdar was awakened by sharp aches in his right shoulder and both knees. He rose and began a series of stretches, with considerable attention to limbering his complaining fingers. Wilda treated Nordil to a lengthy expostulation on his duty to keep her warm all the way through the night. Ian's young joints were no worse for the chill but he did find himself curled tightly to conserve warmth, his face buried in Vladje's fur. When the wolf rose, the cool air felt like a slap to Ian's face.

The smell of Wilda's freshly baked flatbread rose from the cooking iron over the fire where batter bubbled and browned, easing the general unwillingness to rise. Her special recipe included a flour of several grains mingled with seeds and ground nutmeats and she guarded the combination like a royal gold hoard. Combined with strips of dried venison, a convenience when journeying, and fresh berries gathered by Hildir and Vishgar, the warm cakes made a nourishing breakfast. Wulfdar insisted that everyone augment this with fresh greens he had collected. They were slightly bitter and their tang puckered mouths but they were not unpleasant. All was washed down with gourds of water drawn from a nearby stream that fed the Ulava.

Refreshed, the travelers broke camp and resumed the ride toward Gennor, wondering whether the Chegjan had also visited there and how the inhabitants would compare with those of Vorç.

The wind that morning was unpredictable, shifting directions and adding to the chill all felt. Yellow strips of cloth attached to the peace poles snapped in the breeze and Ian could feel the feathers in his hair catching sudden gusts. He drew the scarf Njothila had made tighter about his neck, recalling the icy horror of his nightmare.

The image of her falling prey to despair, or any other power or aspect of the dark demon, was so awful that Ian resolved to do all in his power to prevent it. In spite of the doubts and fears that never ceased to trouble him, Ian's commitment to follow the prophecies and face the Chegjan took on new life.

If Hranild spoke truly, then faith would be his shield against the nagging sense of unworthiness or helplessness. He would believe in the Light, in Hranild, in his comrades, in himself. He would trust the love shown him in both worlds. He tried to recall what he had been taught about darkness not prevailing over the Light—wasn't that in the Last Gospel at Mass? Wasn't this what the star stone tried to teach him also?

Then there were the dedication and faithfulness of those who rode with him—did this not speak louder than words? They had repeatedly shown their readiness to lay down their lives for him. Didn't that call for a like faith from him? There were moments when he felt ready to die for his friends and for this strange world. Might he not recall such proven friendship and loyalty in the times when he felt unprepared?

Ian had witnessed what the Chegjan could do and yearned to see the world set free from its power. He did not care how or by whom this might be accomplished. It certainly seemed foolish to think he could be the one. After witnessing Furk's destruction, the entire venture seemed to be madness. Didn't Zhodor speak of "silly, stupid hope" and ask "whom will you believe"? It felt better to hope and be a fool than to give in to despair and yield all to the demon.

Amid such thoughts, Ian heaved a great sigh and Hildir responded.

"Such a heavy sigh so early in the day. What troubles you, cousin?"

"Ah, Hildir, what can I say? The closer we come to the demon the more I wonder."

"Hmm," Hildir muttered, "I rather think we all do. The closer I come to a battle, the more I consider every possibility, nor do I assume that I will emerge on the winning side. One cannot fight well without facing loss and death. But that only helps me fight more carefully."

"Huh," Ian said, as though considering aloud. "So it is not cowardly to doubt before the conflict?"

"Not at all, lad."

"Tell me, Hildir, what was your most frightening battle?"

Hildir thought for a while, then a quizzical look came over his face and he pondered some more. At last he replied, "There was a mission to the south a few years back, when I was less experienced and the foe especially savage. But I think the one that has haunted me most is yet to come. Do you remember the afternoon in Nimmoth?"

"When we visited the woodworkers?"

"Yes," the warrior replied, "and after?"

"In the alehouse."

"What do you honestly think of the feather woman who approached us?"

"She was beautiful, certainly."

"Anything else?"

"Well, friendly, of course, but she would have to be or have no business."

"You are a wise and clever young man, but what else?"

"She was clever. And natural. She did not seem false, even when she greeted old men who were not very attractive. Do you think she has a good heart, Hildir?"

"That is what I wonder."

Ian wondered where this was going. "Why are we talking about her, cousin?"

"Because I have thought of her many times since then. And that frightens me."

"It is hard for me to think of you frightened of her, Hildir."

"It is because I cannot forget her, Ian, and I think you know that I had not thought of finding a wife this early in my life."

"Well, cousin, you cannot remain a bachelor forever. I know that more than one woman in Vorthall would happily choose you."

"You hear too much gossip. But why does this one woman keep entering my thoughts? Do you think she is a sorceress, like Athnel?"

"I don't know about that, cousin, but she has obviously charmed you. Couldn't it just be the lure of a beautiful woman who took a fancy to you one afternoon in an alehouse?"

"Perhaps. I don't know But if I ever pass through Nimmoth again, I will look for her."

"I never thought such a mighty warrior would be easy prey for a woman's smile," Ian teased.

"Never underestimate us," Meldreth interjected, having heard Ian's latest comment. "Don't you think I could conquer any number of brave men?"

Ian laughed. "I believe you have already done so, cousin Meldreth, but it would not be seemly for you to brag of it."

"Nor shall I," she said as if casually dismissing the topic, then broke out into her hearty laugh. Ian noticed that the brawny and most manly warrior seemed to blush with embarrassment, and he played the gentleman by distracting Meldreth before she could notice.

"I am surprised, lady of golden hair, rosy cheeks, and a most womanly figure, that you serve Vrotni instead of Desh."

"Ooh, listen to the gallant lad," she teased. "You must realize, precocious chap, that serving one star does not mean ignoring the others. I love battle skills too much not to serve the Fierce Mother, but I was born under the sign of the Raven and have always enjoyed the tricks of love."

Emboldened, Ian pushed the conversation further. "You seem to have a great appetite for life, Cousin Meldreth."

"Indeed, I do. Why, I even had the privilege of deflowering the gorgeous hunk of man riding beside you, though he has known many women since then. We never forget our first time, do we, Hildir?"

Hildir finally found his voice and blurted, "I am amazed you can remember that, Meldreth. I was hardly *your* first."

The jovial woman erupted in warm laughter. "True, cousin. I was a curious girl and wanted to try everything before my peers. But I remember my men, every one of them. Can you say the same for your women, Hildir?"

"I am a gentleman and do not discuss the women in my life," the warrior replied, provoking more laughter, Ian joining Meldreth in amusement this time.

"An evasive answer, don't you think?" the warmaiden asked.

"But one worthy of a true gentleman," Ian said in Hildir's defense.

"Men!" Meldreth said, rolling her eyes with mock exaggeration, then rode ahead of them, chuckling.

"Women!" Hildir echoed under his breath. "They are impossible."

Ian picked up where Meldreth left off, taking advantage of Hildir's discomfort. "If the people of Vorthall speak true, you are very fond of the impossible, cousin."

"Well, of course, lad, they are delectable creatures! But they never give you a moment's peace."

"I suppose I shall find out what you mean, cousin."

"Ah, that is right. Your flower has not yet been plucked. No wonder she toyed with you that afternoon. Fresh fruit is especially nice to look at."

Ian completed the saying, "But mature fruit is sweeter to the taste." The older man smirked. Ian persisted.

"I felt like a quick snack in her eyes, but her looks told me you were the main feast. You sensed the same, by the way you kissed her hand. One might think you two had met in court."

Gazing into the distance, Hildir smiled silently.

"Why, Hildir, you are caught in her spell, I am certain of it. And she has not even joined the company of what Meldreth calls 'your women'."

Hildir still said nothing, merely raising an eyebrow in amusement.

"Cousin, you dream! Remember, it was an alehouse, not some baronial castle. She is a feather lady with loyalties to no man. Can you possibly think your paths will cross again?"

"If we return by Nimmoth, you can count on a visit to that alehouse, cousin."

"Hopeless," Ian murmured. "Now *I* am frightened of her, or of her effect on you. Can you focus your mind during combat with this woman haunting you?"

"Easily. All I have to do is imagine I am fighting for her."

"To gain her or on her behalf?"

"Either. Both. For whom would you fight, Ian?"

"For the memory of my family. For the Norrungs and all the people of this world, if I could set them free of this terror. For someone I love."

"And whom do you think you love? Besides your family, I mean."

"Well, those I ride with now, I suppose. You have all become a kind of family to me."

"And you have become one of us."

Ian thought some more. "For my foster-brother, Lord Njothir, and his sister."

"She who gave you your feathers," Hildir commented.

"And the scarf I wound so tightly about my neck this morning," added Ian.

Hildir wondered how many Norrung customs Ian understood. "Do you realize what the gift of feathers means?"

"Is it something special? I know we wear them to signal that we come in peace and that they are sacred. So I assumed she was helping my journey as a man of peace. What else?"

"The giver of peace feathers is usually a grandfather or grandmother. When we are old enough to fight, we are also old enough to walk in peace, so it is something of a rite of passage. If no grandparent or similar elder is available, though this is rare, then feathers are often given by someone who is especially close to you. We expected it to be Lord Njothir, for he is the one who took you under his wing as a brother. I was surprised to see you receive them from Njothila."

"So it was unusual?"

"I think it means she feels closer to you than you suspect."

"Oh."

Ian chewed on this morsel of information. After probing his heart a while, he inquired further.

"So is that why, when we were in the alehouse, you wondered whether I had made any promises?"

"Exactly. And?"

"No, Hildir, I have made no promises to Njothila, nor she to me. But I have thought of her often on this journey. I miss her. She is quick-witted, playful, and very kind. She has become my closest friend because we can talk about anything. Lord Njothir is my brother and friend also, of course, but Njothi has done more than anyone to help me understand this new world. She is also very beautiful. And cautious. I do not think she trusts easily."

"A chief's daughter should be cautious, especially one as lovely as Njothila. Many would win her."

When Hildir said this, Ian realized the thought troubled him. Was he jealous? Yes. He did have feelings for the daughter of Rathdar.

Hildir continued, "Some tribes would bestow her as a political move, to create ties with allies."

Ian protested, "Njothila has made her brother promise not to do that." He was now definitely disturbed. "She will not be given as the Princess Gizli was."

"Relax, cousin. I doubt that Njothila of the Norrungs will be given to any man she does not herself choose. I would not be in Lord Njothir's boots for all the Forest of Norrast, should he not honor his sister's wishes."

Ian now found himself wondering what Njothila's gifts, his scarf and feathers, might mean. How did she view him—as more than a foster-brother? His pulse quickened at the thought of receiving her love. "*Sweet Desh!*" he thought to himself, unsure whether the phrase meant he was praying or swearing.

"But, Hildir," he protested, giving voice to his fears, "can you imagine a chief's daughter with a stranger and orphan?"

The warrior laughed. "I can imagine a chief's daughter marrying a demon-slayer."

"If he returns alive," Ian concluded somberly.

"If you doubt Hranild, you will eventually be proven wrong, cousin. She has an irritating way of being right when things are finally sorted out."

This exchange, in which Ian came to view Njothila differently, was cut short by a shout from Volthir.

The entire company quickened pace to see what he had noticed. Remnants of recent funeral pyres could be seen ahead. Next to them were prayer poles with strips of white cloth, like the one they had seen in Lesser Vish. They were now close to Gennor and smoke was visible rising in the distance.

When they arrived at the source of the black pillar, a mass funeral greeted them. A crowd was assembled around a vast pyre, all the mourners clothed in white. Plangent music mingled with the lamentations of loved ones bemoaning their loss. Ashes darkened most faces. Only small children appeared untouched by the collective misery as they darted among the crowd, making play of the unusual gathering. The rest betrayed the depth of their sorrow with deep, haunted eyes.

The Chegjan had clearly visited Gennor following the harrowing of Vorç.

The people here, however, had not retreated into the shadows but poured out their feelings. Loss, anger, despair, shock—all these were displayed for the world to see. Ian felt as though he were witnessing the heartbreak of an entire town, concentrated in this farewell ritual.

Many cried out to the Veiled One, beseeching her to receive those who now journeyed the star path. Some swore by Wigdor the Just to set the world aright again. Most simply wept. Singers chanted the funeral hymns and Ian noticed that Pjortan and Athnel were softly singing with them. Though the people of Gennor were all strangers to him, Ian felt as though simply being with them might break his heart as well.

CHAPTER 59

The doleful white of death was seen everywhere—on prayer poles, in the clothing of every citizen, flying as flags or hanging as banners. No family was untouched when the Chegjan had taken its toll and moved on. All of Gennor was in mourning and the unrelieved wails rising from every home, shop, and street corner seized upon the demon chasers and seemed to infect their nerves.

Amid tearful exclamations mingled with shock and anger, Nordil managed to extract from a cluster of townspeople that the dark cloud had descended suddenly, ravaged all of Gennor, then headed west as a foul mist.

The riders thus shifted course. Instead of continuing north along the Ulava toward Tlç, Çir, Aolve, and Aonghe, which would have taken Vishgar into the lands of his birth, they turned west along the Gnura River. The Gnura flowed roughly two hundred miles from the mountains of Westwaste, augmented at various points by the Fjolu and Athor Rivers, then merged with the Ulava just above Gennor.

The upper valleys of these rivers were generally avoided. The inhospitable region known as Westwaste was unsuitable for tilling and much of it was considered haunted. Certain portions were allegedly inhabited by gnords and various creatures of whom little was known but much was feared. Although other mountainous areas about the Mere were cultivated, or their forests harvested and riches mined, this alpine portion of the Mither Basin's boundaries had been shunned from earliest times. As unknown territory, Westwaste formed the matter of legends, rumors, and tales of terror enjoyed from a safe distance.

Ian pondered the actions of the Chegjan. Its movements may have initially been random, following the progress of the plague, but at this point it seemed to have overtaken the path of disease and traveled purposefully. Something about its attacks suggested a warped personality coiled at its core, ready to strike like a vengeful and venomous serpent.

Gorselsnakes were unaware of and indifferent to their victims except as threat or nourishment. They lunged without spite, defending themselves or claiming their next meal. The Chegjan, however, demonstrated an alternate quality of indifference. While unconcerned about the damage it inflicted, a certain vicious and taunting pattern seemed to be emerging.

The display on the afternoon of Lord Furk's death was one example, the roiling midnight mass virtually teasing the noble warrior into attacking, then smashing him and his forces in an instant. Instead of staying to move among the onlookers and wreak further damage, the demon dissipated and moved on, as though to lure them into ever more tragedies.

Did this foul thing, whatever it was, take some kind of evil pleasure in inflicting sorrow and suffering? Why was it now heading away from populated centers? Was this simply a random trajectory? Had the Chegjan gathered power toward some peak point leading inevitably toward dissipation in the wilderness where there were no further victims? Or was something more sinister happening? Might it be luring its foes to their certain doom, just as it provoked Furk into rash action leading to his death?

Others in the group had thoughts similar to these as they rode from Gennor along the Gnura Road. Along this lower section the river was broad, snaking its way along the Gnura Plain before emptying into the Ulava. Goats and dairy cows could be seen across the river, content amid the lush green fields from which came the area's rich cheeses.

Wilda observed aloud that the Gnura Road had almost no traffic. Given the intense collective grief of Gennor, one could hardly expect much travel emerging thence in any direction, unless to notify relatives not in the immediate vicinity. The absence of travelers from the west gave rise to unhappy speculation.

"If that starforsaken thing has truly gone ahead of us," Wilda commented, "I shudder to imagine what will greet our eyes in the next town."

"Death, I imagine," Mechdar muttered. "That seems to be the one mark by which we track it."

Vunskridh joined in. "And some sort of madness, I wouldn't be surprised. Folk do not behave normally wherever it touches. Remember the riot that erupted in Siot? We avoided the town, having heard of the violence that flared up and then died down again, as abruptly as it started."

"Gennor may have been as normal as we have seen," Wilda added. "Folks grieve when they lose the ones they love. It's just that no one in the entire town had been spared a loss. I've never seen a whole populace in ashes and white before, but it makes sense, as much as anything does any more."

Pjortan threw in a copper's worth, saying, "I would not exactly call it madness, but the fear in Vorç was beyond all reason. The way the people hid, trembling in fright—I have never heard of the like, nor do I hope to ever again."

"The plague itself was bad enough," Vunskridh observed. "So many people taken before their time…. And then you have the aftermath—folks unable to cope with their losses, just going through the motions of life."

Pjortan, the youth normally brimming with calm faith, raised some eyebrows when he commented, "Frankly, I am amazed we have kept going this far, for each of us lost someone to the fiery death."

At this point Athnel joined the conversation. "Life and death are two sides of one coin, Tanje." Pjortan attempted to stifle a satisfied smile upon hearing himself named so familiarly. He was also embarrassed that she used the diminutive publicly. "All our losses, our daily letting go, you might even say our daily deaths, make way for what is new. All our living is a dying. When we can accept this, much of our vain struggling ceases."

"But…" Pjortan objected, not yet daring to call her Athje, "don't we have to struggle? Why would we be on this quest if it were not a struggle against the darkness?"

"Oh," the lady replied, "there is needful struggle enough. I spoke of vain exertion, our attempts to cling when deep within we know we must let go, our folly in thinking each small death is final when life is trying to break forth, our useless efforts to hold back time. We might as well stand in the middle of the Gnura there and think by wishing we could keep it from flowing."

"I don't know about you," Wilda suddenly changed the topic, "but I may be about to get one of my wishes. Do you see the wagon just approaching?"

A heavily laden cart came from the west, the first they had seen. A woman with abundant dark brown curls cascading over her dusty rose gown was driving the two horses that pulled it. Beside her sat a gangly youth, perhaps a year or two younger than Ian, who would be her son by the looks of his own flowing curls. Together they were singing a river song, occasionally breaking out in laughter. Wilda hailed them and the woman shouted back.

"Well met, travelers! The stars keep you."

Her merry tone and jovial greeting raised spirits. Perhaps the next town had been skipped by the Chegjan. Then again, perhaps not; but for now the party would hope.

The woman, one Vovoni by name, was a merchant and her wagon was full of edibles. Wilda immediately eyed great wheels of cheese as Volthir and Vishgar traded observations on what appeared to be barrels of wine.

"Tjiweth bless me," Wilda said, invoking the Bright Queen and Mother of Life, "my wish came true. Ever since seeing the cows on yonder banks, I have been wishing for cheese. This fine woman and her son…?" Vovoni affirmed he was, indeed, her offspring. "They have brought the riches of the herd our way."

"Cheese is the gift of the rich earth, the green grasses, the sun and rain, the blessed kine, the ripening caves, and the cheesemaker's art. Tjiweth shines on us all with such goodness. Here, let me cut a bit of this one and tell me what you think."

The merchant took out a large knife and loosened a pale yellow wedge from a round near the edge of the cart. Its rind was tan and its texture smooth. A hint of toasted nuts blended with sweet creamy richness flooded Wilda's mouth as she sampled the thin slice Vovoni gave her. The other travelers clustered about the wagon as the woman provided samples of various cheeses.

"And might these barrels contain wine, good cousin?" Vishgar asked.

"Indeed, my thirsty friend, a goodly drink from the vines near Aolve in the north. Have you the silver to purchase some?"

"Ah," Vishgar uttered, deeming her a skilled seller of wares, "I might spare some. What might this coin obtain, my lady?"

Vunskridh noted that Vishgar must call every woman "my lady," regardless of station or relationship. She was not sure what that meant for all the times he had addressed her as such.

Vovoni examined the Thiothi coin, tested it, and answered, "It should be good for a wineskin and I will add a horn's worth in the bargain."

"Excellent!" said Vishgar, promptly bringing forth a large wineskin for the filling. By the time he presented it to her, Vovoni's son had filled a drinking horn and offered it to Vishgar for tasting. The sometime thief exuded delight as he eyed the wine, sniffed it, and took a sip. He rolled it around on his tongue, swallowed, drew a slow breath and exhaled before pronouncing, "Good cousin, you have taken me back to younger years when I drank Aolveni wine with my family. May the stars bless you for such kindness."

Vishgar bowed to Vovoni, then passed the horn around that others might taste what the vintner's skill could do with grapes. The refreshing liquid was greeted with much approval and a couple more skins' worth was purchased. On behalf of the company, Wilda acquired the entire round of cheese they had first tasted. It would provide good nourishment if they traveled into the hills that could already be seen in the distance.

When Wulfdar inquired of the next town, mentioning that Vovoni and her son were the only people they had seen on the road, she found it puzzling.

"I have not come from Bruzhat so I can tell you nothing, good healer. I have come from the wedge of land between the rivers and forded the Gnura at an especially wide and shallow spot just west of where we now stand. My son here was just asking where the travelers and traders were when we spotted you."

"Is Bruzhat the next town along the Gnura?" asked Ringskild.

"It is, cousin," Vovoni replied, giving her great mop of curls a toss. "Are you headed to someplace you know nothing of?"

Ringskild laughed and replied, "You have named it exactly, I fear. You might say we pursue a villain far beyond the lands we know."

The merchant uttered a good-hearted chuckle in return. "I could tell you were not from these parts by your speech and garments. We see few outlanders here. Beyond Bruzhat are only two more towns, then habitations thin and vanish. Some believe the mountains are sacred but most of us simply fear them. You journey toward the frontier where few go and most perish."

"We thank you for the encouragement, cousin," said Meldreth with a smile.

"Oh, I am sorry," Vovoni said quickly. "I meant no ill."

"Of course not," Ringskild reassured her. "We welcome information of every sort. Ignorance rarely assists a venture. Still, we have faced perils before and expect more. We should be on our way, and other customers will await you." The tall warmaiden paused, then added, "You should know, cousin, that an evil blow has befallen the people of Gennor. Many have perished and the whole town now mourns. They may need provisions for funeral meals, and so may you prosper. I thought you should be alerted to what awaits you."

"My thanks, daughter of Vrotni," said Vovoni. "May the stars protect you."

Taking reins in hand, Vovoni set the horses once more on their eastward way. The victual-laden wagon creaked and began to roll once more along the Gnura Road, the rhythm of its wheels echoing in the rhythm of the drinking song she began to sing. Her son joined in the merriment, evidently characteristic of the pair, and they sang heartily as they rode. The Norrungs resumed their westward journey, chatting rather than singing, and still wondering what they would find ahead of them.

CHAPTER 60

True to Vovoni's description, a clearing soon became apparent on the right side of the road, bordered with grasses next to varied shrubs and clumps of willows. A wide track led from the Gnura Road to an especially wide expanse of the Gnura itself, its waters rippling over the shallows. The track resumed on the far side, gradually ascending toward the lush pastures between the two rivers.

Sensing the need for emotional cleansing and refreshment, Ringskild suggested taking advantage of the river. All consented and the company divided, half keeping watch while the others bathed. Pools just upstream from the ford were well suited for the purpose. Uncertain of local customs, the men and women were somewhat more discreet than they might be bathing in the waters of Norrast, yet still more relaxed than anything Ian would ever see in the realm of Queen Anne.

Lady Athnel was clearly accustomed to a more modest setting, as was Princess Çirazel. Zlida held up an expanse of cloth, allowing the princess to bathe while screened from the men and those who kept watch. Waterfowl and a few four-legged animals were graced with a view of the young virgin while Zlida prayed that Elithel would shield her from any human eyes that might be obscured among coppices across the river.

Pjortan, with his Norrung sensibilities, felt perfectly comfortable bathing near any of the warmaidens or the married and motherly Wilda. Athnel's presence altered this ambiguously. When he noticed a smile from her, he relaxed somewhat, though having spotted her amid the waters he found himself drying and dressing quickly with a terse command for Volthir to shut up.

Spirits rose with this well-timed break in the journey. Though nothing else had changed, the demon chasers felt better prepared to enter Bruzhat. Wulfdar busied himself observing the roadside flora and Nordil loosed Fjurthil to stretch his wings. Meldreth's infectious laughter punctuated the ribald tales she loved to tell. Wilda asked the voluptuous warmaiden if she would tell such salty stories after she married.

"By Desh and Eghran, yes!" Meldreth replied, invoking not one but two trickster deities. "Once I catch a man I want to keep him amused and inspired."

"I am sure you will do both, cousin," said Vishgar, prompting more peals of laughter and Meldreth's retort.

"Would you care to be considered, cousin?"

"I am sure that sweet talker is not ready to settle down," Vunskridh abruptly countered.

"What makes you certain of that, daughter of Jornandir?" Vishgar said evenly. "Perhaps my heart is less flighty than you imagine."

"Perhaps bears will start to fly," Vunskridh persisted.

"I don't know," Mechdar chimed in, "we have seen strange things on this journey. I will keep an eye peeled for a large furry thing soaring over the treetops."

More laughter ensued before Vunskridh bowed out of the conversation with a simple, "You do that, Mechdar."

Nordil protested that his Fjurthil would be confused by a bird with fur but would undoubtedly do his best to swoop down upon it.

The merry Meldreth then launched into the story of the widow with six lovers and kept her audience entertained until Hildir spotted the village of Bruzhat.

All they could see at first were a few outlying buildings across the river, the rest being obscured by a small forested island in the river. Just as the riders were craning their necks for a better view they had their second encounter of the day. A man traveling on foot was coming toward them from the opposite direction. He halted and hailed them, waving an arm in invitation to approach.

With the natural caution of warriors, the group rode toward him on full alert, lest nearby thickets prove to be cover for an ambush. Such was not the case, however, and the man proved a friendly ally.

His name was Onvar, his trade farming, and the land he toiled as a peasant was close to Vudheç, the next town upriver. A short, round-faced chap with a bushy mustache, Onvar greeted the strangers on the assumption that they were as good-hearted as he.

"Good to see you coming in peace," he said, a lift of his eyebrows indicating the feathers they wore. "I called you closer because you were almost to the ford here." At that point he gestured to the obvious crossing that could not be seen from where they first spotted him. Ian noticed, as Onvar made a broad sweep with his left arm, that the man's pinky was missing, perhaps lost in some accident.

"We thank you, good cousin," Ringskild said warmly. "I had just wondered where the crossing might be."

"It is easy enough, but it helps to know the river here. We make for the island there, then go to its other end before fording toward the town." A chatty fellow, Onvar continued, "I have come to visit my cousin, Ezni. She's a good woman. Very sad, though. She lost her husband to the fiery death earlier this year. Lives with my uncle and her little girl. I try to see her when I can get away. Family, you know. My sister would come too, but she has too many children to keep track of."

"It is kind of you to visit," said Athnel, breaking into the stream of information.

Out of courtesy, Pjortan invited Onvar to mount behind him and ride across the river. With Onvar's guidance, Pjortan led the way across the shallows of the Gnura toward the island. Vladje seemed to have no problem trotting over the rocky riverbed, and appeared to dart after a fish. If that were the case, the fish made a clean escape and the wolf continued his crossing. Once on land again, they threaded their way along the trail toward the downstream end of the isle. Just before reaching its end, they emerged onto a sand bar deposited there over the years. This led to the next set of shallows and they soon climbed the bank toward Bruzhat.

Onvar's cousin lived near the river, so the group accompanied as Pjortan's mount conveyed the traveler who had come far enough on foot. Onvar commented that he never expected to ride a star singer's horse and wondered if it were some kind of sacrilege to do so, he not being a singer and all. Pjortan assured him the stars would not take it ill since he was riding with, and at the invitation of, a singer. Athnel added that it might even entail a blessing, which caused Onvar to smile.

"Mama, mama!" shouted a child as the riders approached a row of modest houses with shared walls. It was Onvar's niece and he leapt from the horse to run towards her. "Onvje!" she squealed with delight when she recognized him. About then Ezni emerged, at first appearing anxious to know what had excited her daughter. Noticing the large company of riders, her concern grew, but at mention of her brother's nickname her eyes were drawn toward him just as he swooped his niece into his arms.

Ezni shared her cousin's lack of height; though she had an excellent figure and would be a highly eligible young widow did she not bring an aging father with her. Ezni's lively daughter would be a charming enhancement to her attributes as children were so highly prized in a post-plague existence. Whoops of laughter ensued at the sight of her cousin. As she drew closer, Ian noticed her guileless smile and something strange about her eyes. They converged slightly, rendering her cross-eyed.

All this commotion must have roused her father from his nap since a loud male voice shouted "Znizni?" from within.

"It's your nephew Onvar, Father," she replied loudly so the old man could hear. The family members headed toward the door so Onvar could greet his uncle. Onvar gave a quick introduction to the riders who had accompanied him across the river.

"Then they would not know either," Ezni said cryptically.

"Know what, cousin?" Onvar asked.

"Well, something strange happened here yesterday, though I can't rightly say what it was. Neighbors tell me a weird mist drifted over town, sort of like a thin black smoke. They saw it gather and get thicker over the market square then settle. Now they saw this from a bit of a distance and nobody could tell me what happened next.

"When the smoke, or whatever it was, rose again and melted in the air, old Waçda, the one who walks with a cane, continued on her way toward the market. You won't believe what she found, cousin. All the folks in the market square were sitting, or standing, some walking and staring as though they couldn't see a thing. And when she spoke to them, they never answered a word. A few chuckled and a few more cried, but not a soul spoke or seemed to understand a thing. The whole lot of them—lost and with less awareness than a newborn. What do you make of that?"

Ezni finished this remarkable account and looked at the entire company as though daring them to explain what had transpired.

"Have they come to their senses since this happened?" inquired Wulfdar.

"No, Healer," Ezni replied, "their families and neighbors had to fetch them and lead them home. They are alive, but scarce more than that. I have seen this once or twice with the very old, but nothing like this."

Ringskild asked how many were afflicted but Ezni was uncertain. "As many as were in the market at the time, but that could be a few score or a hundred. I cannot say."

"The Mind Eater has tried something new," Nordil muttered.

"So it seems," agreed Volthir.

"What is this you say about a Mind Eater?" Onvar queried.

"Just as the plague has traveled through all our lands," Athnel explained, trying not to distress Ezni, "so has a dark thing called the Chegjan. We consider it a demon for lack of a better word. It spreads despair wherever it goes and it seems to be growing in power. The most any have seen is a dark cloud but it has been known to spark fits of madness and violence, to suck life out of humans and beasts alike, to strike terror, and now to drain all knowing from the living. Outbreaks of public insanity have given it the name 'Mind Eater' but now that seems to have a new meaning, if the foul thing has taken away the minds of those unfortunate enough to be in the marketplace yesterday."

Ezni quickly made a Bjupazhi gesture to ward off evil then asked if anything could be done against this Cheg-whatever. Her daughter, aware only that her mother was troubled, wrapped her arms about Ezni's leg.

Pjortan spoke up. "There have been prophecies that it can be overcome, though none have made clear exactly how. In obedience to those prophecies and our chieftain, we have journeyed from a great forest far to the east, following the demon's path, hoping to hasten its downfall."

"May the stars give you success, by Ulhnut," said Onvar, naming the One Reality beyond all deities in fervid prayer.

"This thing has brought you so far?" Ezni asked, scarce daring to believe anyone would travel more than two days journey from home.

"It has," Pjortan replied.

"Znizni!" cried the housebound elder again and Ezni excused herself.

"How may we help you?" Onvar asked, his generous heart overtaking the resources at hand.

"Perhaps you can help us speak to this Waçda," Ringskild suggested. "You have already helped us find our way to Bruzhat."

"Willingly, lady. Allow me to check with my cousin." Onvar popped into the house, greeted his uncle with exaggerated volume but genuine affection, chatted with Ezni, and re-emerged.

"It is but a short distance from here," he announced. Pjortan offered him a ride again, which he refused this time. Onvar led them to the end of the humble row of homes where they turned left, then left again around the next corner. They soon stood before an old stone cottage with a thatch roof. Onvar hailed its resident.

"Cousin Waçda! It is Onvar, Olvit's son and your neighbor Ezni's cousin."

"Just a minute," came the gravel-throated reply. Moments later a woman emerged, huffing and puffing with the exertion or rousing herself, and leaning on a cane. Her long gray hair was streaked with black and held in a pony tail with a strip of black fabric. A homespun fawn-colored dress lay beneath her ample black apron and rust-toned shawl. She examined Onvar appraisingly and said, "Yes, you look like the family. What can I do for you, son of Olvit? And who is this gang of riders with you? Not from these parts, I can tell."

"No, cousin. They are from far to the east and they hope to do something about the dark thing."

"Ha!" the old woman snorted, "Well, good luck to them." Ringskild dismounted to help put the woman at ease and most of her cohorts followed her example. Waçda assessed them, as she had done to Onvar, pausing at sight of the lovely young princess, who might be from the south but certainly not the east.

"Tell me, war lady," she said to the tall armed figure before her, "have you all lost your wits? Because if you haven't, this thing will take them from you. Mark my words, you don't want to even look at it. Viggi and his wife Hlethar, my dear friends, were both stricken. She had only gone to the market to take him a little meal while he sat at the booth where he always sells the pottery made by his family.

"When I arrived in the market square and saw that something was terribly wrong, I hobbled over to his booth as fast as these old legs and my sturdy stick could carry me. There he was, sitting in the usual spot, staring into the air. Hlethar was standing nearby, still holding the bundle she had brought with a bite to eat. I called their names, but not an answer if the stars depended on it. As though they never knew me! Can you imagine such a thing?

"Well, I thought they might just be dazed and would come out of it any second. But no such luck. And everybody else in the market was the same way! I couldn't help both my friends and move myself, so I scuttled off to their house where Viggi's brother and his family also live. Told them what I had seen and they ran off to the market to fetch the poor things.

"It's too much walking for me, but I wandered over to see them this morning first thing. Nothing had changed. I don't know what the poor family is going to do. If I ever get like that, I hope Ushni calls me and puts an end to it."

Her narrative completed, Waçda caught her breath and waited for the shocked responses of her audience. Onvar shook his head with a sympathetic look on his face but the outlanders seem unimpressed. This disappointed the old woman.

Ringskild not only failed to cluck with pity, gape with amazement, or comment on the sorry state of the world, she only had one question.

"When this thing rose in the air and evaporated, was it drifting in any direction you could notice?"

Waçda pursed her lips in concentration then answered, "It came from downstream because I saw it gathering over the town. Afterwards, I'm not so sure. The way it moved was like smoke but I don't think it was subject to the wind the way smoke is. Nasty business. It might be traveling up the Gnura, but I wouldn't wish that for the sake of Ezni's cousin here." Onvar displayed alarm when he heard this.

"That is in keeping with its westward direction," said Ringskild.

Recognizing the old woman's desire for more reaction, Ian politely spoke up. "We appreciate your giving us a first-hand account, cousin. Everything we learn is helpful."

Several nods from his companions affirmed this and Waçda smiled with satisfaction.

"Always happy to be helpful," she said. "Stars guide you."

"Thank you very much," Ringskild said, prompted by Ian's thoughtfulness. "May the stars keep you."

The party returned with Onvar to Ezni's home. Ezni told them of an alehouse in town where they might find food and drink. They thanked her and Onvar for their help and Ezni's daughter squealed with delight when Vladje gave her a lupine lick on the cheek. Onvar spoke with Ringskild then was left trying to explain away a wolf to his very concerned cousin as the Norrungs rode off in search of refreshment.

"What did Onvar want?" asked Volthir.

Ringskild replied, "To ride with us to his home near Vudheç. If the Chegjan has headed there, his sister's family is in danger."

"You consented, of course," Volthir presumed.

"Naturally. Who could deny him when we have the means? But first we need sustenance."

And so the companions found the alehouse and dined before returning to Ezni's home.

CHAPTER 61

As with all human watering holes, the alehouse was abuzz with the latest excitement. Speculation filled the air along with the smell of onions and cooking meats, the yeasty aroma of ale, and the dense scent of people in close proximity. Simply by being foreigners in Bjupazhi territory, the Norrungs and Hlvi aroused curiosity that led to even more speculation. Vishgar, being native to the lands near Aonghe toward the north, was most like the locals and the most comfortable among them. He worked the crowd with all his charm and verbal skills, helping set the room at ease. The Norrungs were grateful for this service.

Conflicting details muddied the accounts of the Chegjan's visit to Bruzhat. Only a few of those present had seen it gather to descend upon the market square; most had only heard reports. Those gathered to drink were from families largely untouched by the demon's attack and thus were free to socialize. The less fortunate were home caring for the physical shell of their loved ones.

Descriptions of the victims were fairly consistent. Lively, active people of two days ago were unresponsive after the black cloud's visitation. Breathing, sometimes moving aimlessly, sometimes sitting still or fidgeting, managing to eat only when fed, eliminating but often unable to clean up after themselves. All personality had vanished and only the bodies remained. Those inured to the traumas of battle were shaken by this horror.

Wilda's motherly tenderness was especially touched by this latest attack of the Chegjan. Her heart yearned to gather all the lost souls of Bruzhat to her bosom and comfort them. Because she could not, Wilda's tears came easily and she appeared mildly agitated, causing Vladje to stick close to her and occasionally whimper in sympathy.

Wulfdar suggested they had learned enough and urged them to get outside as soon as they finished their repast, which they did. Under the stars, Wilda seemed to regain some of her composure. Zlida conferred with Wulfdar and together they prepared a drink for Wilda from a couple of powders mixed with wine purchased earlier from Vovoni.

Returning to Ezni's home, the travelers thanked the young widow and Vladje allowed her daughter to hug him. Athnel explained a bit about the wolf to Ezni to allay her concerns at this unusual occurrence. Onvar embraced his uncle and cousin, hoisted his niece and whirled her around, then bade them farewell. Having listened to his summary of Waçda's tale, they understood his desire to hasten home. Ezni urged him to give her love to Onvar's sister and her family, which he promised to do.

Instead of riding behind Pjortan for a short while, Onvar was given one of the baggage horses to ride. His small stature made of him a light burden for the animal and baggage was shifted for the horse's sake. Even as day was ending and the almost half-full moon shone in the eastern sky, the companions re-crossed the Gnura and resumed their westward journey along the Gnura Road.

The way was well defined and never strayed far from the banks of the river itself, so traveling by moonlight was not difficult. Even so, they did not wish to overtax the horses or exhaust themselves. Roughly one hour after midnight they pitched camp aside the road, tended to the horses, and got some sleep.

It had been a long day and a few in the party did not awake until Athnel and Pjortan's voices rose in the hymn to the daystar. The laggards quickly rose and prepared to ride. As the party headed west, the way was no longer quiet and devoid of other travelers. Many were heading east, claiming in passing that Vudheç was no longer safe. No coherent tale emerged, only mention of destruction and ominous signs. It was all very vague and the refugees seemed unwilling to say more, even to Onvar.

Onvar's distress grew with every report, no matter how minimal or vague. He could barely contain himself by the time they reached the cluster of dwellings just outside Vudheç where he lived.

"There is my little hut," he shouted then leapt from the horse and ran toward the next dwelling. It was, as the Norrungs supposed, his sister's home and she emerged when she heard him calling her name. She had a babe on her hip and a toddler clinging to her skirt. Other children could be seen nearby though it was anyone's guess if they were all hers or some belonged to neighbors. The poor woman could not understand Onvar's excessive joy at seeing her nor his sudden return from seeing Ezni.

A rapid stream of explanations and questions ensued. Onvar recounted the mysterious disaster that had befallen the marketplace in Bruzhat, reassuring his sister that their cousin and her family were untouched. She, for her part, knew nothing of any misfortunes in Vudheç, only that a large stream of folk could be seen heading downriver on the road barely visible in the distance. She was too busy tending to children to run after news.

When Ian's companions had learned all they were likely to learn and had exchanged greetings with Onvar's sister, they bade the family farewell and returned to the road toward Vudheç. It was only a short way beyond Onvar's home.

The line of those leaving the town had, by then, dwindled to an uneven trickle. Whatever had terrified people enough to make them flee must have lost its power to inspire immediate action. What the travelers saw as they reached the town was a broken city gate.

By itself this might have indicated the eventual consequence of faulty engineering. The town itself was not heavily fortified, its walls forming a hindrance more than a true barrier. A damaged entrance would not be as fatal here as it would be in a stronghold with active enemies. Large dressed stones, a few of them shattered, lay where the arch had collapsed. No fault was evident in what remained of the sandstone columns on either side.

417

Debris had been partially removed, thus allowing entrance and egress, though one had to wind past the fallen stones.

This alone would not have driven inhabitants from the town, so the demon chasers looked beyond the gate's remains, nor did they have to look far. A randomly swerving path of destruction flowed through the town, from its eastern gate through dwellings and business places alike all the way to a breach in the western wall.

Houses were flattened, timbers shredded, the dust of masonry everywhere. In some areas folks were still digging through rubble, looking for either victims or possessions lying beneath the debris. This time there seemed to be no signs of "sheep's death," only the results of a powerful force that had swept through Vudheç without warning. Tales of earthquake in other lands came to mind but the Norrungs assumed this was no earthquake.

The companions made inquiries among the townsfolk who were willing to speak. There could be no doubt that this too was the work of the Chegjan for many references were made to "the dark thing" or "the black cloud."

"A great darkness came toward us," a baker testified, his face and clothing dusted with flour. "Out of nowhere! And it roared like a monstrous beast or a thousand winter storms Oh, everything shook, and by the stars so did I. My hair stood on end, by Wigdor! My poor missus screamed and fainted, so I ran to her. The thing just missed us, knocked over every house on the other side of the street, as you can see. Damn near shit my breeches, I did. You could hear screaming everywhere and folks crying.

"It looked like smoke, you know? But I couldn't smell anything burning until later. I think it sucked the air right out of wherever it struck, but with stuff tossed this way and that a few fires broke out. Being near the river, we ran like madmen with our buckets. Stars be thanked, we build a lot with local stone, and had lots of rains this year. Otherwise, I don't know how much of poor Vudheç would be left."

Nudged by the princess, Zlida asked the man how much of his bread a gold coin could buy. He was delighted to see serious money amid the sudden chaos of his life and the travelers had loaves aplenty when they left him.

Others confirmed the baker's testimony. The Chegjan's direction was obvious and eyewitnesses agreed that it had passed west, moving upriver. A few more purchases of food enlarged the riders' store before they continued northwest along the Gnura.

They had been told in Vudheç that few lived further west. The next town had been hard hit by the plague a few months earlier and held only a fourth as many inhabitants as the year before. Nrvash was the last town on the Gnura and all beyond was wilderness.

Once again the Gnura Road was empty of fellow travelers. The people of Vudheç had fled downstream, not toward the wild uplands. No one seemed to be coming from Nrvash on this particular afternoon.

The area above Vudheç shifted from tilled fields to scrubland, gently rolling hills covered with shrubs and grasses. Occasionally clumps or lines of trees indicated small creeks or underground springs. The air was fresh and redolent of the essential oils of the various plants warmed by the sun. Birds darted about in the brush seeking seeds and insects and hawks could be seen flying over the hills in search of rodents, lizards, or other tasty meals. The hillsides were alive, but not with other humans.

When the company paused at one point to enjoy the shade of some isolated oaks, Pjortan did more than stretch his legs with a short walk. The skilled young runner darted off on an animal trail, enjoying the sheer exhilaration of using his long legs. Athnel watched him run as she sat beneath a large oak with Vladje's head in her lap. Ian stood next to her, observing her as she kept an eye on Pjortan.

"May I guess why you chose to remain with us, lady?" he ventured.

Athnel smiled sweetly and said, "I believe it is obvious. Yes, beyond the fellowship of singing for the stars there is something more. Do you think a man of the forest can live with a lady of the court, Ian?"

"I think any man would be a fool not to try, were he lucky enough to find a soul mate." Ian blushed as he said this and Athnel chuckled.

"Why Ian, you have become quite gallant. If you keep this up you will sound as sweet as Vishgar."

"You tease me, lady. He could talk the feathers off a bird, I think, or the scales off a fish. Still, we all know that Pjortan adores you."

Athnel stroked the wolf's fur and spoke, "You are sweet to say so, and I know he dotes on me, though he can never find words to say it. Are you that tongue-tied when your heart wants to speak?"

Ian was embarrassed by the question. "I have not had the occasion to know. I suspect I shall be as clumsy as any man when the time comes."

Athnel thought a moment then said, "Something tells me you will find the words when you need to. Don't be afraid to speak, my friend. She will be waiting to hear you open your mouth and your eyes will have told each other already." Pleased with her cryptic comment, Athnel smirked at the confused lad.

Pjortan returned from his run and for a moment his eyes flashed at the sight of Ian talking with Athnel and blushing. She, for her part, did not need special powers to recognize a spark of jealousy and quenched it gently, saying, "I was teasing Ian about his future love life and fear I have quite discomfited the poor boy."

Hearing Athnel call Ian a boy made Pjortan feel better and Ian very much felt like a foolish boy at talk of love. He reassured Pjortan further, though unknowingly, when he confessed that matters of the heart were a complete mystery to him and he would leave such things to Athnel and Pjortan. With that, Ian strolled off, leaving the runner at a loss for words.

Realizing that Ian had indirectly named the reality Pjortan had not put in words, the singer took the plunge.

"I…. That is, my…. Well, I don't know how to…"

Athnel rescued him, at least partly. "You are afraid to put your feelings into words, is that it, Tanje?"

Reassured by the endearment, Pjortan nodded and tried again. "I… think about you every waking moment. And I dream about you in my sleep."

She waited to hear more.

"Are you still with us only for the sake of Ian's mission or… have you thought of after that?"

The young singer was no Vishgar, but he was making progress.

"I have given it a great deal of thought and I know what I desire. What I want to know now is what you desire."

She had given the challenge. Their eyes were locked and Pjortan was now sweating from more than his exercise. He licked his lips and tried to answer.

"I don't really know if any of us will return from this journey, Athje." There, he had finally used the intimate form of her name. "But whether we do or not, I do not wish to be without you."

Athnel smiled yet held out a bit longer. "You are a gifted speaker, Tanje, and you sing so beautifully that the stars must weep with joy to hear you. Please continue, for I delight in what you say."

There was the encouragement. But was he ready to say it plainly?

"Athje, I have never known a woman so beautiful nor so holy nor so wise as you."

"Now you will make me blush."

"No, it's true. And…I think I have loved you since we first spent hours talking together. And when the wind blew your dress as we sailed, you were more beautiful than the stars themselves."

She smiled and warned him not to blaspheme.

"Do not mock me, lady. We singers know how to play with words but we may not lie."

"No, and I know you speak true, Tanje, for your heart lies open to anyone to read. Because of the command not to sing alone, I would have remained with you all lest the darkness prevail. But I have a far stronger reason to remain and have never hidden it."

"Me?" he hoped.

Athnel gave him the hopeless look women give men when they are dense and said, "I think I will answer that question when some man tells me he loves me."

"Oh. But you know I love you."

"I know it, Tanje, do you?"

"Yes. Yes. I love you, Athnel of Laoghar, with all my being."

"And so I love you, Pjortan son of Drethor."

They laughed at how long it took for these words to be said and were about to kiss when Ringskild announced to all that it was time to ride on. Athnel gave Pjortan a quick kiss, just a touching of lips, and Vladje followed it with a big slurp as they rose to continue the journey. Pjortan was torn between wiping of the wolf saliva and cherishing the touch of his lady's lips. Grimacing, he decided Vladje was a sacred animal and let the wet kiss remain.

He did not see Athnel smile and wink at Wilda but he did notice the smirks on the faces of his male companions. Finally he could take it no more and looked challengingly at Nordil. "What?" he demanded.

"I only smile at your happiness, cousin."

"I was only smiling, Nordil," Pjortan protested.

"Volthir tells me that smile was preceded by a kiss."

Pjortan felt every inch of his body flush a deep red. Then he realized there were no secrets in this intimate group and confessed, "Well, yes."

"Congratulations, lad. It took long enough," Nordil teased.

"We cheered you on silently," Volthir added.

"I don't suppose you could have minded your own business," the singer protested feebly.

"No more than you could hide your heart, singer." This time it was Wulfdar joining the game.

"It's all right, Pjortan," Nordil reassured him. "We have all known for a long time how you felt about her, and how she feels about you. We've just been waiting for the two of you to admit it to each other. And we are truly happy for both of you."

Volthir spoke in a less reassuring tone: "I even think Ringskild interrupted your kiss on purpose."

"Does she begrudge us that?" the innocent protested.

"Not really," Volthir said, "she knows there will be more. Besides, she delayed our departure until you got to the kiss, so I conclude that she is your ally."

With the revelation that the entire company had been watching this long-unspoken courtship, Pjortan was so thoroughly discomfited he did not know what to think. Finally he yielded to the overwhelming emotion of giddiness in the knowledge that Athnel loved him.

CHAPTER 62

Pjortan's giddiness faded and the other members of the company were sobered as new signs of the Chegjan appeared. Throughout its progress across the lands north of the Mere the demon seemed to acquire and demonstrate new powers. At first there was the sapped energy among plague survivors, a malaise leaving them drained of purpose and any delight in life. Next appeared the life-sucking deformation called "sheep's death." Soon manifestations of violence and mob insanity emerged in the towns and sheep's death appeared among humans as well, most appallingly in the head-on confrontation with the late Furk of Vothnell and his companions. Cannibalism and stars only knew what other enormities were found in its wake.

Since crossing the Ulava the demon chasers had encountered people turned into timorous shadows by terror, an entire town consumed with overwhelming grief, bodies robbed of mind and personality, and buildings cast down. One might have concluded that the Chegjan was like a proud child, showing off its abilities. Now it had begun to leave new tracks: blasted spots of land.

At first Ian thought he was seeing a portion of landscape caught in deep shadow from a cloud, an ordinary sight. Murmurs around him led him to look more closely. There was no cloud overhead to cast such a shadow and the day was bright enough. The dark blotch had not moved. As they rode nearer, Ian could see that the very soil appeared scorched and flattened, as though a fire had blackened all living things yet not spread far.

Vunskridh and Volthir started to ride toward it but Vladje dashed ahead then turned to growl at them. They returned to the others.

More such evil spots appeared on hillsides and one came close to the Gnura Road. Passing nearby the travelers could see that even the rocks were blackened.

Vladje's fur rose as he sniffed about this spot and the travelers proceeded warily, wondering if the Chegjan waited nearby. Scenery that earlier seemed full of life and beauty now appeared untrustworthy, as though late spring flowers disguised some lurking death.

Unable to affirm that they were in any more danger now than before, Ringskild called for making an early camp that day. There had been little rest the night before and she did not want them to head into the mountains exhausted. Now, while the ascent was gentle, they could take refreshment. A roadside shrine to Tjiweth marked the course of a spring and this seemed a favorable place to rest.

Honoring the Bright Queen and Mother of All, Athnel and Pjortan sang an ancient hymn as Zlida and Wilda sprinkled grains about the carved stone pillar and Nordil poured some of Vovoni's wine at its base.

Mechdar was startled to note that Vishgar seemed to be mouthing the words of the hymn as the singers chanted. When devotions were completed, he approached the Ushtethi and asked how he had learned the hymn.

"We all see the snake tattoo on your forearm, but I have never spotted a star on your neck," said Mechdar, asserting that Vishgar was clearly not a star singer.

"Indeed, cousin, I am no singer, but my mother was, and her father before her. I heard many hymns in my childhood and still remember some of them."

"You do not cease to amaze me," Mechdar commented.

"Life never ceases to amaze me," replied Vishgar. "The ways of the stars are mysterious and I can never predict what will happen next. While it is true that my life has probably been more pleasing to Eghran the Trickster than to Wigdor, Dispenser of Justice, I have never lost the awe of the stars that I learned at home."

Mechdar smiled without comment and shook his head.

The fighters among the company opted for martial exercises, seeking not only to maintain strength and agility but also to exorcise anxiety. Attacks and defenses were both so vigorous it was not easy to tell this was an exercise and not true battle. Eventually they halted and cooled down before enjoying a light supper. Alerted by Mechdar, the singers queried Vishgar about his early exposure to star songs and he sang some first heard when his grandfather worshipped. Athnel observed that he knew a couple of songs she had never heard, including an especially lovely invocation to Weltar, seeking wisdom from the compassionate goddess.

Now that Pjortan had been explicitly assured of Athnel's love, he was more relaxed with her speaking well of other men and silently chided himself for petty jealousy. Vishgar was handsome and well spoken but Pjortan no longer viewed him as a rival.

Pjortan suggested a different kind of singing as all sat around the fire. Hildir launched a drinking song while a wineskin was passed around. Fadh the Drinker, deity of wine, mead, and general merriment was extolled in choruses filled with tongue twisters—the entire song designed to lead to laughter, which it did.

Ringskild began the next song, recounting the valiant deeds of Kellat the Fearless, warrior hero of tribes that once inhabited the lands near Tolvith in the far north. The servants of Vrotni joined in praising the valiant Kellat and his superhuman exploits. Glories of battle were followed with amatory exploits as Meldreth launched one of the ribald songs of which she knew so many. After traveling so long together, the Norrungs all knew this one.

The ancient ritual of facing the night with fire and song was thus enacted once more, the faithful band obeying instincts long since formed in the convolutions of the human brain—the drive to band together and face the dark in order to survive and see another day.

A faint haze drifted in as evening drew on, lightly dimming the deities of heaven. The night was mild and spirits were brighter for the early halt in travel and bouts of song and drink. Pjortan watched the stars and, for once, Athnel ignored the sky to watch Pjortan. Nordil and Wilda cuddled and observed the whole company, somewhat as parents might look at their grown children. Hildir and Meldreth teased each other, as they often did, and Vunskridh stared into the flames dancing over glowing red embers while Vishgar looked on.

The fiery deities wheeled overhead and the night passed quietly with the exception of a brief incident when a small boar approached the camp. Volthir and Ringskild were keeping watch and Vladje nudged Ringskild to alert her silently. She stealthily wakened the other fighters. By the time the animal's outline was visible in the moonlight, the battle between instinct and strategy was on. Skills were marshaled on both sides, the boar using every trick it knew to evade pursuers and survive until dawn and the hunters constantly adjusting tactics to outthink the beast. They not only had numbers on their side but also one very agile wolf, which further confused the wild pig. It had never known wolves and humans to operate in concert. Even the dark wee hours could not save it. Soon the boar hung from a tree limb, destined for Wilda's culinary experiments. Vladje enjoyed some fresh kill and as for the humans, the sudden burst of excitement provoked by the boar's intrusion soon subsided into a blend of dreams and hearty snoring.

The next morning was hazy yet pleasant. Camping early the night before produced the desired benefit: a company refreshed and ready to ride again instead of one haggard from long days. Wulfdar had risen early and gathered medicinal plants growing nearby and Wilda had similarly found a few cooking herbs. Ian could smell the volatile oils of wild sage and thyme as Wilda packed her treasures. Hildir took the boar down from the tree and hung it from a pack horse, loosely wrapped to keep insects at bay.

Pines began to mingle with the grasses and mixed bushes of scrubland as the demon hunters continued the gradual ascent of their upriver journey toward Nrvash. Sensing that with the end of organized settlements might come the end of the demon's travels, the riders rehearsed the various events and prophecies that had guided them thus far.

Having served Furk, Athnel was moved at Hranild's words: "Who seeks glory shall lose it." She commented, "Lord Furk was vain yet very brave. For all his bluster and impetuosity, he was a good-hearted man and a fair ruler. He will be missed when the people of Vothnell learn of his death. There is no question that he joined this quest for several reasons. Glory, alas, was one of them, though he also loved adventure and the excitement of new challenges. For all his righteous anger and rash chivalry, the demon destroyed him with no effort."

Ian, whose grief at Furk's loss had both overwhelmed and completely surprised him, protested. "He will have glory, though, for I believe his brave charge against the foul thing will not soon be forgotten."

"True, lad," said Mechdar, "but not the glory of defeating it."

"May his journey among the stars be blessed," added Pjortan in his own way of honoring the dead warrior.

"I understand the hermit's talk of the treeless road," interjected Vunskridh, shifting the topic from Furk. "We had journeyed by the Mere. But what about finding a tree where the one goes?"

"Perhaps we shall enter some rocky place, or land so arid trees will not grow," Nordil guessed.

"Or mount above the tree line," suggested Wulfdar. "The mountains before us may reach as high as the Nivannath. Or higher."

Meldreth suggested some mythical lair the Chegjan knew as home. "The demon may have a great hall where the pillars are not trees, as in Vorthall, but stone like some of the castles we have seen. It may be guarded by terrible monsters, maybe even vurgals!"

Çirazel's eyes grew wide at mention of monsters. Life with her father and brothers had been terrifying enough; she did not relish meeting worse.

Volthir snorted. "Melje, you know vurgals dwell in the waters, not in mountain heights. Or at least that is what all the legends say."

"Please," Ringskild chided, "let us not terrify ourselves with stories and speculation. Our task is to stay alert and be faithful. Let us continue reviewing what we know, not what may or may not be."

"We have watched this darkness grow in power," said Pjortan. "It seems to delight in showing off what it can do, inflicting all kinds of damage wherever it passes. It heads now toward Westwaste. It might enter or cross the high mountains and leave the lands about the Mere alone, but I think the demon takes pleasure in the evil it does. It could easily head south and ravage the lands on the west side of the Mere, maybe even circle the great sea and return to Norrast, many times more powerful than when it began.

"If its powers continue to increase and it does not forsake inhabited regions, there may be no end to its destruction. I say all this to acknowledge what we are facing and how high the stakes are. Yet Hranild told us faith will be our shield and Zhodor not only asked us if we would believe, he reminded us that Senjir dances.

"So long as the Dancer of the Stars weaves her patterns, the worlds exist. This Chegjan, this foul life-destroying enemy of hope, becomes more of threat each day yet the Dance goes on. Zhodor reminds us never to forget the promise of Senjir's endless creativity. At least, that is what I make of Zhodor's words."

"And we must sing for that dance," added Athnel, her green eyes fixed on her fellow singer.

Before Pjortan could mouth the key word from Zhodor's command to sing, several of their companions said aloud, "together." Pjortan turned red and smiled and for once Athnel flushed as well, lightening the moment with her musical laughter.

Renewed gravity came from Wulfdar, the eldest present, who agreed with Pjortan's assessment of the importance of Senjir's dance. "We have no way of knowing what our role in the dance is, or how much it matters, yet I believe we are part of it and should step as well as we can. The hermit along the River Road instructed our singers not to part. I doubt his words were necessary," the healer smiled, "but I thank Lady Athnel for choosing to remain with us and with Thomdar's nephew here. Whatever prophecies may say, each of us has choices to make. I am glad of yours, lady."

"Thank you, healer," she responded. "I am glad of your presence, both for your wisdom and for your skills. I do not think we have seen the last need for what you can offer."

Mechdar spoke up next. "The meddling seer with her noisy raven told us Love will be our chieftain if we will follow it. What in Eghran's name does that mean?"

"Rathdar's son could not lead us on this journey, we know that much," Wilda answered.

Ian spoke up. "We are here because we love. Although we set forth in obedience to Njothir and the council of Vorthall, I believe each of us has pursued this path on behalf of all we love—our family and friends, our tribe, and even, having seen more of this world, all the lands about the Mere. If our hearts were to turn cold and we no longer cared, we would have abandoned the quest. Ringskild has been our wise and faithful captain, but Love is the chief we follow, even to the death."

Volthir blinked and said, "Ian is right. We servants of Vrotni go into battle over and over, fighting for our lives and the lives of our comrades. We risk the fray for the sake of our people, our homes, all we love and hold dearly. Vrotni herself is called the Fierce Mother, her ferocity being an aspect of a mother's love."

Pjortan spoke next. "We singers raise our voices with love of the stars and I would guess that Wulfdar and other healers practice their art for love of those who suffer."

"And for love of life and health," Wulfdar added.

"We know so much and so little," Wilda mused. "I know I came along because I was not going to let my husband out of my sight for so long and there is no doubt I love every one of you. You too, son of Ioreth." Vishgar nodded in acknowledgment of this extraordinary affirmation as she continued. "There are all these clues on how we should approach the demon—walking humbly, not seeking glory, staying in truth, carrying the light. But never a word on what to do in the crucial moment."

"I'm afraid that is something I have to figure out for myself," said Ian.

At that very moment, Fjurthil returned from a flight, bearing no prey but landing on Ian's leather-clad shoulder.

"I was about to say," Nordil spoke with amusement in his voice, "that I truly believe you will know what to do when the time comes. My beloved Fjurthil seems to agree."

"Just be sure you remember that your beloved Wilda had better rank higher than your beloved bird," Wilda rejoined, nudging her husband.

"I thank you, Fjurthil," Ian said to the falcon. Fjurthil let out a cry then flew to Nordil's gloved arm.

Thus they journeyed on, each of the companions pondering which loves fueled this expedition, each seeking how to carry the light. Raucous jays provided a counterpoint to the human conversation. Both species seemed to alternate between weighty matters and bantering until the riders reached Nrvash.

As before, they had encountered no one traveling downriver. Since the fate of the town was unknown, they approached with extra caution. The only sounds were a light breeze filtering through trees and, in the distance, the Gnura rushing over a milldam. No smoke rose from either hearth or pyre, no babble of conversation or noise of children filled the air. Aside from a scorched spot three hundred paces from the town there were no signs of the Chegjan's activity.

Whereas the frightened denizens of Vorç could be glimpsed and their furtive footsteps heard, there was no sign of habitation in Nrvash. In normal circumstances the small town may have been the last settlement on the Gnura before entering the wilderness, but today it was only an architectural testimony to former settlers.

Ringskild ordered a search throughout the houses but no humans were seen. Wilda wondered whether they had all fled but Hildir said they had evidently taken no possessions with them. Food, clothing, utensils, riches—all had been abandoned as though the people had run off with neither plan nor preparation.

Athnel stood for a while with her eyes closed then announced, "There is no one here. We need not linger."

Her magisterial statement was understood as coming from some mysterious power and the company accepted its veracity.

The princess suggested taking advantage of the food and other supplies lying at hand before journeying into the wilderness, offering to leave payment. Lady Zlida took silver coins from the purse entrusted to her by the late Princess Gizli and these were left in case the inhabitants of Nrvash should return. With assistance from Zlida, Vishgar, and Ian, Wilda prepared a hearty meal they could consume that evening, a boar stew flavored richly with pungent onions, recently gathered herbs, and several root vegetables.

Were they not leaving coins in exchange, the warriors would have been pillagers that day, gathering as many useful supplies as possible.

No citizens returned to the town that night as the companions slept in borrowed beds, enjoying the comforts not found when sleeping on the ground. As dawn came, they rode upstream once again, leaving ordinary human society behind.

CHAPTER 63

Birdsong implied an ordinary day to be filled with ordinary events. Bossy jays expressed themselves, as they had the day before. Tanagers, grosbeaks, and an occasional woodpecker punctuated the morning, along with sporadic cries of a hawk. A few buzzards soared in wide circles over the foothills, alert to any carrion feast. Pines appeared more frequently as the ground rose toward the hills and the road eventually faded into a trail. Few traveled this way.

Scars upon the ground—the tell-tale "demon tracks"—were now few and far between. Ian thought they only appeared when the group began to think the Chegjan had ceased to leave marks. When he shared this observation, Vunskridh and Zlida said they had thought the same. Murmurs arose and a new fear insinuated its way among them: did the Chegjan know just when they would suspect they had lost its track and where to blast the earth to encourage their pursuit? What might the darkness know of their minds and hearts?

Pjortan opined that light penetrates darkness and not the other way around, so they ought not to spook themselves.

"The lad's right," agreed Wilda. "Look what one candle can do! The hermit said we carry the light, so we are come to shine on that awful thing."

Nordil, knowing the power of his wife's convictions, dared not gainsay her affirmation though he suspected her speech was mixture of belief and rallying her own spirits. For his part, Wulfdar recalled that Thomdar had suggested Pjortan for his piety. The healer gave thanks for Thomdar's wisdom. The young singer had managed to lift Wulfdar's heart on more than one occasion. Beyond that, Pjortan's utter infatuation with Lady Athnel and her devotion to him were signs of life and hope amid the demon-ravaged lands through which they passed.

Unexpected refreshment came at midday when they came to Lake Gnor where the Athor and Upper Gnura Rivers flowed into a foothill basin. Vunskridh spotted the tiered cascade of Gnor Falls where the lake overflowed to descend toward the plains as the Lower Gnura. Ferns flourished among the mists where mosses formed an emerald backdrop while silver jets of water plunged and boiled over and among boulders. Horsetail grew in ridged stalks springing from sandy soil and several edible or curative plants lined the path as well. The constant spray drifted in a light breeze, cooling the travelers as they passed slowly, taking care not to lead their horses too close to the slippery rocks along the bank.

The trail veered left and away from the falls in a switchback allowing easier progress where the land rose more sharply. Vegetation was thick here with the presence of abundant water and wildlife flourished. Rustling among the bushes and the calls of birds evidenced the vitality in the environs of the lake. Having passed the final switchback of their ascent, the riders finally saw the calm blue surface of the lake, ringed with countless shades of green punctuated by massive rocks at the lake's edge. Ducks bobbed near the rushes along the shore, untroubled by the rare presence of humans.

Mechdar led the way as the companions threaded their way among the trees and rocks, the trail having given way to multiple animal tracks near the shore. Avoiding fallen trees and enjoying the beauty of the place, they rode through shaded groves and across sunny meadows. Eventually they paused to rest and eat. Hildir killed a nearby snake, a large but not venomous serpent with thick black stripes and plenty of meat on it. Wilda swore by Tjiweth she would not cook it and Hildir tossed it aside. Vladje was less fastidious than Wilda and made a meal of it, mercifully out of the good cook's sight.

More to Wilda's liking were a couple of ducks Vunskridh took with bow and arrow and hung to begin aging. "Ah, swift as Iltir," Wilda praised the huntress, comparing her to the Archer, god of lightning.

The meal itself, however, consisted of stale bread, dried meats, miner's lettuce, and several delicacies "purchased" in Nrvash. Fresh spring water was plentiful nearby and all drank their fill.

Following such a pleasant break, the group resumed its journey, following the sporadic blackened patches marking the demon's progress. This led them alongside the Athor River, turning southwest in their ascent toward the haunted region of Westwaste.

Given the natural beauty and abundant game of the area, Nordil wondered why people avoided it. Besides the fresh "demon tracks" there had been no signs of mysterious powers or legendary beasts. Neither Fjurthil nor Vladje had seemed troubled of late and they were more sensitive to such things than the humans they accompanied.

"If there is nothing worse than we have seen this day," Nordil said, "I would gladly live in a place such as this."

"It is lovely, husband," rejoined Wilda, "but we have family back in Vorthall, so don't get any ideas."

"My little pasty," he responded, comparing her to one of his favorite dishes, "I was not making plans, merely praising the place." He then reached across to take his wife's hand and squeeze it, smiling and miming a kiss. Ian noticed some comrades rolling their eyes at such uxorious affection though he knew folks found the enduring affection of the couple reassuring.

Travel that day was uneventful, for which all were grateful. Volthir and Meldreth scouted a secure dry place near the river for that evening's camp. With no fresh tales of terror and devastation, all slept well that night. Athnel, as was her custom, stayed up during part of the night watching the stars. Weltar, the Tortoise and goddess of compassion was visible this time of year. She was also Wisdom personified and Athnel prayed for some of Weltar's sage advice as they moved forward.

435

Vishgar sat beside her, sharing the watch at that time with Ringskild.

"I am in awe of Grandmother," he said softly, gazing in the same direction as the lady singer. "She has seen all things and somehow understands. I have seen so little and yet there is much that makes no sense."

"Perhaps," Athnel replied, also in quiet tones, "it is because she sees all that it makes sense to her. We only know fragments."

"And there are fragments I not only fail to understand, I cannot see how they can be forgiven. Bulçar's cruelty, for example, and his horrid sons, Njlvac especially."

"It is refreshing to know a thief who discerns good from evil," Athnel said.

"You mock me, lady, yet I can tell simple wickedness from true evil. I have been wicked, as you well know, and enjoyed it, I confess. I have taken the riches of others and lived on their efforts. But I would never take another's life or livelihood nor inflict wanton suffering."

"You had Hnaç to do that for you," Athnel reproved.

"True enough. I will defend myself and those I care about as easily as any, but I never had the stomach for taking life. Hnaç was cold and efficient. I justify neither him nor my use of him."

"I am glad you know better than to even try. Do you think you can be forgiven, son of Ioreth?"

"I do not fear Weltar's embrace, for she is our grandmother, and Tjiweth is the mother of all living. Ushni receives every soul in the end but Wigdor's judgment is another matter. He sees the heart and knows what it true. We are all blind to our own faults but I believe my own deceits thrive on the surface. I do not fear the Judge of Heaven piercing the depths of my heart, only the approach."

Athnel scanned Vishgar's face a while before responding. "I believe your instinct is true. There is a core of goodness and decency within you, obscured by the many pretty lies you have spoken and the tricks you have played to prey on the unsuspecting. You have lived off others and pretended your charm could offset the damage done. Now, I think you realize it cannot. There is a judgment you do fear more than that of Wigdor."

"Yes, lady. It is a judgment for which I long and from which I shrink, trembling within. There are eyes before which I feel unarmed, naked, defenseless; yet that is how I long to stand before them. What can any of us bring but ourselves?"

"By the stars, Vishgar, I think Weltar has given you some of her wisdom. I am glad you trust her compassionate embrace and I hope you find such acceptance here beneath the stars. It is a great gamble. Are you really ready to risk so much?"

Vishgar hesitated, turning his gaze toward the stars once more, and replied. "I have no choice, lady. The prize is great. I cannot walk away."

"Desh have mercy on you, cousin," Athnel said, smiling. "I am going to retire now. May your watch be peaceful."

To all outward appearances that watch was indeed tranquil, as was the entire night. Beneath the surface Vishgar's mind churned like the waters at the base of the cascade at the outlet of Lake Gnor.

CHAPTER 64

The gentle peace of the following morning was shattered by a chorus of jays hectoring an owl that should have retired before the dawn. Observing this aerial assertion, Nordil decided Fjurthil would wait a while before being loosed to fly. The band of demon chasers broke camp and resumed their journey upstream. The path veered a ways from the river and rose to run parallel with the water along a bluff. As the daystar neared its midpoint in the sky, the travelers looked down on another lake, smaller than Lake Gnor, less than a mile in length and somewhat narrow. This wide spot in the Athor River was also fed by Gath Stream entering the lake from the side opposite the Norrungs.

The sight of such waters brought a lump to the throat of Ringskild as she thought of the rivers and lakes of Norrast with a twinge of homesickness. She indulged this longing for a few moments, drew a deep breath, and led the descent from the bluff toward the lake below. Tracing their way along the water's edge they came to the point where the river flowed into the lake. There they spent a while with spears and nets, gathering fish for the next meal. Those less skilled at fishing gathered dry wood from higher ground where the river could neither soak nor spray it. The catch was cleaned, spitted, and cooked.

Following the feast of fish, they journeyed further as the Athor rose toward its source in the heights between Mounts Vathad and Rggan. Though the days were still lengthening as the year moved toward midsummer, the sun was setting earlier for the small band as they drew closer to the western mountains. That day they managed to reach the point where the Athor made a broad curve before turning northwest.

In spite of her great love of preparing and enjoying food, Wilda had not relished the fish as she normally would. She felt slightly unwell that afternoon and Nordil kept an anxious eye on her. As the hours passed Wulfdar gave her some willow bark to chew and joined Nordil in watching Wilda closely. As the group made camp, her fever was evident.

Wulfdar examined her and found no signs of injury or infection, confirming her protestations that she had neither. The healer provided more medications and Pjortan sang a hymn to Vuchtall the Healer. Wilda's mind was comforted by the youth's singing and eased into sleep with the help of Wulfdar's potions. Nordil sponged her brow in the night.

Morning found the married couple exhausted; she from battling a fever and he from keeping watch over her. Athnel joined Wulfdar in ministrations, he urging potent medicines and Athnel seeking a magical remedy. Their efforts were only partially rewarded. The hapless Wilda was secured to her horse lest she swoon and fall off. The journey resumed as the band headed for Athor Gorge.

The ground rose as gently as the day before for the first couple of hours then inclined more steeply. The hills on either side rose higher as they advanced and the river cut deeper into the rocks that lined it. The worst of the spring floods had exhausted their raging force and it was possible to journey alongside the Athor, though no passage would have been likely during the ice melt of earlier months.

Raw slabs of rock rose higher and higher as the questers followed the river's path. In spite of the steady climb of the land it seemed as though they were descending into the canyon. Vishgar had seen gorges near the land of his birth but the dizzying expanse of such steep walls were new to the Norrungs.

The sense of confinement was daunting and memories of ambush at the Drush Pass caused the riders to wonder if the granite slabs above them might come tumbling down. Any attempt at listening for ambush was doomed by a constant roar of the water filling the air.

Every shade of gray could be seen in the patchwork of rocks enclosing the river's path—dark slate, hints of rose, a variety of rusts and copper greens. Beside them the Athor leapt over boulders in a frenzy of white spray rushing into turbulent pools of jade. When the river's course led them into shade the air cooled abruptly, a treat to be enjoyed before emerging again into sunlight.

Trees clung tenuously to the stony walls, fed by the trickle of springs, and a few cascades leapt from the canyon's rim to pursue a jagged path toward the Athor. The blue wedge of sky overhead seemed distant, it's bright purity occasionally interrupted by a small cloud or the silhouette of a buzzard.

As the riders rose toward the end of the gorge proper, the way forward involved trial and error, finding passable points among immense boulders cluttered by logs trapped at flood time. The river, at that stage, swirled in a deeper cut some twenty feet below them.

As Ian rounded one cluster of massive stone the fur on Vladje's neck rose and the wolf emitted a low growl. Vishgar, riding behind him, could see Vladje tense but Ian could not hear Vladje's warning for the din of rushing water.

Just as a man leapt at Ian from a ledge, Vladje launched himself at the man's leg, gripping it with his fangs and pulling the man down. A second stranger rushed from behind the rocks, his sword hastening toward Ian's chest. Vishgar intercepted the latter attacker, deflecting the man's sword with his own and engaging the leather-clad foe in single combat. The brigand managed to strike Vishgar's shoulder with a vicious blow but that was his final lucky stroke. Vishgar maneuvered with surprising skill and focus, pinning the man against the rocks from which he had sought to ambush Ian.

Amid this sudden chaos Ian's horse reared and required some effort to calm down. The lad struggled to regain control while Vishgar and Vladje fought on his behalf. When the horse had settled, Ian dismounted, drew a sword, and headed toward the wolf. Vladje had drawn a fair amount of blood from the attacker and the two struggled on the rocky ground, raising dust and further bruising both of them on the hard, sharp stones. Just as Ian sought an opening to strike the outlaw without hurting Vladje, the two rolled off the edge and fell toward the river below.

Ian watched in horror as the two struck a boulder then bounced toward the water. That impact must have either stunned or killed the man, who ceased struggling and plunged inertly into the roiling waters below. Ian gasped and doubted his eyes as Vladje glowed and vanished before hitting the frigid stream below. The lad's eyes filled with tears as he collapsed upon the ledge, he mind confused and his heart aching.

All this transpired so quickly that the rest of the company, spread out in search of the easiest passage through, gathered only to find one outlaw staring nervously at the blade of Vishgar's sword and Ian weeping on the ground. Shouting to be heard over the Athor's roar, the company sought to sort the sudden events. Ringskild ordered a search for others connected with the two attackers while the one captive was securely bound.

No accomplices could be found, making the attack of two on an armed party a total mystery. Ringskild turned her attention to questioning Vishgar's captive.

The man did not appear alert. His dark brows formed a thick horizontal line above darting olive eyes. He repeatedly licked red fleshy lips set among short but straggly facial hair. His skin was sun-reddened, coarse, and marked by small scars. Crudely cured leather had been stitched together with sinew to make his clothing and he was devoid of any ornament. In addition to the sword so recently aimed for Ian's heart, the brigand bore three daggers, one at his belt and one in either shoe.

His speech was halting, as though he were unaccustomed to conversation and thought required effort. His name was Zhrdstvo and the other fellow was his brother Ggivna. They lived off the land, spending part of the year in the cool confines of a small cavern here near the head of the Athor Gorge. They had just arrived there a day earlier and, seeing Ian and Vishgar approach, hoped to steal food and horses from them. Such little conversation as this demonstrated that Vishgar's captive was slow-witted and unlikely to evaluate the chance of prevailing in this effort.

441

The two brothers were part outlaw, part denizen of the wilderness, managing to live where others rarely ventured. Zhrdstvo led his captors to the entrance of cave where, as he had told them, they found signs of habitation but recently renewed.

The question of what to do with the attacker had to be faced. He would hinder the journey and his recent action could not be winked at. In addition to living off the land, the brothers had evidently taken advantage of the unwary throughout their lives. With a silent prayer to Wigdor, Ringskild declared his life forfeit. While Wulfdar tended Vishgar's bleeding shoulder, Vunskridh carried out the sentence efficiently, dispatching the fellow calmly and without unnecessary cruelty. His body was left for scavengers with no ceremonial other than the chanting of Ushni's Hymn, at Pjortan's insistence.

Witnessing the execution, Vishgar wondered what Vunskridh was thinking. Was she avenging the attack on Ian—and himself—or warning Vishgar of her lethal capacity? He was reassured when she approached, along with others, to inquire after Vishgar's well being and to thank him for saving Ian.

Vishgar believed it was Vladje who had saved Ian, his own part was secondary. The cost had been immense. None in the company failed to have a deep affection for this most extraordinary wolf who had guided and protected Ian thus far. Vladje had reassured the entire company in moments of decision and kept them from danger. Now he was gone and Ian was shattered.

Wilda was spared the news as she was too feverish to comprehend. She and Vladje had been fond companions and this news would hit her hard. Since her fever had not lessened, Wulfdar gave her a small dose of poppy wine so she might rest. Still tied to her horse, she rode with the others, unaware of her surroundings.

Once past the area of attack, the riders gradually emerged from the forbidding canyon walls and came to a vast meadow nourished by the river. All were grateful for a resting place. Wilda was ill, Ian immersed in sorrow, Vladje lost, and all had climbed over two thousand feet in elevation that day.

The meadow provided good pasture for the horses. Although Wilda could not cook that evening, the forest dwellers knew how to make the most of the game that had aged over the recent days of the journey. Wulfdar pointed out edible plants to Pjortan, who gathered them, and the great cheese Wilda had gotten from Vovoni added to the meal. A hearty repast nourished the body but a general soul sickness prevailed.

Pjortan controlled his jealousy as Athnel, despite her youth, stepped into Wilda's motherly role and held Ian as he wept for Vladje. When Meldreth joined in comforting Ian, Pjortan relaxed slightly. He did not begrudge Ian the comfort, given his friend's orphan status in a strange world; he only wished Athnel had not volunteered so easily.

Athnel spoke to her fellow singer.

"Tanje, my love, you must never forsake me. If the loss of Vladje pains me this much, I doubt I should survive your loss."

This was all Pjortan needed to hear and he wrapped his arms about her. "Athje, only death could take me from you and I pray that Ushni tarries."

"Do you think it was Morvladh in our midst," Athnel asked.

"Who can say? Vladje was no ordinary creature. Can the gods die?"

"Only Weltar could answer that, though I suspect they are immortal. They may come and go, though, and Vladje appears to have left as suddenly as he appeared."

"Was Ian able to tell you what happened?" Pjortan queried.

"Only that Vladje caught the first attacker, this Ggivna fellow, before he could land on Ian. Ggivna and the wolf fought bitterly until they rolled off the ledge and plunged toward the Athor. Ian thinks Ggivna was dead before he hit the water, having slammed against a rock on the way down, but Vladje seemed to blur or glow then vanish above the churning pool below. Just vanish. As though he had never been."

"After all we seen, I suppose I should not be surprised. You know, I must have thought he would be with us forever."

"Only Ulhnut is forever, Tanje. Even the stars have a beginning in the song of the One."

"I don't want our love to end, Athje. Never."

"Fear not, my joy, love is one thing that may have a beginning but does not have an end."

As the two singers reassured each other, Nordil's attention was on his wife. Wilda still burned with fever, her face flushed and her consciousness intermittent. Nordil wiped her brow with a damp cloth and stroked her sweaty hair. From time to time he spoke softly to her or leaned over to kiss her. Wulfdar urged medicines upon her only but managed to have her swallow small sips.

Volthir, Hildir, Meldreth, and Vishgar assembled a travois so Wilda could travel without being lashed uncomfortably to a horse. She would still be restrained but suffer less physical stress. Athnel suggested the presence of sacred starweed and they proceeded to include some as Wilda was wrapped in blankets. Whether it was the starweed or something else, the sick woman ceased thrashing as soon as the plant was placed upon her breast.

Each member of the party sought to console Ian at the loss of Vladje, though the time was yet too soon for him to be much comforted. When Vishgar told Ian how sorry he was, the chosen youth looked at the sometime thief and said, "You saved my life."

Vishgar gazed back at Ian's brimming eyes and felt embarrassed. "I did what anyone would."

"No, cousin," Ian protested, "you did what a faithful friend and a brave warrior would do. Thank you."

Vishgar looked at the ground, muttering that there was no need to thank him. "I must thank you and your companions."

"What for?"

"For giving me something to live for besides myself. For including me in this quest and showing me what honor is. For...."

Ian tilted his head and listened.

"For not casting me out," Vishgar concluded.

"Why would we do that?"

"Because I have lived a dishonest life. You have every reason not to trust me."

"There is nothing dishonest in what you did today, my brother." Here Ian used a term reserved for closest friends, the term he usually used only for Njothir and his biological brother Steven. "Look, the Norrungs took me in, treating a total stranger from another world as one of them. Why should such a generous people not receive you and give you a chance to start anew?"

"Few would do so, Ian," Vishgar said, not daring to call the lad "brother" in return.

"Few would heed a seer and travel across the world in hopes of achieving the impossible yet these have done so."

"I am glad you are unhurt," Vishgar concluded.

"Aside from the pain in my heart this night, I am well. Thank you again."

"You are welcome." Vishgar paused then added, "Brother." Ian smiled.

CHAPTER 65

Çirazel could barely contain herself the following morning.

"Look, Zlida," she whispered excitedly. "The deer are so beautiful and there are so many of them!"

Lady Zlida had not led as sheltered a life as the princess yet she too was astonished by what she saw through the mists of dawn. At least two dozen deer had gathered in the meadow, moving about on elegantly slender legs, their ears twitching for the slightest sound. They had come to drink from small streams and the Athor itself.

So few intruders came to this meadow that the animals were indifferent to human presence. Generations of wariness had never existed here nor developed into instinctual evasion.

The Norrungs were also amazed at the presence of so many deer, slaking their thirst in seeming unconcern. For a while they simply stared at the abundance of the herd, absorbing their beauty. Meldreth noted several young, just past the spotted stage of fawns yet not full-grown. Volthir focused on a ten-point stag standing just beyond a cluster of does.

With noiseless deliberation the warrior took up his bow and fitted an arrow to it, pulling the string back with all his might and taking aim. The shaft flew true enough to strike the animal's chest. Startled, it registered a slight shock and prepared to bound away when a second arrow zinged through the air and hit its heart. Within a couple steps the stag halted and fell.

By now the herd, uncertain of what had taken place but aware of some threat, sprang into action and vanished into the bushes and a web of trails into the surrounding woods. This sudden movement triggered the flight of birds as well and the silence of the early morning was broken.

Volthir noted that it was Vunskridh who had made the second shot. "Well done, cousin," he said gallantly, though chagrined at not taking the beast himself.

"Well shot, yourself," she replied, "for without his hesitation I should have missed him. I believe we have venison for breakfast."

And so they did, though Çirazel, having just experienced the wonder of deer in the wild for the first time in her life, would not partake. Zlida chided her for foolish sentimentality and reminded her that life feeds on life, for such is the nature of things. The princess simply said, "Another day, Zlida, but not this morning."

As the daystar rose in the east, the stag was hung to bleed and be cleaned. A veritable feast was prepared and Wulfdar supervised the making of a thick and nourishing broth for Wilda. Marrow, bits of meat, fresh greens from the meadow and a couple of healing powders went into it, all blending into a treat for the sick woman.

Wilda was intermittently aware of her surroundings as the day began, though still feverish. Weakened from a day without solid food, she obediently partook of Wulfdar's soup, sipping it slowly from a spoon held by Nordil. While she was still alert, her husband explained the travois and she grudgingly accepted its convenience, allowing herself to be hauled like baggage. Once they resumed the uphill journey, Wilda experienced little indignity, Wulfdar's sleeping powders having lulled her into complacent drowsiness.

It was a difficult day. The companions climbed some five thousand feet in altitude over the course of nine hours. At some points the path required unhitching the travois and carrying it as a litter. In the early afternoon they came upon a small lake. At Wulfdar's suggestion, Wilda was carried from a sandy beach and lowered into the cold waters of the lake to lower her body temperature. The effort paid off for she only had a minor fever after that and was more alert and conversant by the time they made camp that evening.

"Where are we?" she asked and tried to pay attention as the events of the past two days were shared. By common agreement she was almost spared the tale of Vladje's departure but she asked for him. Ian stepped forward, took her hand, and reported how the wolf had tangled with the first attacker, fallen off the ledge, and vanished. Wilda and Ian were both in tears as the tale was told. She finally spoke.

"He saved us both, lad. Never met a nicer wolf. Hah!" she cackled, amused at the thought of meeting a wolf. "Now, be a good lad and fetch my slippers."

Puzzled glances were exchanged and Nordil's face contorted with concern. Wilda had shifted from the present circumstances to the past, speaking to Ian as though he were one of their sons and she were at home. Had her mind gone back twenty years in an instant?

"Nordi? Have you talked to mama today?"

There was no question that Wilda had slipped into a time long gone by. Wulfdar nodded to Nordil, who assured his wife that he had spoken to her mother.

"That's good," she smiled.

Wulfdar spoke quietly with Athnel then fetched a potion he had obtained in Thioth. Athnel urged Pjortan to sing a soothing chant given to humanity by Vuchtall in the First Times. As the singer began to sing softly in his clear tenor voice, Wulfdar gave a small flask to Athnel.

"What a pretty song," Wilda said, her eyes bright but unfocused.

"Yes, isn't it?" Athnel agreed, placing a drop of thick liquid on her fingertip. "And I have a tasty surprise for you. Here, try this." She proffered her finger and Wilda took a cautious lick, savored it a bit on her tongue, and declared it quite delicious.

Wulfdar nodded affirmatively to Athnel, who tendered one more taste to the fevered woman. She corked the flask tightly and handed it to Wulfdar while remaining by Wilda's side. Athnel then joined Pjortan in the chant and laid her fingers lightly on Wilda's temples. As the gentle rhythm of the chant wrapped itself about Wilda, Athnel's eyes closed and a very faint pale green aura surrounded her, visible to a few.

Wilda's eyelids slowly became heavy as the chant continued and those around her began to feel less anxious as well. She slipped calmly into sleep and Nordil sighed with relief. When the song ended, Athnel removed her hands and turned to Nordil and the others.

Nodding toward Wulfdar, she said, "We have been able to ease her mind and grant her sleep, which should last most of the night. But her mind is still disjointed, flitting about in time with very little order. I have no idea what might have caused her illness."

As faces turned toward the healer, Wulfdar added, "Neither do I. It is most strange. She had neither eaten nor drunk anything the rest of us did not share. No accident or injury seems to have triggered it. No bite marks are upon her to suggest the act of a creature. It is an evil mystery. We will do all we can to help her back to health."

Nordil noticed that there was no promise of restored health, only the promise to do what could be done. Grateful for the love that accompanied all efforts, he thanked the healer and the singers then made his own bed next to Wilda and did his best to cuddle with his beloved.

The scenery of the day had been magnificent and several wondered how such a lovely land could be called a "waste." Aside from the occasional demon track there was nothing wasted about the pristine mountain wilderness. For all that, Wilda's illness hung over the companions with an oppressive force similar to the dark mists of the Chegjan. The group retired in their camp among the fir trees with heavy hearts.

CHAPTER 66

Nordil had an unexpected ally in watching over his wife. Princess Çirazel stayed close by and took turns wiping Wilda's brow with cool cloths or fetching water for her to sip. She explained to the anxious spouse that having lost her mother, Princess Gizli, Çirazel had been comforted by Wilda. The young princess did not add that she had no intention of losing a maternal figure so soon after the death of the one who gave her birth.

Zlida was somewhat miffed by the affection the princess bestowed so easily on a foreigner. The slight, received though not intended, was diffused by the reality that Zlida was not only a royal serving lady but also something of an authority figure, having supervised part of Çirazel's training in court protocols. In that role Lady Zlida received her share of fondness and respect but affection was unlikely. Her own sense of what was right and proper precluded expressing private feelings.

As for Wilda, her mind seemed to travel further in one spot than her body had traveled in the last fifty days. Time became fluid and she mistook Çirazel variously for one of her nieces, her mother, or her sister. She knew Nordil but viewed him one moment as her husband and the next as a young suitor with whom she flirted. Sudden fits of anxiety would come over her and Nordil's heart ached to see Wilda in a distress he could not allay.

Wulfdar examined Vishgar's wounded shoulder and made clucking noises. Hoping to preclude infection, he removed the previous day's dressings, flushed it with some wine—with Vishgar heartily protesting the waste of good drink—and sprinkled various medicinal powders on it. These he covered with spider webs before wrapping it all in some clean strips of cloth. The healer accompanied these ministrations with advice on how Vishgar should and should not move his arm during these initial stages of healing.

"See that you mind the healer, cousin," Vunskridh said, startling the wounded man by the positive tone in her admonition. The warmaiden had called the sometime thief many things, but never before addressed him as cousin. Having delivered this stern advice, she rode ahead before he could react and the party set out.

Having ascended so far the previous day, the company moved more slowly in the thinner air, working its way still higher along the Athor's path. Weaving their way through a forest of fir, pine, mountain oak, and bearberry, they had not traveled far when an unusual feeling began to pass among them. The sensation was not like the dread or despair associated with the Chegjan's presence, nor quite the uneasiness of believing oneself watched by unseen eyes. A subliminal tingle announced the presence of something powerful, though one could not say whether the power was evil or benign.

For so much of the quest they had relied on Vladje's instincts to discern whether to trust or be ready for battle. If they had not missed him enough, this made them more aware of his absence.

"You feel it, don't you, love?" Pjortan asked Athnel.

"Very strongly. We are close to something ancient," she responded.

"Do you know what it is?" he pursued.

"No. But we shall know soon enough. We are almost there."

The supersensory knowledge of the singer-sorceress was validated within minutes as the party took a turn in the trail and emerged from brush into a clearing. Grasses and low-growing plants dotted the earth, along with a few stalks of small crimson beardtongue sticking out next to boulders. At the other end of the clearing was a massive flat rock, roughly chest high, with a mound of bones surrounding it. The bones were of every type—skeletons of birds, reptiles, mammals, and some humans as well. Lizards scuttled as the new visitors approached.

"Ushni's veil," Vishgar swore softly.

"Is this an evil or a holy place?" Wulfdar asked no one in particular.

Athnel chose to answer. "Both and neither, I expect, but I will try to discern what I can."

She dismounted and approached the expanse of stone that clearly stood as the focus of the place. Her steps were slow and measured, as though she danced, her arms delicately outstretched toward the slab. Watching her progress, Pjortan was torn between admiration of her beauty and fear for her safety.

The others had dismounted by now. The young princess and the groom looked after Wilda, who babbled softly on her travois while the rest kept their eyes on Athnel. The warmaidens and warriors were alert to their surroundings, hands gripping weapons. Vishgar winced with pain in his left shoulder yet also reached for the handle of his sword.

When she reached the bone-strewn perimeter, Athnel paused, eyes shut and senses alert, then calmly kicked the skeletal debris aside. Nothing happened in response beyond the scattering of dust and the scurrying of insects. Stepping closer, Athnel placed her hands on the rocky surface, feeling the warmth where the morning sun struck and the residual cold of night where the other hand was in the shade.

Her observers were silent as she allowed her spirit to encounter and listen to the spirit of the stone. Minutes passed. The only sounds in the morning air were those of small animals, the swish of horse tails and an occasional equine snort, a light breeze filtering through leaves, and Wilda's half-asleep monologue.

Ian was the first, with the possible exception of Athnel, to notice a vibration that tickled his skin even as nothing seemed to touch it. The odd sensation grew until all could feel it, or wonder if they heard it soundlessly. The lady singer suddenly jerked her hands back from the stone as though they had been burned.

"Ah!" she cried, though none could tell whether from pain or satisfaction. Her eyes were now open, staring in wonder at the rocky expanse. Athnel motioned for the others to draw near, which they did though not close enough to disturb the bones she had so casually brushed aside.

Where mottled stone and a few spots of lichen had appeared quite ordinary before there was now a flowing motion over the surface, a fine network of dark red lines rippling at random. Some of them began to gather in a more patterned manner then formed into an ancient script, wavering over the stone.

"Can you read it?" Ringskild asked anxiously.

"I have never seen a script like it," added Pjortan.

"Once in a very old manuscript I saw something like it, but had no luck deciphering it," Wulfdar commented.

Bits of wonder and speculation were uttered all about her until Athnel spoke. "It is a script not used for generations and I doubt the tongue is much like the one we speak. But since it is a magical communication, I shall try to interpret what it seems to tell me."

At this pronouncement all were once more hushed.

"'Behold Galaghat:' that is how it begins. This is 'the place of bones' and I think we are meant to be in awe of it. We certainly felt its presence before we could even see it."

She resumed her reading, though it was more like listening to the heart of the mountain than reading the incomprehensible marks and squiggles on the stone. As Athnel completed each phrase the quivering runes dissolved and reformed into the next.

"'Sacred to Ushni of the Shadowed Veil' it continues." Athnel's gaze was unfocused, as though she stared vaguely into the heart of the stone rather than at the shifting script before her.

> She who turns none away
> Receives her children here
> Blessed are those who rest in her
>
> She is light and not darkness
> Her heart and hall are both joyful
>
> Those who worship here
> Will know peace

At that point the surface grew darker and the dancing lines thickened and joined as though a film of blood masked the top of the stone. New lines began to appear, their motion less fluid and more agitated. They coalesced in bold black figures then faded to be replaced by the next phrase.

> One shall go
> Two shall watch
> Three shall sing
> The Mither waits
>
> Hold the truth
> Dust is child of the stars
> Dyrn is of this world
> Though not from it
>
> Love is mighty
> Fear is weak
> Only Light is real

Those witnessing the mystical script saw the entire slab turn black when Athnel reached this last phrase. It then lightened as though a stiff breeze blew a thin layer of soot away to reveal the inert gray rock that had always been there. All appeared normal except one seam in the stone from which blood appeared to drip onto the bones below. While others beheld this, Pjortan leapt to catch Athnel who swayed and collapsed at the end of her reading.

The group backed away from the great stone and gathered in small clusters. Çirazel, Nordil, and Wulfdar looked after Wilda while Vunskridh and Zlida joined Pjortan in helping Athnel lie down on a bed of grasses. Vishgar had tried hard to ignore the pain in his shoulder but it seemed to have grown throughout the stone reading. His forehead beaded with sweat and his face had grown pale. Meldreth and Ian had noticed this and urged him to lie down, or at least to sit before he passed out. Ringskild and her warrior brothers stood guard, wondering if they were on the alert for mortals or monsters.

The vibration that had warned the companions of a mystical presence had passed and the day seemed ordinary once again. The only hum was that of insects going about their business. A resinous fragrance of evergreens scented the morning air while small birds chirped and a pair of ravens croaked. Soothing gurgles of the Athor journeying over stones were heard in the background. The peace of the mountains contrasted with the sights and sensations just experienced.

"Are you all right, brother?" Ian queried Vishgar.

"I will live," Vishgar joked. The tension etched in his face did not deny the prognosis but it gave the lie to hearty humor. Meldreth withdrew to ask Wulfdar if he had something for Vishgar's pain. The healer gave her a small envelope of powder to add to a draught of wine. The gold rings in Vishgar's ears danced when he shook his head in approval of this use of wine.

"Much better than pouring it over a wound. I'm glad the old man is coming around to my views on healing."

"You will owe that 'old man' your life before this trip is over," Meldreth reprimanded with false sternness.

"I am collecting many debts, I fear," Vishgar responded. "I doubt I will be able to repay them."

"Sometimes we pass the gift on," said Ian, gently reminding all that he owed his life to Vishgar.

"That is true," injected Volthir who stood nearby, scanning the forest for danger.

"I trust I may pass on the good that has been done for me," Vishgar concluded.

Meldreth laughed loudly and said, "You may yet be worth a good woman, you son of a snake," and pulled back when she realized she was about to slap him on his injured shoulder. She was not prepared for his sober response.

"I pray I may."

"Indeed?" she continued. "Stars be praised, cousin. I would have you myself, even while you were thieving, but I am more of a 'good time' than a 'good woman.' You must be setting your sights high."

"Daughter of Vrotni, you are a very good woman—faithful, brave, and warmhearted. I also have no doubt you could take any man to the stars and back again."

"That I can," Meldreth roared and laughed the more. "You are feeling better, cousin. Next time ask for Wulfdar's help before you turn white and nearly fall to the ground. We need every warrior we have." Before he could reply, she joined the others keeping watch.

Athnel, meanwhile, was solicitously watched by Pjortan while Zlida examined her then crushed a small leaf between her fingers. This she held to Athnel's nose and the pungent fumes roused the singer. Vunskridh, meanwhile, fetched a gourd of water for Athnel to drink.

"Vuchtall be praised!" said Pjortan when Athnel's eyelids fluttered open. The warmaiden raised Athnel's head and offered her the water, which Athnel sipped slowly.

"I am fine, Tanje," she said, reassuring her anxious admirer. "Thank you, ladies."

Zlida queried, "Have you suffered any harm from the reading?"

"No. Some actions drain me of all strength but it is only temporary. I will be ready to go in a few minutes. Might I have a bite of cheese?"

Pjortan dashed off to fulfill her request and returned to find her sitting up and chatting with the two women.

"Thank you, love," she said, taking the slice of nourishment he had fetched. While nibbling she commented that the place had been sacred to the stars for many generations, "Perhaps hundreds of years. Evidently those who die here are so blessed by Ushni that Hjelgi leads them to her hall straightway. Even Wigdor yields his judgment. From the variety of bones I would say that all creatures seek this blessing."

"I would rather face Wigdor than have to travel this far again just to die," said Vunskridh.

"Given the general fear people have of the western mountains, I doubt many do. I only saw a couple of human skulls amid the bones."

"My Hlvi sense," said Lady Zlida, "tells me this is a dangerous place, even if it is holy to the Dark Queen. I shall be glad when we move on."

When Athnel finished her cheese and stood again, Zlida excused herself to wait upon the princess. Vunskridh discreetly left Pjortan and Athnel alone.

"You frightened me, Athje," he said.

"You must not frighten so easily, Tanje. I am not frail, though grateful to have you nearby. Did you catch me?"

"Yes."

"I assumed as much. You know, Eghran and Senjir will not overturn the worlds if you and I are not within sight of each other every moment."

"Are you sure?" he teased in response to this reproach.

"I am a year or two older than you, young singer. Trust your elders!" With that, she slapped his chest and walked away, leaving him to grin with relief at her recovery.

CHAPTER 67

Wulfdar had helped Wilda's anxiety somewhat and eased her to sleep, wondering how much longer she would willingly accept his potions. The companions gathered to discuss the words of Ushni's Stone (as they had come to call it).

Athnel herself could not recall the phrases for which she had been a conduit but the others pieced them together. The first portion carried the promise of the place to all creatures. It was the second half that piqued their interest as it seemed specific to their quest.

"The hermit called me Dyrn," said Ian.

"He did, lad," Mechdar affirmed, "and now we are told you are of this world though not from it."

"But I came from England," the youth protested.

"Perhaps," said Nordil, sparing a glance away from his wife, "your ancestors came from here."

"You mean, found themselves in Yorkshire the way I found myself in Norrast?" Ian wondered.

"All that matters to us, Ian, is that you belong to us now," Mechdar pronounced to a chorus of muttered affirmation.

"Thank you, cousins."

Hildir broke in with the question: "What does it mean that 'one shall go, two shall watch, three shall sing'?"

Wulfdar spoke as the eldest, naming what he knew Ian dreaded. "Ian is the one who must go to face the Chegjan." Watching Ian's face as the youth tried to be brave, Wulfdar added, "Sorry, lad, but we all know it's true. I'd send my old bones in your place if I could."

"I understand, Wulfdar. It's all right," Ian replied.

"And two shall watch?" pursued Hildir.

"Watch for what?" added Volthir.

"Or whom?" Meldreth suggested.

Ringskild confessed, "I have no idea. Ian? Athnel? Anyone?"

All shook their heads and the dark-haired warmaiden assumed a grim visage as she said, "Then we shall understand it and act accordingly when it is revealed to us."

Hildir persisted in his questions. "I expected two to sing; we have two singers with us. How will there be three?"

Athnel came up with an answer to that. "There is one who comes from a line of singers and knows some of the oldest star hymns. He has not been formally dedicated to the stars, but I think it would not hurt for Tanje and me to have another voice."

Pjortan blushed at her blatant public use of his familiar name. Vunskridh noticed the questioning look of reluctance on Vishgar's face as his brows shot up.

"The son of Eslij?" she said in astonishment, referring to the snake tattooed on his arm.

"Vishgar?" was all Athnel replied, looking at him.

"I am hardly worthy, lady," Vishgar stammered.

"None of us is worthy of the stars, cousin," she countered.

"You must," said Pjortan. "Athnel has told me how you learned from your mother and grandfather. We are commanded to sing together."

"He will," declared Vunskridh, a note of threat in her voice.

"I shall obey the stars," Vishgar said, bowing his head so his ruddy curls were highlighted in the sun.

"Thank you, brother," said Ian.

"Yes, thank you," said Athnel and Pjortan almost in unison. Vunskridh smiled, Vishgar blushed, and Ringskild interrupted.

"Amid these thanks, I wish to join my cousin Nordil in thanking the princess for helping to look after Wilda and Lady Zlida for all her assistance in our venture.

"As for the phrase 'the Mither waits,' I would guess the lands about the Mere all long to see this darkness undone. The peoples need to hope and dream and dare to live once more. We have been sent to help that happen. What we do here in this region, we do for all."

Muttered agreement rippled about the circle. Ringskild continued.

"If we are made from the dust of the earth, then we are children of the stars, if I interpret aright. 'Love is mighty; fear is weak. Only Light is real.' These are the words of the stone. Every fighter knows that fear makes us weak. Rulers know that fear can undermine their realm. It eats away at the human heart.

"What makes our hearts strong is love—the love of those we fight for; the love that binds us together; the love of the people and the land and the stars above. I do not know how far this dark thing may lead us but I sense, and hope, we will not need to journey much further. This is a time for brave hearts and for this we have been chosen. Let us love, for Hranild told us love would be our chieftain if we would follow it. When the final moments come, just as our Chief Njothir bowed to the stars and yielded leadership, so shall I. Each of us will have to follow the love and the light within. They are greater than I, and more powerful. And I want you all to know that no matter what may follow, I thank the stars to have traveled with you, my cousins, my companions, my friends."

As she concluded this ringing speech, Ringskild made a point of looking directly at those who had joined the Norrungs: Lady Athnel, Princess Çirazel, Lady Zlida, and Vishgar. She wanted each one present to feel included. Now that all other companions had fallen away, their lives depended on each other more than ever before.

"Only the Light is real!" shouted Volthir, raising his sword in the air as though about to enter battle.

"And the darkness is not," said Ian more quietly.

"The Light!" they all began to shout, raising weapons or fists.

With this affirmation of prophecies and defiance of the subtle dread that Galaghat inspired, the company remounted and moved ahead, still following the Athor River toward the heights.

Within ten minutes of leaving the place of bones they spotted another "demon track." As they paused to look at the scorched grasses and a few blasted trees, a squirrel clambered down a nearby hemlock to dart toward a fir. Just as it crossed the edge of the demon track, the hapless creature dropped dead in mid-leap. Observing this, the comrades looked more closely, without approaching any nearer, and noticed a few birds had also perished in the cursed circle.

The next two thousand feet of ascent were slow going, a seemingly endless series of switchbacks through the fir forest. A bit after midday they reached the point where an icy stream plunged into the Athor, its waters springing from the side of Mount Vathad that thrust its jagged rocks some six thousand feet further toward the heavens.

Wilda still accepted Wulfdar's medicines but they seemed to be losing their effect. Though drowsy, she was agitated and fearful. Çirazel had to take over for Nordil when the frantic woman failed to recognize her husband. Each time this happened he felt a fire explode inside his heart, an ache tearing at his soul. Although the healer increased the dosage, he feared to use much more lest the drugs destroy the delirious woman.

Zlida rode behind the travois that held Wilda and sang for her—songs of Hlv with gentle tunes and comforting lyrics. The noble lady exhausted her knowledge of lullabies, many of which the princess recalled from her childhood, then sang love songs that ended happily and finally returned to a repetition of lullabies. The rocking rhythm of the latter matched the inevitable rocking of the travois and Zlida sought to blend sound to motion.

These musical efforts had partial success, distracting Wilda from the nameless fears that seemed to assail her. Still, she cried out as though in great pain though the only pain was in her mind.

As the riders looked toward the peaks of Mount Vathad and Mount Rggan rising before them, they noticed tattered clouds swept by winds near the summits. Snow still clung all along their crests, now and again flung against the sky by sharp gusts. Not only was the air thinner now but the temperature was far cooler than it had been below. When late afternoon came, Ringskild ordered a halt.

They had come to another meadow, seemingly pleasant. Warmaidens and warriors scouted about it to ensure a modicum of security. No enemy or peril was evident. Fresh water from the Athor was plentiful though game was less so than it had been at lower elevations.

Trees surrounding this grassy field were also fewer and shorter than those below the level of Galaghat. A quick glance up the hillside toward Mount

Rggan confirmed that they had halted just below the tree line. Soon there would be neither cover for foes nor shelter for themselves, save the sheltered side of rocks or an overhanging ledge.

More ominously, they spotted more frequent scorched patches on the hillside above, as though the Chegjan wanted them to see where it had been. Stones themselves had blackened where no fire had ever scorched.

Several gathered firewood from among the debris of stunted trees that had died and kindling from desiccated shrubs. Those with any healing or nursing skills attended to Wilda and to Vishgar's shoulder. In the light of Wilda's suffering, Vishgar felt unworthy of treatment but he was obedient to the healer. Wulfdar also insisted that Nordil take a few drops of one of the medicinal potions, refusing to explain that it was to allay the man's anxiety over his wife. Wulfdar simply said it would provide a sympathetic healing for the one Nordil loved most and, with those words, convinced him to partake.

Practicing for a new role, Vishgar joined Pjortan and Athnel in a hymn to the day's end as the daystar disappeared behind the western slopes. As it did so, evening drew on rapidly. The fire was a great comfort and all donned more and warmer clothing. Though it was summer, woolen war cloaks were welcome about the shoulders of Vrotni's servants and similar garb provided protection for the others.

Ian, as he had often done before in cooler moments, wrapped his throat with the scarf woven by Njothila. He thought of her each time he did so, and of the rosary she had worked into its pattern. Having finally unpacked a war cloak that Njothir had sent for him, the outlander, who now belonged to two worlds, wrapped himself in it with gratitude. Ian's mind turned to Mary, mother of all believers, and to the various mother figures venerated by the Norrungs. Watching bats fly across the early evening sky in search of food, Ian took no notice, his thoughts far away.

He thought of his own mother, Sarah Dyrnedon, the cheerful heart of Hellebore Cottage, holding the family together. William George Dyrnedon, his gruff but loving father, was most easily remembered reading the paper and not to be disturbed. Annabelle, Steven, cousin Harry, Aunt Susan—Ian's entire family crowded his mind. With eclectic devotion, he commended all his families—the one in Dribley Parva, the one in Vorthall, and the one with whom he shared the meadow—to every heavenly mother, to God, and to the stars emerging above him.

CHAPTER 68

"My heart's desire mounts the heavens...."

The voice was that of Vishgar. He had accepted the honor and challenge of intoning the first line of the hymn to the dawn. Pjortan and Athnel joined on the second line as they praised the daystar that morning. Camp had already been broken and the company was ready to set out once the hymn had been sung. Several non-singers joined in the final line—"Shine in our hearts"—as they prepared to meet the being of darkness they had pursued so long.

Ian glanced up at Rggan before him and Vathad toward the right, the two lofty mountains now wreathed in a layer of cloud, pale pink light glinting off their snowy tops. A shiver radiated from his chest when he noticed dark wisps below the white clouds. He hoped they were just shadows or small patches of rain in the shade. They were not.

Soon all his companions were looking up at the vaporous manifestation of the Chegjan. Black tendrils aggregated on the hillside above to form the billowing evil they had seen the day Furk and his warriors fell. An uneasy tension filled the air of the pleasant meadow. Ringskild broke the anxious silence with her order, "Let's go."

As the Athor looped about the meadow it encountered a trail of boulders, causing the river to split into two branches that flowed around a small sandy island deposited over centuries. The river was shallow there and easy to ford. When the riders approached the short stalks of cattails at its bank, horses began to balk and refuse to cross.

Ringskild's charger stepped into the water without hesitation, crossing to the isle. The Norrung captain paused there, her horse standing amid scouring rushes, to look back at her followers. She saw confusion. Nordil and Wulfdar were tending to Wilda, who had to be raised from the travois onto a horse to cross the river. No amount of urging by other riders could get their horses to set a hoof into the water. There were two exceptions besides Ringskild: Ian and Hildir. They crossed to the island with no difficulty. From there the three watched the futile efforts of their friends.

Athnel shouted across the watery divide. "I believe the stars have spoken through our horses—Ian must go and you two must watch!"

"Is it so?" Ringskild shouted back.

"Let me try on foot," said Volthir, leaping from his horse. He was still several paces from the stream's edge when Fjurthil let out a cry. Volthir lost a few of his black ringlets as a falcon shot from the air like one of Iltir's silver shafts, swooping past the warrior's head while claiming its prize and soaring aloft once more. By the time Volthir realized what had happened, his horse stood between him and the water, its broad flank blocking his way.

"I think you are battling the stars, my stouthearted cousin," said Zlida gently.

"Let us be certain before we yield," Volthir responded.

With effort the others restrained the horse as Volthir walked toward the water. Just before he stepped into the shallows, a snake coiled about his right boot with the speed of a whip. Volthir fell forward into the water, bruising the handsome cheeks of which he was a bit vain. He rose from the Athor chastened.

"It appears Ladies Athnel and Zlida are correct," he muttered, shoulders sagging slightly with defeat. Were the issues at hand not so serious, Volthir would have been met with ripples of laughter. Instead his companions looked on soberly, pondering what to do.

"Are you all right, cousin?" Ringskild called from the sandbank.

"Yes!" barked Volthir, not wishing to discuss it further.

Vishgar, whose wound was from battle and not the humiliating actions of birds and reptiles, dared to make a suggestion. "We can pray and sing from here. If stars and beasts forbid our crossing, perhaps the Chegjan will flee no further."

"Can we let them go on without us?" Vunskridh challenged.

"Can we go with them?" the redhead countered.

"My brother is right," shouted Ian. "The time has come. The stars have guided us and will show me what to do. The Light be with you!"

"The Light shine within you!" Pjortan called and the others joined in blessing those whom the stars chose to proceed.

Athnel began a hymn to Hjelgi the Shepherd as a prayer that he would safely guide the three who rode on. Pjortan added his golden tenor and Vishgar's baritone joined on the refrain.

The three crossed the second branch of the Athor to the far side of the meadow. Mechdar's eyes were moist as he watched Ian's back recede. "He's a brave lad," the older warrior said to no one in particular.

"That he is," agreed Vunskridh, dividing her glances between the riders and the darkness on the hillside.

A solemn heaviness settled upon the comrades left behind, each wondering if they would see their friends again, each trying to hold on to hope. Volthir attempted to reestablish some of his dignity by organizing the camp. Since most had felt as he had, not wishing to relinquish Ian from their protection, they honored his leadership, settling in for an indefinite time.

Wulfdar insisted on verifying that the falcon had done no damage to Volthir's scalp, which it had not. The defeated young man submitted to this final indignity because he knew the healer would not rest until the examination was made. A touch of salve for the abrasions on Volthir's face completed the treatment. The tenacious warrior forced himself to thank Wulfdar for these ministrations.

"My brave young cousin," the healer replied, "we all felt the same way you did and you acted for us all. Thank you for trying."

Volthir gave a rueful smile and a nod before heading off to gather additional firewood. Meldreth and Mechdar had set about looking for game. Zlida examined Wilda's food stores to keep the group fed. Before long all seemed normal. Only periodic glances toward the hills betrayed the mingled hope and dread with which the friends beheld three riders at an ever-increasing distance.

The three singers, counting Vishgar, gauged the position of the churning darkness on the slope to the south and the probable time it would take to reach the area. They then decided to work in shifts, two singing and one resting, until Ian got close to the Chegjan. Pjortan insisted that Athnel take the first turn at rest since she had been reading the sacred stone at Galaghat. The beautiful sorceress did not think this was necessary but allowed Pjortan to have his way and took a nap. The men chanted a cycle of short hymns to each deity of the zodiac before moving on to the praises of the One.

"No! Ouch! No! No! No! Noooo!" Wilda cried out now each time she moved or was touched, which raised Nordil's distress level to the point where Wulfdar was urging him to take a stronger potion just to calm down. The princess found herself caring for the husband as well as the wife.

Although she had seen enough suffering as the daughter of Bulçar of Fjorn, it had always been as a spectator. Çirazel now engaged in the tender care of those beset by pain and anxiety, far from the spoiled existence of a ruling family. Lady Zlida was both surprised and proud of the young woman's adaptation to compassionate action and attributed it to the royal blood of Hlv. The more democratic Norrungs acknowledged Çirazel as a worthy daughter of Princess Gizli though they credited human compassion rather than noble blood.

Meldreth watched Vishgar and Pjortan praying in song, the redhead's eyes closed in concentration as he tried to remember lyrics learned in childhood. "Who would have thought," she said, turning toward Vunskridh, "that smooth-tongued rascal had any devotion in him?"

"I certainly would not have suspected more than a handsome face and pretty words, all masking evil intentions," Vunskridh replied.

"You have been hard on him ever since we first met the rascal, and I can't say he didn't deserve your suspicion, cousin. Have you found any better qualities in him since we left Fjorn?"

The easy-going warmaiden eyed her more tightly-wrapped comrade as Vunskridh looked at Vishgar and unconsciously chewed her lip before answering.

"He still speaks far too fair but I admit we have not caught him in falsehoods since we began journeying together." She then gave a slight chuckle and admitted, "You know I have weighed his every word and deed, cousin, as though a poisonous serpent had been allowed in our midst and I waited for it to strike."

"Ay, that you have."

"He has worked hard and played fair, though I confess I find it hard to trust my eyes and ears when he joins with the singers in prayer. I ask you, Meldreth, how does one make sense of such a man?"

"Is making sense our task while we walk beneath the stars?"

"How do we walk the earth if nothing makes sense?" Vunskridh retorted.

A restrained version of Meldreth's deep laugh lightened the moment. "If I waited for things to make sense, I would scarce draw a breath, nor would I have ever known the pleasures of men."

"You are a shameless hussy, cousin," said Vunskridh with a smile.

"There's nothing to be ashamed of. And, speaking of your fantasy of a reasonable world, you know to act when attacked in battle, whether the battle makes sense or not. Why not live the same way?"

"Am I under attack then?"

Meldreth smirked and said nothing, whereupon her friend shot a mock-evil look in the voluptuous warmaiden's direction and shook her head to indicate Meldreth was hopeless, an opinion Meldreth returned in kind.

CHAPTER 69

The terrain altered as Ian and his two companions left the meadow and ascended the slopes of Mount Rggan. Hemlocks and pines diminished until most were stunted. Heathers, replacement shrubs for the bearberry and other bushes of the lower fir forests, thinned also, leaving the scant soil to occasional sedges and grasses.

Initially, Ian divided glances between faithful friends in the meadow below and the stony mass ahead, jutting defiantly toward the stars. At one point he was distracted by the sight of three mountain sheep traversing impossibly narrow ledges. The next time he turned toward the Athor below, it seemed but a silver ribbon and his colleagues mere ants in the meadow. Though they sent the music of prayers toward him, the sound could not reach his ears.

Hildir and Ringskild were subdued, ever alert to the slightest sound or movement about them and constantly seeking to keep Ian between them. The youth guessed that Vrotni had quietly descended upon them. The snarl of a wolverine earlier seemed like a war challenge, so strong was their response.

All three were acutely conscious of the churning darkness on the hillside above. Hildir recited fragments of the cryptic utterances that had provided their only clues on this venture, untangling as much meaning as he could.

"'You shall not overcome it, though it shall be overcome.' Hranild spoke this to Njothir son of Rathdar and the Norrungs gathered for Rathdar's funeral. Njothir was not allowed to join in this battle. Cousin Ringskild, you and I were there when those words were spoken. Though we have been sent on this journey, we will not overcome this darkness."

The warmaiden's long black braid followed the shaking of her head as she acknowledged this. "True, Hildir. We were charged with bringing the Chosen One safely to face the demon and it seems the beasts themselves have designated us as the two who must watch, whatever that means."

"What is this watching, I wonder," the broad-armed man of action pondered. "Zhodor said to 'watch for the dark where the two stand.' Does this mean we must stand when I would rather be fighting?"

"Yes, I think it does," Ian interjected. "Your skills and strength have gotten me thus far, cousins. Whatever I bring to face the Chegjan, it is neither of those. We have seen what happened to Lord Furk. You must not follow his example."

Ringskild and Hildir exchanged glances, acknowledging the note of authority in Ian's voice. Ringskild spoke. "Ian, foster brother of my foster brother, and thus brother to me, I no longer lead. You know that. You were right to remind us the other day that love is our chieftain and I have only been captain of this small company. If, as all the utterances seem to indicate, you must face this thing alone, you must let love lead you."

"I thank you, my sister. That has been much on my mind of late."

Hildir added, "And remember, Hranild said that 'faith shall be your shield if you will but bear it.' We have seen the darkness mock power and bravery. It works with fear and seems to laugh as it swallows up life. Ward it off with faith, cousin."

"I shall do my best, Hildir. I am grateful for the faith of every one who has journeyed with me."

Each of them gave a wistful smile to encourage the others as they struggled to muster every grain of inner faith.

Ringskild recited the next line: "'Hope shall be your weapon if you will wield it' were Hranild's next words. It is a strange weapon and I have no idea how to sharpen its blade."

Ian emitted a chuckle as he quoted Zhodor. "Silly, stupid hope! It will save you, seekers!"

"It has gotten us from the eastern forest to the mountains of Westwaste," said Hildir.

"It's a strange thing, isn't it?" Ian continued. "Hope, I mean. When life is good and reasonable, then it makes sense to have hope but we don't even think about it. But when that happy fabric frays and begins to unravel, nothing makes sense and suffering is all around us—that's when we start thinking about it and talking about it."

"That is when we need it," Ringskild observed.

"Evidently so," added Ian. "Well, then, I have no idea where its handle is or how to grip it, but I shall try to wield hope. The Chegjan's weapon is despair, so I shall meet it with the opposite."

"Well spoken," Hildir cheered.

At that point they turned about to the left, reversing direction as they followed a combination of animal trails and the mountain's contours. The Athor Valley lay below and the sky expanded to a seemingly endless horizon. Its blue vista swept from the northwest at their backs across the winding paths they had followed and on to the southeast where rolling hills descended between the Athor and Ftasha Rivers.

"Tjiweth's beauty!" Hildir exclaimed, invoking the Mother of All Life. For his part, Ian looked at the wild expanse of his adopted world and felt a hand grasping his chest. He blamed the chilly alpine breeze for the tear in the corner of his eye.

Ringskild sounded to Ian like a poet-philosopher when she said, "Whatever strange steps Senjir may take, I cannot fault a dance that results in such beauty."

"Nor I, my lady," Ian responded in mock courtliness.

"Beware, Ian," teased Hildir. "It is very dangerous to confuse a warmaiden with a lady."

'Ah, Hildir," Ian retorted, "they are both women and both can be beautiful."

"Well and wisely recovered," said Ringskild, assuming a fierce tone to match the banter. "And both can be dangerous."

Ian laughed. "Even at my tender age, I believe I have figured out that much."

A few small rocks slid on the hillside to their right, perhaps caused by the smallest movement of an insect or the subsequent chain of motion begun by a gust of wind. The sound terminated all banter and put the three on renewed alert.

The Chegjan continued to hover on the face of the mountain above them, endlessly shifting configurations as though a starless midnight had gathered into a cloud. It did not, however, change location but merely waited where they had seen it condense. The One chosen to go and the Two chosen to watch had no doubt it was aware of their approach.

CHAPTER 70

One of the great eagles of Westwaste could ride a warm draft from the Athor Valley and descend a mere five miles, covering the distance between where the riders paused and their comrades below. It was much farther for those on horseback now crisscrossing the slopes of Rggan in their slow ascent.

They had left the sheltering green of trees behind. Even small streams amid the rocks yielded no more than touches of moss and the barest vegetation. Here the world was denuded and forced to face the elements devoid of protection. Masses of stone defied the heavens as they rose higher and higher. Though huge boulders rested precariously here and there while lesser stones shifted and slid, the mountain itself seemed immoveable, implacable, and far removed from human concerns.

Two jagged shards sliced the blue fabric of the sky like monstrous stone knives. The smooth face of their vertical sides caught the late afternoon sun, giving them a warm glow amid the expanse of leaden gray rubble that covered the upper slopes of Rggan. Ringskild suggested they take advantage of any shelter the monumental fingers of the mountain might provide and spend the night there.

The three approached the area cautiously, knowing well that shelter for the night could also serve as cover for any number of evils. Reconnaissance showed the area to be uninhabited yet closer inspection also rendered the towers more overwhelming than when seen at a distance. Though no signs of recent visits could be seen, the travelers knew they were not the first to stand beside the upright slabs.

At the base of each were weathered carvings. The various signs were almost entirely undecipherable except for crude animal figures and handprints. Geometric designs abounded. The one pattern repeated at the base of each tower was comprised of two sets of eyes, narrow oval outlines with dots in the middle.

"Two shall watch," Ian whispered.

Hildir concurred, also speaking softly as though in a place either threatening or sacred. "So this is 'where the two stand' to watch for the dark."

"Ian," Ringskild said, lapsing from her seemingly casual attitude of relinquishing leadership and resuming her voice of command, "you must rest here tonight before going on. I would not have you face that thing tired. And I would rather you face it when the daystar shines. Night will soon be here."

"I agree, cousin, though I wish this were over with," he replied.

"As do we all," Ringskild agreed.

The three cared for their horses and took nourishment from their stores. They found a slight overhang away from the wind and did what they could to clear away stony rubble. It was not a comfortable camp but it spared them from the night winds. Hildir slipped a dash of powder Wulfdar had given him into Ian's drink to help the lad sleep that night. They watched the stars emerge in an evening sky that extended farther than any of them had ever seen before, then Hildir recited another line, this time from the Stone of Ushni at Galaghat below.

"Love is mighty," the warrior began. Even as he was beginning to nod off, Ian joined in the rest, as did Ringskild.

"Fear is weak. Only Light is real."

Hildir took the first watch, smiling at Ian and Ringskild curled together for warmth. The night was not especially dark. Ruanel, the Pale Queen, was just short of full and her silver light washed the hard stony world so different from the forest depths Hildir knew as home.

The normally playful and carefree man wondered if any of them would return to Vorthall, and if so, would they bear good news? What would "home" seem like after all they had been through? He was strong and healthy and anticipated many years ahead as a good warrior. Was he ready to take a wife and become a father?

Hildir tried to visualize several of the more attractive young women of Vorthall but the face that kept rising in his mind was that of the feather woman from the alehouse. The challenge he then faced was to keep his mind on his watch rather than dwell on her wit and beauty. Alertness, not arousal, was what he needed this night. By focusing on the stars and the slightest noises of the night, Hildir managed to return to the present. It was the first night when only one kept watch at a time; he could not afford to let his mind drift.

The healer's powder did its work. Ian remained sound asleep when Ringskild was awakened by the sound of wind whistling about the rocks in the night. She brought herself to wakefulness and relieved the pensive Hildir. He took his place next to Ian, grateful that Ringskild had warmed the blankets and hides.

The most formidable warmaiden of the Norrungs was glad her people were skilled weavers. She had a great wool cloak wrapped about her shoulders, one woven by her mother years ago. The pattern was subtle and the colors muted but one could not ask for better protection among the exposed rocks on the heights of Mount Rggan.

Ringskild pondered the artistry by which the gift of sheep was transformed into a variety of textiles—the shearing and carding and spinning, the plants and minerals that loaned color to the fibers, the tedious preparation of the warp, and the rhythmic act of sending the shuttle back and forth. Her mother had initiated her into this sacred act when Ringskild was a little girl with big eyes and dark hair.

Ringi, as the family called her, was an unpredictable child. One moment she was all imp, seeking to instigate some new trouble; the next she stood mesmerized by the loom as though worshiping Eslij the Serpent, goddess of weaving. When not lost in the meditation of weaving, she was fierce and full of energy. The entire village of Vorthall was concerned when she and Njothir were not to be seen, so well known was their record of making mischief. They were the ringleaders and other children would follow them without question. This led to not a few bones and other objects being broken and nearly every adult among the Norrungs coming, sooner or later, to a point of exasperation.

Ringskild was now on the greatest adventure of her life, one that could affect the welfare not only of the Norrungs but of the world she had been traveling now for two moons. It did not seem right to be on such a mission without her battle peer and foster brother. Those who accompanied Ian were among the finest fighters of Norrast yet she missed Rathdar's son and her own brother, Rutnir.

Ivor's daughter gave her head a small shake and compelled her thoughts back to the here and now, scanning the jagged bas-relief of rock-strewn landscape, delineated in countless shades from silver to black by the pure moonlight washing over all Ringskild could see. In spite of intermittent breezes the night was still; no motion could be seen.

Ringskild studied the patterns of the stars, moving imperceptibly across the sky in their slow dance. Grandmother Tortoise was prominent this time of year. Tonight she was less obvious because of the Pale Queen's brightness. Next in the year's cycle would be the Veiled One. Would she be receiving Ian on the morrow or would he prevail? Would the demon perish or grow stronger, swooping down to set Hildir and Ringskild on the star path before returning from the wilderness to ravage the inhabitants of new realms?

As she pondered terrifying alternatives, Ringskild noticed a shift in the view before her. It was a shadow moving across the stone. Was the demon descending upon them even now? A quick glance at the sky set her heart to rest on that account, though she could not say what she was seeing. A large shape had flown across the face of the moon, casting its shadow on the ground. Its flight was swift and she could not discern any details, though it seemed far larger than any vulture or eagle she had ever seen. Moonlight glinted off its wings with an opalescent beauty before it sailed out of view.

The vastness of the creature's shadow suggested that it was flying very high and was quite large. Ringskild wondered at first if her mind were playing tricks or if it were some phantasm conjured by the Chegjan. What remained with her, however, was a glimpse of some strange beauty. The moonlit bird, or whatever it was, did not feel like a creature of the darkness and the light on its wings could almost bring tears to the eye.

After another hour she traded places with Hildir again, saving her observations for the morning. Since they were taking watches alone, they kept them short and made one more trade before dawn. While Ian slept, the night passed quickly for those who watched.

CHAPTER 71

Something suspicious was going on in Vorthall and Njothila was determined to find out what it was. She had the most uncomfortable sense that members of her family were keeping something from her. Auntie Gethalen had often been stern but always open and frank; nowadays her words were circumspect and her behavior secretive.

Then there was the old blind woman. Hranild's activities were always ambiguous and unsettling. The seer managed to combine a warm, loving heart with extremely odd behavior. One never knew when she would leave off a normal conversation and begin to speak for the stars. Many avoided her for fear she would get that odd look that came over her when listening to voices no one else could hear. Once that happened, anything might come out of her mouth.

Njothila realized that her brother often counted on the seer's advice in order to guide the Norrungs wisely. She also noticed that her brother flinched as much as she did at the sound of the deer hoof rattles on Hranild's staff.

Several of the other young women of Vorthall had confirmed Njothila's observation that Hranild seemed unusually busy, bustling about in the village rather than staying close to her home on the edge of the Norrung settlement. Hranild's raven also was spotted flying about a great deal, even when the old woman herself was nowhere to be seen. In addition to all this, the seer herself seemed present far too often around the chief's family.

Njothir seemed to know nothing of this except whatever official messages Hranild brought to him or her counsel when he sought it out. Njothila was less certain of her cousins.

Feigning an innocuous visit with her aunt to seek motherly advice, Njothila made a point of appearing at her aunt's apartments suddenly and unexpectedly. Hrek, her cousin's boy, was playing nearby and greeted her loudly.

"Cousin Njothi! Can you play with me?"

"Not today, little cousin. Perhaps later. I wish to see my auntie."

"All right, Njothi."

The boy had been awfully eager for her company, something that made no sense as he usually avoided girls of all ages. He also nearly shouted her name. Njothila wondered if she actually heard scurrying inside or not, but rather than knock she simply opened the door and announced herself.

"Auntie Gethalen? It's Njothi."

"There are you are, dear. How are you?" Gethalen swallowed the young woman up in an embrace, the voluminous folds of a muted lavender gown billowing about her.

"I am fine, thank you. How have you been?" Njothila asked, retrieving herself from the effusive hug and glancing about to see several other women sipping tea. Two women were busy at work with needles, making fine red cross-stitches in black fabric. The chieftain's sister looked inquiringly at her aunt.

"Ah, dear, you have found our little secret," Gethalen said conspiratorially, acknowledging that they were, indeed, working on a groom's shirt.

"And who is the eligible male in our family?" Njothila asked.

Gethalen pursed her lips and raised her eyebrows as if daring her niece to guess.

"Echtil is still too young and cousin Vigna married last year."

Gethalen prompted, "And...?"

"The plague took the others, and you wouldn't be making the shirt for our foster brother, Rutnir," Njothila continued, methodically eliminating possibilities. Then she halted, a look of horror on her face.

"Not my brother!"

"Oh yes, your brother, dear. But even he does not know it yet. You must keep it a secret, especially from him."

Njothila's face screwed up in genuine confusion. "What do you mean he doesn't know? How can he get married without knowing about it?"

At this point a great deal of tension seemed to have gone out of everyone but Njothila. The women who had been drinking tea tittered and the embroiderers smiled.

Gethalen explained. "You must have noticed Hranild's visits, Njothi. Everyone," she emphasized, "notices when the seer comes around. I have seen your own father jump at the sound of her staff, rattling like doom itself.

"Well," the aunt continued, "she told me that we need to start preparing now. When a certain someone comes back from a long journey, my nephew and your brother will finally know his own heart. We won't have enough time if we wait until then. You know how long all this sewing takes."

"You mean Ringskild, don't you?" Njothila asked.

"Well, you know Hranild. She never says exactly what she means. Or she never knows exactly what the stars mean, which amounts to the same thing. But I can't imagine those two being happy with anyone else, can you?"

"No, I suppose not. Did they really get into as much trouble as the stories I have heard?"

"Stars, yes! If there was mischief in Vorthall you could count on those two to be at the head of it. When they weren't squabbling with each other. Perhaps those early battles started them on the path to being such valiant fighters."

Njothila could well believe any rumor of her brother's past—he seemed proud of his misdeeds—but she had trouble taking in the marriage talk. "And Njothir has no idea? Still?"

"The young Lord of Vorthall is brave, just, and wise in just about everything but knowing his own heart, dear," Gethalen said with the indulgent smile of an elder who had seen her share of youthful folly.

Suddenly Njothila's eyes lit up. "Then this means Ringskild will return! And Ian! And the others! Yes?"

Gethalen assumed a cautious tone as she replied, "I trust it means all that. I only know that if Hranild hears the stars aright, Njothir will know joy."

Anxiety flooded into Njothila's heart as she plummeted from the highest of hopes to her darkest fear. "She could return without all who went forth?" Njothila ventured.

"They have gone on a very perilous mission, my child. We Norrungs are a brave people and good fighters, but there is no guarantee of who comes home, ever."

The elder's heart ached to see her niece in distress but saw no way to reassure her, though she was rather certain she knew what Njothila wanted to hear.

"What else has Hranild been up to?" Njothila demanded after a silent struggle to subdue her tears.

Gethalen looked at her niece tenderly and replied, "You will have to ask her that. I have never understood seers myself."

Njothila sighed as she watched the figures slowly taking shape on her brother's marriage shirt. "I wish my brother great happiness. And I promise not to tell him. I have seen signs myself that he is beginning to understand. Did you know," and here her tone became conspiratorial, which caused all the women to lean closer, "that when he calls her 'foster sister' he looks as though he had a mouth full of vinegar? I am certain he no longer thinks of Ringskild as a sister. If...I mean, when she comes back there won't be much time. Hranild is right."

"For good or ill, she usually is," Gethalen said.

"In fact," Njothila added, "when she rides into Vorthall I should be surprised if he doesn't snatch her off his horse and carry her to his bed then and there."

"Njothi!" her aunt reprimanded as all the women burst into laughter and the lewd chat that seems to surround wedding preparations.

CHAPTER 72

Ian's sleep had not been dreamless. While his body nestled in the makeshift shelter beneath the mountain's ledge and rested throughout the moonlit night, his mind roamed unrestrainedly through many pathways.

Memories of childhood flowed together in scenes simultaneously improbable and realistic. Ian recalled the time his cousin Harry fell into a ditch only the water this time was dark as ink. Steven and Ian were desperate to pull Harry out though originally they had debated whether to bother. Steven's face would sometimes melt into that of Rutnir, the warrior who rescued Ian and Gwenda's family from raiders. Gwenda's voice would become that of Ian's mother then shift once more to that of Annabelle confessing to her brother that she was afraid of the dark. Neighborhood dogs assumed the mannerisms of Vladje as they loped through the neighborhood before sprouting wings and taking flight.

Sunlight flashed off the wings of what were now lapis birds darting above early summer fields on their way toward a copse. Ian followed the birds, the smell of warm vegetation in his nostrils as he ran through the fields and entered the lattice of branches at their edge. The dappled light of this secret green world and the buzzing sound of small insects hovering in front of his face suggested sleep and Ian struggled to stay awake. The lapis birds had vanished and the boy found himself in the realm of buzzing and crawling things.

A gorselsnakes raised its head only to prove itself a common garter snake before slithering off. Ian followed it through the shrubbery, wondering why its hissing sound was growing into a roar. The moist shady soil changed texture and became wet sand, as though Ian were on the edge of some body of water. He looked down and instead of proper shoes he was wearing rough boots and his trousers were made of some coarse cloth. Even as he puzzled over this, Ian parted the last clump of vines to see a small pool in the course of a stream. The roaring noise revealed itself as the sound of a cataract falling some seventy or eighty feet from the sheer face of a stone cliff before splashing over rocks and tumbling to the calmer depths of the pool.

In the middle of this stream, standing on a sloping stone, was a young woman with long chestnut hair. She wore a pale yellow shift that rippled in the perpetual breeze stirred by the waterfall. Her face was lifted toward the sun and her eyes closed. Ian was so taken by her beauty that he had to remind himself to breathe. An unknown and indescribable yearning came over him and he longed to reach toward her. As he stared in rapture, the maiden opened her eyes and turned to face toward him. She smiled and took a step in his direction as he began to step into the water.

The maiden's foot slipped and she fell into the water with a small shout of distress. Ian splashed forward, wishing the water's resistance away though to no avail. After a few steps he plunged into the pool and swam toward her, fighting the current. By the time he reached the spot where she had fallen into the pool, she was not to be seen. Ian took a great gulp of air and dove into the clear depths.

The damsel's tresses had spread in the water, moving rhythmically. As Ian swam toward her they seemed more like seaweed in which the youth's frantic arm was fast becoming tangled. He reached for this woman he knew he loved and initially felt nothing but grasping water weeds. Then he touched her hand and clasped it, drawing her toward him.

With the fury of the trapped or dying, Ian kicked with all his might to raise the maid toward the surface. Just when he was certain his ravaged lungs must burst, Ian's head burst into the air and he raised the lovely woman.

They were no longer in the sunlit pool but in a watery cavern lit by a single shaft descending from high above. Ian had lost all sense of direction and had no idea where to find a shore but his foot touched bottom. With this new-found leverage he was able to feel his way toward a slope and bring the maid to a sandy bank. To his infinite relief, she still breathed. He held the dream lady in his arms, marveling at the feel of her, drenched in cold water yet warm and more alive than anything he had ever known.

Their eyes adjusted slowly to the dim light yet Ian was certain she looked at him wordlessly. He gathered his courage and bent to kiss this rare and wonderful damsel. Before their lips could touch, Ian heard mocking laughter and felt a familiar kick. It was his brother Steven, kicking Ian out of bed the way he did each morning. "What are you kissing your pillow for, fool?" Steven mocked.

Ian whirled about, prepared to give his older brother the drubbing he'd wanted to give for a very long time, only Steven wasn't there nor was the maiden in his arms. Ian was lying on a pile of straw in a room with stone walls and floor. He rose and walked toward the fortified wooden door, curious at his surprise when it opened. Why should it not? He stood in a corridor lit by a single small torch.

Ian grasped the light and began to explore, sensing that he needed to leave the place before some unspeakable evil befell him. Whichever way he turned, there seemed to be openings to more corridors, each and all devoid of clues. He could not recall how many turns he had made but knew he was thoroughly lost when he spotted an eagle feather by one of the arched openings to yet one more hallway. Ian followed this until he noticed a second feather by a set of stairs on the left. He picked it up, as he had the first, and climbed the age-worn steps that rose endlessly, twisting and turning as they ascended.

Upon reaching the landing at the stop of the stairs, Ian noticed daylight shining at the bottom of a huge door. He pulled at the handle but it did not yield. Ian tried again without avail. The door seemed stuck rather than bolted and it had no lock, so he exerted all his force several more times. As he prepared for one more great effort a voice beside him said, "Allow me."

It was the lovely maiden, still in the pale shift but completely dry. She smiled and reached for the handle, opening the door easily. Together they stepped into the sunlight, freed of the mysterious castle's ominous embrace.

Ian began to ask the young woman who she was when he remembered the eagle feathers he had gathered and now held. He glanced down at them, recognizing them as the very ones he had worn in his hair. When he looked up again to say her name, Hranild stood in her place.

The old seer's sightless eyes were no hindrance as she reached out and put a finger on Ian's lips to keep him from saying anything. She then set the rattles of her staff ajangle and began to walk on the path that led from strange door recently opened by the maiden's hand. Ian followed obediently, wondering what Hranild could hear in the cries of her pet raven as it flew from tree to tree beside them, croaking excitedly like a village gossip who cannot wait to share every detail of fresh news.

The trail led to Galaghat, the place of bones. There, on the stony slab where Athnel had read its mysterious message, lay a sandy-haired warrior wearing a golden torc. Ian rushed past Hranild in horror to take a closer look. His foster brother lay cold and motionless. Ian swung about to demand an explanation only to see Njothir standing where the seer had been. Njothir laughed at Ian's incomprehension, though with a warm smile.

Beside the chieftain of Vorthall stood his sister, Njothila, only she seemed at least a decade older than when Ian bade her farewell at the start of this journey. She was clad in a green dress and wore a happy expression. When Ian glanced back toward the stone where Njothir had lain there was no body on it, nor were there bones strewn about at its base. Instead there were children of varying ages who now ran toward the three.

A lovely girl of about ten years who looked like a younger Njothila approached Ian and hugged him, as did a slightly younger ragtag boy. Another girl and two boys, younger still, dashed to Njothila with happy voices, causing her to laugh. Njothir also embraced several children as all chatter blended into a musical babble. Ian registered the happy, affectionate tone of the voices but did not understand a word that was said.

The sunny scene at a transformed Galaghat grew faint as a dark cloud congealed in the blue vault above and descended as a fetid mist. The loving arms that had grasped Ian were now clinging vines holding him in place. The terrifying darkness that suggested the Chegjan revealed itself as something more familiar: the hot smoke of a fire. Almost as swiftly as it had formed, the billowing black rose in the air to reveal a purple fire unlike anything Ian had ever seen. A young man about Njothir's age stood facing a wall of violet flame. Whatever this stranger did next was of great importance, though Ian could not tell why, nor did he learn what happened as Ian passed out, victim of the intense heat and tension.

As he came to, Ian felt a great rumbling. Was it Mount Firestorm again, shaking the earth and calling him to this world? No. This was the beat of war drums and the sound of swords beating on leather shields. To his utter amazement, Ian was among the warriors and warmaidens pounding their shields and calling upon the Fierce Mother for valor. With a final shout they spurred their horses and descended a broad hill toward the line of their foes.

Ian's heart leapt as his horse lifted off the ground, having sprouted wings. Together they soared over the battlefield, rising to see forests and valleys spread out beneath them. Rivers and hills unknown to Ian gave the landscape texture. To the east Ian spotted a volcano and wondered it that were Firestorm itself, quiet but smoking. Ian initially gripped the horse's flanks and held its reins with tense fingers for fear of falling, then found himself relaxing as they mounted ever higher

The magical horse flew in a great arc, spiraling ever higher, and Ian could see the shining surface of the Mithermere to the west. His first glimpse of it had been when he and his companions exited the Bay of Mimmoth but at this height he beheld far more of the great inland sea. Ian thought the light danced on the waters like silver stars.

He had hardly formulated the imagery of stars when he felt himself raised up into the midst of the stars themselves, breathlessly enveloped in the living tissue of the cosmos. Colors Ian had never imagined washed across the expanse of the sky as bright globes twinkled and moved in a dance of heartbreaking majesty.

A great pulsing music animated the heavens, the heartbeat of Ulhnut or the drum of Ivra as she thrummed the rhythm of Senjir's dance. Tjiweth herself, the Bright Queen and Mother of All Life, approached and kissed Ian on the brow. Tears filled his eyes at the experience of so much beauty. The lad did not even fear when he drew near Wigdor the Judge, Keeper of Oaths, and Lord of Truth. The Chieftain of Heaven placed a golden torc about Ian's throat, naming him a chief among those who walk beneath the stars.

The dearest deity may have appeared most surprisingly. Ian noticed that he was no longer astride a winged horse but rather a giant wolf. This could only be Morvladh, the Great Wolf, himself. His panting tongue lolled to one side and he bore a considerable resemblance to Ian's beloved Vladje.

Together wolf and human were caught up from the stars into Light itself. Ian no longer gripped Morvladhs's flanks nor grasped his fur. His entire body was relaxed and floating, beyond the realms of mortals and deities, suffused with radiance that exceeded the brightness of stars. He was reliving his experience of the moonstone, tasting what it was to be united to all creation and in blissful communion with the One.

This time there was no dizzying ladder but there was the sensation as he emerged from this vision that his forehead was once again pressed against the mysterious stone in Thioth. Ian blinked his eyes open and found himself in just such a contact. This time, however, his brow was touching a fragment of Mount Rggan.

Unlike Steven, Hildir did not kick Ian out of this makeshift bed. He did say, "Time to rise, my brother. The daystar approaches."

CHAPTER 73

Summits of lofty peaks are among the first to greet the daystar. Ringskild had already glimpsed a gentle wash of pink working its way down from the top of Mount Advat. The world below still lay in shadow as Hildir and Ian joined her. Though none of the three was a singer, much less a star singer, they did their best to intone the dawn hymn when the daystar appeared in the east.

> You embrace the distant isle
> And the snow-capped mountain
>
> Giving warmth and light to great and small

From the heights on which they stood, the companions could appreciate the vastness of Shach's embrace and the indifferent blessings he bestowed on all creation. The beauty of such a visually perfect morning and the threat so near at hand and present in their minds brought tears to their eyes as they chanted. Ian was stirred to his depths at the song's plea—"We are your children; help us walk aright." He still did not know what he would have to do, only that he must do it.

> Bless my morning song
> Bless your people
> Shine over all the earth
> Shine in our hearts

No one who had journeyed with them for the past two moons could look upon their faces that morning and doubt, as the hymn concluded, that light shone in their hearts. Though they began that morning with dread in the air, they offered themselves to the Light and their faces possessed a certain radiance as the first rays of the sun struck them.

They stood a few moments longer in silence, savoring the fresh new day and the preciousness of life. In spite of a mild case of nerves, they managed to eat some breakfast and see that their horses had oats.

Performing simple morning rituals seemed strange when touched by the realization that this might be the last time they ever did so. Each word, each gesture, each wordless action seemed freighted with significance.

Ringskild and Hildir mostly watched as Ian prepared to go where they could not. This time he girded on no sword and picked up no shield. He was dressed as usual on a journey. Because of the elevation he wore his wool war cloak similar to the one in which Ringskild had huddled during the night. About his throat was the scarf Njothila had woven for him with its rosary pattern to remind him of home and faith. When he had put it on, he prayed for faith, hope, and charity, just as though he were beginning to recite the Rosary.

Ian looked at the eagle feathers Njothila had given him and turned to his companions.

"I do not go to meet that thing in peace. What should I do about the feathers?"

Knowing who gave them, Ringskild spoke without hesitation. "Wear them. You shall face that which is Not Peace, but you go as one who bears peace. You may defend yourself and you may defend the peace of the world."

Hildir nodded his agreement and Ian wove them once more into his Norrung braid. When he had finished, Hildir faced him and said, "I am about to do a thing that has never been done when feathers are worn. Our sister is right, you are a bearer of peace and it is fitting that you should wear peace feathers.

But you also go to stand for the Light, and you must be stronger than you shall ever need to be again."

With that he reached out with his forefinger, stealthily dipped in red pigment, and drew the mark of Vrotni on Ian's forehead so that he might go forth as a warrior.

Ringskild initially gasped at the scandalous combination and then beamed delightedly at its very outrage. "Our brother speaks truly," she said. "Such a thing has never been done and I doubt it shall ever be done again. May the Fierce Mother give you courage and strength when you need them."

A tender and infinitely sad expression then came over Ringskild's face, quite transforming this woman of such wild ferocity. For a moment she reminded Ian of the picture of the Virgin Mary his mother kept in her kitchen. She stared at Ian for a while, then said, "Ian, I am sorry we have had to do this to you."

"Please don't sorrow, Ringskild," he replied. "You did not do anything but watch over me well and faithfully. If anything, the stars have determined this and they are beyond blame. Besides, I was given a choice and I chose to do this. It's all right. I finally know why I do it."

They both gave wavering smiles and embraced. As they released each other, Ian marveled that Ringskild had it in her to appear so sweet and loving.

Hildir was also moved, choking back tears as he said, "Stars be with you, lad. You are today the bravest of Norrungs. I am proud to be your brother." He then hugged Ian with those huge, brawny arms and Ian wondered if his ribs would snap.

They stood looking at one another and then turned, nearly as one, to look up to the hillside. The Chegjan had remained in place, waiting, teasing, daring them to make their move. In spite of the clear day and the bright morning sun, now tinting the rocks so they appeared coated in golden honey, the cloud seemed darker than ever, absorbing all light and reflecting none.

The gravelly sound of the scree under Ian's boots as he took his first steps struck his fellows' ears as loud as thunder, for it was the only noise in the morning stillness. Ian walked carefully to avoid stumbling or twisting an ankle on the treacherous rocks. He thought of Zhodor, whom ignorant people called the Fool, challenging: "Try to find a tree where the one goes." The bare mineral landscape he now trod was well above any trees.

There were not even animal paths, only the ravines where the mountain lay in zigzagging folds. Snowmelt would follow these gentle clefts but now they were dry. Ian trudged uphill, frequently righting himself when stones would slip beneath him, upsetting his balance. Occasionally he had to clamber and crawl over a boulder that had found its way into the dry creek bed and halted until some greater force could move it further down the mountain.

As he climbed, Ian silently recited snatches of prophecies, songs, and prayers, feeding his soul on every encouragement he could muster. From the hermit's admonition that we must be who we are, he repeated, "I am Ian Dyrnedon, son of William and Sarah, son of England. I am Ian of Dyrn, woodworker of Vorthall, of the tribe of the Norrungs. I am a child of God by birth and by baptism. I am a child of the stars, befriended by the Great Wolf."

This recitation led to fragments of his dream and eventually he added more affirmations. "I am beloved of the stars. I bear the Light."

The distance between the Chegjan and the youth lessened. In spite of the consuming dark, Ian could faintly make out the cloud's constant motion. Whatever its nature, the demon never rested. Ian breathed deeply and tried to imagine resting in the Light as he had in his visions. Even while holding the thought of rest, he continued his ascent.

> Love is mighty
> Fear is weak

> Only Light is real

This gnomic utterance from the Stone of Ushni became his final refrain, summing all he sought to remember.

The first sign of what lay ahead was the Chegjan's thought tendril reaching out to the challenger's mind with the question whether Ian was remembering great truths or merely trying to convince himself these pretty sayings were actually true.

"I don't care," Ian snarled defiantly and aloud. "I believe they are true and shall live by their truth. And you can go to hell."

The ominous being waiting for him was far more dangerous than his parents or any authority he had known. This was no time to curb his language for fear of reprimand. He was far from society and the issues at stake were more real than English standards of decency. This was one time hell seemed very real to Ian, and very appropriate, and for once he had used the phrase literally.

The next touch of the demon clearly had the force of a dialogue, not merely Ian's inner doubts, for it was a direct response.

"Touchy, are we? You don't expect to be that defensive and face me?"

Ian realized he was being taunted and had probably lashed out too quickly. The roiling miasma of evil was still a ways off. Ian reminded himself to focus not on the darkness that wished to destroy him but on the imperishable Light. He made no response.

"Ah, retreating already. What a shame after coming so very far."

Ian had only retreated inwardly. He continued to climb, scrambling amid the talus to reach the Chegjan. The inner and outer acts were both manifestations of discipline he had learned from the warmaidens and warriors among whom he had traveled.

While still two thousand paces down slope from the darkness, Ian noticed visible tendrils approaching him, like instantly growing vines only these were black as ink instead of the myriad greens of new growth.

The first skirmish had begun.

CHAPTER 74

Wilda's condition continued to worsen. The frantic woman alternated between thrashing and screaming in panic and mumbling in fevered exhaustion. Young Çirazel, the princess turned nurse, encountered fresh indignities daily and sustained a few bruises. Her noble lady in waiting was horrified to witness royalty stoop from being waited upon to dealing with the waste of a madwoman.

Nordil, whose life was bound up with that of his beloved, bore even more marks of Wilda's insane behavior. His face was scratched and he had been struck and kicked more times than he could count. Wulfdar tried every powder and potion in his portable apothecary but most of them seemed to be losing their effect.

All three of the caregivers were drained from tending the tormented woman. Tempers would flare up and then they would feel ashamed in the light of Wilda's agony. Meldreth would join them from time to time, relieving them for a spell. Everyone was so accustomed to her good-natured laughter that they were struck to see her weep silently when looking at Wilda's face contorted with terror.

The singers were not faring much better. Each was grateful for the scheme of initially taking turns so that they had opportunity to rest, but long hours of lifting Ian before the stars through their songs and the outpouring of concern that accompanied them took a toll. It was harder still when they were certain Ian was climbing to face the Chegjan alone.

Athnel signaled the beginning of that final journey, sensing deep within her mystic powers that Ian was taking his first steps up the rocky trail that led to hovering darkness. Though they lacked the eyesight of an eagle to descry the youth trudging uphill, the entire camp could see the black cloud high on Mount Rggan.

Now Athnel, Pjortan, and Vishgar sang together constantly, from that day's Hymn to the Dawn forward. They chanted these praises of the daystar shortly after the trio at the Watch Stones had done so, beginning as the sun's light finally descended down the mountain to touch the meadow where they waited.

They followed that required song with ancient praises to Ulhnut that Vishgar had learned from his grandmother then continued with invocations of every imaginable deity. Though star singers could only use violence rarely and in self-defense, they hymned Vrotni, the Fierce Mother, that Ian might have courage. They also invoked Eghran, the Trickster and God of Chaos, for though they were also forbidden to speak falsely it seemed probable that Ian might need trickery in his dealings. Eghran was also called upon to save Ian from treachery on the Chegjan's part.

Who could keep track of all the reasons, noble and questionable, for which they sang this hymn or that? They only knew they sang for the world itself and the life upon it. When memory fumbled inventiveness took over and they chanted spontaneous litanies. So intent were they on doing their part that they resented it when they had to break from their partners to relieve themselves or take some water.

Those lacking the training or calling to sing to the stars offered their own prayers, heart yearnings for the safety and success of the youth now stumbling on the slope in the distance. Volthir poured out his heart to Shorall while fishing for trout in the Athor, cursing and beseeching with such fervor that fish would not come near the passionate warrior.

Vunskridh had turned to archery in pursuit of game and she found herself praying to Iltir of the silver shafts. Her own desire to slay the demon emerged in a few especially passionate but undisciplined shots, one of which wounded a deer without slaying it. She quickly begged Athna the Hunter and the spirit of the deer for forgiveness, forced herself to take one deep breath, and shot again. This time the injured animal fell and Vunskridh raced to be sure it suffered no longer. She shouted for Mechdar to help her dress the animal. They would eat, but Vunskridh of the swift eyes felt reproach and shame.

Unaware of what was happening in Westwaste, Njothir only knew that he was restless. The night before, Njothila had found him staring at the fire with moist eyes and a pensive look. The Norrungs' greatest fighting man rarely showed tears, so Njothila simply came up to him and slipped her arm around his so they could be together in silence.

Nothing unusual had taken place in Vorthall that day, if one ignored the clandestine activity at Auntie Gethalen's, and Njothila had no idea what troubled her elder brother. In the shadows she could see another companion, sitting at a distance, present for his chief but asking no questions. It was Vorgun of the Badger Clan, Vorthall's eldest councilor since Hordal's death. Tonight he gave no advice. Vorgun simply watched Njothir as Njothir watched the endlessly shifting dance of the flames.

At length, Njothir sighed and glanced toward Vorgun.

"Do you remember, my uncle, when she spoke out before you?"

Vorgun chuckled. "Yes, Lord. She was always rash, that one. So were you, for that matter. I thank the stars you both survived childhood, and even more that Vorthall survived the pair of you."

"You all conspired to keep me from leaving this place," the young chief accused.

"Your place was here, guiding the people," the old man replied. "And it still is, though I know you have chafed every moment since they left."

Njothir reached around his sister's shoulders to give Njothila a sideways hug as he continued to speak with Vorgun. She, in turn, extended an arm about his waist to squeeze back.

"Have you ever forgiven her for speaking out of turn, uncle?"

The firelit wrinkles in the elder's face increased as he smiled and said, "The warmaiden said what needed to be said, nephew, what is there to forgive?"

"Do you remember when she pledged her life to the quest for the sake of all our people?"

"As though it were yesterday," Vorgun responded. "She is, if I make bold to say it, Lord, your equal in bravery."

Njothir replied promptly, less the elder feel offense had been taken. "It is the truth, uncle, and I admit it. Njothila here knows that Ringskild even made me back off on a number of occasions. I suppose that night was one of them."

Njothila gave her brother a pinch of reproach as Vorgun spoke once more.

"You did not retreat before the maiden, my chief. The entire council pleaded with you to remain with the people. All you did was yield to the stars and fulfill your duty as our chief. He Who Comes from Beyond the World could not be safer than to be with the companions who journey with him."

Njothir felt more than heard the slight gasp when his sister heard Vorgun refer to Ian. She finally spoke, having waited as long as she could for the chief and the elder. Her will was probably as strong as Ringskild's, perhaps stronger, but her manners were considerably more polished.

"Do you think they are still safe, uncle?" the maid asked.

"The stars know that, my child; this old man can only hope."

Now that she was a young woman, Njothila did not care to be called a child. Vorgun's years gave him license to call anyone younger than forty a child, so she could hardly take offense.

"I was wondering the same, sister," Njothir said. "I have neither seen nor heard any sign one way or the other. Hranild has told me nothing of use, though the messengers last week said they were well when passing through that city at a river's mouth—Fimmoth, I believe they call it.

"I sometimes want to shake the seer until she rattles like those damned hooves on her staff. She says something that is supposed to help us understand and it only confuses us more. And don't either of you ever dare tell a soul what your chief just uttered." He sighed. "She is a good person with a good heart. If only she could talk straight…. But that is probably the curse that came with her gift."

Njothila stifled a giggle at her secret knowledge though Njothir, with one arm around his sister, could feel the small convulsion. "What?" he demanded.

"Nothing, my brother. It was just the image of," she started to say 'old Hranild' but realized it would be rude to use the word 'old' that way in Vorgun's presence. "Of Hranild shaking until she rattled."

Njothir gave her a sharp look. His sister was clever, sometimes too clever, but not the best dissembler. He suspected she was laughing at something else, but decided not to pursue it.

"You youngsters," Vorgun interposed. "Some of us will dry up and our bones rattle soon enough." It was a reproof but the tone in the old man's voice conveyed humor as well.

"We all pass quickly in the stars' eyes," Njothir observed as his gaze returned to the flames still dancing above the glowing red embers.

The way her brother said this was instantly sobering to Njothila. She looked at his wistful face and wanted to say or do something to comfort him, but could think of nothing. She knew he was worried about all those who had set forth some two moons ago. He finally admitted as much.

"I miss her."

Realizing he may have said a bit too much, the son of Rathdar quickly amended his comment.

"I miss them all, every one. May Hjelgi guide them home soon and safely."

"Stars grant," said Vorgun.

"I miss them too," said Njothila in a voice so faint it was more like a whisper. Njothir squeezed her shoulder while a tear trickled down his sister's cheek.

CHAPTER 75

Ian did not cease climbing when he saw the Chegjan send feelers his way. Since the day he left Vorthall, he had pursued this thing. He would not now wait passively.

A curse leapt from his lips as gravel slid under his feet and he stumbled, catching himself but bloodying one palm in the process. Ian did not want to appear clumsy or unsure before his foe. Nearly falling on his face just now did not shore up his dignity, but neither did it weaken his resolve. He was, of course, unsure of many things. Ian hoped the prophecies were true and the demon might be unsure of a thing or two as well.

The first black feeler, as unsubstantial as smoke yet quite visible, neared him from the right. Like a clinging vine it reached out and coiled around his ankle. At first all Ian felt was a chill, then a slight resistance as though something tenacious but not very strong tried to hold him back. Or haul him in like fish caught in a net, he thought.

Ian wondered what the demon was doing. Taking his measure? Toying with him? Since he had no way of knowing, Ian trudged on as if the snaking mist were not linked to his every step.

The next tendril floated chest-high above the ground and floated toward Ian's heart. Ian reminded himself of Hranild's pronouncement that faith was his shield and made no effort to fend off this or the prior approach. When the misty finger touched his chest, Ian felt a brief but sharp sensation, as though his heart were cold as ice. It passed and he considered whether it might just be an illusion meant to unnerve him. His heart continued to beat and he continued to ascend. Whatever the Chegjan was up to, Ian felt no worse so far.

Ian paused to catch his breath for a moment with no more than six hundred paces to go. When a third feeler neared, he resumed the advance lest it appear that he was waiting for it. This one wafted higher still and touched his forehead with a mild sting.

The three extensions of the powerful but insubstantial thing dissipated after this, leaving only the churning blackness that awaited him. Ian knew only too well that he still had no idea precisely how he was to defeat the demon towering before him, so he focused on what he did know. That had to suffice.

Even with the hill's inclination and the treacherous scree, it did not take long to close the distance. Ian marveled at how bright the day was and how dark the Chegjan seemed amid so much sunshine.

"Love is mighty, fear is weak; only Light is real," he repeated silently to himself, only to hear—though within his mind and not with his ears—a rumbling chuckle. Ian took a deep breath and stepped closer until he was at the boundary between light and darkness.

It was not like looking into a bank of fog or smoke. Those were thin and vaporous; they only darkened as you went deeper. This was impenetrably black at its surface. The demon might be able to see into the hearts and minds of mortals but Ian could not see into it at all.

Thinking once more of his overpowering experience with the moonstone, oneness with Light confirmed by last night's dream, Ian took a few more steps forward, into the darkness itself.

The only sensible reality was the mountain beneath his feet. He could no longer see or hear anything outside himself and the dark. It was like being inside a deep cavern where no light reached. Even there, however, one might hear the sound of dripping water or the flight of bats. The Chegjan, on the other hand, muffled all sounds of the world beyond itself, giving the impression that it was the only reality. Ian could hear his heartbeat and breathing, the scrape of his boot on a pebble—nothing else.

Ian found it hard to believe that anything existed outside himself and the darkness, but he refused to panic. Reason told him this was an illusion though his heart began to quaver. It was too late to withdraw so Ian stood his ground.

If the Chegjan had not destroyed him already then some strange drama was about to unfold. Ian wanted his wits about him in the deadly game they had begun at the first exchange. He seized the initiative and hurled a challenge.

"Have I retreated? Am I defensive now?"

As before, he spoke aloud though certain the demon could discern his thoughts. The Chegjan formed words soundlessly within Ian's mind.

"You are less rash than the late Lord of Vothnell but certainly no less brave. Even so, boy, you are a fool to face me. What can you possibly hope to accomplish?"

"I shall bear light in your darkness, you child of evil." It was a struggle, but Ian remained calm. He wanted to vent endless invective on the force that had caused so much suffering and death across Ian's newfound world. Instead he bridled his tongue.

"I swallow light, boy. How much do you see now that you have entered my sphere?"

The obvious answer was nothing, nothing at all. Ian bided his time before answering.

"Hranild's eyes are dead yet she sees more than most. You may have cut off my seeing but the stars have not ceased to shine."

"You think you see, mortal, but you are a mere pissant and know nothing."

This may have enraged the mighty or the wise but Ian had few pretensions. "My knowledge is a drop in the Mere," he replied, "and the sea is but a drop in the universe. I know very little."

There was no sense in avoiding anything so patently evident, but Ian added unexpected defiance after this confession: "It doesn't matter."

The midnight cloud seemed to quiver with amusement. Ian wondered if there could be such a thing as silent laughter. Given how unbelievable all of this was, he could only assume it was not only possible but actual. The Chegjan found him amusing. Ian was a small mouse between the paws of a very large and very swift cat. He could perish at any moment. The demon was playing with him for the cruel pleasure of it.

"Furk was a real joy," the demon taunted. "He launched himself at me with all he had and his host scrambled to follow him to their doom. They gave me so much fresh power I was tempted to devour you all."

The unbidden and surprising pain Ian had felt when Furk fell, the intense loss of a silly man who loved justice and could not be bothered with fear— flooded back in that moment at the demon's prompting. Ian's heart felt several times larger than normal in his constricted chest as he fought back tears of grief and anger.

"Ah, passion!" the Chegjan acknowledged. *"There is nothing like it to bring out human folly. Will you overstep too, my little pissant, you insignificant grain of sand?"*

Ian took a deep breath and held his tongue once more. He suspected that simply following the demon's lead would trip him up. "I shall not deny I loved and admired the man, faults and all."

The darkness twitched with a felt but unheard snort. *"You humans even admire faults. What hopeless creatures!"*

Ian remembered that hope was to be his weapon if he would but wield it. As with all things Hranild uttered, it made no ordinary sense. But he did know he was not hopeless and that helped.

"And you come against me with no sword or lance. How pathetically you just clambered up to your doom!"

So, Ian considered, it picked up on my thought about a weapon but did not get it exactly right. I am not completely transparent; the darkness has faulty understanding. He smiled in the dark.

"You seem happy to face your death, mortal."

"Not happy. But I do not fear it."

"You should. You seem to be the best weapon of your ragtag company, pitiful as you are. If you fail in whatever it is you could possibly purpose this day—and you will—then I continue freely feeding on the world's pain. You cannot imagine how delicious it is to be nourished by another's anguish."

Ian wondered: Was this how Hranild could see? All his eyes could find was utter, impenetrable darkness with no relief, no ray of light. Yet he could sense the self-satisfaction of this cruel thing, whatever it was, as clearly as if he could see a person smirk. It reminded him of the Bastard's spawn, as Bulçar's sons were known, and the cruel delight they took in torturing others. Ian felt a wave of disgust rise in him, a moral revulsion paralleled by a mild urge to vomit.

He held his ground without responding. The Chegjan continued.

"No, you need not fear for yourself. Your precious Ushni awaits you. Of course, if no living thing has seen her, she might be a hideous and vicious hag hiding behind that veil. You really do not know. But you might fear for your world. For the hundreds and thousands more that will fall either to the plague or to me. And I shall outstrip even the fiery death."

Ian had no idea why the demon continued to toy with him. Perhaps Ian was just a special dessert to be savored after feeding on so many others.

By not rising to the Chegjan's taunts, Ian was either prolonging the game or hastening his own end. He could not tell, but all he could do was face each moment. And do so as truly as he could. True to himself. True to the Light. True to his friends. True to…Njothila.

In that phrasing a new level of clarity came to Ian's thought, reinforcing all his ruminations of the past few days.

"You expect the light to help you, silly boy?" the darkness challenged. *"Do you think I grow weaker?"*

At that point the insubstantial darkness all around him took on the characteristics of a hot, acrid smoke. Ian began to sweat and choke, his lungs crying for air and his whole body desperate for relief of the intense heat. He gasped and fell upon the stony ground, choking as the darkness seemed to grow even deeper, if that were possible.

It felt as though Ian were falling endlessly into some terrifying abyss. This was unlike the ecstatic bliss of floating in Light. Now he was being swallowed by darkness, absorbed into meaningless nothingness, lost forever.

The Chegjan was not through with him, however. Before losing all consciousness, and perhaps his very being, Ian felt the air clear and his lungs gulp great life-giving draughts. He had fallen, but only on the gravel surface of the mountain. As his sense of orientation returned, Ian picked himself up and stood once more before, and within, the monstrous vileness.

It was only a short moment of respite. Whereas he had just succumbed to a burning heat, Ian now could feel a growing chill. It was like the cold of Mount Rggan's stone on a winter night seeping through every barrier to work its way into one's very marrow. This was not as sudden as the foul smoke; it was slow, as though the Chegjan enjoyed the exquisite sensation of the warm life-bearing blood in Ian's veins gradually turning to the water of a cold alpine spring and then forming in crystalline patterns of frost. At any moment it would feel as though ice alone flowed through his body. Ian burrowed into his cloak and pulled his scarf tighter about his neck.

He could not see and now could barely feel, yet Ian knew within his memory and his heart that Njothila had woven this to keep him warm and marked it with a pattern she had seen but did not herself understand. Ian visualized his own rosary and barely had time to think of the joyous mysteries as a whole. They were about light coming into darkness. He forced himself to inhale what seemed to be impossibly icy air and allowed Njothila, the fair maiden of his dream, to warm him with her love.

The demonic cold ceased to chill him and a rising love within his own heart, responding to hers, began to thaw his veins. The frigid ache in his chest began to retreat. Having tasted what it felt like to be turning to stone, Ian relished the sensation of renewed humanity.

To be human, to know simple pleasures and both ordinary and extraordinary pain, but still to hope, and struggle, and love—this was enough. Ian felt fresh rays of light bathing him from within.

"You are a resilient creature," the Chegjan conceded. *"But still mortal. Can you really expect to see the daystar again?"*

"I can," Ian replied, "and I do."

The entire mass of darkness rumbled, whether with laughter or outrage Ian could not tell. The watchers below, standing by the stones and never taking their eyes from the evil mass into which their friend and champion had disappeared, could see it convulse on the hillside.

"You stand before me defenseless and don't even know what you are doing!"

"But," Ian rejoined, for the first time with a determined smile upon his face, "I know why I do it."

"What could possibly give you such an illusion, you pathetic creature? Nothing in the world can stop me!"

The game had turned. Ian knew what the Chegjan did not.

"You are known as the Chegjan, the dark thing, that vile thing, the evil demon, the destroyer of hope, and many such names. Do you know what I am called?"

Once more the darkness snorted dismissively. *"You are called Ian, the chosen, the stranger, sometimes Dyrn, and I call you pathetic,"* the demon replied.

Ian savored the expectant silence in the dark, then added, "I am also known as The One Who Comes from Beyond the World."

There was a definite ripple in the darkness at this.

"I was not born in this world and I am come to destroy you." Ian pulled something from his pocket as the darkness thundered.

"Then die!"

Ian focused every ounce of love he had ever received or given, and then—for his family back in England, for his foster family, for the Norrungs and all the peoples of this strange and beautiful world, for his faithful companions, for the Light, and for Njothila—he flicked open the pocket knife his father had given him and that he had always carried. It too was not of this world.

"For love and the Light!" Ian shouted and plunged the knife into the black air.

Darkslayer – Part Two: The Light Bearers

Be sure to look for the second half of this adventure recounting the long journey home. It should be available before the Mithron New Year (Winter Solstice) 2012.

The Chronicles of Midhris continue to trace the story of Ian and his family in two worlds. This is just the beginning.

DARKSLAYER

INDEX OF CHARACTERS

This index includes persons, deities (stars and planets), tribal and ethnic identities, animals, plants, and monsters. Geographic names are in the Index of Places that follows.

Since persons are known by multiple variants of their names and epithets, the format used here lists the common form, i.e., name and patronymic, followed by the affectionate or diminutive form in parentheses. Next are nicknames and epithets by which that person is also known. Identification of the character by title, role, or relationship follows the dash.

Examples:

Athnel *(Athje), Baroness of Laoghar—star singer, woman of power (sorceress), vassal of Furk of Vothnell, joins the companions of Ian*

Ian *son of William (Inje), Ian from beyond the Forest or Ian from beyond the world, Ian of Dyrn, Darkslayer, Ninefingers, Heart Reader, Starbeloved, Demonkiller— Ian William Dyrnedon, English youth who passes into Mídhris and slays the Chegjan, hero of Darkslayer*

Gelje, *the Eagle—constellation of the Eagle, goddess of visions and of seers*

Gnord—*legendary large bird similar to giant heron with scale-like emerald green feathers on the body and iridescent wings; they communicate telepathically with each other and with other creatures; treated mythically and considered monsters of land and air; home is in Westwaste and the far reaches of Bjupazh; symbol of Ulnor; often mistaken for a dragon-like creature*

Agnar—Baroness of Dhoret, sister of Furk of Vothnell, died giving birth

Anmer son of Njuthar—farmer, brother of Meldreth

Annabelle Dyrnedon (Annie)—Ian's younger sister

Ardiç—council member of Grudhor, serves Prince Stjor

Athna, the Hunter—constellation of the Hunter, 7th sign of the zodiac, god of hunting and game

Athnel (Athje), Baroness of Laoghar—star singer, woman of power (sorceress), vassal of Furk of Vothnell, joins the companions of Ian

Atkriva, the Denier, the Turner Away—wandering star (planet), god of falsehood

Bard Star—nickname for Gwerlut, wandering star (planet)

Bardil daughter of Nugti—village elder of Derwut

Bastard, the Bastard's Spawn—references to Prince Bulçar of Fjorn and his two sons Njlvac and Stjor

Battleaxe, the—nickname of the Lords of Vothnell (from arms: black battleaxe on silver field)

Bibala—mother of Ivor, grandmother of Ringskild and Rutnir

Black Lion, the—nickname for the Princes of Fjorn (from arms: black lion on red field)

Bluthni—warrior, Furk's lieutenant

Bogtar—Hlvi, father of Vazdan

Borthun—prince of Fjorn, father of Bulçar

Bratha—villager of Dinth who comes to Vorthall as refugee from raiders

Brindar—dungeon master of Thioth

Brithir son of Bratha—villager of Dinth

Brona—warrior, captain under Furk

Bulçar son of Borthun, the Black Lion, His Magnificence—brutal warlord prince of Fjorn, husband of Gizli, father of princes Njlvac and Stjor and princess Çirazel

Çara—widowed queen of the Fighi, superior horsewoman, mother of Inwal

Chegjan—demon of darkness and despair that accompanies the "fiery death" (plague) from Norrast across the northern lands, sapping humans of their will to live, growing in power, causing horrific deaths, insanity & violence, sudden dementia; the supernatural and mystical "villain" of the tale; defeated by Ian

Çirazel daughter of Gizli (and Bulçar)—princess of Fjorn and Hlv, rescued by her mother and the Light Bearers from the incestuous attentions of her brother Njlvac

Çorth, the Royal Star—wandering star (planet); goddess of legitimate rule

Çrdna—Fjorni general serving Njlvac

Daghir—father-in-law of Ivor, grandfather to Ringskild and Rutnir

Darkslayer—epithet of Ian, destroyer of the Chegjan

Degh—blustery drinker, Magda's brother-in-law

Demon Chasers—phrase used to describe Ian and his companions

Desh, the Raven—constellation of the Raven, 8th sign of the zodiac, goddess of love (marriage and sexuality in general)

Digrak son of Kortu, Raven of Hlv—King of Hlv, nephew of the late King Glazu, uncle of Princess Çirazel

Djort—would-be rapist slain by Vladje

Djutar son of Fraek—warrior, captain serving Furk of Vothnell, captures the demon chasers

Donal—grandfather of Hildir

Dorgal the Weeper, the Sorrowful Mother—constellation of the weeper; rain is described as Dorgal's tears; she laments those slain by Iltir's lightning bolts

Dragu—count of Stjolvanor, vassal of Thioth, husband of Sjanni

Drak—Norrung warrior mutilated in battle

Drenneth—first wife of chief Rathdar of the Norrungs, mother of Njothir and Njothila, died of the plague

Duka—herald in the court of King Digrak of Hlv

Durwe—sacred blue durwe, a cousin to the soap plant used in making the dye used by the Fighi to color the left half of the face

Echthil—unmarried youth, relative of Rathdar

Eghran the Trickster—constellation of the Trickster, 12th sign of the zodiac, god of chaos, trickery, and new possibilities

Elithel the Virgin—constellation of the Virgin, goddess of young girls and maidens

Eslij the Snake—constellation of the Snake, goddess of weaving

Ezni—widow, cousin of Onvar, lives on the outskirts of Bruzhat with her father and small daughter

Fadh the Drinker—constellation of the Drinker, god of wine, mead, and merriment

Fendir the Heron—constellation of the Heron, god of fishing

Fighi, also known as **Fighshuvli** —tribe inhabiting the region of Fighast; singular forms: Fighe, Fighshuvel; later migrate south to be absorbed in the Druvaith; in religion they favor Shach, the Daystar, over the stars of night

Fintall—hunter, father of Gwenda, established Fintall's Homestead on the southern edge of Norrung territory

Fimmothi—inhabitant(s) of the port city and territory of Fimmoth

Fjorni—inhabitant(s) of the city and region of Fjorn

Fjorvel—second among the star singers of Vorthall, assistant to Thomdar; respected and trusted for her advice and compassion

Fjurthil the Swift—Nordil's falcon, accompanies the demon chasers

Fliç—common thief, cutpurse, nimble-fingered pickpocket, associate of Vishgar

Frythi—inhabitants in region of Fyrth at time of Ian

Fulkar son of Relkar—heir of Dhoret, son of Agnar, Furk's sister, and thus putative heir also of Vothnell

Furin—knight of Laoghar, widower, serves Lady Athnel, father of Hron ("Little Hron"), joins the companions at Fimmoth on the way home

Furk, the Headstrong, the Battleaxe—Lord of Vothnell, impetuous and arrogant warrior with strong sense of justice, insists on joining the demon chasers with his soldiers

Gavron son of Vorn—teenage son of Vorn the traitor and Lady Mirdel

Gelje, the Eagle—constellation of the Eagle, goddess of visions and of seers

Geredh—hunter, husband of Gwenda, injured by raiders

Gethalen (Gethje)—sister of Drenneth, former warmaiden, aunt of Njothir and Njothila

Ggivna—brigand, brother of Zhrdstvo, attacked Ian in Athor Gorge

Gizli of Hlv, sixth daughter of Glazu—princess of Hlv, wife of Bulçar of Fjorn, mother of Njlvac, Stjor, and Çirazel; frees the demon chasers from the dungeon of Fjorn

Glazu of Hlv—King of Hlv, husband of Lalut, father of Gizli; succeeded by his brother's son Digrak

Gleth son of Glendar—honest riverboat captain

Gnord—legendary large bird similar to giant heron with scale-like emerald green feathers on the body and iridescent wings; they communicate telepathically with each other and with other creatures; treated mythically and considered monsters of land and air; home is in Westwaste and the far reaches of Bjupazh; symbol of Ulnor

Gnurshan—merchant of Ulnor, father of Njatha

Gorselsnake—venomous serpent; 3-4 feet long, cream-colored belly, back pale tan with bands of light, dusty jade, black diamond in each green band with a spot the color of lapis at its heart; not especially aggressive but venom paralyzes and is fatal to humans

Grath—warrior, baron serving Furk

Grdna—prince of Fjorn, father of Revith (legitimate) and Bulçar (illegitimate)

Gridnu—minor noble of Hlv, father of Zlida

Gwenda daughter of Fintall—wife of Geredh; mother of Njella, Njedreth, and Sendhor; first person to encounter Ian in his new world

Gwerlut, the Bard Star—wandering star (planet), god of bards and all secular singers; touches the head of Senjir the Dancer when Ian comes to Mídhris

Grozny—people of Gnor on the Island of Hlv

Hornell—elder of Nigel, friend of Jannir

Henry (Harry)—Ian's cousin, son of Aunt Susan

Harked son of Herbal—warrior, companion of Njothir, slain battling raiders of Athna

Hildir son of Volta—warrior, companion of Ian, great mountain of muscles and notorious ladies' man

Hjelgi the Shepherd, Shepherd of the Stars, Shepherd of the Sky, Shepherd of the Dead, Shepherd of the Clouds ("sky sheep")—constellation of the Shepherd, 2nd sign of the zodiac, god of shepherds and guides, invoked to arrive safely at one's destination; comes at time of death to guide one on the star path

Hlethar—peasant of Bruzhat, wife of Viggi, mind eaten by the Chegjan

Hlindavel daughter of Veldir—cousin and lady in waiting of Lady Athnel of Laoghar, joins the companions at Fimmoth on the way home

Hlvi—inhabitant(s) of the Island of Hlv or its territories

Hnaç—cutthroat, companion of Vishgar

Hnakil—wealthy herder outside of Pjall, cousin of Tjorn, father of large family, wary of wolves; shows the companions examples of "sheep's death"

Hordal the Lawkeeper—member of the council of Vorthall, presides at election of new chief

Horstan—Norrung of Vorthall, head of the guild of traveling merchants

Hranel daughter of Ian—firstborn child of Ian and Njothila, born one year after Hranild's death

Hranild the Seer—blind seer of Vorthall; guides the events that defeat the Chegjan

Hrechelfern—a variety of fiddleneck fern used in the manufacture of Fighi face dye

Hrek—young boy, grandson of Gethalen, son of Njothila's cousin

Hriga—sorcerer to the court of Fighast, "reads" Inwal's body to understand his death

Hron (1) son of Furin, Hron of Laoghar, Little Hron—page to Lady Athnel, joins the companions with his widowed father

Hron (2) of Vorthall, Big Hron—large warrior who helps Rutnir capture Turstil

Hrugdal the Landcarver—legendary king of the giants, grandfather of the Seven Giants that were turned to huge stone masses

Ian son of William (Inje), Ian from beyond the Forest or Ian from beyond the world, Ian of Dyrn, Darkslayer, Ninefingers, Heart Reader, Starbeloved, Demonkiller—Ian William Dyrnedon, English youth who passes into Mídhris and slays the Chegjan, hero of *Darkslayer*

Iltir the Archer—constellation of the Archer, god of lightning (characterized as his silver arrows)

Invar the Spider—constellation of the Spider, goddess of sleep and dreams

Inwal of Fighast—prince of Fighast, only son of Queen Çara, seeks to slay Ian

Ioreth of Ushtet—woodcarver, father of Vishgar

Ivna—Norrung elder, mother of Thomdar, grandmother of Pjortan

Ivra the Drummer—constellation of the Drummer, goddess of thunder, accompanist to the dance of Senjir

Jannir son of Stejni—widely traveled and well-liked Norrung trader, serves as guide for Ian and his companions, "Hjelgi of the Light Bearers"

Jean-Louis de la Roche—young lad of some interest to Ian's sister Annabelle, her future husband

Jornandir—father of Vunskridh

Jortel—Pjortan's mother, Thomdar's sister, Ivna's daughter, dies of the plague about the time Ian arrives at Vorthall

Kellat the Fearless—legendary warrior, Ringskild sings a song about him

Kiftak—Hlvi minor noble, father of Zarta, brother-in-law of Pusht

Kirlat daughter of Rather—feather woman (servant of Desh = prostitute) of Nimmoth, meets Ian and Hildir, falls in love with Hildir, joins the companions at Fimmoth on the way home

Kjevar the Woodcarver—master woodworker of Vorthall, Ian's master

Kochtu son of Kordru—Hlvi noble youth

Kordru son of Gridnu—minor noble of Hlv, brother of Lady Zlida, husband of Otharel

Kortu of Hlv—prince of Hlv, younger brother of King Glazu whom he predeceased, father of King Digrak

Lalut of Hlv, the Old Princess—widow of King Glazu, high priestess of Vuoru (goddess of the deep waters), mother of Gizli, grandmother of Çirazel

Lapis Bird—bird with lapis blue wings & body; outline resembles mockingbird & mocker's dusty breast; iridescent turquoise & emerald spots on its wingtips; flight song rises an octave and drops to outline a major chord; trills in challenge

Lazu—porter to Zlida's family in Ktelnik

Magda—skeptic concerning sheep's death, brother's wife to Degh

Mechdar son of Thumnar—seasoned warrior, companion of Ian

Meldreth daughter of Njuthar—lusty warmaiden with robust laugh, teller of tales, seducer of men, one of Ian's companions

Mezdru—Hlvi clan chief, father of Queen Nikra

Miglac—warrior, sergeant serving Furk of Vothnell

Mirdel—Thiothi lady, wife of Vorn the traitor, sent to Fimmoth as widow with children in the charge of Lord Steward Peveç

Mirnel daughter of Vorn—daughter of Lady Mirdel

Mjurni—sister of Donal, Hildir's eldest kinswoman

Morvladh the Great Wolf—constellation of the Great Wolf, companion of Athna the Hunter, appears as mortal wolf to guide and protect Ian, who affectionately calls him "Vladje" (= Wolfie)

Mrdtu—Hlvi clan to which Vazdan the merchant belongs

Neztu—merchant of Hlv, husband of Zigdel, brother-in-law of Lady Zlida

Nikra daughter of Mezdru—Queen of Hlv, wife of King Digrak

Nimmothi—inhabitant(s) of Nimmoth or its territory

Nintel—Hlvi maiden, incognito name of Princess Çirazel as she journeys from Fjorn to Hlv

Njatha daughter of Gnurshan—councilor of Ulnor, spokeswoman for the three who meet the Light Bearers, proclaims Ian a Free Citizen of Ulnor

Njedreth son of Geredh—hunter, with his father and brother he is rescued from raiders by Rutnir's company

Njella daughter of Geredh—Gwenda's third child only mentioned in passing

Njlvac son of Bulçar—prince of Fjorn, nasty piece of work, seeks to violate his sister, slays his mother

Njothila daughter of Rathdar (Njothi), the Snow-skinned, Mother of Nations—daughter of the former chief and his first wife, sister of Lord Njothir of the Norrungs, gives Ian a hand-woven scarf and two eagle feathers when he sets out on the quest, has nightmares about him

Njothir son of Rathdar (Njori), Njothir the Righteous—young chief of the Norrungs, Lord of Vorthall, adopts Ian as his foster-brother; one of the "twin terrors" of Vorthall with his foster-sister Ringskild, together they grew up as the greatest fighters of the Norrungs

Njuf—baron of Ystraf, a vassal of Fjorn, seeks help from Prince Stjor

Njuthar—Norrung warrior, father of Meldreth and Anmer

Nordil son of Kendan—groom, falconer, husband of Wilda, companion of Ian

Norrungs—tribe that inhabits the Forest of Norrast, forest folk skilled in woodwork, weaving, metal and leather crafts; great warriors; they elect their chiefs democratically and find the feudal societies of the west rather strange

Nugti—father of Bardil of Derwut

Olvit—peasant of Vudheç

Onvar son of Olvit—peasant of Vudheç who meets the companions and leads them into Bruzhat where his cousin Ezni lives

Ornathel—chief scribe of Grudhor, serves Prince Stjor

Otharel—minor noblewoman of Hlv, wife of Kordru

Othzli daughter of Kordru—young lady, niece of Lady Zlida

Pelli—cousin and confidante of Njothila, witnesses Njothi's panic attacks

Peveç—Lord Steward of Fimmoth, foster-son and vassal of Lady Rushvin of Thioth

Pjernval the Mighty—chief of the Norrungs, father of Ronir, grandfather of Rathdar

Pjortan son of Drethor—star singer, nephew of Thomdar, companion of Ian, noted for his purity and devotion

Pusht—chief of the Grzni

Pushta of Vorç—inquisitive lad who witnesses destruction wrought by the Chegjan but, unlike all his fellow citizens, dares to encounter the demon chasers

Pwist—chamberlain, maternal grandfather of Lady Athnel

Rachje the Ash Tree—constellation of the Ash Tree, god of woodworkers to whom Ian dedicates himself

Rachthor—legendary monster of the waters, reputed to swim the Mere and large rivers and capable of devouring creatures as large as a cow

Raftor—baron of Othen near the border with Fjorn, vassal of Thioth

Rathdar son of Ronir, the Faithful—chief of the Norrungs, succumbs to the plague at the beginning of the story; had two wives: Drenneth and Vunill

Relkar—baron of Dhoret, husband of Furk's sister Agnar

Rendathel daughter of Rendor—rescued from raiders in Dinth and brought to Vorthall with Bratha her mother

Rendor—villager of Dinth killed by raiders, husband of Bratha

Revith son of Grdna—Prince of Fjorn, Grdna's legitimate son, succeeded by Grdna's bastard son Bulçar under suspicious circumstances

Ringskild daughter of Ivor (Ringi), the Fierce—greatest warmaiden of the Norrungs, sister of Rutnir, foster-sister of Chief Njothir, captain of the demon chasers, joined Njothir in terrorizing Vorthall as a child, a berserker in battle, a highly skilled weaver

Ronir son of Pjernval—Norrung warrior and councilor, father of Rathdar

Ruanel, the Pale Queen—the moon, a goddess

Rushvin—duchess of Thioth, beloved ruler, widow of Duke Thjun; suzerain of Hlfin, Fimmoth, Stjolvanor and other cities; supporter of the demon chasers and giver of noble gifts

Rutnir son of Ivor—Norrung warrior, rescuer who brings Ian to Vorthall, Njothir's foster-brother, "lieutenant," and successor; brother of Ringskild

Shach, the Daystar—the sun, a god, hymned each morning in all the lands about the Mere and almost exclusively venerated among the Fighi; giver of light and the visible joy of creation

Shachfest—the summer solstice, longest day of the year

Sarah Elizabeth Dyrnedon, née Maxwell—Ian's mother

Sendhor son of Geredh, Young Sendhor—hunter, son of Gwenda, interested in Njothila

Sendhor the Elder—hunter, father of Geredh

Senjir the Dancer—constellation of the Dancer, 1ˢᵗ sign of the zodiac, goddess of creation who dances to the music of the One, causing worlds to spring into being

Sjanni—countess of Stjolvanor, wife of count Dragu, pregnant when Ian and his companions pass through

Shlevor—marshal of Thioth, a Tessian warrior, leader of Lady Rushvin's armies

Snith—ferryman across the Wicket, friend of Jannir

Shorall the Fish, Father Shorall, the Father of All—constellation of the Fish, 4ᵗʰ sign of the zodiac, god of fish and of food, of all that nourishes, deity of husbands and fathers

Stavna—warrior, lieutenant of Furk of Vothnell, serves with Djutar

Steven George Dyrnedon—Ian's older brother

Stjor son of Bulçar—princeling of Hlv, middle son who inherits Fjorn when his father, mother, and brother are killed and his sister flees

Shundar—merchant of Gretland who meets the companions early in their quest, friend of Jannir

Susan—Ian's aunt, his mother's sister, mother of cousin Harry

Thiothi—inhabitant(s) of Thioth

Thjothar—anecdotal innkeeper of Nimmoth who is insanely jealous of his highly unattractive wife, subject of humor among travelers

Thjun—consort of Lady Rushvin, deceased at the time of this adventure, his fur robe is given to Lord Furk

Thomdar—chief star singer of Vorthall, uncle of Pjortan

Tjernmor, the—the titular ruler of the port of Mimmoth, accompanied by great pomp and splendor though the actual power lies in a bourgeois merchant council

Tjiweth the Bright Queen, the Mother of All, the Great Mother—constellation of the Bright Queen, goddess of married women and mothers, of beauty, of the earth in her sustaining bounty

Tjorn—sober fellow, cousin of Hnakil, witness of sheep's death, takes the demon chasers to his cousin in order to see examples

Tjurn—trader from Mimmoth who comes to Vorthall and informs Njothir of the Chegjan's ravages on the same day that Hranild announces that Ian is chosen

Torthan, the Gold Falcon—handsome baron of Valcor, vassal and chief tactician of Furk of Vothnell, enjoys discussing strategies with Ringskild and fancies her

Torvu the Stallion—constellation of the Stallion, warhorse of Wigdor, deity of horses and riders

Trno—warrior, sergeant serving Furk of Vothnell

Turstil—warrior of Vorthall, grandson of Hordal the Lawkeeper, collaborator with raiders

Ulhnut, the One—the Ultimate, the Transcendent, the Source and Goal of all that is, the Ground of the music by which creation exists, of Whom all the deities are manifestations [*cf. Brahman in Hindu thought*]

Ulniç—Fjorni soldier serving Njlvac

Urzli daughter of Gridnu—firstborn of Gridnu and Zithanel, Lady Zlida's eldest sister

Ushni the Dark Queen, the Veiled One—constellation of the Dark Queen, goddess of death to whose halls all mortals eventually come; no living creature sees her face, its unveiling is the moment of death, but her face is loving and gracious; Ushni's Lullaby refers to the hymn sung at death with its message "come, my children, and do not fear"

Vartal—Norrung miller who nominates Njothir as new chief following Rathdar's death

Vazdan son of Bogtar—wealthy merchant of Hlv, husband of Zarta, fellow passenger with the companions on the ship to Hlv

Veshnel the Reaper—constellation of the Reaper, god of harvest

Viço—Fjorni soldier serving Njlvac

Viggi—peasant of Bruzhat, husband of Hlethar, mind eaten by the Chegjan

Vigna—Norrung youth, relative of Rathdar's who married the year Ian appeared

Vishgar son of Ioreth from Ushtet (Vishi)—thief, noted for his smooth talk and quick wit, copper-colored hair, snake tattoo on his forearm; his mother and grandfather were singers; keeps crossing paths with the demon chasers, joins them in prison in Fjorn, escapes with them and joins forces with them; wishes to return to Ushtet to see his father and become a woodworker like him

Vjendar—baron of Hlvin, nephew of Rushvin of Thioth and her heir, brilliant ruler who appears deceptively soft, supports the demon chasers

Vladje—the wolf who wakes Ian on his first morning in Mídhris, guides him to people, watches over him, leads and protects the companions; Ian's tutelary deity, an avatar of Morvladh, the Great Wolf of Heaven; he allows himself to be touched by only Ian, Wilda, Athnel, and children

Voltar son of Donal—Hildir's father

Volthir son of Brethir—"black Norrung" warrior, companion of Ian

Voraghel—woman of power (sorceress) and great-aunt of Athnel

Vorgun of the Badger Clan—eldest member of the Council of Vorthall, confidant of Njothir

Vorn—steward of Thioth, long-time servant of Rushvin, husband of Lady Mirdel

Vornel daughter of Vorn—youngest child of Vorn and Mirdel

Vothneli—inhabitant(s) of Vothnell

Vovoni—merchant from north of the Gnura who sells wine and cheeses, traveling and singing with her teenage son

Vrotni, the Fierce Mother—constellation of the Fierce Mother, 5th sign of the zodiac, goddess of new mothers, midwives, and of war

Vuchtall the Bear—constellation of the Bear, 6th sign of the zodiac, god of healing

Vughdor—chief healer of Vorthall, long-time friend of Wulfdar

Vunill—second wife of Rathdar (bigamy allowed for chieftains), second mother of Njothir and Njothila, commits voluntary sati on Rathdar's pyre

Vunskridh daughter of Jornandir (Vunni), the Sharp-Eyed—warmaiden with swift reflexes, good hunter, skeptical view of strangers, companion of Ian

Vuoru, the Foam-Crowned—goddess of the deep waters, worshiped on the islands and coastlines but not by inland folk such as the Norrungs, prominent in the worship of the Hlvi

Vurgal—legendary monster whose descriptions vary; all the stories agree that vurgals had lots of sharp teeth. Some tales mention horns, others fur, and others feathers; their eyes are either as large as a chief's drinking cup or small and shine with a red light. They were monsters that lurked in deep woods or dark places like caverns, their favorite food was human flesh, and parents have terrified generations of children with threats of them

Waçda—elderly peasant of Bruzhat, neighbor of Ezni, and the first to witness those in the main square whose "minds had been eaten" by the Chegjan (essentially a state of instantaneous dementia in which the body functions but the person is non-responsive)

Weltar the Tortoise—constellation of the Tortoise, 10th sign of the zodiac, goddess of wisdom, fertility, longevity, and compassion

Wigdor the Chieftain—constellation of the Chieftain, 9th sign of the zodiac, god of justice, keeper of oaths, deity of boys and young men

Wilda daughter of Tjuva, Mother of the Light Bearers—wife of Nordil, cook and mother figure for the demon chasers, close friend of Vladje, acts as Kirlat's kinswoman

William George Dyrnedon—Ian's father

World Horse—cosmic figure represented by an actual horse at the election of Norrung chiefs, praised and figuratively sacrificed in an ancient ritual

Wulfdar son of Daghna—healer and elder of Vorthall, known for his inquisitive mind, companion of Ian

Zarta daughter of Kiftak—Hlvi noblewoman, wife of Vazdan the merchant, fellow passenger with the companions on the voyage to Hlv, childhood friend of Gizli

Zigdel daughter of Gridnu—youngest sister of Lady Zlida

Zithanel—minor noblewoman of Hlv, mother of Lady Zlida, widow of Gridnu

Zlida daughter of Gridnu—Hlvi lady in waiting on Princess Gizli, priestess of Elithel, guardian of Princess Çirazel until she could be restored to the people of Hlv

Zhodor the Fool—orphan boy of Vothnell who prophesied during fits, is later adopted by Torthan of Valcor

Zoldar—Fjorni captain serving Njlvac

Zhrdstvo—brigand, brother of Ggivna, an outcast who attacked Ian in Athor Gorge

DARKSLAYER

INDEX OF PLACES

This index includes geographic features: towns, regions, mountains, rivers, etc. This list includes places and features in the areas from Norrast to Bjupazh, i.e., the regions discussed in *Darkslayer*. Not all items listed here are included in the narrative.

Persons, deities (stars and planets), tribal and ethnic identities, animals, plants, and monsters are in the Index of Characters that precedes this list.

Without latitude and longitude, geographic location is imprecise. This index identifies proper names with category and some relational indication of location (region or territory in parentheses).

Advat—stream, tributary to Athor River (Bjupazh)

Anfell—fishing village on the east coast of Anvik (Dunfell)

Anvik—island, the most NW of the Dunfell Isles (Dunfell)

Aolve—village on the Ulava River, N of Çir

Aonghe—free city at the confluence of the Croven and Ulava Rivers (Aonghe)

Athor (1)—river, tributary to the Gnura (Westwaste)

Athor (2)—gorge, canyon cut by the Athor River (Westwaste)

Beavish (Lesser Vish)—village south of Greater Vish, abandoned after the plague (Siot)

Beavjos—island on the east side of Vios, north of the city of Vios near the mouth of the River Çorthan; the name means "little Vios" (Vios)

Bjupazh (1)—river flowing east from Bjupazh to join the Ulava River (Bjupazh)

Bjupazh (2)—territory west of Ulnor

Bjupazh (3)—mountains from which the headwaters of the Bjupazh River arise (Bjupazh)

Bruzhat—town on the Gnura River upriver from Gennor (Bjupazh)

Buzhna—village at the confluence of the Ftasha and Bjupazh Rivers (Bjupazh)

Chrun—village on the East Piç River

Chudh—sheltered port on the Isle of Çtor (Dunfell)

Çir—village on the Ulava between Tlç and Aolve

Çorn—stream north of Dinth that flows north to the Lands Beyond (E Norrast)

Çorthan—river arising in the sacred spring of Çorth (goddess of legitimate sovereignty), flowing from E side of Mount Hiovith to the east coast of Vios by Beavjos (Vios)

Crumbly—city on the Mither River N of Nimmoth where Wicket River joins Mither (Nimmoth)

Çtor—island, most SE of the Dunfell Isles (Dunfell)

Cuggl—village on the bluffs on N side of Norrast at its mouth, opposite port of Norden; later becomes one of the free cities and a region known for cattle [Note: anomalous pronunciation, pronounced like English word "cudgel"] (Cuggl)

Çush—fishing village on isle of Hlnik, facing Hlv (Hlv)

Dark Place, the—site of Ian's confrontation with the Chegjan amid scree before cliffs on Mount Rggan, uphill from the Watchstones; the stones at this site turned black at the destruction of the demon (Westwaste)

Denev—village between Nith and Nimmoth (Nimmoth)

Derwut—village at the confluence of the Dirtach Stream and Woodstream River (Norrast)

Dhoret—city and barony in Sendhial (Sendhial)

Dibble Lane—street where Ian lived in England (Yorkshire)

Dinth—village near the source of the Mirfann Stream (E Norrast)

Dirtach—stream that loops around Hildham and joins Woodstream River (Norrast)

Dnth—port city, capital of the loose Dunfell federation, located in bay on the eastern side of Dnvik (Dunfell)

Dnvik—island, the SW island of the Dunfell Isles (Dunfell)

Drggan—island, west central island of the Dunfell Isles (Dunfell)

Dribley Parva—village where Ian's family lives (Yorkshire)

Drith—river flowing north from the N side of Mount Viothan to join the Liavith at Ulnaov (Vios)

Drstvo—village on the Ftasha above and to the NW of Zlava (Bjupazh)

Drush—pass, a narrow stone arroyo W and slightly S of Othen (Thioth)

Dunfell—islands west of Hlv: Anvik, Çtor, Dnvik, Drggan, Plit, and Zhinu; also the loose federation of the island (Dunfell)

Elnath—town and barony of Thioth, S of Uvanor and NW of Mount Twij (Thioth)

Ercoille—river, flows into the Wicket at Siot (Siot)

Fazhvahath—town at confluence of the Bjupazh and Ulava Rivers (Bjupazh)

Fiaghor—river, flows south into the Norrast between Cuggl and Windl (Fighast/Cuggl)

Fighast—city on the Fiaghor, capital of the Fighi at time of Darkslayer (Fighast/Cuggl)

Fimmoth—port city at mouth of the Fiona River (Thioth/later Ulnor)

Finnstream—stream E of Mount Hnorg, empties into Upper Woodstream (Norrast)

Finthan—mountain NE of Hlfin, SE of Thioth, twinned with Mount Hlinnat (Thiothi/Fjorni border)

Firestorm, Mount—volcano located in the eastern mountains E of Norrast and Isenwild (Vovannath)

Fjolnis—mountain NNE of Fjorn (Fjorn)

Fjolu—river, flows into the Upper Gnura River (Westwaste)

Fjorn—city and principate on the Fiona River, N of Thioth, E of Gnura Ulava confluence (Fjorn)

Ftasha—river flowing east from southern Westwaste to join the Bjupazh River (Westwaste/Bjupazh)

Fyrth—town at the confluence of the Fera River and Yldstream (Fera/Isenwild)

Galaghat ("The Place of Bones")—site sacred to Ushni, ancient place of sacrifice on the Advat River (Westwaste)

Gath (1)—stream N of the Athor Gorge, flows into Lake Gath (Westwaste)

Gath (2)— lake fed by Gath Stream and the Athor River (Westwaste)

Gelchoj (1)—town, "Place of the Eagle (Gelje)," western port of Vios with shrine to the goddess of visions (Vios)

Gelchoj (2)—bay on W side of Holy Isle of Vios (Vios)

Gennor—town at confluence of Gnura and Ulava Rivers (Bjupazh)

Gnura—river flowing SE from Westwaste to join the Ulava River (Westwaste/Bjupazh)

Great Mither—large river draining the Mere from SW (Liarroth)

Greater Vish (Morvish)—village on the Upper Wicket River (Siot)

Gretland—town on the Wicket River (Siot)

Grudhor—town and barony on W side of Fiona River (Fjorn)

Gzor—town, fishing town and defensive bulwark on W side of Hlv (Hlv)

Hellebore Cottage—home of Ian's family in England (Yorkshire)

Hiovith—mountain, highest mountain on Holy Isle of Vios (Vios)

Hlfin—city and barony on W side of Fiona River, N of Fimmoth (Thioth)

Hlinnat—mountain NE of Hlfin, SE of Thioth, twinned with Mount Finthan (Thioth)

Hlinnor—town and barony E of Fiona River, S foot of Mt Hlinnat (Thioth)

Hlnik—island SW of Bay of Ulnor, NE of Hlv (Hlv)

Hlv (1)—island SW of Ulnor (Hlv)

Hlv (2)—kingdom centered on the Island of Hlv (Hlv)

Hlvmath—city, inland capital of Hlv built on multiple hills (Hlv)

Hnorg—mountain NE of Vorthall between Finnstream and Nurgen Stream (Norrast)

Invarath—river arising from Invar's Spring on N side of Mt Hiovith and flowing to north coast of Vios (Vios)

Ithtall—stream flowing into Mither River below Nimmoth (Nimmoth)

Jorgil—town on Ulava Plain, W of Othen, E of Vorç, S of the Seven Giants (Thioth)

Ktelnik—port city on N coast of Hlv at mouth of Zhik and Ktol Rivers (Hlv)

Ktol—river flowing from eastern mountains of Hlv past Hlvmath to empty at port of Ktelnik (Hlv)

Laoghar—city and barony at N end of Vothneli lands (Vothnell/later Nimmoth)

Lesser Vish (Beavish)—village south of Greater Vish, abandoned after the plague (Siot)

Liavith—river flowing from the S side of Mt Hiovith to the E side of Vios (Vios)

Little Niggle—stream running through Nigdell (Norrast)

Megh—village located on the West Piç River (Nimmoth)

Mere—large inland sea, center of Mídhris, also known the Mithermere

Mimtor—lighthouse located on a promontory at the W side of the Bay of Nioril (Mimmoth)

Mirfann—stream W of Wivel Stream, flowing S to join the Lower Tilçar (E Norrast)

Mish—town on Mlvanor River in County Norrast (Isenwild)

Mither—great river draining the northern basin of the Mere, emptying at Mimmoth into Bay of Nioril

Mithermere—large inland sea, center of Mídhris, also known simply as the Mere; named for the central northern river (Mither) that feeds it and the large southwestern river (Great Mither) that drains it, conceptually viewed as two parts of one great central river flowing from north to south

Mídhris—the region surrounding the Mere, a term coined by the redactor; the region is commonly called "the lands about the Mere"

Mlvanor—river flowing N from Mish to join the Norrast River (Isenwild)

Mjerth—village, the first village W of Siot

Morvish (Greater Vish)—village on the Upper Wicket River (Siot)

Nialt—free city on the Nija River NW of Crumbly (Nialt)

Niftor—city on Mither River between Nimmoth and Mimmoth (Nimmoth)

Nigdell—village one day's journey W of Vorthall (Norrast)

Nimmoth—major trading center and later free city on the Mither River N of Mimmoth (Nimmoth)

Nimos (1)—bay on N coast of the Mere W of Mimmoth (Mimmoth)

Nimos (2)—city on Bay of Nimos (Mimmoth)

Nioril (1)—bay at the mouth of the Mither and Njor Rivers (Mimmoth)

Nioril (2)—peninsula sheltering the Bay of Nioril (Mimmoth)

Nishtell—town on the Ercoille River between Pjall and Siot (Siot)

Nith—village located on the Ithtall Stream (Nimmoth)

Njim—river flowing N to join the Wicket S of Siot (Siot)

Njor—river flowing SW into the Bay of Nioril (Mimmoth)

Njorc—village on the Upper Njor River (Mimmoth)

Norden—major port city on S side of mouth of the Norrast River, Fighi port at time of Darkslayer, later capital of County Norrast in Isenwild (Fighast/Isenwild)

Norgardh—village located high on the Nurgen Stream NE of Vorthall (Norrast)

Norrast (1)—vast forest E of the mere, N of the Isenwild and S of Eastern Nivannath Mountains, home of the tribe of the Norrungs (Norrast)

Norrast (2)—river S of the Forest of Norrast, flowing W to the Mere (Norrast/Isenwild border)

Norrast (3)—territory roughly coterminous with the Forest of Norrast (Norrast)

Nrvash—village on the Gnura River above Budheç (Bjupazh)

Nurgen—stream flowing from Norgardh to loop around Vorthall and join Woodstream River (Norrast)

Othen (1)—border town and barony W of Fiona River and S of Othen Stream (Thioth)

Othen (2)—stream flowing E into Fiona River and forming the border between Fjorn and Thioth (Fjorn/Thioth)

Paç—town on E side of Ulava River, S of Fazhavath (Thioth)

Piç—river flowing NW to join the Mither River N of Nimmoth, its upper portions form East and West forks (Nimmoth)

Pjall—village on the Ercoille River N of Gretland (Siot)

Plit—island, the central island of the Dunfell Islands (Dunfell)

Rggan—mountain on the slopes of which Ian confronts the Chegjan (Westwaste)

Stjolvanor—town and county on E side of Ulava River, S of Vorç (Thioth)

Shultal—village on the upper Njor River, downstream and W of Njorc (Mimmoth)

Tejth—river with three forks from Mt Vjat and E side of Ulvat, flowing past the Seven Giants and into the Fiona River (Fjorn)

Thioth (1)—city on the Fiona River, capital of powerful duchy at time of Ian (Thioth)

Thioth (2)—duchy encompassing the southern portions of the Fiona River Valley and the Ulava Plain, later part of the territory of the Free City of Ulnor (Thioth)

Three Sisters—three mountains N of the road between Vorthall and Hildham (Norrast)

Tilç, East and West—mountains SW of Mt Nigh; the South Fork of the Upper Tilçar River arises between them (Norrast)

Tilçar—river with three forks near Mt Nigh, flows S into the Norrast River (Norrast)

Tlç—village on the Ulava River between Gennor and Çir (Bjupazh)

Tugdal—coastal city W of Nimos, N of Vios (Mimmoth)

Tugh—river on northern coast of the Mere, debouches at Tugdal (Mimmoth/Vothnell)

Tuvik—southern island flanking the Bay of Gelchoj on the W side of Vios (Vios)

Tvordak—northern island flanking the Bay of Gelchoj on the W side of Vios (Vios)

Twij—mountain W of Fimmoth with steep slopes on coastal side (Fimmoth)

Ulava (1)—great river of NW region flowing S and emptying at Port of (Thioth, Bjupazh, Ulnor)

Ulava (2)—plain through which the Ulava River flows (Thioth, Bjupazh, Ulnor)

Ulnaov ("All Holy")—sacred city of Vios located at the confluence of the Liavith and Drith Rivers (Vios)

Ulnor—free city, port at mouth of the Ulava River (Ulnor)

Ulvat—town overlooking the Ulava Plain, located between Fjorn and the confluence of the Gnura and Ulava Rivers (Aonghe)

Uvanor—town W of Thioth and S of Mt Uvjor (Thioth)

Uvja—river flowing from Mt Uvjor to the Fiona River between Fjorn and Grudhor (Fjorn)

Uvjor—mountain SW of the Forest of Fjorn, NE of the Ulava Plain (Thioth/Fjorn)

Valcor—small town and barony NE of Vothnell (Vothnell)

Vathad—mountain, one of a series of peaks NW of Mt Rggan, source of Avdat Stream (Westwaste)

Vathil—town SSE of Ulvat, WNW of Mt Uvjor, disputed territory (Aonghe/Thioth)

Vathna—village E of Vorthall destroyed by raiders at beginning of Darkslayer; on the Tilçar below confluence with West Mirfann Stream (Norrast)

Vazghla—village, fishing and defensive town on NE coast of Çtor facing Hlv (Hlv)

Vechthall—village on the Tilçar W of Vulth and Mt Nigh (Norrast)

Veshnath—river arising in sacred spring of Veshnel on E side of Mt Hiovith toward port of Vishni on E coast of Vios (Vios)

Vios, Holy Isle of—sacred island at N end of the Mere (Vios)

Viothan—mountain on S half of Vios (Vios)

Vishni—port town on E coast of Vios at mouth of Veshnath River (Vios)

Vjat—mountain N of Ulvat (Aonghe)

Vjoç—island off the Bay of Nimos (Mimmoth)

Vlizhktan—mountain located toward SW end of Hlv (Hlv)

Vorç—town by a ford of the Ulava River between Gennor and Stjolvanor (Bjupazh)

Vorthall (1)—town, capital of the Norrungs, located in curve of the Nurgen Stream (Norrast)

Vorthall (2)—great hall of the Norrungs, the chief's hall in Vorthall (Norrast)

Vothnell—city and county, port between Fimmoth and Tugdal (Vothnell)

Vudheç—town on the Gnura River upstream from Bruzhat (Bjupazh)

Vulth—village on the Tilçar where W and N forks of the river meet, W of Mt Nigh, easternmost village of the Norrungs (Norrast)

Vuorshnik—sacred cliff on SE coast of Hlv where Vuoru is worshiped (Hlv)

Watchers—two hills W of Hildham, gateway from Norrast to Cuggeli territory (Norrast)

Watchstones—two striking vertical rock formation on Mt Rggan above the tree line (Westwaste)

Wenadh—river flowing S to join the Norrast at Windl (Fighast/Cuggl)

Westwaste—uninhabited region at far W of the northern lands, presumed to be haunted

Wicket—river flowing into the Mither River at Crumbly N of Nimmoth (Nimmoth)

Wivel—stream W of Vechthall flowing S to join the Lower Tilçar (Norrast)

Woodstream—river draining central Norrast S into the Norrast River (Norrast)

Ystraf—town and barony ESE of Grudhor on E side of Fiona River (Fjorn)

Zeltar—village, fishing and defensive town on W end of southern coast of Hlv (Hlv)

Zhik—small river on Hlv debouching with other rivers into bay of Ktelnik (Hlv)

Zhiktan—river flowing from Mt Vlizhktan into the River Ktol (Hlv)

Zhinu—island, the NE of the Dunfell Islands, closest to Hlv (Dunfell)

Zlava—village on the Ftasha River above Buzhna (Bjupazh)

Zlinfath—village on island of Hlnik N side facing mainland (Hlv)

About the Author

G. M. Deveril is the name of the fictive redactor of the Chronicles and the *nom de Mídhris* of Paul E. Strid who lives and writes in Albuquerque, New Mexico. He fell in love with words at an early age and takes delight in learning languages. A double dropout, he studied early and medieval church history at UCLA back when these stories began and, decades later, explored multi-cultural and interfaith ministry at several theological schools in Berkeley. *The Chronicles of Mídhris* are probably the true project and doctoral thesis of all his studies. For a decade he served as vicar of St. Cuthbert's Episcopal Church in Oakland, California. Retired from his church career he now works in customer support for federal travelers. His hobbies include cooking, gardening, photography, and enjoying local theatre.

Further information on Mídhris may be found at the Mídhris blog:

http://midhris.blogspot.com/

Readers may comment there and ask the author questions.

Made in the USA
San Bernardino, CA
24 October 2013